The Unseeing

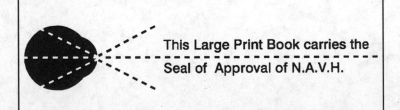

THE UNSEEING

ANNA MAZZOLA

THORNDIKE PRESS

A part of Gale, Cengage Learning

GALE
CENGAGE Learning·

Farmington Hills, Mich • San Francisco • New York • Waterville, Maine
Meriden, Conn • Mason, Ohio • Chicago

GALE
CENGAGE Learning

LIBRARY OF CONGRESS CATALOGING-IN-PUBLICATION DATA

Names: Mazzola, Anna, author.
Title: The unseeing / by Anna Mazzola.
Description: Large print edition. | Waterville, Maine : Thorndike Press, a part of Gale, Cengage Learning, 2017. | Series: Thorndike Press large print mystery
Identifiers: LCCN 2017001925| ISBN 9781410499585 (hardcover) | ISBN 1410499588 (hardcover)
Subjects: LCSH: Gale, Sarah, –1888—Fiction. | Brown, Hannah, –1836—Fiction. | Murder—Great Britain—Fiction. | Large type books. | GSAFD: Legal stories. | Mystery fiction. | Historical fiction g
Classification: LCC PR6113.A994 U57 2017b | DDC 823/.92—dc23
LC record available at https://lccn.loc.gov/2017001925

Published in 2017 by arrangement with Sourcebooks, Inc.

Printed in the United States of America
1 2 3 4 5 6 7 21 20 19 18 17

For Jake

"The investigation of truth, the art of ascertaining that which is unknown from that which is known, has occupied the attention, and constituted the pleasure as well as the business of the reflecting part of mankind in every civilized age and country."

— *A Practical Treatise of the Law of Evidence,* Dr. Thomas Starkie, 1833

PROLOGUE

Through her left eye she could see nothing now. Through her right, Hannah could make out the flame of the one candle that still burned, guttering and shivering low in its puddle of wax. It was only the candlelight that convinced her she was still alive. The fire was dying in the grate and the coldness of the flagstones had seeped into her bones, leaving her as icy and insubstantial as the snow that fell outside.

She knew she should call out: for a surgeon, a constable, or simply someone to bear witness. Otherwise, unless they looked closely, they would read it all wrong. But she was unable to cry out. Her body seemed to have slipped from the grasp of her mind and she had a strong sensation of falling — of the world sliding away from her. She was vaguely aware of the flame's shadows fluttering on the ceiling above her. She saw for a moment her mother's drawn, unsmiling face.

"You shouldn't tell lies, Hannah. They always come back to bite you."

A gust of wintry air blew into the room: the door had opened. Just before she lost consciousness, Hannah heard footsteps coming toward her, footsteps she thought she knew.

In the draft, the candle dipped, swayed, and was finally extinguished. All was dark.

■ ■ ■ ■

PART ONE:
CORPUS

■ ■ ■ ■

1

MYSTERIOUS AFFAIR

Yesterday afternoon, about three o'clock, as a police constable of the T division was on duty near Pineapple Gate, Edgeware Road, his attention was attracted toward an unfinished house, in which he saw at a distance something lying on the ground at the bottom part of the building; he directly approached the spot, and there beheld, tied up at the top, a full-sized sack, which he lifted up, and found to be of considerable weight. Without loss of time he untied the fastenings, and, to his great horror and consternation, ascertained that the said sack contained the dead trunk and arms of a female.

— *MORNING POST,* 29 DECEMBER 1836

27 March 1837
"Murderer!" they shouted.

"Whore!"

"Take her eyes out: it's what she did to Hannah Brown."

Hands battered the wooden roof and sides of the prison wagon, and above the din, Sarah could hear the voice of the driver as he tried to calm the horse and urge it forward. Silently, Sarah willed it too, knowing that if the wagon stopped and the mob got at her, she would be done for. She had heard of such things happening: of a man accused of killing a child, seized as he left the Old Bailey and reduced within minutes to a bloody mess; of resurrection men, chased through the streets, escaping only when a pub landlord helped them over a wall. No one would help her.

The wagon inched through the crowds, away from the magistrates' court and onto a wider street where the horse picked up pace. Through the barred cart door, Sarah could see some of the people running behind them, shouting, shrieking, shaking their fists. Gradually, they fell away, some leaning forward, hands on their knees to catch their breath. The vehicle jolted on over the cobblestones, past the great dome of St. Paul's, and then up a side street where the roar of London was briefly muffled.

They came to a halt and the guard

14

wrenched open the wagon door. "Out!"

Sarah gathered her skirts and stumbled down onto the ground. It was nearly dark now and a thin rain had begun to fall. Steadying herself, she stared up at the high stone arch and, beneath it, the great oaken door, studded with nails and topped with spikes. She had walked past this door several times before, but she had never imagined that she would walk through it, for this was Newgate, the most notorious prison in London.

The guard knocked on the door, and a few moments later, a porter appeared, his face the drab color of tallow. He nodded at the guard and looked briefly at Sarah, his expression unreadable. Without saying a word, he led Sarah through a second door, past a lodge, through an iron-bolted gate, and down a narrow corridor until they reached a door that bore the sign Reception Room. It was not much of a reception. There was no fire in the large stone room and the air was chill. A woman dressed in dark gray sat on a high stool by a desk, writing in a thick, leather-bound book. She pointed at a wooden bench. Sarah opened her mouth to speak, but the woman put her finger to her lips and shook her head. The only sounds were the scratching of the pen, the closing of doors far off, and an occasional undistinguishable shout.

After a few minutes, a taller woman, her face bone white, her eyes small beads of jet, entered the room carrying a wooden box and a bundle of clothing. She was dressed, like the first woman, in a gray dress, gray bonnet, and heavy black boots. However, around her shoulders was a black mantle, and about her middle she wore a wide leather belt with a brass buckle from which dangled a chain of keys.

"Name?" she said sharply.

Sarah got to her feet. "Sarah Gale."

The woman stared at Sarah, her gaze as cold and hard as a knife.

The first woman spoke. "She's the one just been charged with aiding and abetting the Edgeware Road murder, Miss Sowerton. I've written it all down."

"Oh, I know who she is," Miss Sowerton said.

Sarah lowered her eyes but felt the woman's gaze still on her, dissecting her.

After a few moments, the woman held out her hand. "Possessions."

Sarah looked up.

"Give me your *things.*"

From her pocket, Sarah removed the few items she had brought with her — an old silk handkerchief, her locket, and a tortoiseshell-backed brush. The woman took them and put them into the wooden box. To Sarah it felt as though the last pieces of her were being stripped away.

"Undress!"

Sarah looked at Miss Sowerton and then at the other woman, who nodded.

"Do as the matron says."

Slowly, Sarah removed her cloak, gloves, and shoes, then undid the fastenings on her dark-green dress and removed her petticoats until she was standing in just her shift, stockings, and stays in the cold room. Miss Sowerton regarded her steadily, her arms folded.

Finally mustering the courage to speak, Sarah said, "I'm not what you think. I didn't do what they say."

The matron's mouth slid into a semblance of a smile. "Oh, no, 'course not. You're innocent as a babe unborn. None of the inmates in this prison is guilty. The place is fit to burst with innocent souls." Her lips set again into a line. "You're not to speak unless spoken to. We don't want to hear your lies."

She looked carefully over Sarah, as though eyeing a suspect piece of meat at market.

"Dark-brown hair . . . brown eyes . . .

17

sharp features . . . scars to the chest, wrists, and lower arms."

With cold fingers, she lifted Sarah's petticoat.

"A mole above the left hipbone."

The woman on the stool scribbled in the leather-bound book. The matron folded Sarah's clothes, placed them in the wooden box, and snapped the lid shut. Then she handed Sarah the bundle. While the two women watched, Sarah put on the clothes: a blue dress with dark stripes, a blue-checked apron and matching neckerchief, a patched jacket, and thick brown stockings that scratched against her skin. For an instant, she was reminded of her dress fittings with Rosina when they were children: standing before their mother's cold gaze in dark silks and stiff lace. Would it have always come to this?

A thud: two black shoes — old, dirty, and mismatched — had been thrown at her feet.

"Put these on and follow me."

The matron led Sarah along a succession of winding alleyways and down dark, low-roofed passages and staircases, her heels clicking against the stone. They came eventually upon a row of identical doorways and Miss Sowerton paused.

"The condemned cells," she said, watching for Sarah's reaction.

Sarah shivered, pierced with a shard of fear. Condemned: damned, sentenced to death. If the court decided that she should hang, this would be where she would come on her last night. She realized that she had instinctively raised her hand to clasp her throat and she lowered it before the matron could notice.

They walked through another corridor that led onto a large, empty quadrangle, lit only by the sickly yellow light from two gas lamps. This, the matron announced, was "the women's area," with its own taprooms, breakfast room, and kitchen. Sarah was hungry, for she had taken nothing since a few mouthfuls of porridge at Clerkenwell Prison that morning. The smell of the place, though, turned her stomach: a sour smell of unwashed bodies and chloride of lime. It was for the best, she told herself, that George was not here. Some convicts were allowed to take their children into Newgate with them, but this was no place for a child. This was no place for any human. Still, the thought of him without her was a sharp, almost physical pain.

Miss Sowerton stopped before a black door and produced a large key. A rumbling

19

came from within the lock as the key turned and Sarah had the sudden idea of the place not just as a prison, but a terrible creature: flesh and bone, iron and stone.

"Your cell," the matron said.

When Sarah failed to move, Miss Sowerton pushed her firmly into the room, locking and bolting the door behind her.

Sarah's first impression was one of complete darkness. After a few seconds, however, she saw that a few gray rays of light filtered through the glass of a small iron-barred window. Against the far wall, under the high window, was a bed. She felt her way to it and ran her hand over the bedding: a blanket and a rough pillow, so cold they felt damp. There was a stale odor to the cell — a tang of must and sweat and something unidentifiable. Fear, perhaps. She could hear the sound of footsteps in the corridor outside and, from far away, a scream cut short.

On a small table beneath the window stood a jug, a book, a candle, and a little metal tinderbox. Sarah opened the box and struck steel against flint until sparks became flame. In the glow of the candle she saw a three-legged stool, a burnished copper washbasin fastened to the wall with a water tap over it, and, in one corner, a water closet seat.

She knew that most of the other prisoners had to share cells, some four to a room. Evidently, the warders did not trust her with other women. Maybe they thought she would slit their throats as they slept.

A draft, finding its way under the door, caused the candle flame to ripple. In the center of the cell door, carved into the wood, was an eye, complete in every detail — pupil, eyelashes, brow. A spyhole. Sarah bent down to look through it to the corridor outside, but there was only darkness.

2

On Saturday morning, about half past eight o'clock, as Mathias Ralph, the lock-keeper of the Ben Jonson lock on the Regent's Canal, at the World's-end, Stepney, was engaged in closing the lock after a coal-barge had passed through, he found that the falls or sluices would not close, and that there was a space of several inches between both. On examining minutely to ascertain the cause he was horror-struck to find that it was a human head.

— *MORNING CHRONICLE,* 9 JANUARY 1837

Chief Justice Tindal charged the Jury very fully, and very impartially, but rather, as we think, leaning to the impression that Gale may have been innocent. The Jury, however, brought in a verdict of guilty against both.

— *SPECTATOR,* 15 APRIL 1837

Edmund stood in the bright gas-lit doorway and tugged the cord of a shining brass bell, which gave a muted clang. A man in full livery admitted him into the entrance hall and led him to a door with a small glazed aperture, through which Edmund knew he was closely watched. After a few seconds, the door opened, and a second man appeared, held out his arm, and bowed.

"Good evening, sir."

Edmund passed up the richly carpeted stairs to the first floor and made his way to the large, red-curtained gaming room. The place was already full of people absorbed in play. Around a long table covered with a dark-green cloth, twenty or so men sat or stood, their eyes fixed on the dice and the game. Two croupiers faced each other across the middle of the table.

A waiter approached Edmund and handed him a glass of brandy and soda water from a silver tray. Money flowed more freely from a gentleman who had been oiled. The back room contained a large table loaded with cold chickens, joints, salads, and glistening puddings. The gambler need never leave. Except, of course, when his money ran out.

Edmund waited for the next game of hazard to commence and then joined the table, feeling the blood pumping faster in his veins as the dice were cast. He would, he reminded himself, stay only for an hour and wager only a guinea. But one hour became two. One guinea became three. Eventually, Edmund conceded defeat. This was not a quick way to make money; only a fast way to get rid of it. He took the stairs back to the street, cursing quietly. He could not afford to lose.

It was after ten o'clock by the time he left the Regent's Quadrant. The streets were still ablaze with gaslight and revelers dressed in velvet, satin, and lace returned from the theaters or made their way out into the smoky night in search of excitement or oblivion. Edmund cut through the maze of alleyways to the north of the Strand, his feet crunching on discarded clay pipes and broken bottles. Here was a different kind of London. Barely clothed beggars stretched out their hands from the darkness and a pair of drunks — arm in arm — splashed past through the stinking puddles of refuse. A scrawny woman in a tattered cape pressed herself so close to Edmund that he could smell the bitterness of gin upon her breath.

He was downcast and weary by the time he reached his chambers on Inner Temple Lane, where he rented rooms on the second floor of a grimy, once-white building, the stucco facade darkened by decades of smog and soot. He took the stairs quietly, hoping that his wife would already be in bed asleep.

As he opened the door to their rooms, Edmund saw an envelope on the floor on top of the mat. Stooping and taking the letter in his hand, he noticed that it bore a ministerial stamp. He cracked the wax and read the note within.

The Right Honorable Lord Russell requests that Mr. Fleetwood call at his earliest convenience at the Minister's office on Whitehall.

Edmund's heart jumped. Why on earth would the Home Secretary want to see him?

He turned the letter over, but it gave nothing away.

Edmund set off shortly after eight o'clock the following morning, his hair combed, his boots freshly blackened. He walked through the Temple Gardens and left the relative quiet of the inn to meet the chaos and stench of Fleet Street. Omnibuses, hackney coaches, one-horse cabs, and carriages navigated the dung-filled road. At the dirtiest sections, young crossing sweepers ran nimbly between the vehicles to sweep the dirt into piles at the side of the road. Street sellers cried out their wares and steeple bells chimed together to make the noise of London that rose and fell but never stopped.

He joined the stream of clerks pouring into Westminster: middle-aged men in white neckcloths and black coats, some turning a rusty brown with age; younger clerks with flashes of color like tropical birds — pea-green gloves, crimson suspenders, tall shining hats.

As Edmund passed a baker's shop he caught a whiff of the doughy air. He stopped to join the queue and bought a small cottage loaf and a pennyworth of milk.

He paused at the point that marked the separation of the City and the West End, Temple Bar, and stood there to take his breakfast, thinking of the heads of traitors that were once impaled on its spikes and left to rot — a warning to the people. How much had things really changed in the past century? Four hundred death sentences had been handed down in the past year alone.

Making his way down the Strand, he wondered, again, what the Home Secretary could possibly want with him.

Lord John Russell was a small angular man

of five and forty. He sat behind a large walnut desk, covered with orderly bundles of paper tied with different colored ribbons. To his side was a tall, graying clerk with an unnerving face, misshapen like a reflection in a spoon. Edmund stood before the desk in his best waistcoat and a crisp linen shirt. There was a chair on his side of the desk, but he had not been invited to sit on it.

"I have been sent a petition for mercy," Lord Russell said to Edmund, picking up a letter from the table as though it were a dirty object. "It alleges that the prisoner Gale is innocent and that I should look into the matter. Your father tells me you are already well versed in the facts of the Edgeware Road murder."

"My lord, yes, fairly well. I've followed the case since the papers reported the discovery of the torso. I find it interesting professionally."

Professional interest. That was how he had justified to himself his visit to Paddington Workhouse to view the victim's head, preserved in spirits. It was certainly a strange thing: a pale, swollen face suspended in solution, the dark-brown hair floating across it. A pickled head.

"I receive hundreds of these petitions a week from all over the country," Lord

Russell continued. "Most of them are mere appeals *ad misericordiam* — 'Spare oh mercifully my husband,' et cetera, et cetera. Unless there is some glaring anomaly or injustice in the case, we respond with a standard form saying that the law must take its course. We are, after all, a devilishly busy department. Is that not right, Mr. Spinks?"

The graying clerk gave a slight bow.

"But you are aware of the excitement this case has caused, Mr. Fleetwood?"

"Indeed, my lord, yes."

Since Christmas, the newspapers and penny bloods had run red with details of the grisly treasure hunt for the body parts and the search for the killers. Every appearance of the suspects had been attended by a crowd of hundreds.

"In addition to which, there are various names at the bottom of this petition: Miss Fraser; Mrs. Fry. Names that carry some weight." Lord Russell's mouth stretched into a thin smile. "I must therefore be seen to have considered the matter in earnest. This is where you come in. You are to look at the evidence that was before the court and make a recommendation as to whether the death sentence should be carried out. A month should be enough, I would think."

"A month?" Edmund ran his fingers

through his hair. "This is a very interesting commission, my lord. However, in order to do the matter full justice, might I not need a little longer?" He swallowed. "Two months, perhaps?"

Lord Russell pushed his glasses farther down his nose and peered at Edmund over them. "Let us understand each other, Mr. Fleetwood. I am, as you know, attempting to reduce the number of offenses to which capital punishment applies, and I am willing to exercise discretion where there has been an obvious miscarriage of justice. However, this is a crime for which the great majority of the public (the abolitionist lunatics aside) would support a hanging. The jury took fifteen minutes to convict Miss Gale of aiding and abetting James Greenacre in the horrific murder of a blameless woman. You know the state the body was found in?"

"Yes, my lord," Edmund said, thinking of the mutilated face, the eye gone, the neck crudely sawn through, perhaps before she was dead.

"Unlike most of those tried in this country, she was represented. She was given the opportunity to make a statement, but she chose to say virtually nothing at all. There is nothing I have seen," the Home Secretary continued, "to suggest that she has not received a fair trial. However, there are different degrees and shades of guilt and it may be that the punishment here does not fit the crime. I must show that I have considered the matter on His Majesty's behalf, and that is what I am asking you to do. You may have until the end of the first week in June, if you insist, but certainly no more. Mr. Spinks here will show you all you need to see. He will also discuss with you your remuneration. We shall ensure it is more than adequate."

"Thank you, my lord."

"And, of course, if you do well in this commission you may expect further such appointments in future."

For three years, Edmund had been struggling to make a name for himself at the criminal bar and now, at last, a high-profile case was being placed in his hands — a case that would provide at least a temporary solution to his financial difficulties. And yet, he felt a twinge of unease.

"Would it," he asked, "not be normal in these circumstances to ask the police, rather than a lawyer, to look at the matter afresh?"

Again the thin smile. "Mr. Fleetwood, the police have already conducted a thorough investigation. The case has already been tried. Spinks will take you through the papers. Look again, Fleetwood. Look again." He lifted his hand to indicate Edmund was dismissed.

"Just one more question, my lord. Do I take it that it was my father who suggested me for the post?"

"Yes. You know we were at Edinburgh together? He said you were already acquainted with the case, thought you would do a good job."

Edmund did his best to prevent his surprise from showing in his face. If that were true, it would be the first time in all his thirty-two years that his father had shown any faith in him.

The clerk led Edmund into an adjoining room and, from a large cabinet, removed a bundle of papers bound with a red ribbon.

"This is the report from the inquest. These are the affidavits and notes of evidence from the magistrates' court and the defendant's subsequent appearances. You will see that Miss Gale has changed her account slightly on each occasion. Hardly the mark of an innocent soul."

Edmund did not reply. He would draw his own conclusions. "Are there any other papers?"

31

"Here is a letter from the presiding judge, whom the Home Secretary asked to comment on the case. He considered that the verdict, although harsh, was appropriate, given the jury's findings that she helped to conceal the murder and that there is no need to interfere with it. Nevertheless, as Lord Russell said, in a case of such notoriety we must show we have done more than that. This is the petition, and here are the trial notes. You've said you are familiar with the case?"

"I attended part of the trial," Edmund said. In truth, he had sat through the full two days. He had stayed late into the evening, after the oil lamps were lit.

"Did you form an opinion?"

Edmund thought of Sarah Gale's slight figure in the vast dock, the mirror above reflecting a ghostly light onto her expressionless face. "The prosecution did a very good job with the evidence they had," he said carefully.

"You may also wish to look at the various articles that have been published about the crime. Much has been said."

"Yes, most of it pure nonsense." The papers had vied with one another to produce the most salacious and far-fetched stories about Greenacre and Gale. It was no wonder they had been convicted, given what the jury must have read about them.

The clerk raised his eyebrows. "No doubt you know best. If I can be of further assistance . . . ?"

Edmund had the distinct feeling he was being mocked. "Has Greenacre himself not petitioned for mercy?"

"Oh, yes, of course," the clerk said.

"Then, am I not to investigate his petition also?"

Spinks gave Edmund a look of mock surprise. "I thought you were already acquainted with the case, sir?"

Edmund gave a curt nod.

"Well, then you will know that the prisoner Greenacre admitted to having cut Hannah Brown's body to pieces and distributed them around town. The man carried the head on his lap all the way to Stepney. Difficult to see how such a man can deny murder or, indeed, expect clemency."

"Nevertheless, I would like to see his petition. On what basis does he say he is entitled to the King's mercy?"

The clerk gave a shrug. "I can arrange for you to be provided with a copy, but his lawyers merely say the same as they did at the trial: that their client returned to his house to find Hannah Brown already dead

33

and that he decided in 'a moment of temporary insanity' to dismember her with a
carpenter's saw." He smiled. "The Minister
does not intend to appoint an investigator
to consider his case. He is capable of making a decision on the papers."

"Yes, I suppose he is. And does the prisoner Greenacre continue to say that Sarah
Gale knew nothing of the whole affair?"

Spinks nodded. "Yes, same story. She was
entirely ignorant and wholly innocent, apparently. Almost endearing, really, how they
continue to cover up for one other."

Edmund ignored him. "And if I find that
the death sentence is not warranted —"

The clerk cut him off. "The Minister will
make a decision as to the appropriate
punishment, should you recommend com-
mutation: full pardon, penal servitude,
transportation for the appropriate term, and
so on. But he is, as I'm sure you know, attempting to reduce the number of convicts
sent to the colonies. Strangely enough, they
don't seem to want our society's castoffs."

Edmund thanked him brusquely and
asked to be shown out. As he descended the
steps to the outer hall, Spinks called out,
"Might I remind you, sir, of the usual rule
in these matters? Take nothing on its looks;
take everything on evidence. Even the things

you think you know."

The promise of money to come was enough for Edmund to command Flora, their maid, to buy a large joint of mutton for dinner. He opened a bottle of claret and brought it to the dinner table himself.

"Well, Bessie, finally our luck appears to be turning."

His wife looked up from the candle she was lighting and fixed him with her clear blue eyes. "Why? What's happened?"

Edmund explained the commission, speaking hurriedly in his excitement. "It could turn out very well for us. The Home Secretary said that there may be more such work in future; and having my name associated with such a high-profile matter may lead others to seek me out."

Bessie was silent, looking down at her plate.

Edmund coughed and filled his wife's glass, then his own. "Aren't you pleased, Bessie?"

"It's not that I'm not pleased. I'm sure it's a great compliment to you that you should be asked to investigate such an important case."

"*But,* my love?" He pulled at his cravat.

"Well, it's just that it's such a very *awful*

case. I can't help but think that simply by being involved with it, your name will be tainted."

"Bessie," Edmund felt the blood rush to his cheeks, "you don't lose your reputation in the law simply because the facts of a case are . . . unpalatable." He lifted the lid on his leg of mutton, thinking momentarily of Hannah Brown's legs as they were found, protruding from a sack.

"Oh, I'm sure you understand it all far better than I do. I just don't want you to be criticized in any way."

"And I will not be. I will look carefully at the evidence, I will ascertain the facts, and I will make the recommendation that I think is right. Remember: I have been appointed for the Crown, not for Sarah Gale herself."

He cut into his mutton. It was overcooked: tough and fibrous.

"They don't know your own views on capital punishment, I take it?" Her tone had an edge of sharpness.

Edmund looked up. "No, Bessie, they don't, but in any event they aren't relevant. I'm looking at whether Sarah Gale did in fact know that Greenacre had murdered Hannah Brown — and whether the sentence was appropriate, given the law as it currently stands. My own views on capital punishment are immaterial."

His wife did not reply but worried a strand of her fair hair.

"Bessie, quite apart from anything else, it is good money." He reached across the table and took her hand. "You'll be able to buy those things you've wanted for so long. A new gown. Books for Clem."

Bessie nodded, thoughtful. "Yes. He does need some books." She paused. "Your father didn't feel able to assist us, then?"

Edmund withdrew his hand. "He *has* assisted us: it was my father who recommended me to this post."

A shadow seemed to pass over Bessie's face, but she smiled.

"Well, then he must believe it would benefit your career."

"Yes. I suppose he must."

Or was it a test, Edmund wondered. Was he setting him up to fail?

Bessie drew up her shoulders and raised her glass. "A toast," she said. "To the Edgeware Road case and to my clever, clever husband."

Edmund brought his glass to meet hers and took a long gulp of wine, trying to swallow down the anxiety rising within him. The more he thought about it, the more curious it seemed that the Home Secretary should have appointed him to such a complex case. He was known as a good advocate, but he was still junior. And he was no investigator. Edmund turned his glass in his hand, the wine showing dark red in the candlelight.

What had his father told Lord Russell?

3

On Thursday morning, as two laborers were employed in cutting osiers in a marshy piece of ground, situated close to Coldharbour Lane, Camberwell, they observed something tied up in a piece of coarse sacking and concealed amid a heap of weeds and rushes. One of them lifted the bundle, and called his companion to witness the discovery. He then cut the cord which was tied round the bundle and, to the horror and consternation of himself and his companion, the legs and thighs of a human body dropped from the sacking.

— *CHAMPION,* 6 FEBRUARY 1837

24 April 1837
At six o'clock, the machinery of the prison rattled into action: the strident note of the bell, the thud of boots on corridor floors, the rasp of keys in locks, of bolts being drawn back, and the *clank, clank, clank* of

door after door opening, like a train leaving the station. The only voices audible were those of the warders, shouting orders or rebukes.

When her cell door was thrown open, Sarah took her bucket to the taproom to fill at the pump. For a few seconds, she saw the outline of her face reflected in the water: dark eyes, a slit of a mouth. She broke the surface of the water with her fingers and the image disintegrated into fragments.

Once back in her cell, Sarah set to work rolling her bed linen — a core of white sheets, a crust of yellow blankets. Then she scrubbed the floor and rearranged the items that had been allocated to her: a Bible, a Prayer Book, a wooden platter and a spoon, a wooden salt box, a tin pint mug, a chamber pot, a wooden bucket, a short-handled brush, a blue pocket handkerchief, a piece of soap, and a towel as coarse as a nutmeg grater. She had been at Newgate for nearly a month now (two weeks awaiting trial, two weeks recovering from it), and this was how she got through each day, focusing on her routine. Sometimes, however, a chink in her thoughts let in the wider reality like a piercing beam of white light. If she did not work out a way to escape from this wretched place, she would die here — hanged before a baying crowd outside the Debtors' Door and buried within the prison's walls.

The bolt drew back and her door was flung open again. Miss Groves. She was a heavily built woman with a wide, flat face and skin the color of sausage meat. Groves surveyed the room briefly, ran her finger over the bedding, and then turned her attention to Sarah.

"Rubdown. Shawl off."

She passed her large hands firmly down Sarah's body and legs, feeling every rib bone, every inch of flesh.

She took Sarah's chin in her rough palm. "Open your mouth wide, so I can see inside it." Sarah could smell the other woman's breath, a mixture of peppermint and decay.

"You'll do. You may dress."

The words triggered a fragment of memory — an elderly gentleman with white powdered hair and dry, papery fingers. Images flashed, uninvited: panting in the darkness, cold limbs, hot breath. James had saved her from that, at least, whatever else he had put her through.

Sarah followed a line of women snaking through one of the corridors to the long whitewashed breakfast room whose high windows looked into the interior of the prison. She was seated near the warders rather than at the long deal tables with the other prisoners, some of whom she recognized, some not. Most of the women imprisoned at Newgate were kept there only for a short time awaiting trial at the Old Bailey, then moved out to other prisons. A blackboard in the center of the room had the word *SILENCE* chalked across it in large letters. Sarah could still hear the rustle of whispers beneath the slurping of oatmeal and the banging of spoons on pewter. A pasty-faced woman whom she had not seen before pointed at her.

"That's her, ain't it?" the woman said in a loud whisper. "Greenacre's whore: the one who mopped up the blood."

"More than that," another girl said. "Cut up the body. Chop, chop, chop." The girl mimed the slicing action with her hand and laughed.

"Rook! Boltwood! One more word out of either of you and I'll place you on report."

Sarah looked down into her bowl, raising the spoon to her lips again and again without really tasting the gray contents. The important thing was to keep her face expressionless and to avoid the women's eyes so that they could not tell what she was thinking. She had had a lot of practice: she would, she thought, make a good card player.

Back in her cell, Sarah picked up her sewing. It was crude stuff: not the skilled needlework by which she had once scraped a living, but flannel garments for soldiers and for other prisoners. All the same, the familiarity and the repetition of the stitching soothed her: *in and under, back and up; in and under, back and up.* The events of the past months had reduced her, both her body — starved, pinched, deprived — and her mind, which seemed to have turned in on itself. She had not expected the death sentence. None of them had. There was so little evidence against her.

"You really mustn't worry," Mr. Price, their barrister, had said, as they waited for the jury's verdict in the room beneath the Old Bailey. "Women are never hanged these days."

Sarah had been so exhausted by then, after two days sitting in the dock listening to witnesses' evidence and lawyers' arguments and judges' musings: words and more words, running into and over each other while ladies fanned themselves in the stifling air and reporters yawned and offered one another their snuff boxes. She had closed her eyes as they sat in that stone-walled room waiting, her mind empty. Beneath the table, James had grasped her hand tight, like a vice. "It will be all right," he had said. But it was not all right. It was about as bad as it could be.

For a moment, Sarah saw again the jury being led back in, their faces impenetrable. She heard the roar of blood in her head, drowning out the sounds of the courtroom. She saw once more the foreman standing, the spectators in the gallery leaning forward, the clerk placing a square of black cloth over the judge's long white wig, and the judge's mouth opening and closing.

". . . And Lord have mercy upon your soul."

It was not just the Lord's mercy she needed, though. It was the King's. She felt a crushing sensation within her chest as she calculated that ten days had now passed since she sent her petition for clemency, and still she had received nothing in response. What else could she do? What else could she say? *In and under, back and up.* Think, Sarah, think. It was only by piecing everything carefully together that she would escape.

Sarah glimpsed a shadow beneath the door before it was pushed open. Miss Sowerton stood before her, unsmiling.

"Get up. You've a visitor. A lawyer. Sent by the Home Office, so he says."

Sarah's throat constricted. What did this mean? That her petition had been rejected? That it was to be investigated? She tried to smooth out her coarse dress and tidy her hair under her plain white cap. Miss Sowerton watched Sarah with a smirk on her pockmarked face.

"Making yourself pretty for 'im, are you?" she said. "I shouldn't bother. I'm sure he knows what you are."

I doubt that, Sarah thought as she walked toward her and out of the cell door.

Miss Sowerton led Sarah to a small desk in the corner of the legal visitors' room where a man sat, apparently occupied with the papers spread in front of him. He wore a black frock coat, a double-breasted waistcoat, and a crisp white shirt. He had removed his hat, which sat on the table before him, and his chestnut-brown hair stuck up in tufts. Sarah saw that he had a squarish jaw and smooth fair skin — he could not have been much more than thirty. She had the distinct impression she had seen him somewhere before.

"Here she is," Miss Sowerton said to him.

45

"You've a half hour."

"Well," the man said, getting up and smiling. "Then we must get on."

The matron nodded and then seated herself on a chair beside the table.

The lawyer's smile faded. "I am afraid I must speak with Miss Gale privately."

"Not possible," Miss Sowerton said. "Regulations."

"I discussed this with the Governor. It's important that Miss Gale is able to speak freely during our meeting. I hardly think I will be in danger." He glanced around at the other desks occupied with legal advisers and their clients.

"She was convicted of murder."

"In fact," he said, "the charge was aiding and abetting."

From where she stood, Sarah could see that the lawyer had been reading some notes about the trial. The words from her own statement — "That is all I have to say" — had been underlined.

"Whatever the charge was, I can assure you she ain't to be trusted. She'll tell you lies, the world round and the heavens broad, to save 'erself. And she's deceived cleverer than you."

"Thank you for your concern, but I'm sure I would be able to deal with any situation that should arise."

The matron fixed him with a look of contempt. "Suit yerself," she said, getting up. "I'll be keeping a close eye on you, Gale."

"Please sit," the man said to Sarah, gesturing to a wooden chair. He took out a rich brown leather-bound notebook and then looked up. "My name is Edmund Fleetwood. I'm a criminal barrister."

Sarah looked at him closely. Fleetwood.

"I've been commissioned by the Home Secretary to investigate the circumstances that led to your conviction."

"I might be pardoned?"

"It's one of the options, Miss Gale. That's all I can say at present. It's possible that the Secretary of State could grant you a reprieve or at least commute your sentence. However, I need to investigate the matter fully, as fully as I can in the time available. I have only seven weeks."

His voice was unnatural somehow, as if he had deepened the tone. It occurred to Sarah that he was a novice: he was on the back foot.

She looked directly into his eyes. "And what is it you want from me exactly, sir?"

"Simply your story, Miss Gale. Your own

account of what happened. You said very little at the trial and you have not, so far as I am aware, given a full account elsewhere. I would like you to tell me in your own words what happened last December."

In your own words. She had heard that before. And her own words had been twisted against her. Sarah's hands, which she clasped in her lap, were cold and clammy, but when she spoke her voice was level.

"It happened as I said during the trial, sir. James told me to leave his house before Christmas to make way for Hannah Brown, whom he intended to marry, and I did so. I returned on Boxing Day as he asked me to. I didn't know at that stage that she was dead and knew nothing of his hiding the body."

"Yes, Miss Gale, I'm aware of what you said in your statement for the trial. However, it doesn't make a full account."

Sarah adopted a blank expression while she waited for him to explain. It was best, sometimes, to let a man think he was cleverer than you.

"For example," he said, "can you explain how you came to have pawn tickets for Hannah Brown's silk dresses, and why you were wearing her jewelry when you were arrested?"

"As I've said before, sir, the jewelry was

48

mine. The earrings weren't expensive: just little drops of carnelian in gold filigree."

"Is there anyone who can confirm that?"

"You may ask my sister, Rosina, for it was she who bought them for me. Or you may ask those who knew Hannah Brown, for they will know she never wore such things."

"I believe that her family have already been asked and that they confirmed that they did in fact belong to Hannah Brown."

Sarah shook her head. "You mean her brother. He's lying. She told me they hadn't seen one another for months. He would have said anything to get me convicted."

The lawyer made a note of this but did not respond to the accusation. He emitted a good clean smell, she noticed, of shaving soap and boot polish.

"And the rings?" he said.

"The rings were mere thin bands of gold."

For a second she saw Hannah Brown's large, workman's hands, the close-bitten nails.

"My son dug them up out of the ground some months ago while he was playing in the garden. If you look on the inside, you'll see that one reads 'From AF to SW.' "

As the lawyer wrote this down in his notebook, she noticed that the elbows of his coat were worn to a shine. He was not rich.

"What about the dresses?" he asked.

The dresses. Hannah Brown had shown her the embroidered silk gown she planned to wear on her wedding day. She had spread it out before Sarah on the bed, and Sarah had thought it the purplish-red color of a heart or a kidney. But she would not tell him that.

Instead she said, "James told me that they'd had a falling-out about financial matters and that he'd broken off the marriage and asked her to leave. He said Hannah had given him the dresses as part payment for money she owed him. I had no reason to disbelieve him."

"Did you not think it rather strange that she'd left even her *clothing* at the house?"

"No, not really. She had other dresses. And James was always a man of business. If someone owed him money, he'd make sure that he was paid. In whatever form."

"So you accepted that she'd simply quitted the house and left her belongings behind?"

"Yes, I did."

After a long moment of silence, the lawyer said, "You have a young son, do you not? Four years old."

"Yes. George."

The very saying of his name hurt her deep

inside. A gnawing, empty feeling.

"Then for the sake of your son, Miss Gale, tell me the truth about what happened last Christmas. It may be that I can help you."

She looked up into his eyes — bluish-gray with a circle of darker blue around the iris. Did he really mean to help her? So far, everyone who had offered help had meant something else altogether. The charity ladies who visited had wanted her merely as a curiosity: a macabre specimen to discuss with their friends. The journalist who claimed he would tell her story had printed only lies. Her lawyers had said they would defend her, but were interested only in furthering their own reputations and protecting the man who was paying them. When she had tried to speak to Mr. Price, he had placed his sinewy hand over hers to stop her midsentence. "As you know, Miss Gale, we act for both you and Mr. Greenacre. You would not, I am sure, want to put us in a position where we were unable to represent you. It is far too late for that. Do not lose faith at this hour."

How did she know that this lawyer was any different?

Sweat beaded Sarah's upper lip. "I am telling you the truth, Mr. Fleetwood."

He nodded slowly. "Maybe the thing is to

51

start from the very beginning in order to gain the complete background. We can make it into a full affidavit — a statement of evidence. It would be a way of giving you a voice in all of this. I may not use it all, of course, but it would be helpful for me to understand how the situation came about."

The situation. He meant the murder. He meant, how had a woman ended up beaten and mutilated, the floor washed with red?

"The beginning, sir?"

She wondered where on earth he thought the beginning was. When she was born? When she first met James? When he first tired of her? When James first met Hannah Brown? When the first blow was struck?

As Sarah watched the lawyer dip his pen into his inkpot, she felt a sharp stab of anxiety. Everything she said would be written down, black on white — her words turned into a book of evidence.

Perhaps it was fortunate that at that very moment the bell rang out, marking the end of visiting time. From all around them came a scraping of chairs and rustling of papers as the solicitors got up to leave.

The lawyer's face fell. "Well." He screwed the top back on his pot of ink. "We will need to start on your statement tomorrow. In the meantime, maybe you could think about what you would like to say."

Yes, Sarah thought. She would think about it very carefully.

4

"He said the correspondence was broken off between him and Mrs. Brown, and he wished me to come back again — That is all I have to say."
— Statement of Sarah Gale, Proceedings of the Old Bailey, 10 April 1837

Back out on Newgate Street, Edmund was hit by the stink of horseshit and cesspits, the shouts of hawkers, the clatter of hoofs, the crack of a coachman's whip. It was a relief, however, to escape the prison walls. He had visited the men's side several times before and had on each occasion been revolted by the place — by its odor of neglected bodies, rotten food, and disease; by the casual violence and constant dismay of its inmates — some seasoned felons, some young pickpockets, all fighting and drinking together. The women's side was very different: an ordered and muted domain. But Edmund sensed that beneath the surface coursed the same violence, the same despair.

He walked briskly past the crowds thronging outside the Old Bailey, then down Ludgate Hill and into Fleet Street, until he reached the turnoff for the Temple, a haven of calm with its quiet squares and green lawns. He opened the door to his chambers carefully and climbed the stairs to his study.

Against the far wall of the study was a little bookcase of volumes on law practice and a row of law reports, and under the window was a mahogany desk, on which stood a stick of sealing wax, a variety of pens, a box of wafers, and a writing pad. From this room a door led off, first to the bedroom that he shared with his wife and then, beyond, to a closet room that served as both wardrobe and washroom.

Edmund removed his coat and waistcoat, washed the city's grit from his hands and face, and seated himself at his desk. He needed to identify the gaps in the evidence and formulate the questions that would draw out the truth. He dipped his pen into the inkwell and pressed the steel nib onto a piece of paper, enjoying the clean and fluid way in which the words formed: "The Edgeware Road Murder: Eliciting the Evidence."

As a younger man, he had nurtured ideas of becoming a journalist, exposing political corruption and inequity. His father, a senior Chancery barrister, had quickly and firmly squashed such ideas: "I did not fund your costly education so that you could sully the family name with cheap writings." Since he had to be a lawyer, Edmund had resolved that he would at least be the sort that made a difference. He would bring people to justice, defend the innocent, provide recompense for those who had been wronged.

Things had not gone as planned, however. Although quick-witted and eloquent, Edmund struggled to compete with the brasher and better-connected men who vied for the same criminal work. He took whatever briefs came his way, but the fees were insufficient to cover his and Bessie's living costs. He was creeping further and further into debt, and was by no means sure that his father would keep him from the debtors' prison should the bailiffs come calling.

This case could change things for him, however. If he could bring to light evidence that the authorities had missed — if he could get Sarah Gale to speak — then maybe his name would be made.

It was difficult to know what to make of her. She was slight of figure, with an angular, elfin face and large dark eyes, which she had kept cast down for most of their interview, staring at her raw hands. Handsome, yes, but there was something sharp and sly about her, like a wild animal, hunted.

Throughout the prosecution she had kept her silence. She had said nothing during her examinations by the magistrates, and only a few words during the trial at the Old Bailey. What exactly was it that she had said? Edmund tried to place himself back in the courtroom where he had sat in the dimly lit gallery among politicians, women in veiled hats, and scholars still in robes. James Greenacre alone had been worth the price of admission: he played to the crowds, sitting with his arms folded and his legs apart, like a man watching a cricket match, shaking his head violently when witnesses spoke against him, and laughing audibly during the prosecution barrister's closing speech.

Sarah Gale, however, had remained almost motionless and expressionless throughout. Price, the barrister for the defendants, had read out a short statement on Sarah's behalf, saying that she had not been at the house on the evening of Hannah Brown's death and that she knew nothing about it. Price had been moving on to another point, when the judge had stopped him and, unusually, spoken directly to the prisoner.

"Miss Gale, is there anything you wish to add to that statement? Is there anything else you wish to say?"

Sarah Gale, however, shook her head. "Thank you, sir," she said quietly, "but there is nothing else."

Nothing else. Edmund had struggled then to understand why she did not take the opportunity to retaliate against the Crown's case, so much of which had been speculation and supposition. Now, as he sat at his desk, he wondered why, even though she stood in the shadow of the gallows, Sarah Gale refused to speak out. It was not, he was sure, that she was resigned to her fate. He had seen the hope in her eyes when she realized why he had come to interview her: she understood that he represented a way out. What was it, then? Was she afraid? Ashamed? A memory floated before him of his own mother, covering her face with her hands as his father took out the cane to beat him. She had not spoken out for him then, and he had not spoken out for her later, even though he had screamed inside.

Or perhaps it was something else. For most of the trial, Sarah Gale had kept her eyes to the ground, her expression unreadable. Occasionally, however, she had looked up and stared intently at Greenacre.

There was a murmur of voices from the floor below and Edmund heard footsteps proceeding up the stairs. His door burst open. It was his clerk, Morris. He wished the man would knock. Morris slapped a pile of papers onto Edmund's desk.

"The brief. Not very brief, unfortunately." Even indoors, Morris still wore his dented stovepipe hat.

"What is it, Morris?"

"It is, sir, a spanker," Morris said, putting his thumbs into the pockets of his bottle-green waistcoat.

"But what kind of case?"

"A regular stunner, sir, the like of which you've never seen." Edmund picked the top page off the pile and scanned it. "You're right, Morris. I have never seen such a case, because it's a family matter, and I am a criminal lawyer."

"No, no, Mr. Fleetwood. It's about a family, but it's a criminal case all right." Morris took the paper from him and began to jab at certain sentences with a dirty forefinger. "Look, sir. Child theft!"

Edmund took the paper back and skimmed the introduction. It detailed the case of a woman who had absconded with her children after her husband refused her access to them.

"I'm afraid there's very little we can do for this Mrs. Pickton. She has no defense. What her wretched husband is doing is perfectly lawful." He should know: his own father had done it.

"That's why we'll win, sir. We act for *Mr.* Pickton."

Edmund looked up. "No, Morris, we most certainly do not."

"But, sir, I 'ave agreed it for you with his solicitor. And I 'ave secured an *hadvance payment*!"

To prove this, Morris removed a small pouch from his pocket and shook it so that Edmund could hear the coins chinking. "Three guineas, Mr. Fleetwood." He lowered his voice. "I know you 'as your principles, sir, but you also need to eat."

Edmund rubbed his face. "Morris, you will have to return the money. This is not a matter that I can or want to assist with."

Morris sighed and took back the piece of paper. "Very well, sir. We will let someone else dine off this good man's money."

"Besides, I have to concentrate on the Edgeware Road case."

"Oh, yes, that one's caused a stir. Old Paulson thinks it should 'ave been 'im what got your investigator brief. Not that he could investigate his way out of 'is own dressing gown."

Paulson had been Edmund's pupil master. He had trained Edmund mainly in the art of procuring cheap port.

"Well, evidently they wanted fresh blood," Edmund said, although he felt again a twist of unease. For the same fee, the Home Secretary could easily have procured someone more senior. "I thought you might be interested to see this, sir." Morris handed him a slightly soiled pamphlet entitled "The True Confession of James Greenacre to the Murder of Hannah Brown."

"Another one? But there have been at least three already."

"And all three 'ave been great sellers, I hear," Morris said. "This one claims to be the true one, penned by Greenacre 'imself."

Edmund thought this unlikely. If what the Home Secretary's clerk had said was correct, Greenacre still maintained that he had returned to his house to find Hannah Brown already dead. He began to read the pamphlet.

"You know she's a ladybird, sir?" Morris said in a lowered voice.

"A ladybird?"

"A night flower, Mr. Fleetwood. A dollymop." He leaned forward. "A *tail*."

"You mean a prostitute."

"I would not be so uncouth, sir."

"I know the papers have written it of her, yes, but that doesn't make it true. I met her this morning. She doesn't strike me as the type."

Morris wiped his nose with his cuff. "She might not 'ave been a three-penny-upright, but she were living with Greenacre as 'is convenient, weren't she?"

"She believed herself to be his common-law wife, Morris."

"Wife in watercolors, more like."

"What on earth does that mean, man?"

"It's a fashionable expression."

"I'm sure," Edmund murmured.

"Means a woman who it's easy to, you know, get rid of — dissolve. Like watercolors. A mistress."

Easy to dissolve. Edmund would have to hope she was.

On the cover of the pamphlet were two drawings: one of Greenacre, shown surly and menacingly handsome; the other of Sarah Gale. Her face was sketched in shade beneath her bonnet and her eyes were drawn dark and pained, her lips pursed, her hands at her chest as if praying. It looked absolutely nothing like her.

All the more pressing, then, that he got the true account and painted a more accurate picture. He took another sheet of paper and began to jot down the outline of a statement.

5

The body without head and legs on which an inquest was lately held, was exhumed. The head now under examination was placed with two cut surfaces in opposition. They were found in every way exactly to correspond, even to the superficial cut noticed at the inquest as existing on the right side of the neck.

The profile struck them as being very much that of the lower order of Irish.
— *MORNING CHRONICLE,* 10 JANUARY 1837

It was Jane Hinkley who unlocked the door to Sarah's cell that morning. She had a narrow face and a gentle pink mouth, with a smattering of freckles over her snub nose. She must have been about five and twenty. The other warders referred to each other and to the prisoners only by their surnames, but Miss Hinkley had introduced herself by her full name. This seemed to Sarah a kind-

64

ness — an intimacy.

"Time for your exercise in the yard now, Sarah. Get some color in those cheeks."

She led Sarah along a succession of poorly lit corridors, through huge barred doors, past the cells of those awaiting trial, and on to the women's exercise area. Sarah ducked under the doorway to emerge into a light so sharp and white that it hurt her eyes, which had grown accustomed to Newgate's gloom. She breathed in deeply. Although the London air was heavy with the smell of horse dung and coal smoke, it was a good deal better than the human stench of the prison. She could hear clearly the cacophony of life from Newgate Street. The sounds of the street musicians and the rush of carriage wheels seemed unbearably close, and Sarah felt a tightness about her heart at the thought of all those free people, just yards away.

Outside the door, a group of women stood in line waiting to be led back into the prison. They stared steadily at Sarah, turning their heads to follow her as she walked by. One prisoner — her face pallid and fleshy like uncooked pastry — made a low hissing noise. As Sarah made to move past, the woman stuck out her foot. Sarah stumbled briefly and put out her hand to stop herself from falling, catching the white skin of the prisoner's shoulder. The woman grabbed Sarah's wrist and brought her face right up to Sarah's so that she could feel the woman's breath on her cheek.

"You're lucky today," she whispered. "The warders are watching. But they don't always see. They don't always want to."

It was the new prisoner who had whispered about her in the breakfast hall: cold gray eyes and hair as dark as soot. Her breath stank, of rotting teeth and cheap gin. Sarah pulled away from her and moved on.

For her half hour, Sarah paced the yard in her ill-fitting shoes, around and around the demarcated circle with the other condemned prisoners. She walked behind a tall woman whose dress came only to her calves, her thin white ankles protruding from heavy black boots. There were three rings around which the prisoners moved at the same pace. It was strange to see so many different types of women all in the same blue striped clothing, all walking at the same speed and with the same hopeless expression on their faces. Here, as everywhere in the prison, silence was ordered but unenforceable. Voices hummed along the lines like the wind in the trees.

Sarah kept her head down, but when she

thought no one was watching she raised it to stare hungrily at the faces of the other prisoners, at the sunlight reflecting on puddles of rainwater, and at the pigeons, puffed against the cold, their plumage shining green and mauve. Now and again, she looked up at the sky — cornflower blue with threads of swift-moving white cloud running through it. What was George doing at this exact moment, she wondered. Was he outside playing? Was he safe?

"You must keep him in sight at all times," she had told her sister. And Rosina had understood why.

When she was sure that the warders were looking elsewhere, Sarah studied the strong iron spikes atop the black walls. How would one escape? The walls must be fifteen feet high. They had been scaled before, but not by a woman. She did not have the physical strength to pull herself up, especially now, after weeks of inadequate food and little sleep. No, it was not with her hands that she would escape these walls.

"Someone else has come to save you today." Groves stood in the doorway, resting her considerable weight against the doorframe.

"Who?" Sarah asked.

"A meddlesome Quaker woman. One of

Elizabeth Fry's do-gooders, so help me God."

Sarah suppressed a smile.

When Sarah entered the lady visitors' room, a small fragile-looking woman stood up and clutched her hands together. She was clothed all in black save for a dark-purple bonnet trimmed with velvet.

"Miss Gale," she said, as Sarah approached. "I'm so glad to finally meet you."

Groves snorted. "She is become quite famous, is our Miss Gale. I'll be just over there. Shout if she tries anything."

The woman smoothed her skirts and sat down. Her movements were swift and cautious, like a bird.

"Please," she said, gesturing toward a chair, "sit."

Sarah sat.

"Miss Gale, I'm Miss Pike — Verity Pike. I work with the British Ladies' Society for Promoting the Reformation of Female Prisoners."

The woman had large brown eyes, which darted about as she spoke, and a small upturned nose. She did not look well.

"I wrote to you," Sarah said. "It's kind of you to come."

"Kindness has nothing to do with it, Miss Gale. We knew you needed our help. I attended your trial. I saw with my own eyes what you endured before those men, and I saw clearly that it was you who were the victim in all of this."

Her darting eyes were now fixed on Sarah's.

She, the victim? That was a first.

"What exactly do you mean, Miss Pike?"

"It's the curse of Eve," Miss Pike said confidentially.

She was leaning forward now, her dark eyes gleaming. She spoke in a hushed but urgent tone.

"Ever since Eve, we have been doubly punished. Once for committing a crime, once for being a woman. I've worked for the Society for many years, Miss Gale, and during that time I've seen many women — some little more than girls — punished more harshly than their brothers, husbands or lovers precisely because they were women."

She put both of her hands on the table.

"It's always assumed, you see, that women can do no harm. That they're instinctive nurturers, mothers, wives, carers. So if they hurt, or kill — for whatever reason — they're seen as turning over the natural order of things. They become monsters."

Sarah thought of all the names that had

been applied to her in the past months: witch, whore, murderess, demoness . . .

"I know what you've been through," said Miss Pike. "You were forced into a situation over which you had no control." She reached forward and encircled Sarah's wrist lightly with her thin fingers.

Sarah flinched. It was so long since anyone had touched her except to push or pinch or handcuff her.

"You don't understand," she said.

"Oh, but I think I do," Miss Pike replied, not releasing her hand from Sarah's wrist. "I've witnessed many in your situation: too in thrall to another to speak out against them. But we can help you, Miss Gale. We can help you find the strength."

The woman was gazing at Sarah intently. She was misguided, but a good person, Sarah thought. She was the sort of person Sarah herself might have been, had not the good in her become shrunken and sealed in, like an insect imprisoned in amber.

"Then you'll support my petition?"

"My dear woman, I've already written to the Home Secretary. Several other people of prominence have been approached, and we intend to speak with the appointed investigator to convince him of the merits of your case."

Sarah bit her lip. "The investigator — he came to see me yesterday."

"Oh, yes? Who is he?" Miss Pike asked.

"A young lawyer. His name is Edmund Fleetwood."

Miss Pike furrowed her brow. "I've not heard of him. How does he seem? What sort of man is he, do you think?"

Sarah considered this. He had seemed genuine, but she had no idea where his allegiances lay, nor what he really wanted. "It's difficult for me to tell," she said. "My experience with lawyers has not been positive, but he said he wanted to hear my side of the story."

"Well, that's a good start, certainly," said Miss Pike. "But of course you must tell him the right story. We will do what we can to support you, but ultimately it's you who hold the cards." Miss Pike smiled at her.

Sarah forced herself to smile back, but she felt a twist of fear. She was not at all sure that she had the right cards, nor whether it was the right time to show them.

6

"As described at recipe 1019, this bird is variously served with or without the head on; and although we do not personally object to the appearance of the head as shown in the woodcut, yet it seems to be more in vogue to serve it without. The carving is not difficult, but should be elegantly and deftly done."

— *Mrs. Beeton's Book of Household Management,* 1861

It was a Tuesday morning and Edmund pushed his way through the crowds of Cornhill and the Royal Exchange, turned up Bishopsgate, and walked briskly to the police station. He found Inspector Feltham sitting in an armchair before a fire wearing a dark-blue buttoned-up frock coat.

"We conducted a very thorough investigation, Mr. Fleetwood. I hope you're not suggesting otherwise."

"Inspector, I assure you I'm not here to pick holes in your investigation. However, the Home Secretary has tasked me with analyzing the evidence, and I therefore need to make sure I fully understand the facts."

Feltham looked at him stonily. "Let me explain them to you, then: Greenacre killed the woman. Gale helped 'im cover it up."

Edmund bit the inside of his cheek. "You are certain that it was Greenacre himself who killed Hannah Brown?"

"Oh, yes, it were 'im all right. He was heard arguing with her that night. And we knew 'im already."

"What for?"

"Assault, fraud, abandonment. And there were rumors of much worse."

"Such as?"

"You know both his wives died young?" Feltham raised his eyebrows. "The first, he done up so bad that she died of 'er injuries."

"I thought she had consumption."

Feltham shrugged. "Depends who you ask."

"Did you investigate it at the time?"

"No. Seems he hooked it to America just after she died."

"And the second wife?"

"Took ill of a sudden and jacked it before the doctor could get there. Now there's a

73

coincidence for you." Feltham took a long pull on his pipe.

"Greenacre claimed, didn't he, that he returned to the house to find Hannah Brown dead?"

The inspector snorted. "Oh, yes, that's what 'e *claimed.* Said he'd gone out for an hour and come back to see her lyin' on the kitchen floor. But by that stage he'd already admitted to cutting up the body with a carpenter's saw. Let me ask you, sir: If you came home and found a dead woman in your house, would you call for a constable or would you slice the body up and cart the pieces all around town?"

For a moment, there was silence, save for the dropping of cinders in the grate.

"It was you who arrested him, wasn't it?"

"It was. We'd got word that Greenacre was lodging in a house in St. Alban's Street, Kennington. I got there at 'bout half-past ten o'clock on a Saturday night. It's best to do these things at night, when the suspect's in bed or in liquor. Sure enough, we found him in his shirtsleeves, half-cut, and Sarah Gale was there with 'im, sitting up in bed. We took 'em both down to the station, her little boy too."

"Why did you arrest her?"

"I saw she 'ad some rings on her fingers

74

that she were trying to hide. It was that gave me the idea she was part of it all. And then we found the pawn tickets and the earrings in 'er pocket."

"Did she say anything at the time to explain why she had them?"

"No, she were very quiet. Kept silent for the whole trip to the station, save for whisperin' to her little boy."

"How did she seem? Was she shocked, do you think? Might that have been why she didn't speak?"

The inspector looked at him shrewdly. "In my experience, Mr. Fleetwood, when a cove don't speak it's 'cos they've got something to hide."

Edmund nodded. "Do you have a list of all of the witnesses you interviewed?"

"Not a list, as such."

"Would it be possible to have one drawn up?"

Feltham grimaced. "I can assure you we spoke to every man and woman in the area."

"Nevertheless, it would be useful to see a full list."

Feltham eyed him coldly. "I suppose I'll 'ave to get one drawn up, then. Was there anything else? I do 'ave other things to be getting on with."

"I'd like to see the earrings and the rings

that were found in Miss Gale's possession. She maintains that they're hers."

"Well, she would, wouldn't she?"

"Nevertheless, I would like to see them and to show them to people who knew Miss Gale."

"That won't be possible. Those particaler exhibits went missing before the trial."

"Missing?" Edmund struggled to keep the surprise from his voice. "Were they stolen?"

"I've drawn no conclusions, Mr. Fleetwood. In the event, they wasn't needed. Miss Brown's brother'd already viewed 'em and confirmed that they belonged to her."

"I see," Edmund said, although in fact he did not see how police exhibits could have gone missing before trial, and the matter not have been raised during the proceedings. If Sarah Gale's lawyers had had half a cup of sense, they would have had all evidence on this point thrown out.

"One last thing," he said. "Had Sarah Gale ever come to your attention before all of this? For soliciting, perhaps. Some of the newspapers reported she was a fallen woman."

Feltham shook his head. "As far as we could make out, she 'ad no criminal history — no antecedents, nothing. But then, the best criminals don't."

■ ■ ■ ■

Hart Street, Covent Garden, was not a good address: the street was known for the cheapness of its brothels, the stench of its cowsheds, and the rowdiness of its public houses. However, number forty-six itself was an attractive enough two-story brick building, the lower part a grocer's shop furnished with barred sashes and painted woodwork. Above, dormer windows projected from the steep slope of the slated mansard roof. The sound of laughter rippled down to Edmund as he made his way up the stairwell to the apartment.

Rosina Farr opened the door in her apron. He knew immediately that it was her, for she had her sister's large, brown, darklashed eyes and her high cheekbones. Rosina looked much younger, however, and her skin had a pinkish bloom in contrast to Sarah's Newgate pallor.

"I'm afraid you've caught me in the middle of preparing our tea," she said, once he had introduced himself, "but please come in."

Rosina led Edmund into the kitchen, where she was making a pie of some kind. The room was spare and barely furnished

— a small fireplace and a coal box, some cheap pottery ornaments and a pair of brass candlesticks on the mantelpiece, a few earthenware cups and plates on a small shelf — but it was warm and clean and neat.

At the table, cutting out shapes from the pastry, was a little boy with dust-colored hair and a thin, floury face. This must be Sarah's son — indeed, he looked familiar.

"George, say hello to Mr. Fleetwood. He's helping your mama."

Edmund wanted to tell Rosina that he was not helping Sarah; he was investigating her case, but it seemed wrong to say anything at that moment. Perhaps, in any event, she was only saying it to comfort the child.

George looked at him with wide eyes but said nothing. Edmund bent down to his level. "I see you're assisting your aunt with the dinner."

The boy looked to Rosina for reassurance and her face broke into a wide smile, forming dimples in her cheeks. When she smiled, she looked very different from her sister, but then, it occurred to Edmund, he had not seen Sarah smile.

"I'm sorry to interrupt, Miss Farr, but I wanted to ask you a few questions. It shouldn't take too long."

Rosina wiped her hands on her apron and

untied the strings. "George, be a good boy and go and play in your room for a few minutes while I talk to this gentleman."

The boy looked at Edmund suspiciously before doing as he was asked.

Rosina gestured to Edmund to sit down at the table and she took a seat opposite him. With George gone, she at once became serious. "Please tell me: how is she? They won't let me see her."

Edmund shifted awkwardly in his seat. "She is . . . unharmed," he said, trying and failing to come up with a more positive description of her state.

Rosina looked at him searchingly. "Where is she kept? Is she given enough to eat?"

Edmund hesitated and she shook her head. "I knew it."

He spread his hands. "Newgate is not as bad as some have described it, at least not anymore." This was not a lie. Some of the descriptions he had heard of the women's side before Elizabeth Fry's intervention were horrific: naked screaming babies, born in filth; women packed into cells, sleeping in dirty straw; jail fever rife, prostitution common. The place was awful, but perhaps not as nightmarish as it had once been. Then again, maybe it was simply a different kind of hell.

"Have they hurt her?"

"So far as I know, your sister has not been mistreated there."

Again, not an untruth.

"Forgive me, sir, for interrogating you, but I've been so worried about Sarah and they won't let me visit her, nor even pass a letter to her."

"No, well, the nature of the charge means she isn't entitled to visits from family or friends."

Rosina smiled bitterly. "There are no friends. There's just me. And George."

Edmund nodded, imagining for a moment how Bessie would bear it were she to be cut off from her son and her sister. He brushed the thought aside: he needed to be careful not to get drawn into this; that was not why he was there.

"I wanted," he said, "to ask you about the jewelry that was found on your sister's person when she was arrested. There's a difficulty in that the police have mislaid the items, but I was wondering if you could describe to me the jewelry you know your sister to have owned."

"They say they lost the jewelry?" She squinted at him.

"Apparently so. Before the trial."

"Maybe they never seized it."

80

Edmund pressed his lips together. "At all events, they don't have it."

Rosina frowned. "Well, Sarah had very little. There were two thin gold bands that George dug up in the garden a while back while looking for fairy gold." She gave a half smile. "I remember Sarah showing me the engraving on the inside of one: initials. We discussed whose they might be. Then there were the earrings — some gold and carnelian drops that I bought for her myself. They're the only decent present I ever bought her, so now to hear they've been used against her . . ." She shook her head. "And she had a locket, a silver one with a portrait of our brother inside."

"Thank you," Edmund said. "And Sarah was with you on Christmas Eve, wasn't she?"

"She was with me during the day, at my employer's house on Camberwell Grove. She left in the evening to put George to bed."

"What sort of time was that?"

"About half after eight o'clock, I'd say. She didn't want to go back to that nasty lodging house, but I couldn't let her stay with me. I would have been dismissed."

"I see. I also wanted to ask you about James Greenacre." Her expression darkened. "What of him?"

"What do you think of him?"

"That he has no more heart than an iron file. That the sooner they hang him, the better."

"Did you think that your sister's relationship with him was . . . a normal one?"

"Depends what you mean by normal. There are many women who put up with all manner of things from their men." She looked away from him, toward the fireplace.

"It would help me," Edmund said, "if you could tell me more about their relationship."

Rosina met Edmund's eyes then. After a moment, she said: "You were appointed by the Home Office, weren't you?"

"Yes, by Lord Russell." Was she wondering, perhaps, why he had been selected despite his relative youth? Was she questioning his authority? But it was not that at all.

"Could you ask Lord Russell to let me see my sister? Could you ask him to allow George and me to visit her? It's very important, you see, that I talk to her."

When Edmund did not immediately reply, she continued, "We couldn't do any harm, and it's not right, Mr. Fleetwood, for a four-year-old boy to be kept away from his mother all this time. If you would just ask . . ." She held his gaze, her brown eyes steady and shrewd. Was she bartering? His assistance for her information?

Edmund sat back in his chair. "I could certainly *ask,* Miss Farr. Like you, I cannot see that any harm would come of it, and I am sure that your sister's state of mind would be much improved by a visit." Maybe, in fact, Rosina would encourage Sarah to talk. Maybe seeing her son would inspire her with the confidence to speak out. "But I cannot promise that the Home Office will grant any such request. It isn't the normal procedure."

"No," Rosina said thoughtfully, "but then your investigation isn't normal procedure either, is it? How often do they appoint someone to investigate a petition for mercy?"

"Very rarely, so I understand."

She nodded. "Did the Home Secretary select Sarah's case because he thought there'd been a miscarriage of justice, or was it simply because the case has attracted so much attention?"

Edmund was surprised by her boldness. "I really can't discuss the terms or reasons for my appointment. I can, however, assure you that I take my duties very seriously and that I'm doing my utmost to get to the truth of the matter. That's why it's important that you answer my questions as best you can."

Rosina nodded slowly. "Well, as far as Sarah's relationship with James went, it certainly wasn't healthy. It didn't make her happy. It turned her into a miserable, cowed creature — not my sister at all."

"You think he manipulated her?"

"I think he did his best to destroy her: to make her feel that she wasn't worth a straw. Some men do that. Makes them feel good about themselves." As she spoke, she kneaded a piece of pastry, crushing it into the table. "James tried to stop her seeing me, you know. He wanted to isolate her so she couldn't get away."

"Do you think she covered up for him?"

Rosina stopped kneading the pastry. "No. My sister is a good person. She's always protected me. She wouldn't have helped him."

"You really believe she didn't know what he'd done?"

"She was blind to what kind of a man he was, Mr. Fleetwood. I tried time and time again to show her, but she couldn't see it. Or didn't want to."

"Would she have lied for him?"

For a few moments, Rosina did not speak, and then she said, "I don't believe she'd have done anything to assist him with covering up another woman's murder, no matter what power he might have had over her. And James has maintained throughout all this that Sarah played no part in the death. I can assure you he isn't saying that out of the goodness of his heart or out of love for my sister. He must be saying it because it's true."

There was, Edmund thought, something else. Something she wasn't telling him. "Is there —" he began, but Rosina held up her hand to stop him.

"George," she called, "are you outside the door?"

The door opened a crack and a small face peered through it. "I'm hungry," the boy said.

"Yes, I must get on and finish cooking. Mr. Fleetwood, you're welcome to stay and join us. The pie just needs half an hour in the bakehouse."

Standing in the flour-filled, sweet-smelling kitchen, Edmund was almost tempted. "Thank you, but I must get home to my own luncheon. I have a little boy myself, a few years older than you, George."

"Well, then," Rosina said, "you'll know how important it is for a boy to have his mother with him." She looked at Edmund, her gaze hard as flint, and then quietly she said, "Please get my sister out of there. We need her here. We need her home."

When Edmund returned to his chambers, he found Bessie and Clem at the table, finishing their meal. Bessie gave a strained smile as he entered the dining room. There was a darkness beneath her eyes that made her seem older than her twenty-seven years and Edmund wondered if she might again be pregnant. He would not ask. Clem was the only one of four babies she had carried to term and Bessie held her grief close and silent.

"You're late, Daddy," Clem informed him brightly as Edmund took his seat.

Looking at Clem, so well fed and self-assured, his blue eyes clear and untroubled, Edmund could not help but compare him with Sarah Gale's son: pinch-faced and wary.

"Yes, I'm sorry about that, but I've been meeting with another small boy, one rather less fortunate than you."

"I'll bet he doesn't have to eat Flora's tapioca pudding."

"Admittedly no," Edmund said, eyeing the lumpy mess in Clem's bowl. "He is not so unfortunate as that."

"Oh, very well, Clem," Bessie said, removing the napkin from his collar. "You may leave your pudding, so long as you promise to be good for Miss Plimpton."

Their son, although nearly eight, was still schooled at home by a governess: a young, rotund woman with startled-looking eyes behind thick glasses. Edmund supposed that in a year or so they would have to send him to public school, but he shied away from the idea. Even now, remembering his early years at Harrow caused a sharp pain around his heart. He had thought that his father's strict regimen would have inured him against the cruelties of small boys, but it turned out that there were parts of him that could still be hurt. He had no wish to inflict that on his own child.

"Why have you been meeting with small boys?" Bessie asked, once Clem had left the room.

"Sarah Gale's son."

"Surely you weren't interviewing him?"

"No, I had to speak with his aunt — Sarah's sister. I was hoping she might throw some light on what happened."

"And did she?"

"Well, she was adamant that her sister wouldn't have helped Greenacre, but what woman would not say that to save her sister from the gallows?" He lifted the lid on the soup tureen and spooned some clear broth into his dish. "She did seem credible, however. And at least she was willing to talk, which is more than can be said of Sarah Gale."

"Does she not answer your questions?"

"Oh, she answers them, but without giving very much away. Which may be because she's afraid. Or it may, of course, be because she's guilty as the devil."

"Or it may be that she doesn't trust you."

"I'm quite sure she doesn't. I suppose that's hardly surprising. The question is how to convince her to tell all."

"Well," Bessie said, her expression thoughtful, "why does any person trust another? Why did I learn to trust you?"

"I'm sure I don't know," Edmund muttered into his soup. "Because my father told you to?" Bessie was the daughter of one of his father's clients. It had been he who had introduced them.

"Edmund, you *do* know. You took me seriously, even though I was full of sugar and nonsense. You listened to my tedious worries and hopes and acted as though they meant something."

He looked at his wife and, for a moment, saw her as he had first known her: luminous and confident and with plans for their future. Was it him and his own defeated hopes that had changed her?

"I suppose," Bessie said, "trust is about thinking that the other person will take seriously what you tell them. Perhaps Sarah Gale will only confide in you if she thinks you're on her side."

Edmund suppressed a surge of irritation. "Bessie, the point of my being the investigator is that I remain neutral. I do not take sides." He picked up a bread roll. "But maybe you have a point. Maybe in order to gain her trust, I need her to think I believe her."

During their second meeting, Sarah Gale seemed even more wary than when they had first met. She glanced nervously at the other prisoners seated nearby: a pale-faced woman with raven-black hair who sat sullen and silent with her arms folded, a stocky girl in urgent conversation with her solicitor.

"No, I never took it," the girl was saying. "Strike me blind if I did."

"Do you know these women?" Edmund asked Sarah, by way of prelude.

She looked at him with what he thought might be contempt. "We're not allowed to speak to one another."

"I see," he said. But that did not answer his question. He tried again. "I visited your sister."

She sat up straighter at that. "Oh, yes? How is she? Did you see George?"

There was an edge to her voice. Was it fear?

"Yes, they both seem well. Rosina looks very like you."

"You are polite, Mr. Fleetwood. She is younger and far prettier than me. And George, did he seem . . . unsettled?"

"No," Edmund lied. "He was perfectly content. They were making pastry together."

Edmund thought he saw the gleam of tears in her eyes, but her voice remained steady.

"What did Rosina tell you?"

"She confirmed, as you said she would, that the jewelry was yours. And she indicated that she was no great admirer of James Greenacre."

"No," Sarah gave the ghost of a smile. "They do not much like one another. I'm sure he will tell you that himself."

"You were with Rosina on Christmas Eve, weren't you? The day of the murder. At what time were you there?"

"From about two o'clock, I think. I visited James's house in the morning and walked from there to the house of Rosina's employer, in Camberwell. She was working then for a family, teaching their daughters. George and I stayed with her until about half past eight o'clock."

Her story matched Rosina's, but that in itself meant little.

"Is there anyone who can confirm where you were after that?"

"Mr. and Mrs. Wignal, the couple who owned the lodging house where I was staying at that time. I saw Mrs. Wignal in the evening before I took George up to bed."

Edmund made a note of this.

"And you saw James Greenacre at the lodging house on Christmas Day, the day following the murder. Did he give nothing away?" Edmund did not say it, but it occurred to him that Greenacre must have come to Christmas dinner straight from chopping up the body. He had a horrible vision of him carving the roast.

"No, not that I noticed," Sarah said. "He was perhaps a little melancholy, but I put that down to his having broken off the relationship with Hannah."

"And you accepted him back immediately?"

Sarah lowered her eyes. "Yes."

Edmund thought about this. "Greenacre

threw you and your son out of the home you shared with him a few days before Christmas so that he could marry this other woman. Then, only two days later, he invited you back to his house. Hannah Brown was gone, but all of her possessions remained. Yet you returned at once to live with him and didn't question any of this?"

"You forget, Mr. Fleetwood, or perhaps do not understand, that my situation was precarious. I had virtually nothing to live on, nowhere to stay, and a boy to feed." She looked at him. "You know what happens to people in my situation, don't you? They end up in the workhouse, separated from their children. Many would sooner die."

Yes, Edmund had read all about the workhouses: the institutions intended to punish the poor for their poverty and discourage them from seeking help. Children were kept apart from mothers, husbands from wives. Food was scant and disease was rife. You did not go into a workhouse unless you had absolutely no other choice.

"So I was grateful to have him back," Sarah continued. "It was never what you might call an equal relationship. I'm not proud of that, but that's the way it was." She spoke curtly and turned her face away

92

from him.

There was a long pause. Edmund could hear a young girl at the next table whimpering. After a few moments he said, "The statement you provided at trial was very short. Why was that? It was your only real opportunity to put forward your side of the story."

"I had very little to say," Sarah replied. "Simply that I wasn't there when Hannah died and that I knew nothing of it afterward."

Edmund nodded slowly. "The difficulty is that most people think you must have known."

"Yes," she said tightly. "I've heard again and again that I must have known, that I must have suspected, that no woman could have lived in that house and not have known what had happened there. All I can say to that is that I did *not* know." She still spoke quietly, but there was a violence in her voice that unnerved him.

"I did *not* know he had cut her up there in that house where I lived with my son. If I'd known, I would have left. And I certainly wouldn't have gone about town seeking to pawn the dresses of a woman I knew had been murdered."

Edmund conceded in his own mind that

93

this was a good point. She would not have wanted to draw attention to herself. He decided to try a different tack.

"Explain to me how it was decided that you should go abroad. Greenacre intended to take you to America, didn't he? Was that a surprise to you?"

Sarah folded her hands in her lap. "The speed of it was, I own, a little unusual, but not the idea itself. James had talked for years about going there. And now he was offering to take me with him — to pay for George and me to travel and start life afresh."

"How did he explain why it was necessary to leave so quickly?"

"He said that a business investment had gone bad and that he owed money, so needed to leave immediately. That seemed plausible enough, as I knew the same had happened a few years before and he'd gone to America then too."

That must have been just after Greenacre's first wife had died. Did Sarah know that? Did she know, when she returned to live in that house, precisely what Greenacre had done to Hannah Brown? Could she even have helped him? Edmund looked closely at her. A strand of hair had escaped from her white cap and curled down her face like treacle, dark brown against her milk-pale cheek. She did not look, he thought, like a criminal, but was it really possible to tell?

"Were you pleased the relationship with Hannah Brown had ended?" he asked.

Sarah rubbed at her jaw. "Yes, to be honest, I was glad she was gone. Without James, I'd have been back to where I was before — virtually penniless and friendless and with nowhere for George and me to go but a lonely lodging house." She looked up at him quickly. "But I didn't wish her dead."

"No, indeed," Edmund said, although it occurred to him that she might very well have done.

"Now," he said, "you'll remember that yesterday I asked that you relate your personal history. I wondered if you could tell me about your childhood. It would be helpful — for the statement."

He saw her body tense. "There's not much to tell," she said. "I had a fairly strict sort of upbringing, I suppose."

"Strict in what sense?"

"The usual sense," she said, her tone flat. "We were to be meek and mild and fearful before God; He was watching us at all times and judging us. You know, that sort of thing."

"Oh, yes, only too well."

She looked at him sharply.

"My father was another firm believer in original sin," Edmund explained. "He rather made it his mission to work our wickedness out of us."

He smiled, but there was no happiness in the memory of it, of being lectured, disciplined, and dragged to various terrifying locations — deathbeds, hospitals, poorhouses, and prisons — all as part of his education on the importance of seeking salvation. As a boy, Edmund had found it difficult to separate the idea of Our Father in Heaven from his actual father. Both were remote and frightening, capable of bestowing love but also of meting out punishment. Both were sometimes arbitrary as to which they dispensed.

"So, yes," he said. "We knew all about God's wrath."

She looked at him with what might have been interest, but which might also have been suspicion. "We?" she said.

"I had a brother. Jack."

His unsmiling ally. It had always been harder for Jack: he was gentler, more bruisable.

"What happened to him?"

"Jack always wanted to run away, to escape our life in London. Just after he turned twenty-one, he did it — secured a position in Bombay, serving in the infantry with the East India Company. I think he decided that fighting the natives was easier than fighting my father." He gave a short laugh. "He'd only been out there for a few months when he contracted typhus fever. There was a letter . . ." He swallowed, remembering the day that letter had arrived, his mother's screams.

He realized that Sarah was looking at him intently. Her face seemed to have softened. Was this the key, then? To feed her pieces of his own story in return for hers?

"You and your sister," he said after a moment. "You're very close. She was worried about you — has tried many times to visit you."

"Yes," Sarah said. "Well, as children we only really had each other. We've always had to look after one another."

For a moment her expression was quite open, as though the mask had slipped.

"Tell me about that time," Edmund said. "Tell me how it was."

7

"A woman without a tongue is as a soldier without his weapon."

— *The Old Wives' Tale,*
George Peele, 1595

"I suppose," Sarah said, "we should start where I did. By the seaside. My father was a cloth merchant with a small factory in Lyme Regis in Dorset. It was there that I was born and there that we grew up."

Sarah recalled Lyme as a solitary and insular town surrounded by steep hills. A narrow road led down to the shore and to the square in the center of town, which housed the Three Cups Inn, the Lion Inn, and the assembly rooms. From there, shops and houses spread out along the coast and up the river, with the Shambles market sprawling up Broad Street.

"We lived in a large, slate-roofed house at the top of Silver Street. From the bay window in my bedroom I could see the Cobb: the long gray stone wall that curves out of the water creating a harbor.

"My sister and I were cared for by a succession of nursemaids. We spent our time in the nursery, in our secluded garden, or on the beach, collecting shells and looking for fossils. We saw very little of our parents. Father seemed always to be occupied with his work and our mother was either busy with her social engagements or lying in the parlor with one of her headaches.

"They were very different people, my parents. My father was a dark, austere man who spent his days writing in ledgers and on charts and graphs. My mother, however, was like a shining jewel, the hard sides polished bright. When she was well, she liked nothing better than to play hostess: arranging tea parties and dinners and balls."

Sarah's main memory of those years was sitting at the top of the stairs, listening to the tinkling music of laughter, the piano, the clashing of cutlery, and the chinking of glasses — feeling shut out and lost.

"Occasionally, Rosina and I would be dragged out for my mother's parties, awkward in starched petticoats and ribbons. We were never expected to speak — only to curtsy and smile and perhaps to play a piece at the piano. If we behaved well, we were given a treat — a sugar plum, an orange water ice."

She did not say what happened when they failed, and fail they did: crying, or sulking, or flinching when kissed. Then they would be locked in their room without a candle, assured that the devil would come for them if they cried out. Sarah had never forgotten the thickness of that darkness, nor the quality of that fear. She would whisper stories to Rosina to calm her: of children who overcame strange beasts, of woodland animals who outwitted their hunters.

"When I was seven, our mother had another child: the son she had so long wanted. Both Rosina and I are dark, of course — brown hair, brown eyes like our father — but Oscar was a little blond boy with pale blue eyes and skin the color of cream. I remember this as a happier time. Mother spent less time prone on the chaise longue, and sometimes came up to the nursery. She commissioned a portrait of all three of us together."

Sarah paused. She could see the picture now as though it were before her: she and Rosina in white lace, their eyes cast demurely down. Oscar in between them, rosy-cheeked, dressed in black velvet with a white lace collar, staring straight out.

"A year after that picture was painted, however, when I was eleven years old, both Oscar and I took ill with scarlet fever. I can remember the heat and the terror and the searing pain in my throat. But while I grew better, Oscar became more and more ill. They shaved his little head and covered it in wet rags. They bled him and bathed him and fed him broths and potions, but it was no use — the fever had spread to his brain.

"Oscar died in the autumn of 1814, faded as the leaves fell from the trees. Rosina and I were not permitted to attend his funeral, nor to speak of him after that. His little clothes were folded away into a trunk and moved into the attic. And that was the end of the happier time."

Sarah swallowed. It felt strange to speak in full sentences after a month of only monosyllables — *Yes, Miss. No, Miss.* Her throat felt dry as sandpaper, her tongue spongy and tired.

There was much more she could have said, of course. She could have told him of how, for weeks after her brother died, their mother had kept to her rooms; of how the house was suffused with an unnatural hush; of how they walked the halls like ghosts, afraid of the sound of their own footsteps.

When her mother eventually emerged, something was gone. After a while, she had to mask her grief and return to society life. Children died all the time, after all. The parties began again, and the picnics, but it was as if a veil had come down over her. And the glazed look, which Sarah had noticed on occasion before, took up residence as her permanent feature. Although her mother never said it, Sarah knew that she thought God had saved the wrong child, or that she had somehow tricked fate. Indeed, Sarah herself came to believe that Oscar's death was in some indistinct way her own fault, just as it was their fault that Jesus had died, sacrificed for their sins.

The picture that had been commissioned of all three of the children together was removed from sight. Instead, her mother took to wearing a mourning brooch, typical of its time but always, to Sarah's mind, strange: a miniature painting, surrounded with pearls, of Oscar's eye.

Sarah noticed that the lawyer had stopped writing. While she had been speaking, he had been scribbling things down in his little book, but now he was watching her closely.

"It must have affected you deeply, your brother dying like that. Particularly at such

102

an impressionable age."

She shrugged. "It was a long time ago."

"Nevertheless."

Perhaps she should not have spoken of it at all. She had little left now but her own secrets. And besides, she did not want him to think her damaged.

Edmund closed his notebook. "Your sister asked that I do something for her."

Sarah straightened her back. "Do what, sir?"

"She pleaded with me to apply to the Home Secretary so that she might be allowed to visit you, with your son."

Sarah felt the blood rush to her face and her heart quicken its pace. "And you —"

"And I agreed to make that application and in fact did so this morning." He looked at her levelly. "I cannot promise that Lord Russell will grant the request, but I put forward to him the reasons why I thought such a visit might be beneficial."

Sarah tried to read what was written in his eyes. What did he mean by beneficial?

"I am most grateful to you, Mr. Fleetwood. You didn't need to do that."

"No," he said slowly. "And you didn't need to tell me all you have this afternoon. But you did."

Sarah forced a smile. Had he believed

what she had told him, or was he letting her know he could not be fooled? He too smiled as he got up to leave, but the smile, she noted, did not reach his eyes.

We are like two chess players, she thought, as he walked away. Each trying to anticipate the other's move.

"Special privileges, is it now?"

Sarah gave a start. Miss Sowerton was standing to her right, only a foot or so away.

"Miss?"

"There's many in 'ere would like to see their families and aren't able, whose crimes are far less serious than yours. What about Eliza Sharpe?" The matron nodded toward a raw-boned, thin-lipped woman seated close by. She looked up when she heard her name. "Five children she's got," Miss Sowerton said, "and she ain't seen 'em for months."

Well, let her see them, Sarah thought.

"But then," said the matron, her lip curling, "there's not many can tell a story as pretty as you can, are there, Gale? Was that what your governess taught you, eh? Fancy sewing and lying?"

So that was it. This woman did not hate her for her crime, but for her learning and her supposedly privileged past. "You should not have been listening to our conversation," she said quietly.

"Oh, is that right, Gale?" Miss Sowerton lowered her voice until it was little more than a whisper. "I'm in charge here. I'll listen to whatever I want, whenever I want. And you *dare* talk back to me again and you'll be locked in the dark cells quicker than you can blink."

The dark cells: that place of utter blackness beneath Newgate where those who refused to keep silent were shackled to the wall, gagged, and then left to their own private hell.

Sarah looked away from her. She was stupid to have responded at all.

"I'll speak to the Gov'ner," Miss Sowerton said. "If I 'ave anything to do with it, the next time you see your family will be on the gallows steps."

8

It might almost be considered that some plan was arranged to place the different portions of the body as far as possible apart: certainly, had the Map of London been taken as a guide, and three equidistant points dotted off in the suburbs, none could have corresponded to the angles of an equilateral triangle more exactly than the three different places we have mentioned. The three points are full seven miles from each other: twenty-one miles must therefore have been traversed.

— *LONDON STANDARD,* 8 FEBRUARY 1837

James Greenacre was not what Edmund had expected. He had envisioned an ogre. What he saw was something far more subtle. When Edmund entered the legal visitors' room, Greenacre rose to greet him and extended his hand.

"Mr. Fleetwood. Do sit down."

Greenacre was flanked by two warders, despite Edmund having asked the Governor to ensure there was only one guard, seated out of earshot.

"You mustn't mind these two," Greenacre said, noticing Edmund's expression. "This is Villiers, and this Crowe. They're good men. They're merely doing their job."

"I'm sure. I had hoped to talk to you alone, however."

"I assure you I can speak freely in front of these men. I have no secrets now."

Villiers, a thickset man with dark whiskers, nodded and echoed Greenacre. "No secrets."

Edmund frowned. He felt as though he had walked into the King's chamber to consult with his advisers.

"Mr. Greenacre, you're aware that I have been appointed by the Home Secretary to look into the conviction of Miss Gale and whether there is any reason to question it."

"I am, Mr. Fleetwood. The Governor and I have spoken about it. And I say to you what I said to him, which is that I will do my utmost to ensure that that wretched woman's conviction is overturned. It was a shocking and unnatural verdict."

"Why do you say that, Mr. Greenacre?"

"Because I made clear from the very

beginning that she knew nothing about the death of Miss Brown and that she played no part in it. Why would I have said that if it weren't true?"

This seemed to Edmund to be an odd question to ask. He might have all sorts of reasons for saying what he had.

"I understand that you have also petitioned the Home Secretary for clemency."

Greenacre nodded. "I have."

"On what grounds?"

"On the grounds, Mr. Fleetwood, that it was not *me* who killed Hannah Brown."

"You have new evidence to support that claim?"

"You're a criminal lawyer, aren't you? You must know that no one should be found guilty unless there's clear proof that they committed the crime. I conceded that it was me who disposed of the body, but that doesn't mean that I murdered the woman."

Edmund looked closely at Greenacre. It was difficult to understand how he could be maintaining this fiction. Did he believe it himself, perhaps?

"So you still say that she was dead by the time you arrived home?"

"I do," Greenacre said levelly. "We spoke. I broke off the marriage. I left. When I returned, she was dead."

Edmund coughed. "It was more of an argument than a conversation, wasn't it? Some of your neighbors, Mr. and Mrs. Callow, reported that they heard shouting."

"Some of my neighbors wanted their time in court, Mr. Fleetwood. And they were willing to say anything to get it."

"I see." Edmund paused, remembering the words from Mrs. Callow's statement.

"We'd heard arguing plenty of times before from that house, but not like that. Nothing like that. We should have known something terrible would happen."

"Mr. Greenacre, could you explain to me what your relationship with Miss Gale was?"

"Well, it started mainly as a business arrangement. You will forgive me for using the language of commerce, but I am a man of business. It began on the basis that Sarah would cook and clean for me and so on, and in return would receive board and lodging for herself and her son. In time, a relationship developed between us."

"You did not marry."

"I did not consider it to be necessary."

As Greenacre spoke, he gesticulated with his large hands.

"And can you explain why you told Miss Gale to leave your house?"

"As I said, I am a man of business, and I

was offered a business proposition in the form of Miss Brown. She agreed not only to marriage but to putting her property toward my business interests."

"What reason did you give to Miss Gale for asking her to leave?"

"Oh, I told her the real reason. She always understood that the nature of the arrangement between us was, let us say, conditional. She appreciated the position."

"She must have been upset, however. You were turning her and her young son out onto the streets in the middle of winter."

Greenacre set his jaw. "I don't much like your choice of words, Mr. Fleetwood. I did not 'turn them out,' as you put it. I ensured that Sarah and George had a place to stay — a lodging house in Walworth. I helped her move her things. I assure you it was an amicable parting."

"She must nevertheless have felt some resentment, perhaps toward Miss Brown as well as yourself."

Edmund thought he saw something flicker across Greenacre's eye.

"If she felt any resentment, she did not express it."

"No," said Edmund. "No, I can believe that." But that did not mean she had not felt it.

"And did you intend to continue to support Miss Gale financially?"

"I had no obligation to do so," Greenacre said. "There was no legal tie between us, nor any moral duty. The child, as I'm sure you're aware, is not mine."

"So Miss Gale had been left alone and in poverty all because of Miss Brown's intervention."

Greenacre frowned. "I resent your implication, sir, that she had motive. It wasn't argued even at the trial that Sarah did anything more than assist me to conceal the body, which of course she did not."

"I'm merely trying to understand the state of things at the time of the murder, Mr. Greenacre."

"And I'm telling you that there was no animosity."

Edmund paused. "You described your relationship with Miss Gale as a business arrangement. Why, then, are you so anxious to extricate her from any role in the murder?"

"Because I am a fair man, Mr. Fleetwood, and I believe in justice. Sarah has been wrongly accused and convicted. I am simply doing what I can to remedy that."

Edmund nodded, but he didn't believe a word of it. "You'll recall that one of the pieces of evidence used against Miss Gale was the scrap of fabric found in the bag with Hannah Brown's torso." Edmund watched Greenacre: he did not flinch. "Fabric that the prosecution claimed matched a piece of clothing belonging to Miss Gale's son."

Edmund recalled the moment when the prosecution barrister passed the piece of bloodstained calico to the jury box, together with one of George's frocks. *"You will note, gentlemen, that they are an exact match. Clear proof, we say, that the prisoner Gale knew about the murder and helped to conceal it."*

Edmund looked closely at Greenacre. "Can you explain how that piece of fabric came to be with the body?"

"Yes, quite easily. After I found the body and carried out the . . . clearing up, I needed something to stem the blood. I used some scraps from a box of rags that Sarah kept in the kitchen. I didn't know at the time that some of the scraps came from George's old clothing, but that was all there was to hand. They then ended up in the bag, which I hid under a paving slab off the Edgeware Road."

"And when did you dispose of the body pieces?"

"I dealt with the legs on Christmas Eve."

"You left them in a ditch off the Coldharbour Lane."

"I did. I do not deny it. I was in a frenzied state," Greenacre said calmly.

"And the other body parts?"

"The trunk I took to Pineapple Gate on Christmas morning. The head I carried via omnibus to Stepney on Christmas Day eve."

Edmund paused. "So the head was still in your house when you went to see Miss Gale at her lodging house for Christmas luncheon?"

"That is correct."

"I see." Edmund took a moment to absorb this. He looked at the warders to judge their reaction. They seemed unmoved. "And tell me: in what condition was the house by the time Miss Gale visited you on Boxing Day?"

"Oh, very presentable. I'd cleaned everything most thoroughly."

"Even though you were, as you put it, in a 'frenzied state'?"

"I have always worked quickly and efficiently," Greenacre replied. "Even when under stress."

"Surely she would have noticed that things had been moved about?"

"Absolutely not. I was very careful to ensure that all of the furniture was in its usual position and that there wasn't a spot of blood anywhere. It was essential that Sarah didn't guess what had happened, as I wished her to return to live with me. To resume our former understanding."

"Yes. Which, rather surprisingly, she did."

"Surprisingly?" There was a note of menace in Greenacre's voice.

"I think most women, having been asked to leave their lover's house and replaced with another woman, would have hesitated before returning."

Greenacre regarded him coldly. "Sarah Gale is not most women."

"No, indeed. And she was, of course, dependent on your goodwill and your money."

"I think that sums up most relationships, does it not? Married women can own no property, after all."

Edmund smiled thinly. The man was not stupid. "But in your relationship the imbalance was even more marked, wasn't it? As you have yourself acknowledged, Miss Gale had no hold over you legally or morally, and you evidently thought fit to dispense with her and then invite her back into your home when it suited you."

Greenacre narrowed his gray eyes.

"Many men," Edmund continued, "would be tempted to take advantage of such an imbalance of power. To misuse the woman and perhaps bend her to his will."

Greenacre leaned forward so that his face was only a few inches from Edmund's. "I treated Sarah well. With kindness and generosity. Ask her yourself and that's what she'll tell you."

"I'm asking you."

"And I'm telling you that you mistake me." Greenacre's voice was low and dangerous. "I'm no brute. I've seen men stamp upon their wives and break them till they're brittle as tinder wood. I am not one of those men. Sarah and I have a deep understanding." He folded his arms and turned away from Edmund.

"What do you mean by a deep understanding?" Edmund asked.

Greenacre gave no reply.

"Miss Gale's sister," Edmund said, "believes you bullied and ill-used her."

Greenacre snorted. "Rosina Farr would malign any man who so much as touched her precious sister. Rosina Farr is as mad as Bedlam."

Edmund thought of Rosina's warm smile, of her bright, shrewd eyes. "When I spoke to her she seemed perfectly lucid," he said coldly.

Greenacre turned to look at him. "Yes,

Mr. Fleetwood. The maddest often do."

Edmund thought back to Greenacre's words as he sat writing up his notes that afternoon. To what "deep understanding" was he referring? Why were Sarah and he covering up for each other?

He was roused from his work by a rap at the door.

"Come in!"

Flora slouched into the room, her cap askew on her head. Edmund wondered if she might be drunk.

"Your post, sir." She dropped two envelopes onto his desk and dipped unsteadily into a low curtsy.

Yes, there was a definite smell of the gin-house about her. He would have to speak to Bessie.

Once Flora had left, Edmund unsealed the letters. The first contained a note from his father asking him to call on him at his earliest convenience, presumably to express his views on how the investigation should be conducted. Edmund put the letter to one side. The second envelope contained the list of witnesses that the police investigation had identified. Most of the names he recognized as those called at the Old Bailey: the brick-layer who had found the trunk, resting in a pool of frozen blood; the lockkeeper who had fished the severed head from Regent's Canal; the laborer who had found the last piece of the jigsaw — the legs — poking from a sack in a ditch in Camberwell. Then the friends, relatives, and neighbors of the deceased: the people who knew Greenacre had broken off his marriage to Hannah Brown on Christmas Eve, those who had heard them shouting, and others who had seen Sarah Gale return to Greenacre's house on Boxing Day.

At the trial, Adolphus, the lead prosecution barrister, had built the Crown's case on circumstantial evidence — on the argument that Mr. and Mrs. Callow had overheard, on the boxes belonging to Hannah Brown that were found in Greenacre's house, on the jewelry and clothing in Sarah Gale's possession when she was arrested. Adolphus had made much of the water that Sarah had borrowed from a neighbor, *"doubtless used to wash the blood from the floor."*

Although the prosecution had skillfully glossed over it, the fact was that they had no eyewitness — no one who had seen the deed being committed or who could say with certainty what role the prisoners had played in Hannah Brown's death. They could not even place Greenacre or Gale at the scene of the crime when the murder occurred. Casting his eye down the witness list, Edmund wondered if all of these people were telling the truth. Surely someone had seen something.

The strongest evidence against Greenacre was, of course, his admission that he had cut up the body. Edmund had previously wondered whether Greenacre might have disposed of the body parts in order to protect someone else: the true killer. But, having now met Greenacre, he was quite certain that the man only acted in his own interests. He would not have put himself at risk of death in order to protect another.

Which made it all the more strange that he persisted in his claims that Sarah knew nothing of the murder. Greenacre had spoken of their relationship in the language of business, not of love, and he admitted he had not helped her in December, financially or otherwise.

Why defend her now?

At dinner, over their roasted fowl and potatoes, Edmund broached with Bessie the subject of Flora and her drinking.

Bessie pressed her fingers to her forehead. "Are you quite sure, Edmund? Might she not simply have been . . . tired?"

"Bessie, she smelled like a gin still at three o'clock in the afternoon. I can talk to her if you'd prefer."

"No," Bessie closed her eyes for a moment, "I should do it, but I don't understand it: her previous employer gave her a good character. He wrote such a nice letter."

Edmund turned his plate so that the chipped side faced away from him. "Yes, well, what one person says of another isn't necessarily true."

He thought again of Greenacre and his claims that Sarah had taken the news of his engagement to Hannah Brown calmly. She must, surely, have been furious.

"I just hope she doesn't leave," Bessie said.

Edmund inspected a desiccated leg of chicken. "Would it be so bad if she did? She's not exactly faultless."

Bessie did not look at him. "Nor is she exactly expensive, Edmund. And, unless I have misunderstood our current situation, we are not in a position to employ someone better."

Edmund felt a flush of shame spread across his face. He had assured Bessie that his practice would flourish; that they, like so many other barristers' families, would soon be able to move to better lodgings outside the Temple; that they would take a tour of Europe together. And now here they were, reduced to eating from chipped china and to employing a surly drunk as a maid.

"Things will change soon, Bessie. I will see to that."

Late on Friday afternoon, Edmund traveled to Walworth, to the south of London, to meet the couple with whom Sarah had stayed after Greenacre threw her out: the people who she had said could confirm her alibi. The lodging house was a narrow, dirty building on a terraced street. The door was opened by a scrawny woman with a mouth that turned down at the corners. This, it transpired, was Mrs. Wignal, the lady of the house, which smelled of damp, dogs, and old cooking. She led him into a small, dingy parlor where jars of faded rose leaves attempted to conceal the smell of mildew and a miserable-looking linnet pecked at its cage. She brought weak tea and some thinly sliced seed cake and sat opposite Edmund on a low settee next to her husband.

"Miss Gale came to lodge in our house on the twenty-second of December," Mrs. Wignal said. "She took the back parlor, unfurnished. Told us she was a widow woman." She exchanged a knowing look with her husband, a loose-fleshed man with small black eyes in a wide face the color of lard.

"I first saw Mr. Greenacre the following morning. That was the twenty-third. He came again on Saturday the twenty-fourth of December. Neither of us much liked him, did we, Mr. Wignal?"

Mr. Wignal shook his head. "A coarse kind of man, to my mind."

Edmund took a bite of cake. It crumbled like sawdust in his mouth. When he was able to speak again, he said, "And Sarah Gale? What sort of a person did you think her? I'm trying to understand her character."

Mr. Wignal snorted. "I think poor Hannah's mutilated body should give you a pretty good idea of what kind of woman she is."

Edmund thought of the torso, upright in a pool of blood, of Hannah Brown's pale, sightless face floating in solution. "Mrs. Wignal, Sarah Gale says that she went out on the morning of the 24th, but came back in the evening. She told me that you saw her return. Is that correct?"

"Yes," said the woman. "I saw 'er with my own eyes. She brought the little boy back at about nine — far too late for a child of that age to be up. I saw her carryin' him up the stairs as I came back into the house."

"You said good night to her?"

"I did. We was always civil."

"And she didn't go out again?"

"I'm sure I should have heard if she did. I listens out for these things, just in case a lodger tries to shoot the moon, as we call it. She struck me as the type to try and leave without paying."

"I see. Well, I am obliged to you." Edmund got up to leave.

"It's my opinion," Mrs. Wignal said, "that she played more of a role in the crime than she pretends."

Her husband nodded. "You've got to wonder whether she weren't the guiding hand in the whole business."

"Why do you think that?" Edmund asked.

"Just call it a hunch," said Mr. Wignal, putting his thumbs in his waistcoat, "but it were odd, weren't it, that she was gone from his house such a very short time. Left the house just afore the murder and came back the day after he got rid of the body."

Mrs. Wignal sucked in her cheeks. "You might almost 'a thought they'd planned it together."

Edmund's eyes rested on a bluebottle that had become stuck to a flycatcher sheet and was wriggling furiously to free itself. They were right, of course, that Sarah was gone from the house for a fairly short time, but did that mean she had been instrumental in the killing — some kind of Lady Macbeth character — or simply that she was operating at Greenacre's beck and call?

He excused himself and stepped out into the darkening evening. At least he could say now with certainty that she had not been at Greenacre's house on the night of the murder. The Wignals had no reason to protect Sarah: they evidently despised her.

Outside, the wind had picked up. As he walked back toward the main street, a door creaked on its hinges and swung shut and a dog barked. Thinking he heard the light tread of footsteps close behind him, Edmund turned back, but saw only rags hanging on washing lines overhead, moving in the breeze like phantoms.

9

"Before the rest of the dura mater can be seen, the brain must be taken from the head. To facilitate its removal, let the head incline backwards, whilst the shoulders are raised on a block, so that the brain may be separated somewhat from the base of the skull . . . For the division of the nerves of the brain, a sharp scalpel will be necessary."

— *Demonstrations of Anatomy; Being a Guide to the Knowledge of the Human Body by Dissection,* George Viner Ellis, 1840

When she opened her eyes, Sarah saw a split face before her, the skin so pale it was almost translucent, the setting blood a deep crimson. The right eye protruded from its socket. The other stared right at her, glassy, accusing. She shook herself free of the image and sat up, shivering in the cold air. It was nearly dawn and a watery light trickled in through the small, dirty window. All at once, she was gripped by a sense of dread and fear: how many more dawns would she see before her time was up?

She would ask to see the Ordinary today. Having witnessed his sermons in the prison chapel, Sarah knew that he had little love for the felons of Newgate, but maybe she could soften him. She was good at that. Maybe, given the right words, he would help her get out of this place.

At nine o'clock Dr. Cotton arrived. Close up, Sarah could see that his nose was pitted, his surplice grimy. His gray eyes grazed over her briefly. He did not smile. He did not sit down.

"You asked to see me?" He refused to meet her gaze, but instead stared over her shoulder.

Sarah's stomach fell. She considered saying then that there had been an error — that it was someone else who wanted to speak to him. But she had to try to convince him, undignified though it might be.

"I wanted to ask for your assistance. I wondered —"

"You're the one who helped James Greenacre, aren't you?" he said across her. "Cut that woman's head off."

"No, it wasn't like that. It's not what you've heard."

"Ah, another innocent. The authorities really should be more particular as to whom they lock up."

"Reverend, I did not do what it is claimed."

The Ordinary looked at her then, in the eye. "Unlike people, and unlike courts, God cannot be fooled, Miss Gale. He watches us, all the time."

"I know that, Dr. Cotton. I'm telling the truth. I seek your support in persuading the Home Secretary to pardon me."

He stared at her coldly. "You seem not to have accepted the reality of your situation — the inevitability of your fate."

Sarah wondered how he thought she should demonstrate that she recognized her predicament. Did he want a display of emotion and supplication — wailing, beating her chest, tearing her hair, perhaps? But then he would say she was mad.

"I'm fully aware of the reality of my situation," she said. "That's why I'm seeking your help. I don't know what else to do or who else to turn to. I have a young child, you see, who would be all alone —"

"If you want to save yourself," he said, interrupting, "then you must repent and beg the Lord's forgiveness. Then you must confess. Then you must provide restitution. That's the procedure, Miss Gale. That's how it works." He made it sound like the application procedure for some insurance scheme. "So, are you going to confess?"

She looked at him, at his fleshy, red-veined cheeks and swollen drunkard's nose. He wanted her confession to make into a pamphlet and sell: her story for ready money — it was one of the perks of being prison Ordinary. "But, Reverend, I cannot repent for something I did not do."

The Ordinary turned away. "Then you're wasting my time. Without contrition of the heart there is nothing I can do for you. You are past redemption."

She stood up to protest but realized it was futile. She did feel remorse, of course she did, but she could not provide him with the confession he wanted.

He cast her a final look of scorn mixed with disgust and then left the room, shutting the door hard behind him.

Later, in the large, stone-walled bathhouse, Sarah held on to the cold slippery sides of the trough and lowered herself into the tepid brown water. The bottom of the slate bath was covered with a curious cement material, slimy against her skin. She used the pitted bar of yellow soap to clean herself, feeling the sharper lines of her body where the fat had fallen away. After a few weeks of Newgate's regime, she no longer looked much like a child-bearing woman. She was beginning to resemble the skeleton she would become.

Sarah looked carefully at her hands, at the tendons standing out from the bone, the tangle of blue veins visible beneath the skin. She imagined the flesh melting away, decay setting in, the bones picked clean by animals or maggots. Or would she be anatomized — the skin peeled from her face and the organs removed from her body, specimens for the study of others? *This, Gentlemen, is what an evil woman's heart looks like: observe how strangely it is formed. This is the kidney of a murderess — you see how the infection took root long ago.*

She turned her hands palm up to expose the latticework of tiny cuts on the soft underbelly of her arms. What would they make of these when they examined her cold body? *A sure sign, Gentlemen, of a diseased and dangerous mind.*

James had declared that, if he was indeed to hang, his corpse should be given over to science. How like James that was. Most

128

other people would be horrified at the prospect of being cut into pieces after death: that was why surgeons had to resort to paying resurrection men to procure corpses for them. But not James. No, he would like the idea of being preserved for the education of others, of his organs and brain being labeled and catalogued and discussed by students and academics. He was thoroughly modern, or so he would have others believe. When they had first met, he was full of plans to travel to Hudson Bay and make his fortune in trading. She was to come too, with George, and they would create new lives for themselves away from the stench and squalor of London. At other times, James would return late from the White Lion Radical Committee Room, inebriated, overexcited, and full of schemes for his future political career.

She traced a thin scar that ran from her neck down to her breastbone: a memento of the nights when he came back in a different temper altogether. It was a shard of mirror, he had used: a piece of the looking glass he had found her looking into. "Not so pretty anymore," he had said, when it was done. As time had gone on, those nights became more frequent, more brutal, and she had grown increasingly sickened by her own willingness to tolerate it all. She remained brittle on the outside, but hollow, like an empty shell worn thin by the tides.

Lying motionless in the now cold bath, Sarah cursed herself for not having left him long ago, for not having recognized their relationship for what it was — a cesspit of manipulation and obsession. And her punishment was that she was to be dragged down with him, drowned in another woman's blood. Unless. Unless she could somehow wriggle out of the net that had been cast. Unless she could convince Edmund Fleetwood that she should be pardoned. She was still unsure whether he was really looking for a way to help her, or whether he was merely playing a game. Did he seek her story only as a trophy — the proof of his cleverness? She wanted to believe him good, but she could not be sure. He was, after all, an ambitious young man. A case this famous must be a rare prize, the breaking of a convicted criminal rarer still. And yet his face was gentle.

As she dried herself with her coarse towel and stepped back into her clothing, Sarah felt herself watched. She turned and saw that the prisoner who had threatened her in the exercise yard stood to the right of the doorway, her back against the wall, her arms folded, her pale face half in shadow. For how long had she been standing there?

Sarah hurried to dress, struggling to pull on her stockings and shift over still-damp skin and stealing glances at the other woman, who regarded her with narrow eyes, gray and cold as a winter sky. Emily Rook: charged with battering another woman with an iron bar.

"Nasty piece of work, that one," Hinkley had told Sarah in a whisper. "She's been in 'ere a few times since I started — always for violent offenses. I'd keep well away from 'er if I were you."

But now there was no way of avoiding her. She would have to pass Rook in order to leave the bathroom. Sarah kept her eyes ahead and her back straight as she walked across the wet stone floor.

When she was a yard or so away from Rook, the woman said quietly: "What? Think yourself too good to talk to me?"

Sarah refused to look at her.

"Well, I've been watching you, Gale. I've seen you simpering and sniffling and batting those dark lashes of yours." Rook spoke in little more than a whisper. "You might be able to fool him, but I know what you are."

Sarah carried on walking, not looking

back, her heart hammering against her chest.

"Yes, that's right, Gale, you run along." The woman spoke more loudly now, seeming not to care whether the warders heard her. "But there's nowhere in here I can't get to. When I want you, I'll find you."

That night, when Sarah finally slept, it was to dream of a surgeon's chamber, pure white, with a high stone table upon which a body lay shrouded. Approaching the table, she knew it was Hannah Brown beneath the cloth, her gray-tinged feet protruding from the end of the sheet.

The surgeon was the red-whiskered man who had given evidence at the trial. "You must not be afraid," he told Sarah. "It's the only way."

She realized with horror he meant to anatomize the body before her. He drew from his coat a knife, which glinted silver in the white light of his room. When the man spoke again, he was not the surgeon, but Edmund, dressed in a surgeon's coat.

"The truth is inside, you see," he said. "It's a matter of finding it and cutting it out."

As he drew back the sheet, she saw that it was not Hannah at all but herself, lying motionless on the table. About her neck was the mark of the hangman's rope, cut deep into the skin. She tried to move to show Edmund she was still alive, but her limbs would not respond and even her eyes remained shut. She tried to scream but it was merely a rasping in her throat, and, no matter what she did, she could make no sound. The knife approached but there was nothing she could do. She knew with terrible certainty that she would die. As the cold blade touched her skin, Sarah opened her eyes.

10

"Trial by jury is generally an admirable institution . . . but it sometimes fails, the commonest source of failure being that the conflict of evidence does not bring out the whole truth."
— *A General View of the Criminal Law of England,* Sir James Fitzjames Stephen, 1863

When Edmund arrived at Carpenter's Buildings, he found Greenacre's house boarded up, the door bolted. Outside, a group of children played at hopscotch and a small boy in a torn blue jacket and dirty cap lingered near the gate.

"Do you know who looks after the house now?" Edmund asked him, but the boy did not answer. Instead, he backed away from him and ran.

After a few minutes, a woman in a cheap print dress approached Edmund.

"You want to look at the house?" She had a tired face, lined by age or hardship. "They 'ad to board it up to stop people traipsing through it all the time," she said. "The landlord ran tours of the place till a few weeks back, but people kept thieving bits, as souvenirs. It's for sale, you know." She pointed to the bill in the window.

Edmund smiled. "I'm sure it will be for some time."

The woman shrugged. "It's a shame — it's a fine house. The best one in this street. Not that that's sayin' much."

"Do you live here?"

"Yes, just across the way, at number eleven."

"You knew them, then?"

"Mr. Greenacre and Miss Gale? Yes, I did — least I knew Miss Gale."

Odd, thought Edmund. He had been told that everyone in the area knew her as Mrs. Greenacre.

"Did you know her well?"

The woman's expression hardened. "Are you a newspaper man?"

"No, no," said Edmund. "I've been appointed to investigate Miss Gale's appeal for clemency. I'm trying to work out what happened in that house."

She eyed him suspiciously. "There was a

man here before said he was investigatin'. Asked me questions. I'm sure he was with the newspapers."

They both stood staring at the shuttered windows awhile.

"I can pay you for your time," he said.

"I have a key," the woman said shortly. She drew a ring of keys from her pinafore and selected a steel one, which she inserted into the lock of the wooden door. The smell when they entered was of wood dust with a hint of something else that Edmund could not identify.

The woman wrinkled her nose. "Well, this is it," she said.

There was a fireplace, a rocking chair, and a table with two wooden chairs drawn up to it. A burned-out candle, melted down to a puddle, stood on the table. Already, spiders had begun to make the place their home and cobwebs covered the hearth. The woman opened the shutters so that a box of light fell across the table.

"What's your name?" he asked her.

"Mrs. Andrews."

"You gave evidence at the trial," Edmund said. "I remember you now."

The woman shuddered. "I could tell they'd made up their minds 'bout her from the beginning. She didn't stand a chance."

"You don't think Sarah Gale knew about the murder?"

"She couldn't have. She weren't at the house when it happened. And if you knew her as I did, you'd know she couldn't've taken the dead woman's dresses, or jewels, or helped him hide the body or any of them other things she's supposed to've done." Her voice was thick with anger.

"My mind remains open, Mrs. Andrews. It's because of that I've come to look at the evidence myself, rather than assuming what was said at trial was correct."

She looked at him uncertainly.

"Why do you say she couldn't have taken Hannah Brown's possessions or helped Greenacre?"

"She's a kind soul — softhearted. She was always giving bits of money or food to the poorest children around 'ere, even though she 'ad next to nothing herself."

"You saw her here the day after Christmas Day, didn't you?" Edmund asked.

"Yes, I saw her on the day before Christmas, in the morning, and the day after, on Boxing Day."

"How did she seem?"

"No different from usual."

"From what I understand, most people here don't seem to have spoken to Miss

Gale, except perhaps to say 'Good morning' now and again. And most assumed she was Mrs. Greenacre."

"Well, that's London for you, ain't it? People don't notice their neighbors and takes no time to get to know them."

"How did you come to know her?"

For the first time the woman smiled, exposing broken teeth. "Sarah came to our house one day asking for some water. Our side of the way is better supplied than theirs, see. We got to talking, and it turned out we was both trying to make a little money by sewing and shoe binding. My husband, Joseph, is a shoemaker, but he don't make much. After that, we'd often lend things to each other and I'd come fetch her when I knew the water was on."

So Sarah had often borrowed water, Edmund thought. That meant that the fact she had borrowed water after the murder was not, as the prosecution had claimed, proof she had cleaned blood from the floor.

"You were in similar circumstances," he said.

"Maybe. We was both poorer than many in this area. And we both had young children. I'd often mind her little boy if she had errands to run."

"What kind of a man was Greenacre?"

Her eyes narrowed for a second. "I didn't really know 'im," she said.

"Did you believe him capable of murder?"

"I believe there's plenty capable of anything round 'ere."

"But you didn't see or hear anything that you feel you ought to tell me?"

"No, sir, I didn't. And I fancy that those that claims they did was more interested in the rewards than the facts."

"What do you mean? No reward was offered."

She raised an eyebrow. "Well, p'raps they just realized they'd remembered it wrong, then."

"You mean the Callows? They changed their story?"

Mrs. Andrews looked at him appraisingly for a moment, as if assessing a hand of cards. "First off they claimed it was women they 'eard shouting. It weren't until the trial that they decided it were a man and a woman arguing. You ask me, they didn't hear nothing save for the clink of their own gin glasses."

"Do they still live on the road?"

She shook her head. "No. Long gone. Good riddance to bad rubbish." She stepped forward. "You'll want to look in the back room."

They descended a step into the workroom, which connected to the kitchen. It still contained some of Greenacre's tools and buckets of old varnish and paint. Planes of wood were stacked against a far wall and there was still a whiff of turpentine in the air. At the back of the room was a heavy oak table. Edmund caught the woman's eye for a second but she looked away. This must have been where Greenacre had cut up the body. Edmund ran his hand over the table-top, which was covered with a fine film of dust, and imagined Hannah Brown clamped to the table; he heard in his mind the sound of metal on bone. There was a darkening of the wood in the center: a bloodstain, or simply the grain of the wood?

Edmund wondered whether Sarah could really have lived here in this house and not known. To him, the air seemed filled with death, but how much of that was from what he knew, from what he had heard and read?

Mrs. Andrews left Edmund standing in the front garden staring back at the house, thinking. It was a fairly long strip of garden overlooked by several other houses. If Greenacre had, as he claimed, left the house and returned to it by the front door late in the evening, surely someone would have seen him.

As Edmund left, he had the distinct feeling of being watched. Looking across the street, he saw the flash of a face in the shadow, a dark blank oval, and then heard feet running.

"Who's there?" he shouted, briefly afraid.

But it was, he realized, only a child's footsteps.

Mr. Price was a tall, murderous-looking individual, dressed entirely in black, which accentuated the pallor of his long face. Occasionally, his tongue would flick out and run along his upper lip as though he were tasting the air.

"I did what I could, but the jury were swayed by Adolphus' rhetoric. Now, there is an advocate." He took a bite out of a mutton chop.

They were dining in the Angel on Coldharbour Lane, the public house where Hannah Brown had planned to have her wedding breakfast. Price himself had chosen the location, apparently finding the notion amusing. The taproom in which they sat was crowded with Windsor chairs and decorated with a curious assortment of brass trinkets and ugly Toby jugs. Tobacco smoke hung thick in the beery air.

"And of course juries aren't keen on men

cutting women up. In fact, they disapprove of it strongly. So I knew the odds were stacked against them from the beginning."

"Then why did you take the case on?" Edmund asked, looking unenthusiastically at his own meal: rump steak with oyster sauce.

"Because James asked me to. I'd acted for him before, you know, on business matters."

"You're not a criminal lawyer?"

"Oh, I dabble, I dabble."

Edmund clenched his jaw. This was hardly the sort of case in which a lawyer should "dabble." Two people's lives were at stake.

"And he was having some difficulty finding anyone else who would act for him," Price continued. "It wasn't exactly an attractive brief. After all, how does one defend a man who has admitted to cutting up a woman and dumping her body parts all over London?" He smacked his lips, which were covered in meat fat.

Edmund pushed his food around his plate. "You claimed at the trial that Greenacre had returned to the house to find Hannah Brown dead and decided for some reason to dispose of the body."

"Yes. James's evidence was that he was gone from the house for an hour or two and returned to find her sprawled across the floor."

"Who, then, do you say killed her?"

"If you recall, I said that she'd probably fallen from a chair and hit her head."

"Oh, come now. You know that's not what happened. How do you explain the specific injury to the eye?"

"I'm not a detective, Mr. Fleetwood, I merely put forward an argument."

"Because that's what your client told you to say."

"Of course."

"But you didn't believe it yourself."

Price said nothing.

"How," Edmund asked, "could you have put forward a defense you knew to be false?"

"Mr. Fleetwood, you're a lawyer. Do you always believe the views you advance on behalf of others?"

"I would never put forward an argument I believed to be a lie."

"Ah, well, maybe that is why your name is not better known, Mr. Fleetwood!" Price laughed. "But in fact, I have no idea what happened. Even if James did kill the woman, it may well have been an accident."

"The neighbors heard them fighting, didn't they?"

"The neighbors thought they had heard *someone* fighting. They couldn't say for sure that it was James and Hannah."

143

"But they'd heard them fighting before."

"So they said. Hannah Brown was a rash and headstrong one, apparently. Flew into a furious temper at the slightest thing."

"Yes, so you claimed at trial. As I recall, you made various attempts to undermine the victim."

"I did, yes, but it didn't work. All of our efforts to discredit Hannah Brown failed. Contrary to James's claim that she was drunk, no alcohol was found in her stomach contents."

Edmund put down his cutlery. "He claimed she'd deceived him as to her property, didn't he? What exactly did he say she'd done?"

"She told him she had considerable portable property. I forget how much. It was on that basis that James made the offer of marriage. However, he then found out that she'd been trying to buy certain items in his name at a shop in Long Acre. He was, let us say, displeased."

"Evidently. And how did Greenacre find out about her deceit?"

Price shrugged. "I'm not sure I ever discussed that with him. There were more pressing matters."

"Yes." Edmund looked at Price's bony face, his pale slender fingers. "You made a long speech about Greenacre but said very little on Miss Gale's behalf. Why was that?"

"To be honest, I wasn't particularly worried about her. She has a young child, it was her first offense, and there was no hard evidence that she knew of the crime. It never occurred to me that they might hang her for it. Women are never hanged these days." He took a gulp of wine.

"Well, evidently you should have been more concerned." Edmund spoke levelly but he was furious. "She has now been condemned to death."

Price sighed. "Yes, well, it's always easier to see things after they've occurred."

"Did you not see it as a conflict, acting for both Greenacre and Gale?"

"No, not really. Their versions of events were very similar."

"Almost identical, in fact," said Edmund. "Didn't that make you suspicious? Arguably it was a sign that Greenacre was telling Miss Gale what to say."

Price picked up another chop. "It's not for me to second-guess what my clients tell me."

"It is if you think they're being coerced."

Price bit into his chop. "That is not what I thought."

"Why did you not press Miss Gale to

make a full statement? Her statement for the trial was extremely short."

After a pause, Price said, "In the circumstances, I considered it best that she said as little as possible."

"What circumstances were those?"

Price inspected his knife. "There's only so much we can do for certain clients."

"Clients who won't give you instructions?"

Price curved his mouth into a smile. "Clients whom we believe to be guilty."

For a while, Edmund did not speak. A gale of drunken laughter came from a group of men and women who sat at a large table in the center of the room swigging beer from pewter pots.

Eventually, he said, "Why did you think that, Mr. Price?"

"Oh, just an instinctive feeling."

"So she never actually said or did anything to indicate she had helped to conceal the murder?"

"Of course not."

"Did you press her?"

"Mr. Fleetwood, if she'd confessed I wouldn't have been able to act for her any longer."

No, thought Edmund. And then you would not have been paid.

"This 'feeling' of yours, then," he said coldly. "On what exactly was it based?"

Price put up his hand to call over the waiting boy. "All that discussion about blood-drenched floors and dismembered limbs and she never once raised an eyebrow. She was a cold one. Unfeminine. If I ever met a woman capable of covering up such a horrible business, it was her."

11

"The noble science, as fox-hunting is called by its votaries, is, by common consent, allowed to be the perfection of hunting. The animal hunted is just fast enough for the purpose, and is also full of all kinds of devices for misleading his pursuers."

— *Manual of British Rural Sports,*
John Henry Walsh, 1856

"No touching, Gale!"

Sarah had instinctively stretched one of her hands through the iron bars toward George. After so many weeks of longing to see him, to feel him, she could not quite believe that her son was standing before her, fidgeting. She had forgotten how small and vulnerable he was — his little sparrow neck, his narrow shoulders. They were in the family visitors' room, one side of which was railed off into a large roofed cage, fenced with wirework, through which the prisoner could talk to her visitors for a short time. Having grown used to the muted colors and sounds of Newgate, Sarah was startled by the sight of so many ordinary people: men, women, children; the reds and pinks and greens of their clothing; the smells of smoke and horses and the outdoors that they brought with them; shouts, laughter, a baby's cry. Amid all of this walked Miss Sowerton, surveying each person in turn to ensure that nothing was passed between convict and visitor save for words.

"Look at you," Sarah said to George. "As smart as sixpence."

He was dressed in his best clothes and, as she watched, he pulled at his collar and scratched at his stockings. It was the first time Sarah had seen him since she was arrested and it was a terrible effort to appear composed.

"Are you being a good boy for Rosina?"

He looked for affirmation to his aunt, who stood beside him. She smiled. "Always."

Rosina wore a straw bonnet and a blue print dress with a woolen shawl. Her face, Sarah noticed, was thinner and more drawn than before: a mirror of her own.

"You're learning your letters?" Sarah asked George.

"And his numbers, aren't you, poppet? He's clever — like his ma."

George refused to look at his mother. Could he be turning against her? Maybe he had heard the stories and believed them. Or maybe he was simply punishing her for her absence. He had done the same after those nights she stayed out walking the streets looking for custom, leaving him locked in their room with a rushlight and a cup of milk. Then, as now, she had been unable to fully explain — that she did what she did for him. His behavior was probably a normal reaction in a young child, but it stung like vinegar on a cut. She wanted so much to hug her son — to wrap her own body around his like a protective cage — but she could not even touch him.

"I came to the prison the day after your arrest," Rosina said, "but they wouldn't let me through the lodge. They wouldn't so much as pass a message to you. That cat . . ." She glanced toward Miss Sowerton. "She refused even to tell you that I'd tried to see you."

"It's part of my punishment," Sarah said. "To be cut off not only from the other convicts but from my own family. I wasn't sure I'd get to see you at all."

"You know it was the lawyer who arranged

this? Mr. Fleetwood." She raised her eye-brows. "Is he . . . ?"

They looked at one another in silence for a few seconds.

"Well. Do you think he believes you?"

Sarah chewed her lip. "I don't know. I really don't know."

"He arranged for us to meet. He must be on your side."

Sarah pursed her lips. "Oh, I'm not sure about that. I wouldn't assume anything."

Her sister's shoulders sagged. "Then you must tell him," she said.

Sarah shook her head. *Not here. Not now.*

She stared at George, trying to drink him in: his smooth milk-white skin; his dark blond hair, fine like goose feathers. Eventually, he looked up at her. She smiled at him. Her boy.

But, almost immediately, her burst of joy gave way to anxiety.

"Have you noticed anyone near the house?" she asked Rosina quietly. "Anything out of the ordinary?"

Rosina shook her head. "I promise you, I'm being very careful. You must stop worrying."

They stood in silence for a while, listening to the people around them chattering, bickering, crying. There was so much they

151

needed to discuss but it was impossible to do so here.

"I lost my situation," Rosina said eventually.

"Oh, Rosina, I'm so sorry."

She shrugged. "I didn't much like it at that house in any event. They treated me little better than a servant."

"But what will you do? Did they give you a character?"

"Of sorts, yes."

"They don't know?"

"No, they've no idea you're my sister. Only that I needed to take care of my nephew, which is the reason I gave for needing to live out. I told them you were ill."

Which in a way I am, Sarah thought.

"You must be nearly out of money."

"I have a little kept by," Rosina said. "From selling . . ." She trailed off.

"Yes, but that won't last long." Sarah frowned. "There's a lady helping me," she said after a moment. "Miss Pike. She thinks me good, or at least savable. I'll see if her Society can get you some money for food and clothes."

"That reminds me." From beneath her shawl, Rosina removed a small parcel. "It's just a few things to eat," she whispered. "You look half-starved, Sarah." However, as she made to pass it through the bars, Miss Sowerton — perhaps noticing her movement — began to walk in their direction and Rosina hid the parcel again beneath her shawl.

Rosina breathed out, frustrated. "What about *him*?" she said. "Can't he help us? He owes you well enough."

"He has helped, in his own way. That's why all this has happened."

"But does he know —"

Sarah shook her head again. "Hush! There are eyes and ears everywhere in this place."

The bell rang out, marking the end of visiting time, and Miss Sowerton walked toward the exit. All around began the sounds of farewells, tears, and recriminations. Sarah kissed her own hand and transferred the kiss to George, feeling the smooth curve of his cheek.

Rosina stepped forward so that her face was touching the bars of the cage. "Sarah," she whispered, "you must act now, before it's too late. This is madness!"

Sarah looked about her to check no one was watching them, and then moved closer to her sister: "And then what?" She grabbed Rosina's hand. "I know what I'm doing. I promise you."

Rosina's eyes shone with tears. She

squeezed Sarah's hand and released it. Then they were gone.

As Sarah walked back along the corridor to her cell she heard footsteps close behind her and felt the shiver of breath on her neck.

"Just like you, ain't she, your little sister? Only unspoiled."

It was Rook, her speech fast, her breath, as before, tinged with liquor. Where was she getting the drink from, Sarah wondered. Who was helping her?

"Maybe I'll pay 'er a visit when I get out," Rook said, when she did not respond. "Hart Street, ain't it?"

Sarah snapped her head round to look at Rook. Who was this woman? What did she want? What did she know? But Rook had pulled back and now gazed at the floor.

Miss Sowerton caught Sarah's movement. "Head in front, Gale. Get to your cell."

That night the chilly hush of the prison was broken by the sobbing of another woman. It penetrated through the wall into Sarah's cell: a miserable choking interspersed with cries like those of a wounded animal.

For a long time, Sarah lay awake, her stomach twisting with hunger and anxiety, listening to the sound of the other woman's anguish. Although she tried to push the thoughts from her mind, memories came to her of those nights when she had lain in her childhood bed, weeping. Her cries, however, had been silent.

"This will be our little secret," her father had told her the first time he visited her room. And it still was.

Sarah curled herself under her gray blanket, clutching her knees to her chest in the dense darkness of the cell, trying to put the memories from her mind.

She did not know how long she had lain like this when she sensed a presence. She was not alone. The air had grown even colder. On the stool in the corner she thought she could make out a figure, although she knew it could not be possible. Had she fallen asleep? She could hear breathing, labored and thick.

"Who's there?" she whispered into the blackness.

No answer, but still the heavy breath.

"Who are you?"

Sarah sat up in bed, keeping the blanket wrapped around her. She scrabbled for the tinderbox and, despite her shaking hands, managed to light the char cloth, the blaze of fire illuminating the room and throwing shadows bouncing off the walls. She saw a woman on the stool, facing the door. Even before the woman turned, Sarah knew who she was. She willed herself to look away as the face was lit up by the flame's glow, one eye gone, the other shining bright. Before she could light a candle, the flame was extinguished and the room was swallowed in darkness. Once more, she was alone.

When Hinkley unlocked Sarah's door the following morning, the vision was still with Sarah as an uneasiness in her stomach; a residue on her skin. She was, she realized, terrified of being left alone in her cell again.

"Miss Hinkley," she said, as the warder made to leave, "who is the prisoner I heard crying in the night?"

The warder shook her head. "It's a sad one, that." She spoke in a hushed voice, for the warders were not supposed to converse with the prisoners — only to bark orders or directions. "She's a young girl, accused of killing her own baby. They brought 'er here yesterday from one of the county jails. She won't eat a morsel; says she just wants to die. It's a sorry business."

"Why did she kill her child?"

Hinkley lowered her voice still further. "She was a maid and hid from her master the fact of her being with child. As many do. They found 'er at the bottom of some stairs with a knife, a pool of blood, and a dead baby. I don't sanction it, Sarah, Lord knows I don't, but you can't help but feel a bit of pity for the poor thing. She would've lost her situation and the baby would've probably been taken from her, so I s'ppose she decided the baby had to go. Happens often enough."

"Does she admit that she killed the child?"

"No, 'course not. As you know very well, no one in this place admits anything. She says that the knife were to cut the cord and that the baby were dead when it came out."

"Well, maybe it was."

"Maybe it was, and maybe it weren't. The end result is the same."

"Did anyone hear the child cry?"

"Bless my soul, Sarah, I don't know every bit of detail. I only know she ain't eaten a thing since she got here — just weeps. They should've turned a blind eye to it, that's what I says. Let her get on with her life."

Turning a blind eye: Sarah knew all about that. As she sat at her sewing, she thought of her mother, her mother who might not have cut off her breath at birth, but had instead stifled her slowly, first with discipline and prayer books and a corseted, conditional kind of love; then with advice books, etiquette manuals, and silence. Sometime after her father's visits began, Sarah's image of herself began to warp, like a reflection in a distorted looking glass. In her eyes, her body became bloated and monstrous, her thighs ugly pale slabs of meat, her face puffy and disfigured. She would starve and pinch her flesh to punish it, leaving dark bruises on the soft white skin.

Her mother must have noticed her weight loss, but did nothing about it. Perhaps she approved. After all, she herself was rake thin, picking at food at meal times and boasting that she had no appetite. Laudanum does that.

Meanwhile, Rosina began to draw strange things: dead birds. Children without faces. Men with the heads of beasts. Sarah listened at the door of the parlor as their drawing teacher, a shrewd green-eyed woman, told their mother that Rosina's mind was disturbed.

"There's evidently something distressing her, Mrs. Farr. Have you considered what it might be?"

"And tell me," Sarah's mother had replied, "what qualifies or entitles you to comment on anything other than my daughters' drawing?"

Up until that point, Sarah had wondered

how much their mother knew: whether she was oblivious, or whether she was aware of what was going on, but drowning it all out with a brown fog of laudanum and false laughter. That conversation confirmed what Sarah feared: that her mother knew, but had chosen not to see. Was this punishment, perhaps, for her brother's death? Or had she always hated her daughter? Sarah's heart bunched into a tight fist. The process of hardening had set in.

12

"The head thus cured is very highly flavoured, and most excellent eating. The receipt for it is new. It will be seen that the foregoing proportion of ingredients, with the exception of the treacle, is for one half of the head only, and must be doubled for a whole one."

— The Art and Mystery of Curing,
Preserving, and Potting All Kinds of
Meats, Game, and Fish,
A Wholesale Curer of Comestibles, 1864

The omnibus traveled past the warehouses and workshops of the Edgeware Road and turned left onto Harrow Road. This must, Edmund thought, be the same route that James Greenacre had taken that night, holding Hannah Brown's head, wrapped in brown paper, on his lap. Edmund could imagine him, descending from the omnibus in the darkness, walking through the falling snow to the Regent's Canal, and dropping his parcel into the black water.

Edmund alighted at Paddington Green and walked past the tall elms to a handsome brick house looking onto the east of the Green. He was shown up to a beautifully decorated parlor, where a man with red hair sat writing at a bureau. The man rose from his chair when Edmund entered the room and shook his hand firmly.

"We've met before, haven't we?"

This was Dr. Girdwood, parish surgeon for Paddington: the man who had carried out the original postmortem on Hannah Brown and confirmed that the body parts fitted together.

"You came to view Miss Brown's head when I put it on display in Paddington Workhouse."

Edmund felt his cheeks blaze. "Yes, well, it seemed an interesting opportunity. I'd been following the case, for professional reasons."

"Then you must be pleased that this commission has fallen into your lap. A stroke of fortune, is it not?"

Edmund was no longer so sure of this. He smiled but did not reply.

When they had settled beside a low japanned table, he said, "Dr. Girdwood, the questions I want to ask you are rather grue-some in nature, so you must forgive me."

"Mr. Fleetwood," the doctor laughed, "I spend my days with the dead and the dying. I doubt you can unnerve me. Please go ahead."

"Well, first, you said at the trial that you thought that Hannah Brown had died from an injury to her right eye."

"Yes. There was a wound in the eye itself, above the pupil, and there was a mark, a round ecchymosis, surrounding the eye — an extraordinary black eye, if you like."

"What do you think caused the injury to the eye?"

"It's difficult to say. The circumstance of the eye being ruptured would imply great force. It might have been the result of a blow with a fist, or it might have been a hard object. I'm sorry I can't be more specific."

Edmund nodded, thinking of Greenacre's large hands, balled into fists.

"Thank you. My second question may also be rather difficult to answer. Greenacre admits that Hannah Brown was killed in his house on the evening of the 24th of Decem-ber and he says that he cut up the body in his workroom. Assuming that's true, how much blood would have been spilled during the killing and the cutting? Is it likely he could have had the place spotless two days after the murder such that Sarah Gale could have had no inkling as to what took place there?"

"Good gracious, man, you might want to be talking to a butcher rather than to me!" Girdwood's tone was good-natured. "How much blood would there have been? In short, a huge amount. Greenacre slit the woman's throat shortly after death — possibly while she was still alive — and then cut the body to pieces with a knife and a carpenter's saw. The head, when I saw it, was drained of blood. He may, of course, have used a vessel to catch the blood, but he maintains that he didn't. If that's true, then the floor would have been covered in blood. There have been experiments to show that blood will flow for up to sixteen hours after death."

The doctor poured himself a measure of whisky.

"I'll also give you my opinion that Greenacre didn't kill her in the kitchen, as the prosecution argued. There were traces of blood found in the main bedroom when the police checked it nearly three months after the murder."

Why, Edmund wondered, had the police not mentioned this to him? "Were the stains obvious?" he asked.

"They were small specks, but visible to someone looking carefully. As to whether Sarah Gale would have noticed, well, that's a very tricky question to answer. We don't know how well Greenacre covered his tracks. However, you may have heard one of the witnesses — I forget her name now — talking about how she visited the house some weeks after the murder and the place stank of brimstone."

"Miss Edmonds," said Edmund. "She said that there was an overwhelming smell of sulfur."

"That's it. Now, why would that be?"

"I assumed it was to do with his furniture making. I understand that molten sulfur is sometimes used to produce decorative inlays."

"Perhaps," said Dr. Girdwood, "but it's also used to fumigate rooms after disease. Greenacre might have done so in this instance because he was concerned that the house was not rid of the smell of blood."

"The house Sarah Gale had been living in."

"Exactly. And of course there were the boxes belonging to the dead woman that had been left in the house. She must have seen those."

"She says Greenacre told her that Hannah Brown had left after an argument and that the boxes and their contents were part payment for money she owed him."

"I'd find that a hard pill to swallow," replied the doctor, "but we don't know what Sarah Gale was going through at that time. She seemed during the trial to be in a state of denial, perhaps even hysteria."

"Hysteria?" Edmund was surprised. "Wouldn't that demonstrate itself in a more agitated appearance?"

"Not necessarily," Girdwood said. "Malaise of the female mind can take all sorts of forms. I was struck by how unnaturally calm she appeared to be for the majority of the trial and yet on occasion she seemed to be seized with panic."

Edmund thought back to Sarah's demeanor in the courtroom: outwardly composed, if pale. He had not seen the moments of panic, but maybe his attention had been diverted. Perhaps he had not been looking carefully enough.

"She may," the doctor continued, "be suffering under some sickness of the mind such that she is unable to put the pieces together unable to see what should have been obvious. It's even possible that she witnessed the killing and has since erased it from her

165

mind. I've seen that sort of thing before, usually in men returning from the horrors of war. They shut out certain events because they're too painful."

"But do they forget them completely?"

"In some cases, yes. Or they remember them only in dreams or as hallucinations."

Was that possible, Edmund wondered. Could that account for her anxiety? He had visited her twice more in the past week and had noticed that, whenever he asked her directly about Hannah Brown, she grew tense and agitated.

"Thank you," Edmund said. "I am much obliged to you." He stood up and removed his hat from the table.

The doctor remained sitting. "I haven't formally examined Sarah Gale so of course I can't offer a proper medical opinion, but my suspicion is that she's not altogether there. There's something missing. If I were you, I'd be very wary of accepting her version of reality."

Edmund had persuaded the Governor that he needed to see Sarah in a private room. He hoped that without the warders circling the room like crows swooping for carrion she might feel freer to speak her mind. He had not, however, expected to be taken to her cell.

"There's nowhere else for you to meet," the matron told him shortly as she led him through the watchful silence of the women's quarters. "If you'll insist on a private meeting, we need to make sure it's somewhere where we can keep an eye on her."

Edmund smiled viciously at her back. "And why is that, Miss Sowerton? Has she carried out any acts of violence during her time here?"

He could almost feel the woman bristle. She half turned to him so that he caught her blunt face in profile. "In my experience, sir, it's the ones that seem calm and quiet that are the most dangerous. But of course, you wouldn't know that."

They arrived at a low black door and the woman drew back a shutter and leaned forward to peer inside the cell. Then she drew out one of her many keys, unlocked the door, and pulled back the bolt.

When Edmund entered the room, the first thing he noticed was a strong tang: the animal smell of tallow candles mixed with damp. Sarah stood before them in her normal blue prison attire, but her cap was slightly pushed back and several strands of her hair had come loose. Edmund saw that her skin was even paler than usual, her brown eyes even darker and larger by contrast. Her long lashes shimmered as if she had been crying. Perhaps the doctor had been right about her mental state: perhaps she was broken.

"Mr. Fleetwood wanted to see you in your cell, Gale."

"As you know, Miss Sowerton, I simply wished to see Miss Gale somewhere more private than the legal visitors' room so that we could discuss matters relating to the investigation without . . . interruption." He looked about the sparse room: the whitewashed stone walls, the miserable little window, the small cluster of battered objects. "There is only one stool," he said.

The matron gave him a blank look. "Then you will have to sit on the bed, sir, won't you?"

She turned and left the cell, slamming the door closed behind her. Edmund heard the bolt slide back into place and felt for a moment the sharp terror of imprisonment. This was a mistake, he thought. They were too close together in the confined room and he felt that he was trespassing on Sarah's private space. It was almost as though he had come upon an animal in its lair.

Sarah had not moved since he entered the cell, but stood rigidly. Now, however, she gestured to the stool and said, "You must sit down, sir. I can stand."

"No, no. I won't hear of it."

"Well, then I will sit here." Sarah perched on the end of her bed and took up a piece of sewing. She seemed slighter than she had before; her face sharper, paler.

"Miss Gale, you will forgive me, I hope, for saying that you do not look well. Are you ill?"

She glanced up. "I'm just a little tired. I've not been sleeping well."

Edmund wondered if she was kept awake by nightmares, by the resurgent images that Dr. Girdwood had mentioned as a symptom of trauma. "Bad dreams?" he ventured.

When she did not respond, he said, "Some say that dreams are made up of the things we dare not think about during our waking hours. Do you think that's what your dreams are, Miss Gale?"

She licked the tip of a piece of thread and passed it deftly through the eye of the needle. "Others say dreams are the means through which the spirit world communicates with us."

Edmund gave a bark of laughter, but Sarah did not smile. "You don't believe in a spirit world, Mr. Fleetwood?"

He spread his hands. "I'm a lawyer. I only

169

believe in things for which I have clear evidence."

"There are people who firmly believe they've seen and heard spirits."

"Oh, people often think they have seen things that they can't possibly have seen. Ask any barrister and he'll tell you that three witnesses can see the same event and yet give three completely differing accounts of it under cross-questioning. Throw in the lights and smoke and other deceits used by your average medium, and it's no wonder people believe they've seen ghosts."

He could see from Sarah's expression that he had annoyed her and he cursed himself for not having taken her more seriously — she might have revealed something.

After a few moments, he said, "I must ask you, Miss Gale: the day you and George returned to Greenacre's house — Boxing Day."

"Yes?" She was still looking down at her sewing, making tiny, neat stitches.

"It was only twelve hours or so after Greenacre had disposed of Hannah Brown's head and cleaned the house of blood. You said that you noticed the boxes, and that he explained those, but did you not notice anything else strange about the house? The smell of sulfur, for example."

170

Sarah shook her head and continued her stitching. "There was no smell of sulfur that I recall. And yes, James had cleaned the house and washed the floor, but he said he'd done that for my homecoming — to make it nice for me."

"And you thought that plausible? The man who'd thrown you out less than a week earlier?"

"I dare say it seems very foolish now, but at the time I believed James was genuinely sorry for his behavior toward me." She raised her eyes. "He could be kind, you know."

Kind. A man who had dismembered a woman's body with a carpenter's saw and calmly distributed the pieces about town. Edmund found it difficult to believe that such a man was capable of kindness.

After a few moments, he said, "Miss Gale, I have just come from seeing one of the surgeons who gave evidence at your trial: Dr. Girdwood. You remember him?"

She nodded.

"He told me that when the police searched Greenacre's house they found spots of blood in the bedroom." He looked at her. She had stopped sewing. "You'd been cleaning the house, hadn't you? And staying in the bedroom?" He paused. "You must have

171

seen them."

Sarah put her sewing on the bed beside her. After a time she said, "It was not Hannah Brown's blood."

"How do you know?"

She breathed out. "Because it was mine. From an old argument."

Edmund blinked. An image flashed before his eyes of Sarah's head, thrust back against the wall, her face wet with blood. "Why on earth did you stay with him?" he asked, almost without meaning to.

Sarah twisted her hands together. "Mr. Fleetwood, it's difficult to explain to a man like you why I'd stay with a man like him. You wouldn't understand."

Edmund thought suddenly of his own mother, her spirit sapped by years of his father's sarcasm and silence.

"In fact," he said, "I think I would."

Sarah's expression suggested she did not believe him, so he continued.

"You see, someone very close to me was ill-used. Not physically, but . . . let us just say that I recognize that a person may stay with another in circumstances that are not . . . ideal."

Sarah stared at him for a moment. "And this someone . . . Did she stay?"

"She was not, as it turns out, given the

opportunity."

When Edmund was thirteen, his mother had been exiled from the family, after his father had discovered she was having an affair. At least, he assumed that was what he had discovered. It had never been discussed. His father had taken Edmund and his brother to Scotland to visit a cousin's estate. When they returned, their mother was gone and they were not to speak of her.

"Suffice to say," Edmund continued, "that I appreciate that you might have stayed with James Greenacre for reasons that are not immediately obvious to me."

She was still watching him. "Yes." Her brow creased. "You'll have seen only the side of James that the press has chosen to print: the villain, the brute, the fraud. But he could also be eloquent and charming and sometimes tender." Sarah rubbed at her raw knuckles. "And I don't want you to think there were many arguments like that. He just lost his temper sometimes. Besides, if I'd left, where would I have gone? I had very little money and a young child to feed and clothe. The alternative would have been to throw ourselves upon the scant mercy of the parish, or . . ." She looked away.

Edmund thought of the women who stood in the shadows of Haymarket, in faded silk dresses and rouge. He thought of the woman who had pressed herself against him in the alleyway off Fleet Street; of the girls with bruised faces in the slums of St. Giles. "Would those options have been worse than staying with Greenacre?"

"Yes, Mr. Fleetwood," she said firmly. "They would."

"Some of the newspapers," Edmund said, choosing his words carefully, "referred to you as a fallen woman."

Sarah gave a lopsided smile. "It's a funny expression, isn't it: 'fallen woman'? As if women fall by themselves, by accident." Her voice was sharp. "Most, I think, are pushed."

Edmund waited for her to say something else, but she did not. "So, you . . . ?"

"So I stayed with James, despite everything. I came to think of his little outbursts as the price I had to pay for security. But of course it was no security at all, for once he found a woman whom he thought had money, he turned me out of the house." Her tone had grown cold, her expression hard.

"Then why go back the moment he asked you, if you knew by then that he would drop you in a trice the moment he had a better option?"

"I was afraid — of him; of what would become of George and me on our own. I suppose I'd come to depend upon him, and not just for the money. Without him I was . . . nothing."

A memory surfaced in Edmund's mind of him being taken, as a child, to some tearooms somewhere — all green drapery and mahogany — to see his mother. Perhaps it was the first time he had seen her after her enforced exile. Edmund recalled the smell of wood polish and the expression on his mother's face when she had seen him and his brother.

"You mustn't worry about me. I'm really not worth worrying about." He gazed now at Sarah's delicate face, the graceful line of her throat. He felt a sudden overwhelming tenderness toward her: a need to protect.

"Is that why you've kept silent for Greenacre?" he said softly. "Because you're afraid he'll hurt you? You know he can't harm you here."

He saw her body tense.

"I'm not keeping silent for him," she said. "I didn't speak out about Hannah Brown's death because I didn't know about it." Her expression closed. The vulnerable Sarah had disappeared; the defenses were back in place.

Edmund pressed his lips together. "I see."

Sarah looked him straight in the eye. "I'm

telling you the truth."

He nodded slowly. He had thought he was getting somewhere.

"Let's go back to before all of this happened, shall we?" he said. "You told me before about your early life in Lyme. Why did you leave Dorset?"

For a moment, she was silent, chewing her lip, but then she looked up at him. "The same reason your brother left London, Mr. Fleetwood. We needed to escape."

13

"It follows that, so far as crime is determined by external circumstances, every step made by woman towards her independence is a step towards that precipice at the bottom of which lies a prison."
— *A History of Crime in England*,
Luke Owen Pike, 1876

"It all started," she said, "when the war ended."

In 1815, when Sarah was fourteen years old, a quarter of a million soldiers and sailors came back to a country that had no jobs for them. That, combined with the beginnings of mechanization, led to an economic crisis of proportions not known in her lifetime. Riots began in Kent in June and by mid-November they had spread to Dorset.

"When we had people to dinner they spoke of laborers breaking machines, of crops set on fire, of a tenfold rise in poaching and theft. It didn't occur to me then that any of that might affect us.

"The following year was the year without a summer. I remember the rains and the cold and the news of the harvests failing. That was the summer my father disappeared. I came down one morning to find my mother on the hall floor, weeping. All I knew then was that he had gone. Only later did I find out that my father had invested all his capital in ruinous speculations and left us with almost nothing."

Sarah looked at her hands: at the broken nails and chafed skin. "At some point, I suppose my father must have realized things were going wrong with his business. At some stage he must have known that we were close to financial ruin. And yet he never made a contingency plan. For all his calculating and planning and writing ledgers, he never created a scheme to protect his family if things went wrong. He simply abandoned us, and the whole house of cards collapsed."

Sarah pictured their mother's white face and glassy eyes as she explained to her daughters that they had to leave the house. Although they had known that things would change, neither of the sisters had appreciated the magnitude of it until that afternoon in the front room, the curtains drawn. Her mother told them that they were going on an adventure. Sarah understood that they were being thrown out of the house. That beautiful house that she had always assumed they owned was in fact only rented from a woman who had long ago lost her patience over the many bills that had been left unpaid.

"Before we left, Mother walked slowly about the house, touching the things we had to leave behind: the leather-bound books, the glass baubles, the velvet chairs, the piano. Because it turned out none of them actually belonged to us.

"We packed our clothes and books into trunks and took the stagecoach to London. We set out at night so, I suppose, that our neighbors wouldn't see our disgrace as we left."

It had taken them two days to reach London. Sarah remembered waking early to see the mist-shrouded fields turn into a tangle of streets and alleys. The chimneys grew taller and the threads of smoke thicker, and then the dome of St. Paul's appeared over the brow of the hill. Not that she knew what it was then. Nor did she know the meaning of the dark cloud hovering above

179

it, black in the center and bottle-green at the edges. Only later was she told that it was London fog — that dark cloak of coal dust and dirt that hangs in the air like a canopy shrouding the city. At the time, she supposed it to be a presentiment of doom, which in a way it was.

They reached the outskirts of the city in the early morning and London was already awake. It was the smell that hit her first, an exhilarating smell of ordure and people and life and death. Then the noise: the clash of hoofs and rolling of wheels, the shouts of costermongers, the ringing of church bells.

"Our mother had secured us lodgings in Golden Square, an area north of Piccadilly Circus where many of the properties are let out to families and single gentlemen. It was a considerable step down from where we'd lived before, but still a decent place with two bedrooms and a front parlor.

"Those first days were ones of excitement. My sister and I wandered about the Pantheon on Regent Street and the Burlington Arcade in Piccadilly looking at the displays in the illuminated shop windows — sparkling jewelry, silks and velvets, fancy stationery." She saw in her mind the baker's shops with cakes and jellies gleaming from behind the glass like splendid jewels; the

180

sweet shops stacked with tier upon tier of Berwick cockles, Kendal mint cake, and candied fruits — delights that now seemed unimaginable. Sarah spent her days at Newgate in a state of almost constant hunger, a gnawing sensation only briefly abated by the inadequate meals. What she wouldn't give now for a suck of sherbet or a mouthful of delicate, cream-filled pastry.

"It was only after we'd been there a week or so that our mother told us that we were nearly out of money, and then things of course became rather different. We moved into smaller and meaner lodgings. My sister and I began taking in sewing to make a little money. Our mother visited friends and relatives of my father's to try to secure their assistance, but either she didn't make our situation plain enough to them, or they wanted nothing to do with us. Either way, no money came."

She glanced up at Edmund.

"That must have been very humiliating," he said.

"Yes. For my mother especially. In the space of only a few months, she'd been reduced from a society wife in a small town to a penniless nobody in a city of faceless thousands. Her husband had deserted her, and her friends had turned the other way.

181

She sank fairly quickly after that into a haze of alcohol and laudanum and kept mainly to her shabby little room."

Sometimes, when Sarah knew her mother to be drugged beyond comprehension, she would stand next to her bed and whisper things to her.

"Did you hear him creep to my room at night? Did you know what it was he was doing to me? Were you too weak to confront him, or did you simply not care, you miserable bitch?"

There had been one evening, toward the end of her mother's illness, when Sarah looked up midsentence and caught her sister's reflection in the looking glass above the mantel. She had been listening to every word. Sarah froze. For a few seconds Rosina held her gaze. Then she stepped forward and placed her hand on the back of Sarah's neck.

"I should have done something to stop him," she said. "I will never forgive myself for not doing anything."

"Miss Gale?" The lawyer was looking at her and she realized she had been staring at him without seeing him.

"You were telling me about your mother."

"Yes, I'm sorry. She died fairly soon after that."

"How did she die?"

Sarah paused, thinking of the sickroom table with its stock of medicines and powders. "From the symptoms, they supposed it was disease of the liver."

"And your father?" Edmund said. "Did he come back?"

"No, he didn't."

"He abandoned you?"

"Yes, I suppose he did."

"What happened to him?"

"I don't know, Mr. Fleetwood. I never heard from him again."

"Surely he must have heard of your mother's death."

Sarah lowered her eyes so he could not read what was written in them. "I don't know, sir," she said. "But at all events, from then on, we were truly on our own."

Long after Edmund had left, Sarah continued to think of that time, of her mother's cold body as they dressed her in her one good dress. By then, all of the jewelry had been sold, save for the eye brooch, and the gold and pearls from that were needed to pay for the burial. The miniature, however, Sarah kept.

They buried their mother in the burial ground at St. James's, for that was all they could afford once the doctor and the pharmacist and the clergyman had been paid. There was a reason the place was cheap. The graveyard, packed with the broken bodies of the poor, bulged several inches above the level of the street and the air was thick with the stench of decay.

The sisters stood close together, the only mourners, the black from their newly dyed dresses leaching out in the rain, as the clergyman mumbled through an abridged version of the Order for the Burial for the Dead.

"And though after my skin worms destroy this body, yet in my flesh shall I see God: whom I shall see for myself, and mine eyes shall behold . . ."

The sexton, holding a handkerchief to his face, began to clear the muddy soil away with his spade.

"I held my tongue and spake nothing," the clergyman intoned. *"I kept silence, yea, even from good words."*

The sexton dumped their mother's shrouded form into the shallow grave and sprinkled it with lime.

"Thou knowest, Lord, the secrets of our hearts," continued the clergyman. *"Shut not*

thy merciful ears to our prayer . . ." He was backing away from the grave, his hand over his mouth.

Rosina put her arm around Sarah, who, by now, was shaking. The sexton shoveled a few inches of earth over the body and threw down his spade.

"The grace of our Lord Jesus Christ, and the love of God, and the fellowship of the Holy Ghost, be with us all evermore."

As the clergyman spoke the final words, Sarah pulled away from Rosina and retched into the mud.

"Amen."

14

"It might, perhaps, be thought that if any law were required to regulate the relations between parent and child, it would be found innate in the human breast. But human nature has so many weaknesses, to say nothing of positive evil impulses, that we cannot allow ourselves to trust to it alone."

— *Cassell's Household Guide,*
circa 1880s

He was at the bottom of a well. He knew that someone or something was coming for him and that he needed to get out. It was wet and cold and black as pitch. Water dripped onto his face and all around was a strange smell of fungus and decay, of unknown things rotting or growing. He tried to find some crevice in the slimy walls into which he could dig his fingers so as to drag himself up, but he could get no purchase on the moss-covered bricks and his fingers ran with blood from where the stone had torn at them. Somewhere in the distance he could hear a woman singing but he could not make out the words. He knew that it was Sarah. He knew that there was an important message in her song and wanted desperately to be able to go to her but the walls remained slippery and impossible.

Edmund wrenched himself from sleep and lay upon his sweat-soaked pillow, gradually filtering the fragments of dream from reality. He realized that he had left one of the bedroom windows open the previous night and a cool morning breeze ruffled the curtains and the chintz hangings of the bed. From the street below came the sound of a coster girl, singing:

O ye tears! O ye tears! I am thankful that
   ye run;
Though ye trickle in the darkness, ye shall
   glitter in the sun.
The rainbow cannot shine if the rain refuse
   to fall,
And the eyes that cannot weep are the
   saddest eyes of all.

Edmund turned to look at Bessie, but her side of the bed was empty, and the sheets, when he felt them, were almost cold.

"What were you dreaming?"

He saw with a start that she was sitting in a chair to the side of the bed, watching him.

"I was dreaming . . ." He hesitated. "I don't remember. Something ghastly."

"All that blood," Bessie said, looking out of the window. "All that evil." She drew her silk dressing gown closer around her. "It's no wonder you have nightmares."

"No," Edmund said. "Perhaps not." But it was not the crime itself that had seeped into his dreams. It was the woman. Perhaps Bessie knew that, because her gaze, when she held his, was sharp as a knife.

"You must be careful, my love."

"May I take those for you, sir?"

A porter in a faded uniform hung Edmund's coat and hat on a peg and led him into a dark wood-paneled room where conversation was in full flow around a large rosewood table.

As he entered the room, an ample-chested woman stood up to greet him. She had a broad red face that suggested a liking for the brandy bottle. "Mr. Fleetwood, please come in. Seat yourself. I am Miss McAdam — I chair the meetings." Edmund had, after receiving several requests, agreed to meet with the British Ladies' Society for Promoting the Reformation of Female Prisoners.

A second, slighter woman dressed entirely in black came forward and took his hand. "Do make yourself comfortable. I'll order us some tea."

"Thank you, Miss . . . ?"

"Pike. But you must call me Verity. I've been assisting Miss Gale and supported her petition. I'm very pleased you could join us." She smiled and then disappeared into the vestibule.

"Mr. Fleetwood, tell us," the red-faced woman said, "are you convinced of her innocence yet?"

Edmund took a seat at the table. "You'll appreciate that I cannot divulge my thinking to you at this stage. It's a complicated case."

"On the contrary, young man, it's perfectly simple. Woman A leaves house. Man kills woman B. Woman A comes back to house and knows nothing of the whole wretched business. There's not a shred of evidence against her."

"There are factors that argue against Miss Gale. The pawn tickets, the jewelry, the fabric —"

"Yes, and you know what they call such factors? Circumstantial! You will be pleased

189

to hear, Mr. Fleetwood, that I myself have read extensively on legal matters."

Edmund's heart sank. Fortunately, Miss Pike returned at that moment with a tray and he insisted on helping her with laying out its contents: a silver teapot, a dish of sandwiches, a plate of orange segments sprinkled with powdered sugar.

"I do apologize, Mr. Fleetwood," she said in an undertone. "Miss McAdam thinks she can win arguments by increasing the volume of her voice."

"I'm a barrister. I'm used to that."

Miss Pike smiled at him, exposing a row of neat little white teeth, shiny like a string of pearls.

"You will find that we are split into two camps here," she said to him confidentially. "There are those who subscribe to Miss McAdam's theory that Miss Gale knew nothing of the murder and there are those who, like me, think that Sarah may have known something of the horrid affair but was prevented from speaking out. I've seen this sort of thing before, and I believe James Greenacre wore her down with months of cruelty, emotional and physical." She poured some tea into a china cup.

"The problem with that theory, Miss Pike, is that Miss Gale doesn't herself appear to subscribe to it."

"I appreciate it's difficult to understand, but you see, her spirit has been crushed. Her mind is disordered. She isn't responding as you might expect her to. I know she can at times seem distant, but I think that's a sign that she's protecting herself. I dealt with a similar case a few years ago."

"A woman accused of concealing a crime?"

"In a way. It was a dreadful business." She leaned in closer. "The Parish took a little girl away from her mother, claiming she had badly beaten the child. Initially, the woman refused to defend herself and was really quite hostile when we tried to help. Over time, however, it became apparent that the real culprit was the woman's lover. It took us months to persuade her to speak out against him."

"But I don't have months, Miss Pike. I have four weeks. If I am to find in Miss Gale's favor, she must give me the information I need."

The woman sat back and looked at him shrewdly. "And what exactly *is* the information you need, Mr. Fleetwood?"

"If Sarah Gale can prove that she acted under duress — that Greenacre forced her to act as she did — then she may have a defense. That is all that I can say at present."

"You must agree, sir," said a long-faced woman in black bombazine, "that this is a case that demonstrates the complete lunacy of capital punishment. How can they send a woman to the gallows on such flimsy and disputed evidence?"

Edmund did in fact agree. He had never believed in the principle of *lex talionis* — an eye for an eye. He could not, however, discuss these things freely here.

Instead, he said, "The problem is that the jury found her guilty, notwithstanding the circumstantial nature of the evidence. In order for me to recommend that that verdict be overturned, I need something more than mere conjecture."

"But it is the wrong way around!" said Miss McAdam, her red face even more flushed. "You're asking her to prove her innocence, when the prosecution failed to prove her guilty!"

"But she was found guilty."

"Oh, by twelve imbecilic men who had already made up their minds before they heard a word of what was said in court. Put twelve *women* in a jury box and they would never have found Sarah Gale guilty. It's simply ludicrous that we have no criminal

192

court of appeal. No offense to you, sir, but there should be a proper process for challenging this nonsense."

"Miss McAdam, I fully support the idea of an appeal court, but as we are where we are, I must do the best I can."

"Indeed you must, sir. The power has been placed in your hands. You must use it wisely."

For the next half hour, the women impressed upon him the arguments as to why Miss Gale should be pardoned: she had been blinded by love; she was entirely ignorant of the whole affair; she had been coerced into silence; she was the unwitting victim; she was unsound of mind and thus incapable of seeing what Greenacre had done. Edmund made his way through the sandwiches, murmuring assent where appropriate and responding where to do so would not be to give away too much. As he chewed, however, it occurred to him that if Sarah was indeed mentally disordered, as both Miss Pike and Dr. Girdwood seemed to believe, that might mean not that she was oblivious to Greenacre's crime, but that she was, as Price had said, precisely the sort of woman who was capable of covering up a murder and plotting her way out of prison.

■ ■ ■ ■

He escaped from the meeting a little after two o'clock on the pretext of having another appointment. In a way, he did. He was already in Mayfair, only a few minutes' walk from his father's house. Over the past few weeks, his father had left several notes requesting that Edmund call upon him. He could postpone it no longer.

Edmund made his way to Grosvenor Square and climbed the stone steps to the grand house. Only a few seconds after he rang the bell, the door was opened by the small maid, her scrubbed face bunched into a nervous smile. She bobbed down in greeting.

"Mr. Fleetwood, sir."

"Hello, Milly. I'm here to see my father."

"Yes, sir," she said, scuttling off around the corner.

He took off his hat and walked down the wide, dark hallway into the library, his boots clicking on the polished wooden floor. Nothing had changed. The same tall bookshelves stood against the walls filled with leather-bound legal volumes — Hansard, Halsbury's, and Acts of Parliament. On the walls hung engraved portraits of previous

Lord Chancellors and other celebrated lawyers of the last century. To the right was a cabinet of parchment scrolls and by the window stood a large mahogany desk with a shaded green lamp. The only sound was the clinical tick of the library clock.

It was in this room that his father used to punish Edmund and his brother for what he perceived to be their misdeeds. *"Spare the rod and spoil the child, Alice."* He remembered the thwack of leather on skin, the smart of pain, the sting of tears in his eyes.

"You took your time."

He started at the voice close behind him.

"I'm sorry, Father. I wanted to come sooner, but I've been busy lately."

"Yes, I'm sure you have." His father appraised him briefly. "You'll have a drink with me?"

"No, thank you, Father."

"Yes, you shall. Milly!" The maid was there within moments. "Two rum and waters."

"I really don't —"

"Come, now. We are celebrating, are we not?"

"Celebrating?"

"Your appointment, Edmund! The salvaging of your legal career."

Edmund regarded his father. Although he

was nearer now to seventy than to sixty, he still cut a clean figure, slim-built with silver hair trimmed short. He was dressed, immaculately as always, in a blue coat, striped waistcoat, and dark trousers. Edmund wondered for whom he was making the effort.

"My career didn't need salvaging, Father," he said quietly.

"No? Then why did you write to me asking for money?"

Edmund felt his face blaze. "A temporary issue. I haven't been paid for all my work of late."

"Well," his father said, with false levity, "now you won't need financial assistance, will you? And you stand a chance of making a name for yourself — raising your profile on the back of a fallen woman."

Edmund swallowed. "I'm not sure that she's what you'd call a fallen woman."

"Come, come, Edmund. *The Times* describes her as an 'unfortunate.' We all know what that word means."

"She was living with Greenacre as his wife."

"Ah, but she was not in fact his wife, was she? No. Then there is little difference between her and a common street prostitute."

There was a pause. Edmund listened to the slow tick of the library clock. He wished himself anywhere but there. "That is not what she stands accused of."

"No, indeed, she was convicted of something far worse. You see, once a woman has begun to descend the slippery slope of immorality, there is no limit to what she's capable of. *Falsum in uno, falsum in omnibus.* Remember that, Edmund. Once a woman has lost her sexual scruples, then she will stop at nothing." He smiled tightly. "I would know, of course."

"Father, that's unfair. That was hardly the same thing." Edmund was still not entirely sure what crime his mother was supposed to have committed, but he hoped it had given her at least some brief happiness.

Milly came back into the library with a silver tray bearing two crystal glasses, which his father picked up. He planted one in Edmund's hand.

"To your success." His father knocked back the rum and returned the glass to the tray. "Edmund, are you not grateful? Do you refuse to toast your own appointment?"

The smell of rum made the bile rise in Edmund's throat. He had always hated the stuff. Milly hovered nervously with the tray. Resignedly, he put the glass to his lips,

197

closed his eyes, and gulped down the liquid, trying his best not to gag. He placed the near-empty glass back on the tray.

"Thank you, Milly."

She bobbed into a brief curtsy and then rushed from the room. There was an uncomfortable silence.

"Have you heard from your mother?"

"Not for a while."

Edmund had in fact received a letter from her only a few days ago, but it was best to avoid any conversation about her. As a child, his father had prohibited him and his brother from speaking of their mother at all. At first, Edmund had made the mistake of asking his father where she was and whether he could see her. He recalled the look on his face, the sound of the air compressing as his father's hand landed flat on his cheek. He did not ask again.

"Well, it's good to know you don't care to visit either of your parents."

"As I said, Father, I've been busy."

"Yes, yes. Your new case." His father moved over to one of the wing chairs and sat down. "Tell me: how is it progressing? What methods are you using?"

Edmund also took a seat. "I'm obtaining an affidavit from Sarah Gale regarding her history while at the same time questioning her about the key events."

"I see."

"You don't think that the correct course of action?" Edmund asked, irritated.

"Personally, I wouldn't have thought her life story particularly relevant. What matters is what happened that night. And there is a danger that you will be drawn into her narrative. But of course it is your investigation."

"Yes, Father, it is."

After a long moment, his father said, "And do you believe her version of events?"

"There are some inconsistencies, but as a witness, yes, I find her credible."

His father laughed. "Ah, you mean you find her attractive. It is true that she is handsome, then?"

"Do you mean to imply that I have been drawn in by her womanly charms and am incapable of forming an unbiased judgment? Really, if you think so little of me, why did you recommend me to the post?"

"Oh, Edmund, Edmund," his father said, placing his hand on his son's arm, "I was only toying with you. I'm sure you're doing a perfectly decent job. I just want to ensure that you do the best you can. It is not only your name, after all, that will be associated with the outcome."

Edmund moved his arm away. "Why put

me forward if you were worried about how it would reflect upon you?"

"Well, it could work out to the advantage of us both. I am at that point in my career, remember, where they will be considering me for judgeship. They will no doubt consider my life — my family in the round. And if you were able to impress the Home Secretary —"

"Of course. I should have known this was about furthering your own interests."

"Really, would it be such a chore to assist your own father? The man who has paid for your education and upbringing, who has assisted you even in the matter of procuring a wife?"

His father placed an emphasis on the last word that stung Edmund to the quick. For not only had he introduced him to Bessie, but he had spoken to her father when Edmund wished to court her. At the time, Edmund had thought it a surprising act of kindness. Only later did he understand it was simply a further means of controlling him.

"I must make the decision that I believe to be right," Edmund said. "Not the decision that is most likely to secure your advancement, or my own. After all, there is a woman's life at stake. But perhaps you had not considered that."

He declined the offer of supper and left shortly afterward, his pulse racing, a pain in the back of his throat. While he wanted to believe himself different from his father, the truth was that it was not just Sarah Gale's fate that concerned him: it was his own.

15

"The visionary lies to himself, the liar only to others."

— Friedrich Nietzsche

That night the cry came again, a thin strangled sound.

For a few minutes, Sarah lay on her side, listening, thinking. She climbed out of bed, wrapping the blanket about her, and walked over to her water basin. The room was ice cold.

"Stop crying," she whispered.

Silence. Then a frightened voice. "Who's there?"

"My name's Sarah. I'm in the cell next to yours. I'm speaking through the pipes that connect the basin to the wall. Go over to your own basin."

Footsteps. Then a faint voice. "Can you hear me?"

"Yes. It's Lucy, isn't it?"

"Yes, Lucy Grimshaw."

Sarah had seen the girl that morning, washing in the taproom, her pointed shoulder blades protruding from her stained prison chemise as she sponged herself with water from a bucket. Although her frame was childish, there was something determined-looking about her, a wiry strength.

"You know what I'm in 'ere for?"

"Yes," Sarah said. "I know that you deny it."

For a few moments, neither woman spoke.

"I hear you crying every night," Sarah said eventually.

"I'm sorry. I try not to; I promise you I do." There was a pause. "It's my fault, you see. I prayed every day that he'd die — that I'd lose the baby."

"You don't need to —"

"I do need to, though. I'm going out of my wits in here with all my thoughts and fears and not a soul to talk to."

Sarah crouched on the ground and rested her chin on her arms.

"I willed him dead," the girl said, "but I didn't kill him. That's the God's honest truth."

"You don't have to prove anything to me. My name is Sarah Gale. You know what I was convicted of."

"Yes."

There was silence save for the sound of water dripping. Sarah knew that the girl was waiting for her to speak out and deny the crime. Instead she asked, "Was he still-born?"

"I think so. He never made a peep."

"There was no movement?"

"No, nothing, but they say I should've called a doctor," Lucy whispered. "Even if I thought he were dead. They say he could've been alive. An' maybe he was; maybe I got it wrong."

The girl had begun to cry again, quietly.

"What color was his skin?" Sarah said.

"Miss?"

"I was a nurse, Lucy. I've seen stillborn babies before. What color was his skin?"

The girl had stopped crying. "He were a deep pink."

"With red lips?"

"Yes, that's it. Cherry red. I tried to wash his face, but the skin . . . it were like I was washin' it away."

"Then he was dead, Lucy. Dead long before he came out."

No answer.

"Do you understand?" Sarah asked, louder. "You didn't kill him. He died in your

204

womb. You don't need to feel guilty."

Sarah wished there was someone who could tell her the same: that none of this was her fault. That it would be all right. But no one had ever told her that. It had always been her fault.

"Will you tell them that?" Lucy said finally. "Will you tell the beaks what you just told me, 'bout how he must've been dead if he looked like that?"

In the darkness, Sarah smiled. "I would, Lucy, but it wouldn't do any good. They wouldn't believe a word I said."

For some time after that, Sarah lay on her mattress, her body curled into a ball, thinking of her own baby. Rose, she had called her, after her sister. She had never known what caused the child to die — whether it was the poverty of her own diet, or the squalor of her surroundings, the walls that bloomed with damp, the bed that crept with bugs. Either way, she came into the world dead, her tiny body distended and broken, her perfect mouth blood-red. Sarah had wrapped her in a blanket and held her and held her until the midwife pried the child from her arms.

Sarah squeezed her eyes shut. Lactational insanity, they had called it: the darkness, the panic, the searing hatred like a fire in her brain. Best not to think of that time. Push it from your mind.

She tried instead to imagine George, a soft, warm presence in bed beside her just as he had been those nights when they lived alone in that little room. *"Will you tell me a story, Mama?"* But the image warped and twisted and she could envision him only as he would be if the worst should happen: alone, hungry, and afraid.

Eventually, abandoning the idea of sleep, she drew the gray blanket around her shoulders and kneeled on the stone floor at the foot of her mattress. All at once she was a child again, kneeling next to her sister in the nursery, breathing in the smell of freshly laundered sheets, head down, hands pressed together, whispering:

Have mercy upon me, O God, according to
    thy lovingkindness:
According unto the multitude of thy tender
    mercies blot out my transgressions.
Wash me thoroughly from mine iniquity, and
    cleanse me from my sin.

What a thing to make a child recite. Perhaps it was no wonder she had turned out as she had.

Miss Pike was one of the first visitors to arrive the following morning. Her cheeks were flushed and her eyes glistened black.

"I have met with Mr. Fleetwood," she told Sarah. "He is on our side, I can tell, but he needs to be persuaded. I did what I could, but he will only truly believe it when he hears it from you."

"Hears what from me, Miss Pike?"

The other woman gave her a hard look. "You know what Mr. Fleetwood is, Sarah?"

Sarah considered this. She was still not sure she could pinpoint him: simply ambitious, or ruthless? Caring or cunning? But Miss Pike was not really waiting for an answer from her.

"He is an *idealist*," she said. "He wants to improve society. He wants to reform the criminal justice system. I wouldn't be surprised if he were secretly an abolitionist. We're incredibly lucky that he was appointed. Another man might well have decided against you from the outset, but Edmund — Mr. Fleetwood — he positively *wants* to be able to recommend that you be pardoned."

Sarah looked up. "Did he say that?"

"Not in so many words, but I could tell.

We had an . . . an instinctive understanding."

It occurred to Sarah that Miss Pike was a little in love with Edmund. She was surprised to feel a twinge of jealousy. She realized she had begun to think of him as hers, although she was aware that was ridiculous.

For a while neither woman spoke. Around them, other visitors conversed in low tones. An old lady in a black bonnet read from a Bible to a young girl. A red-haired woman sat slumped forward, weeping onto her arms. And, on the far side of the room, Rook sat sullen-faced before a lady in a green dress who seemed to be lecturing her. From time to time, Rook glanced across at Sarah, her eyes gleaming with malice.

"Sarah," Miss Pike said quietly, "Mr. Fleetwood doesn't believe that you didn't know about the murder. It won't matter how many times you tell him, he will still think you must have known what happened."

Sarah was silent.

"I'm not a lawyer," Miss Pike continued. "However, my understanding is that if a woman can be shown to have acted under duress, or under the influence of a man, then that may give her a defense. And, as I said, I think that Edmund — Mr. Fleetwood — is sympathetic to your plight."

Sarah raised her eyes. "But Miss Pike, I *didn't* know, however implausible that may seem to him, or to you. And even if I were to tell Mr. Fleetwood that James had made me do . . . certain things, you cannot be sure that he would recommend a pardon."

Sarah noticed that Rook was now leaning forward, speaking to her visitor. She could tell from the movement of Rook's face that she was practically spitting out the words. The woman in green pushed back her chair and stood up.

"There are never any guarantees, Sarah," Miss Pike said. "You have to think about what the drawback would be of *not* speaking out. Do you stand to lose anything?"

Sarah looked at Miss Pike in her funny little black bonnet and checked shawl fastened tight around her shoulders. There was so much she did not understand. Did she really think that Sarah had not considered every possibility? That she did not lie awake at night, twisting and turning and trying to fathom how to extricate herself?

"James is a powerful man," she said. "Even now."

Miss Pike folded her hands. "That's what he wants you to believe, Sarah. That's what he's always wanted you to believe: that he's the one with the power. That it's him that's holding all the cards. But you're a strong woman, stronger than you think."

When visiting hour was over, the prisoners were ordered to line up against the lime-washed wall by the door while the lady visitors left the room. Perhaps because she was still considering Miss Pike's words, Sarah did not realize until the other woman spoke that Rook was directly behind her.

"Look at 'em," she said, jerking her head toward the women. "They think they can save us with a few lines o' scripture. They don't know that women like you and me, we're bad down to the bone."

Sarah turned briefly to look at her. "I'm nothing like you."

Rook's expression set. "No, you're right. You're not. 'Cos I at least admit what I am, while you, you're like a bad coin, with the shine worn off."

The woman screwed up her mouth and, too late, Sarah brought her hands to her face. A globule of spit hit her cheek and Sarah wiped it away frantically with the back of her sleeve. When she looked up she realized that Miss Sowerton was standing, watching, only a few feet away. Instead of reprimanding Rook, however, she gave a barely perceptible nod, and turned to leave the room.

16

"Women are greater dissemblers than men when they wish to conceal their own emotions. By habit, moral training, and modern education, they are obliged to do so."
— *Tacita Tacit,* Jane Vaughan Pinkney, 1860

After a breakfast of coffee and hot rolls, Edmund caught the omnibus to the village of Dulwich to see his mother, taking the iron ladder to the roof to sit on the outside in the spring sunshine. He read his notebook as he traveled until the jerking of the coach over stones made him feel nauseated and he stared instead at the changing scenery, the brick and soot of London giving way to the meadowland of Camberwell, Herne Hill, and Dulwich.

He alighted at Mill Pond and walked along the tree-lined street to the Picture Gallery, arriving at the gray stone building twenty minutes after the agreed meeting time. He found his mother in the main gallery, seated on a velvet-covered sofa and staring ahead at a portrait of a dark-haired woman. His mother did not look up as he approached and he had a few moments to appraise her. She seemed to have aged since he had last seen her, or maybe it was simply that distance had made his vision clearer. She was still elegant — narrow-waisted in a peach satin dress and neat straw bonnet, but her face sagged with tiredness and sadness. The image at which she gazed showed a strange woman, both cold and sensual, turning away from the artist.

As soon as she saw Edmund, his mother's face broke into a smile and the tired, dejected woman was quite gone. "Edmund!"

"I'm so sorry I'm late, Mother," he said as she got up and clasped his hands.

"Oh, fiddlesticks' ends. I've been quite happy sitting here. Now, how are you? How is my delightful grandson?"

He took her arm and together they wandered through Sir John Soane's gallery, looking at the paintings, before moving to the tearooms, where they sat amid the tinkling of silver spoons and ripple of conversation.

"And you?" he asked her. "How are you?"

"Oh, I'm quite well. Ethel does such a good job of looking after me and I have everything I need, really."

Edmund knew this was not true. His father paid her a meager allowance, which she used carefully, and Ethel, her maid of all work, was now too rheumatic to carry out all of the household chores alone. He must buy his mother a new dress when he had some money himself.

"You're not . . . lonely?" he asked.

She had retreated from society after his father had cast her out, mixing only with a small group of spinster ladies who were unlikely to judge her.

"Well, you know how it is," she said. "I have my visits from Mrs. Pemberton and Mrs. Curling. And, you will laugh, but I have joined a choir. In any event, I want to know about you. How is your new case?"

"It's certainly interesting, but it's difficult to tell who is lying and why."

"What does Miss Gale say happened?"

He picked up the sugar tongs. "She claims not to have known what James Greenacre had done."

"But you don't believe her?"

"Well, she is clearly an intelligent woman, and an observant one."

"Yes, but, as I understand it from the newspapers, she is also a woman who had been abandoned." His mother pursed her lips and poured more tea. "It may have suited her not to see certain things if it meant that she survived."

"You mean she decided not to notice."

His mother dabbed her lips with the laced edge of her pocket handkerchief. "Not necessarily. Think of what she'd been through, Edmund. That monster Greenacre had thrown her out onto the streets with a young child, hadn't he?"

"Yes," Edmund said quietly, "but at least he didn't try to take her child away from her." He met her eye.

His mother smiled tightly. "That is all a long time ago now, Edmund. And everything turned out well in the end."

"Despite my having done nothing to help you."

"You must stop blaming yourself for things that are not your fault. You were a child."

She put her hand over his and squeezed it. In some respects, he thought, she was like Sarah. She, too, had fallen from grace and was now imprisoned in a way — in her limited society, in her pretense that everything was quite all right. And perhaps Sarah, like his mother, had grown practiced in the art of suppressing emotions — of concealing what she truly felt.

"Do you really think, Mother, that a woman could not know that her lover, or her husband, had murdered another woman? Even if it was in their own house? Even if she had seen him only a matter of hours later?"

She smiled thinly. "I think it very possible, Edmund. People only see what they're capable of seeing at that particular time in their lives." She pressed her hands together as she cast about for the right words. "I suppose it's like that painting by Holbein *The Ambassadors* — that we saw at Longford Castle. Do you remember it?"

Edmund nodded. It had been one of their last outings together before his brother went abroad. They had walked the long corridors of the stately home in a companionable but sad silence.

"Well," she said, "you look at it and at first you think it's just two handsomely dressed young men, don't you? It's only when someone shows you where exactly to stand that you realize that, in between those two men, is a hideous human skull." She folded her handkerchief into a neat square. "People only see what they're expecting to see."

■ ■ ■ ■

It was early afternoon by the time Edmund reached the Temple. Turning onto Inner Temple Lane, he saw a woman walking quickly toward him. As she neared him, he saw that it was Sarah Gale's sister in a plum-colored cloak.

"Miss Farr. Is everything all right?"

"Sir, you must forgive me for approaching you outside your chambers."

He waved this away. She seemed agitated, he thought. The pinkish bloom to her cheeks had faded and her dark eyes were troubled.

"I'm very grateful to you for arranging it so that I could visit my sister." She was breathing rapidly — she had evidently been walking quickly. "But," she continued, "it confirmed what I feared. She is so thin and nervous that I'm sure they are treating her cruelly there. I tried to pass some food and some clothing to her, but the warder wouldn't allow it."

"No," Edmund shook his head. "It's because she's a condemned prisoner." As soon as he had spoken the words, he saw the pain cross Rosina's face and cursed himself inwardly for reminding her of her sister's sentence. "They don't allow prisoners convicted of certain crimes to buy or receive additional food. I realize it seems harsh."

"Not *seems,* Mr. Fleetwood. Is. They're not providing her with enough to live on. She'll starve or take ill before your report is done. I know it's asking a lot of you, but if you could just take her this . . ." She removed from her cloak a brown-paper-covered parcel. "It's just some food and a blanket. They won't question your giving this to her."

Edmund met her gaze and considered his response. "I will do this for you, Miss Farr, and I will try to bring her further food despite the fact that I myself may be reprimanded, but in return you must help me." He saw fear flicker in her eyes. "I know that your sister is keeping something back from me. I want to believe her, but she is not being entirely truthful. Who is she protecting?" Rosina flinched and Edmund knew at once that he had touched upon something. "Is it Greenacre?" he asked. "Because if it is, she is doing herself no favors in covering up for him. He will hang now, no matter what he claims. She is only making things worse for herself."

Rosina shook her head. "I can't help you,

sir, I really can't." Edmund could see, however, that her grip on the package was so tight that her knuckles showed white through her skin. "You must tell me, Rosina. If there is something you know that could save your sister, then you must speak out now."

Her expression was now one of deep distress. "Please, Mr. Fleetwood, if I could say something now that I thought would get us out of this situation then I swear to God that I would." She touched his wrist. "You must listen to what she tells you and you must believe it."

"Daddy!" Edmund turned to see Clem running toward them, his governess running as best she could to catch up with him.

Edmund looked back at Rosina and saw that she was staring at his son intently. When Clem was only a few paces away, she thrust the bundle at Edmund and said, "Please, Mr. Fleetwood. I beg you." She took one last look at Clem and hurried away, her cloak billowing behind her.

"Who was that, Daddy?"

"That was . . . That was." He stopped and looked at his son, his pointed little chin and rosebud mouth, and wondered what about him could possibly have alarmed Rosina. "That was the sister of the woman whom

219

I'm investigating."

"Why was she here?"

"She wants me to help her."

"Will you?"

"I'm not sure yet."

Clem poked the parcel. "What's in there? A head?"

"No, some food, apparently."

Clem looked at the package distrustfully. "Can I see inside?"

"You most certainly cannot."

"Mr. Fleetwood, sir," Miss Plimpton said, finally catching up with her errant charge, "I do apologize." She paused for breath. "He saw you and just made for you though I tried to stop him."

"That's quite all right, Miss Plimpton. No harm done."

Edmund looked back the way that Rosina had hurried off. She was on the edge of the Temple Gardens now, visible only as a flash of purple moving through the green.

On Monday morning, Edmund walked across the dense traffic on Ludgate Circus and past the slender spire of St. Martin's church to reach the London Coffee House on Ludgate Hill. He took a seat in a booth in the wood-paneled back room and ordered coffee and a jug of water.

After a few minutes, he saw the man he had come to meet: Hannah Brown's brother. Edmund recognized him from the trial. He was a tall, long-bodied man with a fleshy, oblong face.

Edmund approached him. "William Brown?"

The man nodded but did not smile. "We'll have to keep this short," he said. "I'm due back at work in half an hour."

He sat opposite Edmund, took off his black gloves, and put them in his hat, then extracted from his waistcoat a gold pocket watch, which he placed on the table before him.

The coffee Edmund had ordered arrived, black and sweet, its steam curling into the air.

"I appreciate you have a busy schedule," Edmund said — he had been trying to secure an interview with Brown for over a week — "but there are several things I need to ask."

"I told the lawyers everything I knew at the Old Bailey," Brown said. "And I told the police before that." His voice was flat, with an edge of contempt.

Edmund took a sip of his coffee, which scorched his tongue. "Of course, but it's important that I investigate thoroughly."

221

No response.

"It was you, I believe, who identified your sister's body."

"I identified her *head.*"

"Yes, I'm sure that wasn't a pleasant experience," Edmund said, not mentioning that he, too, had seen Hannah Brown's head, preserved in liquor.

Brown made no reply.

"You had not, however, seen Hannah for some time before she died. That's correct, isn't it?"

"Yes, that's correct."

"Can I ask why?"

"We'd been at variance for some months," he said.

"What was the cause of the rift?" Edmund asked.

The man looked at him coldly. "What possible relevance can it have?"

"It's difficult to say, without knowing the cause."

Brown sighed. "My sister was prone to fits of temper. That is all."

"Yes, that was something that was mentioned during the trial. Greenacre's barrister claimed she had previously attacked Greenacre physically. Had she ever attacked you?"

"She was not a lunatic, Mr. Fleetwood;

she could simply be a little forceful. In any event, you're supposed to be investigating that Gale woman's ridiculous claims, aren't you? Let's get on with it. As I say, I want to keep this short."

"What was the state of your sister's financial affairs?"

"She did well enough. She kept a laundry, as you'd know if you've read up on this case at all, and business was prospering."

"How do you know that if you were, as you put it, 'at variance' with your sister?"

Brown scowled at him. "She still saw my wife occasionally. Maria. She kept me informed."

"Can you explain, then, why Miss Brown tried to claim credit in James Greenacre's name shortly before she died?"

"Slander and rumor," the man said brusquely. "Hannah had no need of that man's money. She had property of her own."

Edmund turned over a page in his notebook. "It was you, I'm told, who identified the jewelry that was found on Miss Gale as having belonged to your sister."

"What of it?"

"I understand that the earrings were fairly inexpensive things made of gold filigree and that the rings were thin bands of gold."

"And?"

223

Edmund smiled. "If your sister was prospering financially, why was she wearing such cheap jewelry?"

"I am not an expert in women's spending habits," the man replied. "Do you have any other questions?"

"Yes. I believe there was a message on the inside of one of the rings. 'From AF to SW.' Do you know what that meant?"

"No, I have no idea."

"Only, it does not appear to relate to your sister, does it?"

The man glowered at him. "Nor does it appear to relate to Sarah Gale, as was made clear during the trial."

"Did you know that the jewelry has gone missing?"

Brown's face betrayed no emotion. "Has it? How unfortunate."

He knew, Edmund thought. Maybe he and Feltham had agreed that it would disappear. Or perhaps Rosina had been right: perhaps the police had never seized it.

"Did your sister wear that jewelry frequently?"

"What has that to do with anything?"

"Well, it doesn't sound as though it was very distinctive," Edmund said. "Just some gold bands and small jade earrings. I am wondering how you recognized the items, particularly when you seldom saw your sister."

"I do hope you're not accusing me of lying, sir."

"I'm simply asking a question."

"I have a good eye for detail, Mr. Fleetwood. I can only hope that the same is true of you. And now," he said, taking his gloves out of his hat, "I must return to my office."

The man had never seen the earrings; Edmund was sure of it. Sarah and Rosina had said they were carnelian: red.

"One last question, Mr. Brown, if you'll oblige me. Your sister agreed to marry James Greenacre very quickly. She moved into his house after only a few weeks of knowing him, and while there was another woman present. Do you know why that would be?"

William Brown stood up, slipped the gold watch back into his waistcoat, and put his hat under his arm. "Mr. Fleetwood, I would have thought you would be capable of working that out for yourself. She was over forty. She was not an attractive woman, physically or otherwise. She married the first man who asked her. It's just regrettable that he turned out to be a murderer."

Edmund remained seated and watched Brown as he walked rigidly toward the door. For the first time since he had accepted the

commission, Edmund felt a surge of pity
for Hannah Brown.

17

" 'Not a particle of evidence, Pip,' said Mr. Jaggers, shaking his head and gathering up his skirts. 'Take nothing on its looks; take everything on evidence. There's no better rule.' "

— *Great Expectations,*
Charles Dickens, 1861

The waitress banged the plate down on the table in front of him and lifted the lid: kidneys with steaming marrow pudding.

"What do you make of her, then?" asked Edmund's father. "Guilty or not guilty?"

They were in a chophouse on the Gray's Inn Road, sitting on wooden benches amid the chatter of lawyers, the clashing of cutlery, and the crashing of plates on tables.

Edmund tucked his napkin into his collar. "It's still very difficult to say."

"Well, you must have some inkling. Have you not challenged her?"

"Father, it's not a simple matter of dragging the information out of her. I'm doing the best I can — and she's much more forthcoming than she was at the outset — but I suspect she's keeping something back."

"Oh, I'm sure she is, Edmund. I'm sure she is. Not that that necessarily makes her a criminal. What woman tells the truth about her private life? What man, for that matter? Everyone lies."

"Not everyone, Father."

Arthur Fleetwood ignored him and reached for the saltshaker. "The important thing, as in any case, is to sift the insignificant lies from the important ones. She may well be keeping something back, but that does not of itself mean that she is lying about the murder."

"I had no idea you were such an authority on criminal investigations," Edmund said.

His father, impervious to his sarcasm, continued, "Remember that, while women are often very good liars, they are generally less capable of independent and complex thought. It will therefore be necessary to subject her account to rigorous scrutiny — test her on each point, push her, catch her out."

Edmund clenched his teeth. "Perhaps you would like to interrogate her yourself."

His father frowned. "I don't think that would be appropriate. I am merely giving you a few pointers to help you draw out the true version of events."

He poured himself more wine.

"Of course, it's possible she is telling the truth. Perhaps she really did not know that Greenacre murdered the woman."

Edmund shook his head. "She was surrounded by Hannah Brown's possessions. She's an intelligent woman."

"Even the cleverer ones are easily led, Edmund. If Sarah Gale was used to accepting everything Greenacre said and acceding to his every whim, would she really have had the tenacity to question why the other woman's belongings remained in their house? Think of Bessie. Does she challenge your every word and action?"

Edmund felt his face grow hot. "I fail to see what Bessie has to do with any of this."

"Ah," said his father with a slight smile, "I see I have hit upon a sore point. Bessie always was a little willful. As a young girl, she talked back even to her own father."

Edmund bit the inside of his cheek. His father never missed an opportunity to remind him that he had known Bessie first.

As Edmund walked to Newgate, he wondered whether his father could be right: whether Greenacre had oppressed Sarah to such an extent that she ceased to question what he said and did. It was typical of his father to expound on the wrongdoings of others without realizing that he was guilty of the very same thing. Even as a young child, Edmund had recognized the insults and snide remarks that his father made to or about his mother, in public as well as in private: she dressed inappropriately; she ate too much or in the wrong way; she was losing her looks; she spoke foolishly. He had a distinct memory of his mother in a deep red dress, her hair elaborately coiffed, diamonds at her neck, descending the spiral staircase to the hallway, ready to greet the guests who were arriving for some dinner or ball.

"Good gracious, Alice," his father had said as he looked up at her. "You might be a gentleman's whore, not his wife."

Edmund had never seen him hurt her physically. In fact, he had rarely seen his father touch his mother at all. His abuse was of a different kind. Like Sarah, his mother had put up with it, gradually worn down to a husk. Like Sarah, she had stayed until she was thrown out. And the worst of it all was that he knew his mother had done it for them — she had stayed for him and his brother. Why had he not stood up for her? He had realized what was happening, but had felt powerless to stop it. He was not powerless now, however.

Once again, Edmund was taken to Sarah's cell, where at least a chair had been provided for him. It was several days since he had last seen Sarah and, in that time, she seemed to have grown thinner, her face sharper. Her sister was right that they were effectively starving her. There were dark smudges under her eyes and her collarbones protruded through her clothing. And yet there was something about her that stirred him. Something dangerous and dark and beautiful.

When the warder had left and he believed that they were not watched, he passed Sarah the parcel that Rosina had given him, together with a fruit tart that he had purchased on the way to the prison. She looked up at him in surprise.

"Your sister came to see me," he said in explanation. "She is worried, with reason, that you are cold and hungry here and I agreed to give these things to you." He did not mention that it was he who had bought the fruit tart lest it should seem like some form of a bribe or, worse, a lover's gift.

231

Edmund saw her waver as she considered whether to eat some of the food in front of him, but evidently hunger won over. She removed a piece of the tart from its paper, and bit eagerly into it, cupping her hand beneath her chin to catch the falling crumbs.

"Would you prefer that I returned later?"

She finished chewing and wiped a hand across her lips, which were moist with jam. "Thank you, but I would rather that you stayed."

There was a pause.

"What would you like me to talk about today, Mr. Fleetwood?"

Edmund stared at her. It took him a moment to remember what he had intended to ask.

"We talked last time we met about how you came to London. I wondered . . . what happened after your mother died? It must have been a very difficult time."

Sarah gave him a strange look, which he could not read. "My mother and I were never close." She hesitated. "I was not, I suppose, a very good daughter."

Edward gave a lopsided smile. "How strange. Only just now I was thinking that I haven't been much of a son to my own mother."

"Why do you say that?"

"Well, I don't see her as much as I ought." Edmund shifted in his seat.

"Because you are so busy?"

"Partly. Partly because . . ." Because what? Because he felt he had failed her? Because he was ashamed of her? "I'm not sure, really," he said. "I have no excuse, and she is quite lonely. My father and she parted ways some years ago." Why was he telling her this?

"And your father disapproves of your continued contact with her?"

Edmund looked at Sarah, unblinking. "You are very perceptive, Miss Gale."

Sarah gave a half smile. "Not, it seems, when it really matters." She met Edmund's eye. Maybe it was true, he thought. Maybe she really had not known about Hannah Brown.

After a pause, he said, "What did you do after your mother's death?"

"We moved to some cheaper rooms on the Ratcliffe Highway. You know of it, I suppose?"

Edmund nodded. The Ratcliffe Highway ran from East Smithfield to Shadwell High Street. He had visited the area several times, seeking out witnesses on other criminal cases. He had seen the thin children playing in the gutters and the women with bloated faces waiting on street corners for trade.

"It's a rough sort of place," Sarah said, "but we couldn't afford anything better by that stage. The obvious thing would have been for both Rosina and me to find positions as governesses: that's what most middle-class women turn to when their lives fall to pieces. But it would have meant we were apart. Instead, we found employment at a local dressmaker's, sewing being about the only useful skill we'd been taught. It was hard work: long hours in poor conditions and no reliable pay. During the Season, ladies expected their new balldresses to be delivered the day after they'd ordered them, which sometimes meant sewing for twenty hours or more straight off. We couldn't continue like that."

"So what did you do?" he asked carefully. Was this, he wondered, when she had become the "unfortunate" the newspapers spoke of? He knew that many dressmakers and seamstresses had to subsidize their earnings by going to the streets.

"A woman who lived on the floor below us suggested that Rosina and I might try our hand at nursing. It isn't generally considered to be a suitable profession for young women, of course, but we couldn't have the same expectations as before. We could only hope to survive.

"I found a woman in Walworth, Miss Vetch, who'd set up her own school, teaching the basics of nursing and midwifery to a roomful of girls. We attended her school during the day, and by night we took in needlework and lacework. It wasn't easy. Part of the training involved attending patients in the workhouse and walking the wards in the poor hospital." She shook her head. "The stench of the place . . . It stayed with me for days: sickness, dirt, and despair.

"It was too much for Rosina. She was only fourteen then and she became . . . ill. I wrote to our old drawing teacher, who agreed to put her forward for a governess position, and she went to look after two little girls in a decent house off Portland Place."

"Leaving you on your own."

"Yes." Sarah picked at her lip. "It was the first time we'd been apart. We were both very lonely, I think; but at least I knew Rosina was safe. And I saw her every other Sunday. Not long after that I obtained a situation as a private nurse in one of the big houses in Marylebone, caring for an old gentleman. I won't pretend it was pretty work, but it was fairly paid and . . . well, that's how it was for a time."

Edmund tried to read her face. She was

not telling him the whole story, he was sure of it.

"Why didn't you become a governess yourself?" he asked. "Or some kind of schoolmistress? Surely that would have been preferable."

"I couldn't find a position early on. And then, well, I'd been at low jobs for so long that I couldn't get a character for work as a governess."

"There was nothing else you could do? You had been educated, after all."

Sarah gave him a blank look. "I was educated to be a gentlewoman, a wife. I was educated so that I should *not* work. There were very few options open to me."

Edmund nodded slowly. He suspected he knew the real reason she had been unable to get a character: she had sold herself, to save her younger sister.

"When did you marry?" he asked. "I assume Gale is your married name."

She frowned. "It was a few years later, when I was three and twenty. Charles, his name was, though everyone called him Charlie. He was a sailor so I saw him only for a few months of the year, but it turned out that was plenty enough."

"What do you mean?"

She paused. "Charlie wasn't always a kind

man, especially when he'd been at the bottle, and he resented my learning, meager though it was. He thought me above myself and he made it his business to take me down a peg or two."

"What happened to him?"

Sarah gave a thin smile. "Two years after we married, when I was with child, he taught me my final lesson: he disappeared altogether. Sailed off on a cruise and never came back. For months, I tried to find him, but when I discovered that he'd absconded at Cape Town I gave up any hope of ever tracing him.

"I'd lost my situation by then, being big with child, and was nearly destitute. Rosina brought me garments from her employers and their friends to sew and mend: dresses, shirts, bonnets. I was laid up, exhausted with the baby at that time and if Rosina hadn't helped me, I . . . well, I don't know what would have happened."

"And the child . . . ?"

"It was a little girl. She was born dead."

"I'm very sorry," Edmund said, thinking of Bessie's doomed pregnancies, his own grief. But then something else occurred to him. "That means that George is not your husband's son."

"No," Sarah said curtly. "He wasn't."

Edmund waited for her to say something further. When she did not, he said: "He's not Greenacre's son either, is he? You didn't meet Greenacre until after he was born."

"No, but James was often kind to George," she said quickly. "He told him stories and sang to him, and sometimes he'd take him to the pleasure gardens and the zoo at Walworth."

"And threw him out of the house in the depths of winter."

Sarah looked away from him. "I said he was often kind. Not always."

"And often was enough?"

"No, of course not. But I always hoped that things would get better. I wished that —" She stopped herself.

"What was it that you wished, Sarah?"

Sarah was looking at her hands. "I suppose a part of me thought that one day James and I would marry. That we would be a proper family. But of course it didn't work out like that."

"No. No, it didn't." Edmund considered his words carefully. "Tell me about James," he said. "How did you meet him?"

18

"Attentive and silent observation will frequently give an early insight into the game, and enable you to play your hand to more advantage, than by adhering to more regular maxims."
— *Advice to the Young Whist Player,*
Thomas Matthews, Esq., 1808

"It was in the August of 1835. Do you remember how hot it was that summer? The roads were covered in dust and the whole of London stank like the inside of a tannery. One Sunday afternoon, Rosina and I decided to escape the heat and stench and travel down to Camberwell Fair, as a treat for George, and for ourselves."

Sarah remembered it clearly. A tavern ranged from one end of the Green to the other, ornamented with chandeliers, lamps, flags, and banners, and from a distance the whole thing looked like a glorious multicolored patchwork quilt. Walking closer, they saw fortune-tellers and donkey rides, weighing machines and theater booths, drummer boys and acrobats, peep shows and freak shows. The Green swarmed with people in high spirits, many of them drunk, and men and women selling nuts and toffee apples walked through the throng carrying baskets and shouting out their wares, their calls mixing with the sounds of the musicians and the babble of the crowd.

For a time, they wandered about looking at the shows and at the stalls; at the hand-wagons piled high with oranges, gingerbread, brandy snaps, and oysters. At dusk, the bands began to play, and Sarah and Rosina seated themselves in the tavern to take some beer and to feed George some warm milk and pieces of apple. A man approached their table and, without prelude, asked Sarah to dance. It was his hands she noticed first: large and capable with the nails clean and neatly cut. He had a coarse sort of face with a thick nose, but eyes that seemed to glint. James.

"He was very charming to all of us," Sarah told Edmund. "Making jokes and giving compliments and even paying for George to have a turn on the roundabout."

And even then, Sarah thought, Rosina had

seen through him. "I met with James often after that. He brought me gifts: a bundle of oranges tied up in a handkerchief, a bright bird in a cage. He noticed me. After a time, we agreed it made sense for me to move into his house and to cook and clean for him. No doubt you'll think that was improper as we weren't married — I know many did — but I was still Charlie's wife so far as the law was concerned, and I had a child. I suppose I could hardly have expected James to marry me." She twisted her fingers into the fabric of her skirt. "And anyway, I was poor; I needed somewhere to stay."

"He was married before he met you, wasn't he?" Edmund asked.

"Yes, James had had two wives, both of whom died. I know the press has claimed that he dispatched them both like some monstrous Bluebeard character, but the reality is far more mundane. One died of a putrid throat and the other, I believe, fell from a horse."

Edmund cleared his throat and Sarah looked up at him. His expression suggested he did not believe her. Perhaps he had swallowed the newspapermen's stories. Perhaps he was imagining James burying his previous wives in the cellar, as he then said:

241

"When did you move into his house?"

"In September of that year, not long after James himself had moved to Carpenter's Buildings."

"And were you . . . content there?"

"Well, it wasn't a particularly lovely house — it's in the poorer area of Camberwell and, when the wind blows from the north, you can smell the fumes from the glue factory nearby. However, it's surrounded by fields of corn and meadowland full of wild flowers. After the Ratcliffe Highway, it was a sort of paradise."

She could picture the house now: the kitchen with its copper saucepans and little stock of crockery, the bedroom with its iron bedstead and hip bath. She would stand at the window looking down onto the garden, where she had planted flowers with George: sweet briars, summer jasmine, snapdragons. It felt like home.

"We lived together there fairly happily at first, so it seemed to me," Sarah told Edmund. "I did all of the housework and the washing, and took in pieces of sewing to work on in the evenings. George stayed with me in the mornings and was cared for in the afternoons by a woman who also minded some of the other children in the area. Aside from her and a couple of others on the road, I didn't speak too much to people. Most assumed I was James's wife, which was fine with me. In my mind, we were married, really, even if we'd never gone through the ceremony. Of course, the judge held that against me later."

For an instant, she saw before her the judge in his long, white wig: *"You had united yourself to him, sharing his society and bed, without being joined to him by any moral or religious tie."* As though that were proof enough of her criminal depravity.

"What did you think of James at that stage?" Edmund asked.

"I suppose I knew from the beginning that he was an impulsive and ambitious man. He left his father's farm in Norfolk when he was little more than a boy and came to London with nothing. Yet by the time I met him, he was prospering: as well as his carpentry work, he was running a large grocery shop in the Kent Road and he had several other properties in Camberwell. He always had schemes as to how he would make money or make his name. James couldn't just be a cabinetmaker, you see: he had to be a politician, a person of standing." Sarah smiled bitterly. "I should have foreseen that as soon as he was given the opportunity to enrich or improve himself, he would take it, even if that meant hurting me."

"Hence casting you aside for a woman he believed could help him with his business."

"Exactly."

"But, in fact, she lied about that, didn't she?"

Sarah lowered her gaze. "James thought Hannah Brown had been dishonest about her property."

"He claimed, didn't he, that she'd been trying to claim credit in his name at a shop on Long Acre? That's what they were arguing about."

Sarah did not answer, but thought only of Hannah's anxious face: *"He'll understand, won't he? I'll tell him when the time's right."*

Edmund was watching her intently. "Did it surprise you to learn that's what sparked his anger?"

Sarah licked her lips. "James is a proud man. No doubt he felt that she'd insulted his intelligence. He didn't kill her, though."

"Miss Gale, you don't believe that. You know what happened: he lost his temper, as he had done so many times with you, and he struck out. Perhaps he didn't intend to kill Hannah Brown, but he did."

Sarah felt tears filling her eyes. "No," she said quietly. "That's not what happened."

Edmund frowned. "Miss Gale, it was one thing not to give evidence against Greenacre at the trial, but now that you have both been sentenced to death, you must reappraise your situation. They will not reprieve Greenacre, no matter what his petition claims. In refusing to speak out against him you are harming only yourself."

Sarah gazed at him through a film of tears. If only it were that simple.

That night Sarah lay in the dark listening to the whispering of other women in nearby cells. She could not hear what they were saying; it was just a sound like leaves rustling in the wind or skirts dragging along the ground. She thought of how she and James used to whisper to one another, lying in that room that smelled of tallow and rosewater and of their own bodies. Sweet things, kind things, things that made her hot and shivery inside. James would trace the outline of her features — her jaw, her neck — with his rough hand and tell her how beautiful she was. It was as if she were being seen, truly seen, for the first time.

When had it begun to change? Somehow, the sweetness turned, like milk gone bad. And he was so far inside her that when he twisted the knife she felt every turn. James had a way with words: he always knew what to say to buoy people up and make them trust him. But he also knew what would cut the deepest. He began with little slices, barely perceptible, and then, when she was broken down, moved on to the bigger incisions. It became a game for him, she thought. How far could he go? How much would she bear?

Toward the end, Sarah felt she had been carved out from the inside. Hollow. By the time he told her about Hannah Brown, she did not even have it in her to be surprised. Why would he want her any longer — a worn-out whore? And yet the jealousy still tore into her flesh and took root. It was from there that the hatred began to sprout, growing into something over which she had no control.

Hannah Brown. Tall and high-chested, with a thick rope of hair. She might have worn satin and a velvet hat with feathers, but she had a plain, peasant's face and dull brown eyes, the color of the filthy Thames.

A scream pierced the silence.

A few moments later, Lucy's voice came through the pipes.

"What in God's name *was* that?"

Sarah climbed out of bed and ran over to

the sink. "It's probably just a new girl, frightened," she said. "Or maybe someone with the drunkard's terrors."

Often, women were brought in drunk and left to dry out, shaking and shouting and hallucinating alone in their cells. This scream was different, however; it was more like a howl of pain. Perhaps, Sarah thought, the woman was in the dark cells, those cells that she had never seen, and which she was not even sure existed save for in the prisoners' whispered stories.

Another scream came, then another and another until it was almost constant. Sarah screwed her eyes tight shut and tried to stop herself from imagining what punishments the prisoner might be undergoing, but through her closed lids, she saw flashes in the dark: manacles, twisted limbs, lacerated flesh.

Lucy, perhaps thinking something similar, said uncertainly, "It could be poor mad Mabel, couldn't it?"

Mabel was one of the many convicts who should, by rights, have been in an asylum, not a prison: a woman with frightened eyes who would sometimes crouch on the ground and moan like a wild animal. But this was not one of Mabel's cries.

Abruptly, the sound stopped, as though

247

the woman had been struck down or gagged. The empty silence that came after was almost worse than the screams.

"How's a woman supposed to keep herself sane in this god-awful place?" Lucy asked after a time. "I'm going stark staring mad within these walls. If I ever get out, it'll be in a strait-waistcoat."

Sarah rested her head against the stone. "I've begun to think of it as a game, Lucy. A horrible game, but a game I have to win."

"What kind of game?"

"A bit like Deerstalker. Remember that one?"

"No, I never heard of it, but then my family was never much of a one for games."

"It was a parlor game my sister and I played as children," Sarah said softly. "Both the deer and the stalker are blindfolded and then guided to opposite ends of a large table. When the game begins, they move as softly as they can around the table, the stalker trying to catch the deer and the deer trying as best as she can to escape. The quieter you keep, and the more carefully you move, the more likely you are to win."

For a moment, a silence hung between them. "And are you winning, Sarah?"

"I don't know yet, Lucy, but I hope so. My life depends on it."

248

19

"Criminal women, as a class, are found to be more uncivilized than the savage, more degraded than the slave, less true to all natural and womanly instincts than the untutored squaw of a North American Indian tribe."

— "Criminal Women," M. E. Owen,
Cornhill Magazine, 1866

4 June 1837

It was dark by the time Edmund headed home, and raining again. For the past week, the streets of London had been almost constantly wet, turning the filth of the roads into a river of muck that splashed onto his trousers and seeped through the stitching of his shoes as he went from one interview to another, meeting the people who might have seen something, who had known Hannah Brown or James Greenacre, who had opinion after opinion but no solid evidence. As he made his way back along the lamp-lit street, trying to work out what his next step should be, he heard the whoosh of wheels and turned to see a flash of light, before the carriage accelerated through a puddle, splashing him with foul, stinking water. So much for the start of summer.

Once back in his chambers, Edmund struggled to remove his boots. His stockings were wet through and clung to his feet.

He reminded himself that at least he was warm and well fed, his belly full from a hot meal in the Old Bell Tavern and a fire already blazing in the grate. Sarah, however, would be cold and fearful in her damp, dark cell. It was in the evenings that he thought of her most, imagining her sewing by a solitary candle. Edmund had visited her several times in the past few weeks to put further questions to her as they arose and to eke out the rest of her story. He knew her well enough now to know that she recognized that she was running out of time: she grew increasingly agitated and, he noticed, had begun to pick worriedly at her lip. And yet, despite that, and despite her evident desperation to see her son and sister, she continued to hold something back; she continued to shield Greenacre.

Just as he managed to remove the second

boot, there was a knock at the door. Edmund cursed quietly and struggled to get his boots back on. Bessie was away visiting her sister and he had given Flora the evening off. His boots squelched slightly as he made his way downstairs.

When he opened the door he saw a tall man in one of the new, blue police uniforms standing outside. The man took off his leather-topped hat so that the rain fell onto his hair.

"Officer. Do come in," Edmund said.

The policeman stepped over the threshold and wiped his shiny black boots carefully on the rug before following Edmund into the parlor. He stood awkwardly, holding his hat in his large hands.

"I understand that you're looking into Miss Gale's case."

"I am," Edmund said. "Won't you sit down?"

The policeman sat stiffly on the edge of the sofa. In the lamplight, Edmund realized he was younger than he had first thought. Five and twenty at most. His features were small and round, almost babyish.

"I was one of the officers on the investigation. I was there during the arrests, in fact."

"Yes, I remember you from the trial," Edmund said.

"I hear you're reinvestigating the matter," the officer said.

"Not reinvestigating exactly, but looking again at the evidence to ensure the original conviction was correct. As I explained to Inspector Feltham, I'm not attempting to second-guess the police or —"

The policeman put up his hand to stop him. "I'm here in a personal capacity rather than as an officer of the law."

Edmund nodded. "There's something you want to tell me?"

"Yes." He paused. "I was a bit concerned when we found Miss Gale that she might not have been quite herself: that she might have gone along with what Greenacre said because . . ." His voice trailed off.

"Because?"

"Because he made her."

Well, Edmund thought, this was worth putting his boots back on for.

"Go on."

The policeman scratched his head. "When we arrested Greenacre, he told us he'd never heard of Hannah Brown — that he'd never met her. Eventually, he admitted they'd been engaged to be married. Sarah Gale, when we spoke to her, seemed startled and grew tearful when Inspector Feltham talked about the body pieces being found.

When we asked her when she'd last seen Hannah Brown, she claimed she couldn't remember. We left the two of them in the room alone for a few minutes in order to dress, though we kept a close watch outside. When they came out, Miss Gale's neck and chest were blotched red and she looked like she'd been crying. She changed her story after that. She gave a statement at the station, saying she hadn't seen Hannah Brown since the twentieth of December."

The policeman removed a paper from his jacket and passed it to Edmund. Edmund held the document under the lamp and read through it quickly. It conflicted with the statement Sarah made subsequently when she said that she had last seen Greenacre and Brown the day before the murder — not something she would have forgotten. The language was quite clearly not hers.

"Why have I not seen this statement before?" Edmund asked. "And why is this the first time I've heard that Sarah was shocked and distressed on learning of Hannah Brown's death?"

The policeman squirmed in his seat. "I think it was felt by more senior officers that the information wouldn't help the case."

"Because it suggested that she was ignorant of the murder? And that she was saying whatever Greenacre told her to say?"

The policeman was silent. Then he said, "Sir, this must be kept between us."

"Inspector Feltham asked you to keep quiet about it, presumably."

"We were under a lot of pressure to get the convictions. He said that she was putting on an act when we arrested her. If the original statement was disclosed, it would just have confused things."

Yes, thought Edmund. It would have undermined the prosecution case.

"Well. You have been most helpful, Officer . . ."

"Sir, I ask you again not to use the statement. I fear for my position."

Edmund looked at the policeman; his baby face, broad shoulders, his large hands. He remembered his name now: Pegler.

"I understand," Edmund said. But to understand was not to agree.

The following morning, Edmund sat alone at the breakfast table trying to identify inconsistencies in Sarah's witness statements.

Flora appeared as he was pouring himself more coffee. "Your father for you, sir," she said in her usual monotone.

"My father? Are you sure?"

"That's what 'e said, sir. I didn't ask for proof. 'E's in the parlor."

When Edmund entered the room, he saw his father standing awkwardly looking at the books on the bookshelf.

"Father, this is . . . unusual. Has something happened?"

"No, no. I was just on my way to court and thought I'd call to find out how you were all getting on. Where's Bessie? Where is that grandson of mine?"

Edmund regarded him suspiciously. "They're staying with Bessie's sister in Kent for a day or two."

"I see. Anything wrong?"

"No," Edmund said, although it struck him that perhaps something was wrong.

Bessie usually visited her sister only when there was some particular occasion: a birthday, a ball. There was no such event to draw her to Kent now. "They merely wanted to get away from London for a few days, and I of course needed to stay here to complete my work."

"Yes. I'm sure. In fact, I wanted to check —"

"That I wasn't making a mess of it."

"Merely, Edmund, that you had everything you needed. If you wanted any assistance, I'm sure it could be arranged."

"Thank you, Father," Edmund said tightly, "but I have everything I require."

"You have formed a conclusion?"

Edmund felt his chest tighten. "I have not, but there is time yet."

"Not very much time. Your report's due by the end of this week, isn't it?"

Edmund struggled to contain his annoyance. The last thing he needed was to be reminded of the deadline. "I am drawing close."

"She has not confessed, I take it. You need to push her into a corner, Edmund. Trap her. Make her realize that this is her last chance for salvation."

"Father, I appreciate that you would prefer her to be guilty and have decided she is so on the basis of newspaper articles, but you have never met her. And, as I have told you, my conclusion will be based on the truth, not on what might be convenient to your reputation."

His father tutted. "I would be more concerned about your own reputation, my boy. John won't be granting you any more commissions if you don't provide a clear answer on this one."

"I can manage without any further commissions from the Home Secretary."

"Oh, yes? You have alternatives, have you?

Well, I hope you're not expecting any handouts from me. I am not a bottomless well. I have other commitments."

"I assume you're not referring to Mother's allowance," Edmund said quietly. "It is, after all, very meager."

"Edmund, we have discussed this before. It is more than adequate."

Edmund wanted to say something further, harsher. He wanted, in fact, to shout in his father's face: tell him what a mean-spirited, selfish blackguard he truly was. And yet there was still something of his schoolboy's fear in him. He felt the ghost of an old pain, the edge of the cane, the burn of wood on flesh. *"You will do as you are told. You will not answer back."*

"Now," said his father, turning to the door, "I have a court hearing to attend. And you, of course, have work to do."

As Edmund followed the warder along the winding corridors — corridors that should have become familiar, but which still filled him with a vague dread — he rehearsed in his mind the questions he needed to ask Sarah. They had run out of time. He needed her to understand that he could not gloss over the truth. As things stood, he could not recommend that she be pardoned, no

257

matter how much he might want to.

When Sarah arrived, she did not greet him, but said, "There's a girl in the cell next to me who's accused of killing her own baby."

Edmund put down his papers. It was the first time in all their meetings that Sarah had initiated a conversation with him about life in Newgate.

"I think I've heard of her," he said. "This is the girl said to have murdered her child in order to keep her position?"

"Yes. Will they hang her for it?" Sarah asked.

"I doubt it. If it's deemed to be murder the judge may hand down the conviction, but in the vast majority of these cases the Home Secretary grants a reprieve. There's considerable sympathy for women in her situation. If she'd kept the child she would have been cast out from her job and had no means of feeding herself and her baby. There was an awful case last year of a woman who killed both herself and the child as she couldn't bear to have it taken from her."

"What would have happened if the baby wasn't quite dead when he was born, but she didn't call for a doctor?"

"There's a distinction between allowing

someone to die and helping them die. If she'd purposefully left the baby out in the cold to die of exposure, as often happens, then that would be murder. But if she failed to fetch a doctor directly upon seeing that the child was in distress, I doubt that would do it. Ironically, in English law, to stand back and watch someone die without fetching help is not a crime." He paused. "Does she claim that is what happened?"

"No, no. This is all conjecture on my part," Sarah replied. "Please forget that I said anything."

"Yes, well, she may wish to think carefully about what she says. She has no lawyer, I assume?"

"She has no money."

"No. She may be given a dock brief on the day of her trial, but that will be all. She certainly won't want to confuse the man with complicated defenses. The jury probably won't convict her of murder, anyway. They rarely do in infanticide cases. The most she'll get is manslaughter or concealment of the child."

"Concealment of the child?" said Sarah. "As far as I know she didn't actually hide it."

"Perhaps not, but she didn't report the birth or the death, did she? Legally, it amounts to the same thing."

He looked at Sarah. Why was she asking him this, now? "You mustn't concern yourself about her. You have your own worries." He picked up a copy of the statement Pegler had given him and put it on the table before her.

"You made this statement to the police just after you were arrested. In it, you said that you had last seen Hannah Brown on the 20th of December."

Sarah looked at the statement and then at him, her dark eyes seeming to reproach him. He picked up the second statement and placed it alongside the first.

"In this statement, made only a few days later, you had suddenly remembered that you saw her on the morning of the twenty-fourth, the day she was murdered. Why did you lie originally?"

Sarah said nothing.

"Well?" Edmund said.

"James told me to say that. He said they were trying to trap him."

"You must have realized when Greenacre told you to lie that he had done something."

"I thought he'd defrauded her in some way. Not that he had killed her."

"So you were willing to help him cover up fraud, but not murder. Is that it?"

"No! No, that's not what I meant. I was confused. I didn't really understand what was being asked of me. It all happened so quickly. James said they were just making trouble for him for political reasons and that I should stay out of it. He would deal with it."

"Did he tell you what to say in the second statement as well?"

"No."

"That's odd, because I've looked carefully at the statements you made and several sentences in your statement are almost identical to what was written in his."

Sarah said nothing.

"You knew by that point that he had murdered her."

"I knew she was *dead.* He said it was an accident."

"So you continued to back him up."

"No."

"You see, Sarah, the problem is that these statements appear to confirm that you were willing to change your story in accordance with what Greenacre told you. How, then, do I know that you did not conceal the murder simply because he instructed you to?"

"Because I could never have done something so terrible for him. Do you really think

I could have continued to live within walls that I knew were marked with a dead woman's blood? Do you really think I could have continued to share a bed with a man I knew to be a murderer? *I did not know!*"

"Why should I believe that when the jury did not?"

To his horror, Sarah covered her face with her hands and began to weep, her body shuddering.

"Please, Miss Gale." Edmund leaned forward and touched one of her shoulders. He could smell her: a rich smell of salt and ripening fruit. "Help me help you. I must complete my report by this Friday. If Greenacre forced you to act as you did, you may have a defense. Just tell me what happened that night."

"I have told you everything I can," she said, her voice hoarse. "The only way you can help me is by believing me."

20

"There are two ways to be fooled. One is to believe what isn't true; the other is to refuse to believe what is true."

— *Works of Love,*
Søren Kierkegaard, 1847

Sarah woke to a howl of rage. Somewhere on the ward a woman was screeching and shouting. She sat up in bed, drawing the covers around her shoulders. It was that cold sharp time between night and morning and a pale, gray light filtered through the greasy window.

The noise intensified, as though a door had been opened.

"Damn you!" she heard. "Damn your eyes!"

The shouting became more muffled as the woman moved farther away and, after a minute or so, Sarah heard a scream far off followed by the clang of a door being shut.

Sarah sat tensed, but no further sound came, only the whispering of the women in the nearby cells. She stepped gingerly out of bed, the cold stone chill against her bare feet, and moved over to the basin. "Lucy?"

"I'm here. You reckon it's a breaking out?"

"Breaking out" or "smashing up" were the terms the warders used for when a convict ran mad. It made it sound like a sport, Sarah thought. A blood sport. Breaking out was not unusual. After weeks of deprivation and silence, women on Sarah's ward occasionally exploded in anger and frustration, some beating their heads against the stone walls, others tearing at their own skin with their teeth. This was the third time Sarah had heard a breaking out, but it was no less terrifying for that.

"It might be Eliza Sharpe," Lucy whispered. "Apparently they told her yesterday she was for the rope, and her with all them little 'uns. No wonder she's telling them to damn their eyes. I'd tell 'em a deal worse if it were me. They've no heart, no heart at all."

Sarah was silent but her heart raced. Eliza Sharpe: convicted of robbing a milliner in order to feed her children. She had petitioned for mercy shortly before Sarah had. No one had expected she would hang.

Later that morning, when she came to inspect Sarah's cell, Hinkley confirmed it. "Yes, she found out last night that her petition had been refused. She's for it next Monday. You'd have thought they'd have had some pity for her, what with the young ones, but they'll be for the workhouse now."

"Is there really no one else to look after them?"

Hinkley shook her head. "The father's dead long ago and, so far as I know, there's no one else will take 'em. It ain't right, Sarah. I suppose it's no wonder the poor woman's gone off her head. She was quiet when she received the news, but then early this morning she fell into a real frenzy. Nearly frightened me out of my five wits when I heard her."

Sarah was thinking, still, of the children.

"And you should see her cell," Hinkley continued. "She's destroyed everything: bed, trencher, Bible, even her own clothing and bed sheets. All in strips and fragments over the floor like some wild beast's been in there. It sends a shiver through you to look at it."

"Where is she now?" Sarah asked.

Hinkley averted her eyes. "She wouldn't quieten down so they took her to the dark cells."

Sarah felt a shudder pass through her. She imagined Eliza shackled to the wall and screaming into the blackness.

"Is there no chance," Sarah asked, "that they'll reconsider? That they'll pardon her?"

Hinkley shook her head again, sadly. "I shouldn't think so. It's too late. All she's got now is prayers."

The news of Eliza Sharpe's imminent death cast a shadow over the whole of the women's side that morning. There was little communication over breakfast and the warders went about their duties somberly, without speaking to or even looking at the women. Hinkley's eyes were red from crying, as were those of several of the younger prisoners. Even Rook and Boltwood left off their usual taunting.

Eliza Sharpe had not been particularly liked. It was more, Sarah thought, that each prisoner could imagine being in her place — could feel her silent scream of pain searing through the darkness below them.

As she sat at her sewing, Sarah thought about the people who had been hanged since she had arrived. In the ten weeks she had been at Newgate, she had seen four men led to the scaffold. On Monday mornings, the women watched through the dining room windows as the condemned left the prison and walked the short distance to the gallows, their arms pinioned behind their backs. The first to die had been a broken old man who had wept and dribbled piteously. The second was little more than a boy who shook so much he could barely walk. Sarah had turned away, unable to bear the sight of him begging and pleading with the jailers as they passed him to the executioner. The third was an older felon, well dressed in a black frock coat. He appeared calm, though dejected, as though he had always expected his life would come to this. But the fourth, Rudge, fought like a devil to the end.

Three jailers had dragged him, kicking, struggling, and shouting, up the scaffold steps and then pinned him to the ground, lying across the man's arms and legs as the executioner slipped the noose around his neck. It was one of the ugliest things Sarah had ever seen — the violent struggle to stay alive. Even in the noose, Rudge did not give up, but managed to catch hold of the scaffold beam as he dropped. The executioner and jailers tussled with him for several minutes to pry his fingers off the beam, finally sending him shooting through the trap door to his death.

It was rare for a woman to hang. That was what had kept Sarah going — the belief that she might well be reprieved. This, however, had focused her mind. If the authorities were in the mood to hang a woman who had robbed out of necessity, the mother of small children, then they would have no qualms about sending her to be launched into eternity. Unless. She sat at her sewing: *in, out, and over, in, out, and over.* All morning, she sat at her sewing and she thought.

At ten o'clock, Groves arrived to take Sarah to the legal visitors' room. She stood with her back against the wall of Sarah's cell, her expression unreadable in the half-darkness.

"Your time 'ere's nearly up, Gale. Worked out which way you're going to leave this place?"

Sarah felt a cold fear slice at her. "I will leave alive," she said, more to herself than to Groves.

"Will you? That ain't what they're saying. Everyone round 'ere thinks you're next."

Sarah felt for a moment the rope about her neck, the scratch of hemp, the hangman's hands.

Groves moved out of the shadows and walked toward the door. In the light, her face was pale as a grub. "Best tell 'im something good today, eh, Gale?"

Sarah followed Groves along the dimly lit passageway, her mind whirring. As they approached the stairs, she felt a presence to her right. Rook.

"What does it sound like?" the woman whispered.

Sarah did not reply and remained facing forward.

"What does it sound like, to cut through bone?"

Sarah winced inwardly but refused to turn to look at the woman.

" 'Cos that lawyer might believe your lies, but I know you were there, right in that room."

Sarah turned, wanting to read the other woman's expression.

"Yes," Rook hissed, "that's right. I know people who *know*. And what d'you think'll happen when I tell?"

Sarah felt her heart contract.

"If they'll hang Sharpe, they'll stretch your pretty neck quick as winking. And what'll become of your little boy then, eh?"

All at once, Sarah leaned in to Rook, close

enough to smell the sour unwashed scent of her. "If you're so sure you know what I did, hadn't you better be worried about what I might do to *you*?"

Groves whirled round. "No talking! If I catch either of you saying another word you'll both be on bread and water for the next week." She grabbed Sarah's arm and dragged her up the remaining steps. Sarah glanced back at Rook. Did she really think she knew something or was she, too, just playing a game?

Sarah watched Edmund as he opened up his notebook and thumbed through the pages to find his place. He looked tired today, she thought. His face was unshaven and she fancied he was wearing the same shirt as the previous day. He must know, as she did, that they had come to the heart of her case. Indeed, he dispensed with all preliminaries and said, "I want you to tell me today about Hannah Brown: how you met her, and how you came to leave Green-acre's house last December. It's important that I understand what happened."

"I don't know all of the details," Sarah said. "In fact, I'm not at all sure how James came to meet Hannah in the first place. You'd have to ask him."

"This is for your statement, Sarah," Edmund said, opening his notebook. "I need to know what *you* knew of Hannah Brown."

Sarah bit her lip. What did she know of her, really? She had heard her name so many times, in the police station, in the magistrates' court, in the court room — had it shouted at her in the streets. She had shared a roof with the woman; washed her clothes — and yet she knew precious little of what kind of woman Hannah Brown had been.

"The first I heard of her was in early December. James told me he would be bringing a woman to the house — a woman who he was considering marrying."

Edmund looked up from his notebook. "That must have been a shock."

"In a way it was, yes. The plain way he said it. But I'd known for a while I was losing my hold on him. He no longer found me as attractive as he once had."

She touched her cheeks briefly, remembering James's words the night he had smashed her looking glass. "I thought you a peach when I first met you," he had said. "But maybe even then you were overripe." He had thrust her tear-stained face before the broken mirror. "Now look at you."

Edmund was watching her closely, but he

did not say anything. She felt suddenly vain and foolish. What did it matter what she looked like? Before long, her face would be seen only as its death mask.

"What did you say when Greenacre told you he was bringing this woman to the house?" Edmund asked.

"There wasn't much I *could* say. I knew I had no claim over him. We weren't married. He'd never actually promised me anything. By that stage, I didn't really believe I was worth anything. I think I just asked who she was and when she would be arriving. James told me he'd invited her over the following evening and said that I was to cook for them and to pretend to be only his housekeeper."

Edmund squinted in disbelief. "He wanted you to *cook* for them?"

"Yes."

Sarah's face flamed. What a fool not to have left him there and then. Things might have been so different.

"And you agreed?" he asked, incredulous.

"I was living there. I didn't have much choice. I had a child and nowhere else to go. It was winter, remember."

It was a power game on James's part, she knew that. It amused him to test to what extent she would bow to his will.

Edmund shook his head. "What happened

when she arrived?"

Sarah remembered opening the door. Whatever she had been expecting, Hannah Brown was not it. She must have been near five and forty, maybe older, with hair far grayer than Sarah's, a colorless, plain face, and a large flat forehead. For a second, Sarah had wondered whether this could truly be the woman who was usurping her. But then she noticed the clothing: a green satin dress, the color of wet grass; a merino shawl of the best quality; a black velvet feathered hat and — when she stretched out her hand — beautiful black kid gloves, wrinkle-free.

"I showed her in and James introduced me as his housekeeper, as we'd agreed."

But Hannah Brown was no fool. She looked Sarah up and down, appraising her in an instant. She seemed to take in her cheap print dress and worn shoes and say, *Yes, I'm better than that.*

"And then?" said Edmund.

"And then I laid out the food for them and left them to eat." Sarah had stayed in the bedroom and listened to the low buzz of voices, the occasional burst of laughter, and the scraping of cutlery. It had reminded her of being a child, sitting at the top of the stairs listening to one of her parents' dinner parties in the dining room below: the same sense of isolation but compounded with humiliation and rage.

"She wasn't a handsome woman, was she?" Edmund said. "The witnesses at the trial were not flattering in their descriptions of her."

Sarah thought back to the trial — to all the people who had spoken of Hannah. Not one, she realized, had spoken of her with any affection or warmth.

"No, Hannah wasn't handsome," she said. "He wanted her for her money."

"Do you think she knew that?"

Sarah considered this. She thought of Hannah showing her the wedding dress, smoothing her hand over the red silk. And she thought no, Hannah Brown did not really know. James's flattery and fine words must have made her believe, as they had made Sarah believe, that he truly cared for her. She felt the unexpected sting of tears in her eyes. Hannah Brown had fooled herself into thinking that James loved her.

"No," she said simply. "I don't think she knew."

"When did she move in?"

"Not long after that. Maybe the second week in December. James helped her carry two trunks of belongings into the house."

"All my wordly goods!" Hannah had said, affecting an air of levity. And Sarah had thought: then you are not so rich as all that.

"You were still living there at this stage?" Edmund said.

Sarah averted her eyes, a flush of shame spreading across her face. "Yes, I moved into George's little room. I had a mattress on the floor. There was nowhere else for us to go, you see."

That was not exactly true. She could, she supposed, have moved into a lodging house immediately, although it would have meant they had very little on which to live. However, she had stayed because she had hoped even then that it might somehow be all right. That she might somehow learn to accept her new lot of second woman.

At night, lying on her straw mattress, Sarah listened for telltale sounds from the bedroom next door. She held her breath, expecting to hear groans of desire or exertion, but there was only ever muffled talking and whispering, the creak of the floorboards. Mostly, there was silence. It was this that kept her from outright despair. If James was not sleeping with Hannah, then it was still possible that she herself could serve some purpose. If he only wanted Hannah for the money, then there might yet be room

275

in his life for her. Looking back now, she knew it was a ridiculous way to have thought and an awful way to have lived: squeezed into a tiny room, clinging on to a thread of hope.

Each morning, she would rise at six o'clock and prepare breakfast for Hannah and James. When Hannah descended the stairs the two women would exchange a few stilted words while Sarah stirred the coffee in the saucepan, and then Sarah would find a reason to leave the kitchen.

"Did Hannah Brown know about the relationship between Greenacre and yourself?" Edmund asked.

"Officially, no, but I'm certain she guessed. She was sharp as steel, that woman."

Sarah was equally certain that Hannah had wanted her and George out.

"When did Greenacre tell you to leave his house?"

"It was about a week before Christmas. He said I'd have to suit myself with other lodgings as they'd arranged to be married on Christmas Day. So I took George and most of our possessions to a boarding house nearby, off the Walworth Road. It was a nasty, damp place. The landlady looked me up and down and raised an eyebrow at

George in his shabby clothes. She reckoned me a night flower, I think."

"Yes," Edmund said. "I've met Mrs. Wignal. I can imagine she wouldn't have been particularly welcoming. How did you leave things with James?"

"There wasn't much of a saying of good-byes, although James did ruffle George's hair and tell him to be a good boy for me. I won't pretend I wasn't bitter, but there was no point in saying it." And she had not wanted James to have the final satisfaction of knowing how deeply he had hurt her.

"What did you do after that?"

"I got on with my life as best I could. George and I spent those days mainly in our little parlor, which had a fire, thankfully, as it was biting cold by that time in December. I'd taken in some sewing and shoe binding from the neighbors, and the money from that kept us fed, albeit not very well. I had to live more slenderly than ever now that I was paying the rent."

"And did you hear anything further from Greenacre?"

"Nothing. I thought James might at least come and check on us, but he didn't. I went back on the morning of the 24th of December to pick up the rest of my belongings."

In part, it had been pretext to see whether

James still intended to go through with the wedding. She could not quite believe that he would do it.

"Did you speak to him?"

"No, he wasn't there." She paused. "I saw Hannah Brown, though."

"And?"

"We sat together and drank tea in the kitchen. It's odd to think of it now. We'd never been friends. She told me that they were to be married on Christmas Day at St. Giles's church and that they'd arranged to dine with some friends of hers beforehand on the Coldharbour Lane. She showed me the dress she intended to wear. I wished her the best for it, took my things, and then went to Rosina's for the rest of the day."

"You didn't try to tell her that James only wanted her for her money?"

Sarah thought back to their conversation. It had seemed to her then that Hannah was gloating.

"He'll like it, won't he?" she had said, running her hand over the red dress. "He's been holding himself back for our wedding night, but he'll think me handsome in this, won't he?"

Sarah had believed then that Hannah was trying to rub salt in the wound, but wondered now whether she had been seeking reassurance.

"No," Sarah said to Edmund at last. "I didn't. I didn't say anything to warn her. I don't suppose she would have believed me had I told her, but . . ."

"But?"

Sarah moistened her dry lips. "Well, I think now that I should have said something."

Edmund had stopped writing. He was looking at her intently. "You didn't say anything then, but you can say something now, Sarah."

Sarah opened her mouth, the words forming in her mind, but there was something in his eyes that stopped her. A flash of something cold, like the edge of a blade.

Edmund fixed his gaze on her. "You couldn't save Hannah Brown, but you have an opportunity to save yourself. Think about it. Think about it very carefully, because by the end of this week I must make my decision."

Miss Sowerton had assigned Sarah to laundry duty.

"It'll be nice for you to get out of your cell, won't it?" she had said, drawing back her lips to expose stained teeth.

Laundry duty involved a stint of up to five

hours in a stiflingly hot room, washing and wringing and sorting the thousands of sheets and flannels and items of clothing that had come from all over the prison, some dripping in lice, others riddled with disease.

After luncheon, Sarah took her allotted place next to the huge trough in which the clothing received its first rinse, to remove the vermin and the worst of the dirt. The air was already thick with steam and with the smell of washing from the morning session. Twenty women were employed in the laundry at any one time: some to sort it into bundles, some to stir the vats, others to work the mangles, others to dry, fold, and iron. Sarah saw with a shiver of fear that Rook and her friend Boltwood had been put on the wringing team. Sarah felt their gaze on her like the brush of a moth's wings. She knew their low-toned conversation was about her.

Sarah had never seen the two warders on duty before. She thought they must be inferior warders who lived outside Newgate, unlike Sowerton and Groves, who had rooms within the prison. Sarah could not imagine that being a live-in warder or matron was much better than being an actual prisoner. They woke within Newgate's forbidding stone walls and could only leave for a half day every other Sunday. For the rest of the time, they resided alongside the damaged, the dangerous, and the impoverished, working ten to twelve hours a day for scant pay and little thanks. It was no wonder that these women had themselves turned to stone.

By three o'clock, Sarah's clothing was drenched with her own sweat and with moisture from the dank air. As she stirred the increasingly dirty water with a ladle, she thought of Hannah Brown in her own laundry. She would not have carried out any of the washing herself, of course, only supervised the other women; but her hands — red and calloused — betrayed the years of labor it had taken her to get to that stage. That was why, Sarah had realized, she wore those soft kid gloves, just as she covered her lined face with powder and colored her sallow cheeks with rouge.

Of course she had jumped at the opportunity to marry James, and of course she had wanted Sarah and George safely out of the way. Only at the trial had Sarah learned that Hannah had never been able to conceive — the surgeon who carried out the postmortem gave evidence that, very unusually, she had no uterus. So she had nothing to offer. No looks, no prospect of childbearing — nothing except her money, and even that was less than she claimed.

Sarah was roused from her thoughts by a change in the atmosphere of the room. Looking about, she saw that the two turnkeys had disappeared. In their absence, the women had begun to murmur to one another and had largely left off their work. The mangles stood motionless and vats had been left untended. It was too quiet.

With a jolt, she realized that someone was standing directly behind her. Before she had a chance to turn, she felt hands on her neck and on her shoulders, and she was thrust head-first into the filthy brown murk of the vat before her. Sarah struggled and twisted but hands held her down beneath the surface of the water until her chest ached. Abruptly, she was hauled back up where she gasped desperately for air, then forced deep down again, her mouth and lungs full of the dirty soapy water as she panicked and thrashed. Again, she was dragged back up and again she was held under, until she could no longer stop herself from trying to breathe, and her mouth opened and, in desperation, she sucked water into her lungs.

Eventually came a moment of calm: I will

die, she thought. I will die not at the end of the rope, but here, drowned in the dirt of other prisoners.

She was pulled back and dropped onto the ground, where she lay choking, coughing, flailing. She managed to crawl onto her hands and knees and retched onto the floor. Once she could breathe again, she saw before her two black boots. Peering up, past the sodden woolen stockings and brown dress, she saw Rook's face, strands of greasy black hair plastered across her forehead and a malevolent smile on her lips.

Someone else was behind her, Boltwood presumably. Sarah pulled herself unsteadily to her knees, her hand on the side of the laundry vat, her chest heaving.

The other prisoners stood motionless, watching her, before they returned silently to their tasks.

Sarah was soaked through, her clothing heavy and clinging to her skin. She felt Rook's eyes run over her frame.

"No one threatens me," Rook hissed. "Especially not a dissembling whore like you. You think you can frighten *me* into keeping quiet? The only reason I haven't spilled your secrets already is because I'm keeping you here, to play with."

Rook bent down and brought her face

close to Sarah's, so close that she could see the tiny blood vessels in the whites of her eyes.

"But I'm getting tired of you, Gale. So sooner or later," she whispered, "I'll finish you."

21

"Ding, dong, darrow,
The cat and the sparrow;
The little dog has burnt his tail,
And he shall be hang'd tomorrow."
— *The Nursery Rhymes of England,* 1842

Edmund stared at the haddock on the plate before him. The report for the Home Secretary was due in two days' time and he had still not determined what he would say. Anxiety constricted his chest and he had no appetite for his breakfast. He pushed his plate away, the food virtually untouched.

Bessie looked up. "Edmund, are you unwell?"

"No, my dear. I'm just a little distracted."

"It's this case, isn't it?" she said, removing the bone from her own fish. "You've gotten too close to it."

"A woman's life is in my hands, Bessie. You expect me to remain unmoved?"

285

"No, of course not, and it must be very difficult for you," she said stiffly. "Only . . . you must retain a distance, mustn't you? You're the investigator, not her lawyer, after all. And she did get herself into this situation, whichever way you look at it."

"How sisterly of you, Bessie, to have such sympathy for Miss Gale's plight."

Bessie frowned at him. "Maybe you should stop feeling so sorry for your Miss Gale and have a thought for poor Hannah Brown. It seems to me she's been entirely forgotten in this whole business."

"And maybe you should refrain from giving advice on subjects you know nothing about."

"Edmund, please don't patronize me. The whole of London knows about your case: it's been all over the newspapers. I can have an opinion on it just as anyone else can."

"I am simply saying that you cannot judge the situation without knowing the full facts."

"But even you don't know the full facts. You've told me as much yourself. Which is why it's all the more important that you retain your distance."

"First my father seeks to advise me on my investigatory role, now you. How fortunate I am to be surrounded by such experts."

"Edmund, it is simply that I know how

you are when you want to believe something, when you want something to work."

"Bessie, I work as hard as I can to make
things happen. There was a time when you
admired me for that, but perhaps you have
forgotten."

Bessie's cheeks grew pink. "I still admire
you, Edmund," she said quietly, "but I also
worry about you. I worry about us."

"If you are worried about our financial
situation, I appreciate you are used to better, but I have told you that things will
improve. It is merely that I can't take on
more work until this case is over. And it
soon will be."

"Edmund, you misunderstand me. I admire your zeal, truly I do, but I worry that
you have been drawn in by this woman, that
you are helping her for the wrong reasons."

Edmund regarded her coolly. "Have you
been speaking to my father?"

"What?"

"Have you been speaking to my father
about this?"

"Well, I spoke to him briefly. He called
the other day when you were out, as I told
you."

"And you discussed my case." He could
imagine them together, sipping tea, agreeing on his shortcomings.

"Among other things, yes, but I don't see what that has to do with anything."

Edmund stood up. "No, I don't suppose you do. Now, if you'll excuse me, I'm taking my coffee to my room. I have work to do."

In his study, he went back through his notes, reread the police file, and wrote up a list of witnesses and key figures, summarizing what each had told him and what it meant for the case. Although he had made considerable progress, he was still missing key information. He had been unable to trace the witnesses who claimed to have heard arguing on the night of Hannah Brown's death, and, despite speaking to numerous people in the area, he still had no solid piece of evidence that could of itself undermine the pronouncement of the court. The Home Secretary had made clear he would require some convincing before he overrode the guilty verdict.

The problem was Sarah. She had not, as he originally feared, refused to talk to him. Going back through his notebook, he acknowledged that over the course of their interviews she had told him a great deal. But she had refused to shift from her position that she simply did not know anything about the murder, a position that had become increasingly untenable as the fuller picture emerged. Edmund was convinced that Sarah knew of the murder but that Greenacre had terrified her into remaining silent, and, somehow, was continuing to suppress her. He felt he was getting close, however. He just had to reel her in, as one might a fish, keeping the line taut so she did not spit out the hook.

Shortly before eleven o'clock, Flora entered the room in a stained apron. She had grown even grubbier and surlier in the past few weeks, but no more sober. "A Mr. Spints for you. Or maybe Spanks. Says you'll know who 'e is."

Edmund found the Home Secretary's clerk standing in the parlor, his complexion tinged a sickly green by the turquoise walls. For a moment, Edmund saw his home through the clerk's eyes: the sad display of peacock feathers over the mantelpiece, the faded silk flowers on the rosewood table, the terrible shabbiness of the place.

"I do apologize for intruding, Mr. Fleetwood, but I have some information that I thought I should pass to you as soon as possible."

Edmund forced his mouth into a smile. "Oh, you're not intruding. What information do you have for me?"

"It's been brought to my attention that there was a witness who gave evidence at Walworth police station who has subsequently disappeared. He did not therefore provide a statement to the magistrates." Spinks passed Edmund some papers. "These are the original notes. A boy called Thomas Clissold told the police that on the 26th of December, Greenacre approached him in Bowyer Lane and asked him if he wanted a job. He was then tasked with collecting Greenacre's belongings and taking them to the docks. You'll find the relevant paragraph on the second page. Here." Spinks pointed to the passage with a fingernail yellowed by tobacco.

Yet another piece of evidence the police had failed to mention. Edmund sat down and read the notes to himself.

When I got to the house, I found everything was packed up: boxes, bedsteads, and bedding, all bound and ready. Greenacre was very much agitated at the time. He was assisting me to tie the things in the truck. After the things were tied up, he said, "Now I am going to leave the country. All is right." The woman Gale was by the side of him. And when he made that observation, Gale exclaimed, "Ah! You have done for yourself."

"Well," Edmund said, "if she did indeed say that, then she must have known Greenacre was fleeing from justice. But she may not have known what charge he was fleeing from."

"Strange that she said it out loud, though, wasn't it? A woman who has since been as quiet as a rat asleep in its hole." Spinks paused. "There is a different way of reading it."

"And what might that be?" Edmund said, annoyed that the clerk seemed to be testing him.

"Perhaps she said it on purpose to incriminate Greenacre."

"Why would she do that?" Edmund said.

"To deflect attention from herself."

"You're implying she murdered the woman."

Spinks tilted his head to one side. "She had a motive, hadn't she? Hannah Brown had stolen her paramour." He put an unpleasant emphasis on the last word.

"Then why, Mr. Spinks, would Greenacre himself have sought to extricate her?"

"Because he himself didn't know she was responsible. Remember that he said at the trial that he returned to the house to find Hannah Brown dead."

Edmund shook his head. "I don't think that's plausible. If she really did say those words in order to incriminate Greenacre, why would she later deny all knowledge of the crime rather than claiming he had murdered the woman? No, I'm sorry: it doesn't piece together."

Spinks raised his thin eyebrows. "Merely a theory, sir. No doubt you are correct. But in any event, I thought you would want the notes."

"Yes, of course. Thank you." Edmund's mouth smiled, but his eyes did not.

"I presumed you would also want to know that the Home Secretary has refused Greenacre's petition for mercy. He will hang next week."

"That's no great surprise, but Lord Russell decided the matter very quickly."

The clerk's smile reminded Edmund of the snarl of a wolf. "The Minister needs to have a good reason to commute the sentence of the court. A very good reason."

When Edmund showed Spinks out, he found Morris leaning against the outside wall, eating walnuts out of a paper bag.

"Have you heard about the topping, sir?"

Morris said, as he watched Spinks retreat into the distance.

"The topping?"

"The nubbing. Greenacre's to be topped on Monday. He'll be on his way to the salt box by now, I shouldn't wonder."

Edmund grimaced. "Oh, the hanging. It's a horrible thing, Morris."

"I don't know, sir. There are worse ways to go. If the executioner calculates the distance you have to drop right, it's over in a trice, your 'ead snapped sideways by the knot. Not that it's much fun for the audience if they go that quick. Depends how much Greenacre's got to tip Calcraft with. Get it wrong and they can wriggle like a fish on a hook for several minutes."

"Delightful."

"And 'e's croaked."

"Croaked?"

"Confessed, probably to try and get a last-minute reprieve."

"What? The Home Secretary's clerk didn't mention this."

"No, well, it's only just 'appened. I got word from my man at Newgate." Morris tapped the side of his nose. " 'Parently Greenacre admits now that he killed Hannah Brown but says it were an accident. According to my man, Greenacre told one of the turnkeys that he walloped her and she fell backward off 'er chair and hit 'er head or something. Then he says he panicked and cut 'er up. Still claims your Gale woman knew nothing about it." Morris popped a walnut into his mouth. "He's certainly a rum customer, that one."

"Thank you, Morris. I need to talk to Greenacre again. I'll go to him straightaway."

James Greenacre had been moved to one of the condemned cells and was no longer allowed to attend the visitors' rooms. The brick-roofed cell was empty save for a wooden bedstead, a table, a stool, and a slop bucket. One of the warders brought in a chair for Edmund and then took up his seat again outside the cell. Greenacre was now under constant watch. He was thinner than when Edmund had last seen him, but his pale gray eyes were clear and he was freshly shaven, with his hair combed back.

"I was sorry to hear your petition had been refused," Edmund said, although he thought nothing of the kind.

"There's still time for the Home Secretary to change his mind," Greenacre replied.

"I understand you've given a new version of events in which you admit to having killed Hannah Brown."

"Yes, she attacked me and I retaliated, but I didn't intend to kill her. She fell."

"I see." Edmund did not in fact see how the injury could possibly have been caused by a fall. "Can I ask why you decided to confess at this hour?"

Greenacre smiled slyly. "Perhaps I have found God."

Edmund ignored this. "And does the rest of your story stay the same? Do you still say that Sarah knew nothing of it?"

"I see you are on first-name terms now. How pleasing. She's an alluring woman, isn't she? Not pretty exactly, but there's something about her."

Edward tensed. "Can you answer my question?"

Greenacre gave an exaggerated sigh. "Yes, my story in that regard remains the same. I assume hers does too. But of course you wouldn't be here asking me that question if she'd said anything else." Greenacre spoke as if to a child. "I say, as I have from the very beginning, that she knew nothing about Hannah Brown's death or of my disposing of the body." He paused. "Sarah loves me, you know. It would never have occurred to her that I could have killed another woman."

Edmund could not resist. "Even though

you regularly beat her?"

Greenacre's smile vanished. "Is that what she said?"

"It's simply what I have inferred."

"Investigators don't infer. They analyze the evidence and sift the facts from the fiction. I looked after Sarah. I'm looking after her now."

"What do you mean by that?"

"That I'm trying to get it into your dull brain that she played no part in the death."

"Tell me, Mr. Greenacre," Edmund said crisply, "why are you so insistent on that fact, when you evidently cared very little for her?"

"If I were you," Greenacre said, "I would not presume to understand another man's relationship. You're married, aren't you? Do you think your friends or relatives have any idea what goes on between you and your pretty blonde wife when the doors are closed and the curtains drawn?" Edmund grew suddenly cold.

"It is not," he replied stiffly, "my relationship with my wife that is at issue here. I am asking you why, in your final days, you continue to maintain the innocence of a woman who you cast out of your house the moment a better proposition came your way? A woman who you mistreated to such an extent that she lost all sense of her self-worth. Could it perhaps be that you are attempting to disguise the fact that you bullied her into silence? That you are guilty not just of murder, but of threatening the only witness to your horrific deed?"

Greenacre clapped his hands slowly. "Oh, very good, Mr. Fleetwood. Very noble. But entirely wrong. You will not help Sarah, nor damage me, with your theorizing; you'll succeed only in making yourself look a fool." He stood up so that he towered over Edmund. "You've tried to be too clever. The truth has been staring at you since the beginning. Sarah simply did not know. If she's now suggesting something else, it's because you, not I, have persuaded her of it."

He walked over to the door of his cell. "Guard! Mr. Fleetwood wishes to leave now."

Edmund remained seated. "Did I say that I had finished questioning you?"

Greenacre smiled. "I'm not a witness for you to cross-question. You have no power to compel me to answer your questions. I spoke to you only because I wished to help Sarah, but you've now exhausted my patience. This interview is over."

Edmund stood up and gazed levelly at

Greenacre. "They will not pardon you, no matter what you say now."

"No? Well, then I had better get on with praying to God to have mercy on my eternal soul, hadn't I? I will pray for you also, Mr. Fleetwood. 'To open their eyes, so that they may turn from darkness to light.' "

Greenacre put out his hand and gave a slight bow as if showing Edmund from his parlor. "Good day, Mr. Fleetwood."

22

"I promise before Almighty God that the evidence which I shall give shall be the truth, the whole truth, and nothing but the truth."

— The Promise, English law

"What are you playing at, eh?"

Groves stood in the doorway, her large frame filling most of the space, her arms folded.

"Why d'you still not speak out, you foolish woman?" she hissed. "You'd be out of this place in a week."

"It's no business of yours."

"Oh, but it is. Because it's me who'll have to prepare you for the scaffold. Any idea what it's like, Gale? To 'ave your arms pinioned against your back? To 'ave the hood placed over your head so you can scarce breathe? The rope tightened beneath your chin? To feel the trickle of piss running down your leg?"

Sarah shivered. "It will not come to that," she said quietly, more to herself than to the warder.

"No, you're right; it won't. Not if things carry on as they 'ave been." The warder tilted her head to one side. "You wouldn't be the first prisoner that's met her maker at the hands of another convict." She paused. "Not by any means."

Sarah felt her heart thumping in her chest.

Groves shook her head. "I don't know what your game is, Gale, but right now you look set to lose."

Groves closed the cell door and, as Sarah listened to the clipping sound of her footsteps receding, she felt fear rising within her, hot and dark, stifling her, constricting her chest, and choking her. She's right, Sarah thought. I will die in this place. I will be stabbed in my bed or strung up by the neck and I will never see my son again. She felt again the noose tightening around her neck, the fibers cutting into her skin, felt the cloth of the hangman's hood against her lips as she struggled to breathe.

She slid to her knees and clasped her hands together.

"Please, God, teach me to do what is right. Lead me in thy truth, and teach me."

■ ■ ■ ■

Less than an hour later, Sarah sat opposite Edmund at the small table. His face was pale and creased with agitation.

"Sarah, I have only forty-eight hours left to submit my report and at the moment we have you in Greenacre's bed shortly after the murder, surrounded by Hannah Brown's belongings, and without a credible explanation for how you could not have known what he had done."

Sarah could feel sweat prickling on the back of her neck.

"I cannot recommend that you be pardoned unless I can show that you had a reason for not speaking out. Did he threaten you, Sarah?"

She felt her heart hammering against her chest. "I've told you: I wasn't there; I knew nothing of what had happened."

"But no one believes that, Sarah. No one believed it at the trial. They took all of fifteen minutes to convict you. You have to do better than that." He removed the notes of Thomas Clissold's interview from his bag and read the passage to her.

" 'You have done for yourself.' How do you explain that?"

"I didn't say that. He's lying."

"Why would he lie?" Edmund asked. "He had no reason to lie. *You do.*"

Sarah did not reply.

"You cannot keep silent for Greenacre forever," Edmund went on. "He will hang next week in any event."

Sarah looked up. "Are you sure?"

"I'm sorry. I thought you would have been told. The date has been set for Monday."

Monday. Five days. Five days and he would be dead. All at once, the room pitched and tilted. Sarah leaned her head forward and closed her eyes, seeing darkness swirl beneath the lids.

"I'm sorry," Edmund said again. "The Home Secretary refused his petition for clemency. And Greenacre has confessed."

"What do you mean?"

"He admits that he killed Hannah Brown, albeit unintentionally. He says that he struck her and she fell, hitting her head on the floor."

"Why would he say this now?"

"Sarah, you must have known."

She did not respond. She did not know what to think.

Edmund put out his hand as if to take hers, but then let it drop. "People often confess at the last minute in the hope that their sentence will be commuted. In Greenacre's case, however, I think it very unlikely that the Home Secretary will lift the death sentence. It is too little, too late."

Sarah felt a heaviness seeping through her. After a few moments, she became aware that Edmund was gently touching her shoulder. "If you would like some time alone . . ."

"It's all right, Mr. Fleetwood. In the circumstances, I think you're right. We had better get on with it. What is it you need me to say?"

Edmund put his notes back down and smoothed his hair. "You have to tell me what he did to you, Sarah. He coerced you, didn't he? Made you go along with what he said. What happened?"

She bit her lip until she could taste the blood.

"Sarah, let me explain something to you: the law in this country makes merciful allowance in dealing with the female offender where it can be shown that she has been impelled to act under masculine influence. Had you been married, you might even have had a complete defense. You weren't lawfully wedded to Greenacre, but you lived with him as his wife, didn't you?"

"Yes, I believed him to be my husband, or

close to it. I'd always hoped that he'd ask me to actually marry him, but he never did. That's why it was so painful when he chose to marry Hannah Brown."

"Yes, yes. And you were under his control?"

"He had a certain power over me. I was afraid of him. I'm afraid of him now."

"I understand that, Sarah, but you must tell me what really happened. This is your last chance to save yourself. I cannot help you if you will not help me."

He was right. This was it. She had come this far. She might as well finish it. She dug her nails into her palms.

"All right," she said. "I will tell you how it was. Late Christmas morning, about eleven o'clock, James came looking for me at the house in Walworth. He told me he'd thought better of his marriage to Hannah Brown as it turned out she had no money after all. It was me he wanted, he said, and he was very sorry for the way he'd treated me those past weeks. He'd brought a bag with him containing some food, some paper hats, and a small parcel. We were to have a superb Christmas dinner together, he said: a leg of pickled pork, a pair of roast stuffed fowls.

"I know I should have thrown him out and told him it was too late. I can't quite believe

304

that I didn't. But I was very lonely then and I didn't believe anyone else would have me. My situation was precarious. I'd nearly exhausted our supply of money and would have had to turn to the Parish for assistance shortly. So you see, I was relieved that he wanted me back. I suppose that had been James's intention: to wear me down until I was willing to accept anything. I cooked the food on the little stove in my room and we ate it with some port, James trying all the while to be jolly. It was an odd sort of Christmas."

"When did you go to his house?"

"The following day. I knew as soon as I stepped over the porch that something was wrong. Hannah Brown's boxes were still there, all bound up with cord. When I asked why, James told me she'd left them in payment for money she owed him and that she'd gone to stay with her family. However, I knew from my few awkward conversations with Hannah Brown that those boxes contained all the property she possessed in this world, and I knew also that she didn't have much of a relationship with her brother and sister — they hadn't even been invited to the wedding."

"So you knew he'd killed her?"

"Not at first, but then I noticed the sharp

smell of chloride of lime. He'd cleaned the floor, and very recently. James never cleaned the floor. He never cleaned anything. It was clear to me then that something awful had happened there."

"Did you confront him?"

"No. I was too afraid to do that, but I told him I wasn't staying in that house. I tried to leave, taking George with me. James begged first: grabbed my hands and said it had all been a terrible accident, that he'd been a fool to throw me away, and that he needed me now more than ever. His grip on my hands grew tighter and he said, 'If you love me, Sarah — and I know you do — you'll be a good girl and keep quiet about this. Then we can get on with our lives.'

"When I refused, he became angry and shook me, accusing me of betraying him. I tried to pull away from him, all the while trying to get him to lower his voice so as not to alert the neighbors and not to distress poor George, who was watching from the other side of the room.

"James drew me even closer then, so that I could feel his breath on my face. It would be all the same, he whispered. Because if I spoke out, he would say I was there. He'd say I'd done it myself. I still had some spirit at that point. I told him that no one would ever believe that I — a nurse, a mother — could kill someone, and another woman at that. His hands went round my throat then and pressed.

" 'Sarah,' he said, 'if you don't keep your mouth shut, I'll make you regret it for the rest of your life.' And then he shifted his eyes toward George.

" 'You wouldn't hurt him,' I said, though I could barely breathe.

" 'I'm telling you, you have to keep your silence,' he said, 'or it will be over. For all of us.' "

Sarah looked at Edmund. "What could I do then but what he asked?"

Edmund had been making notes while Sarah was speaking, but was now still. He looked her straight in the eye.

"So he threatened you into keeping quiet? You had no other choice?"

Sarah thought of George's terrified face.

"I had no choice. I had to do it. If I'd betrayed him, it would have been the end of me and of George."

Edmund nodded and returned to his notes. It was done.

After a few moments, Sarah said, "What I've just told you, is it enough?"

Edmund looked up. "What do you mean

'enough'? It's everything, isn't it?"

"Yes. I mean: is it enough to save me?"

"I cannot promise you anything, Sarah, but I will certainly be recommending that you receive a full pardon."

She put her hands to her throat. "I would be released?"

"Yes, assuming the Home Secretary agrees with my recommendation. It's possible, of course, that he will reject it in its entirety but I think that very unlikely. It's also possible, I suppose, that he will come up with some alternative — a stretch of imprisonment, for example."

"Here? In Newgate?" Sarah could not stay in this place.

"I am setting out the worst possible eventuality. I think it likely that Lord Russell will accept my recommendation. He's a sensible man. He will see, as I do, that you had no choice but to act as you did."

"It's important, Mr. Fleetwood, that James doesn't come to know that I've spoken out against him."

"Sarah," Edmund said, "he's in one of the condemned cells, under close watch. He can't harm you here."

She shook her head. "You don't understand what influence he has. What friends he has. Someone could get to George. And

308

if James were to be reprieved . . ."

"He won't be reprieved, Sarah, no matter what he says or does. The mere fact of him cutting up the body was enough to warrant the death sentence, and he cannot deny that now."

"But still, if he were to find out . . ." She shuddered.

Edmund put his hand over hers, his palm warm on her marble-cold fingers. "I'll ensure that the information is communicated in absolute confidence to the Home Secretary. No harm will come to you or George. I promise."

Edmund walked briskly back to his chambers. He should never have doubted himself. He would always have persuaded her to talk. Now he had the material to prepare the report: Sarah had to go along with Greenacre or she herself would have ended up on the cutting table, her son too. He did not doubt that the man was capable of it. It was satisfying to think that this information would not just save Sarah, but crush any last chance Greenacre might have of a reprieve. He was guilty not only of murder but of threats to kill a mother and child.

Once back at Inner Temple Lane, Edmund rushed up the stairs to his study and began preparing his writing implements. He rang for Flora to bring him some refreshments: a few biscuits and a little wine. After eating, he brushed the crumbs from the foolscap paper and dipped his pen into the inkpot, pausing briefly before commencing his assault on the paper. Now that he had the truth, he had no time to lose. He must finalize Sarah's affidavit and draft the report to the Home Secretary.

Three hours and two drafts later, he flexed his hand and leaned back in his leather chair. He had distilled Sarah's story into five pages, which explained why an educated and intelligent woman such as Sarah could never have voluntarily aided and abetted a murderer, and why Greenacre's manipulation and threats had meant that she had no choice but to keep silent. There was something pleasing in speaking out on behalf of a woman who had been subjugated and silenced by a powerful and cruel man. He had not stood up for his mother, but he could do his best for Sarah. Reading back through the affidavit, he had a vague sense that something was missing but he could not place it. He picked up his pen and wrote out the statement of truth at the bottom of the document. It was a work of art.

Outside, it had turned into a ghastly

evening. Rain hurled itself at the windows and a furious gale blew, rattling the casements and contorting the branches of the trees. After a hasty dinner of boiled beef and greens, Edmund returned to his study to complete his report to the Home Secretary, taking a glass of mulled sherry with him. The more he wrote, the more certain Edmund became that the report would be approved. There was no real evidence to support the idea that Sarah had assisted in the crime. There was, in reality, very little evidence at all. She ought never to have been convicted. The police had suppressed information that might have helped the defense, skewed the evidence in order to justify the arrest, and then conveniently lost the jewelry, knowing that she could prove it was her own. The jury had been inherently prejudiced against Sarah by the inaccurate and sensational reports in the press, and they had not been presented with a true and full account of Sarah's story, partly because of her own fear of Greenacre and partly because of negligent legal representation. He hesitated to criticize Mr. Price in his report — it was always unattractive for lawyers to disparage one another — but he had seen the man's performance with his

own eyes. Price had failed his client appall-
ingly.

"My own careful analysis of the evidence,"
he wrote, "shows that although — for the
reasons outlined below — Sarah Gale did
not speak out against the crime, she did not
actively help Greenacre conceal the murder,
as was claimed at trial."

When considered properly, each piece of
evidence that was used against her falls
away. First, the jewelry that the prosecution claimed she had stolen from the
deceased was in fact her own property, as
has been confirmed by her sister. In any
event, the prosecution evidence on the
point should have been discounted at trial
as the exhibits had been lost.

Secondly, the fact that Miss Gale borrowed water to clean the house on the
26th of December proves nothing, as Mrs.
Andrews of number eleven Carpenter's
Buildings has confirmed that Miss Gale
regularly borrowed water with which to
clean. Thirdly, James Greenacre has
admitted that it was he who took the
scraps of child's clothing (that were later
found with the body) from the kitchen
without Miss Gale's knowledge.

As regards her failure to report the crime

312

or to subsequently give evidence against Mr. Greenacre, it is clear that Miss Gale acted, or rather failed to act, out of necessity. Mr. Greenacre, a man with a confirmed history of violence, including against Miss Gale herself, had threatened the lives of both her and her young son. In those circumstances, I submit that the failure to report the death did not amount to concealing a murder.

It irked Edmund that the criminal law in this area was ambiguous. Despite having spent hours researching the matter in the Inner Temple Library the previous week, he could find no case or authority that expressly stated that necessity or coercion were in fact a defense to aiding and abetting a murder. But then, this was no longer a court case.

Edmund ended his report by respectfully recommending a free pardon or, at the very least, that Sarah's sentence be reduced to a short term of imprisonment.

He laid the last sheet to dry. The ink glistened in the lamplight. For a minute or so, he watched the rain beat against the dark glass and finished the rest of his wine. He reread the report, paused for a moment, and then signed his name.

PART TWO: CAPUT

23

"A thousand gazing eyes are there,
And a thousand anxious breasts:
And many a knee, in pretense of prayer,
On the threshold rests.
But it is not to worship the mighty God,
To pour out a contrite heart,
To bow to the throne, to kiss the rod,
For the sins in the soul that smart.
'Tis to look on the man of shame and
    crime,
From the law of his God who hath swerved,
To see as he stands on the verge of time,
If his spirit be yet unnerved."
— "Lines written in the Chapel of Newgate,
previous to the Condemned Sermon, on
James Goodacre," *The Stage: Both Before
and Behind the Curtain,* Alfred Bunn, 1840

It was Sunday. The day of the condemned
sermon.

After supper, two of the younger turnkeys

hurried Sarah over the moss-green cobbles of the yard into a whitewashed room and then into the chapel itself. She had been into the chapel twice before. It was plain and ill-lit with grimy windows and galleries for the male and female prisoners lined with shabbily painted benches.

As Sarah entered, she saw that not only were almost all of the benches already taken with other prisoners, but the galleries were packed to bursting with men and women in regular dress — vibrant blues, purples, and pinks, parasols, hats, and cravats. These were paying members of the public who had come to gawp. There must have been five hundred people in there, maybe more, chattering excitedly. As she walked past, the turnkeys keeping a firm hold of each arm, people turned toward her, watching and whispering.

"His accomplice!" she heard from a woman in the gallery above, and there was a collective gasp and a rustling as people stood up to look. So that was why they had brought her here.

The pulpit and reading desk had been hung with heavy black velvet, and tall candles had been placed at either end. The King's arms, a splash of red, blue, and gilt, was spread across on the wall above. The sheriffs, in their gold chains, sat to the right of the pulpit, the Governor to the left, his face skeletal in the candle's glow. Above him, the Commandments on the wall had worn away and were barely legible.

Sarah realized that James Greenacre was already there, in the condemned box: a huge pen, painted black. He sat on a chair in the center, facing the front of the chapel so that Sarah could not see his face, though he was clearly visible to those in the galleries above. He leaned forward slightly, his hands on his knees, as if praying. They said that even the atheist would pray when faced with imminent death.

Sarah was seated on a bench to the right of the chapel between the turnkeys. Perhaps they thought she would try to run to him, for they sat so close that she could feel their hipbones through their skirts. She willed James to turn round and look at her but he remained facing forward, motionless.

The chapel quietened as the Ordinary entered. He wore a long black cassock with a white cravat at his throat, giving him the appearance of a pompous puffin. He looked about him, wordlessly ordering the crowd to be silent. When everyone was suitably hushed, he began.

"O thou great and glorious Lord God!

Thou high and holy one who inhabitest eternity and despises not the meanest of thy works, we humbly beseech thee to look down in compassion on us, thy poor vile and sinful creatures who now present our prayers and supplications unto thee."

Although the chapel was packed full with bodies, his voice carried and resounded from the stone walls, uncomfortably loud.

"O Lord, have mercy upon us. Blot out our transgressions, and remember our sins and iniquities no more."

Sarah looked up at the statue of the Virgin Mary in the chancel to her right. The paint had peeled from her face and she stared blindly back. The Ordinary finished the prayer and moved on to his sermon.

"There are few more affecting things in this world than to visit a man sentenced to death on the last night of his sentence." His voice had dropped and the crowd leaned forward to catch his words.

"Occasionally, men remain hardened to the last, clinging to their wretched disbelief in God, but this is rare. Most often, as with our subject here, although he has eschewed the Christian ways his whole life, once he knows he is standing on the very brink of eternity, *then* he clamors for forgiveness!"

The Ordinary raised his voice as he said

320

these last words and there were mutterings from the gallery. So James had found religion. Maybe in his last days he had grown desperate, his confidence trampled by the advance of death. Or, more likely it was a ruse to procure a last-minute reprieve. Sarah wished she could see his face so as to catch at what he might be thinking.

Raising his arms, the Ordinary continued: "Ladies and gentlemen, stretch your imagination to the utmost, and try to picture what must be the state of mind of such a man the night previous to his execution. He knows that in a few hours he will meet his Maker. He knows it is too late to atone for his actions. He knows, as David did, that the wicked shall be turned into hell!"

He expounded upon the qualities of hell: lakes of fire and brimstone, wailing and gnashing of teeth. His words were like blows, all raining down on James, who sat only a few yards in front of him, his head bowed. Sarah wondered what the Ordinary had said to James when they were on their own. If he viewed her, as an accomplice to the crime, as past saving, then he must think James would burn in the fires of the hell he described. But looking at the Ordinary now on his podium, waving his arms about for the crowds, she suspected he did not believe any of it. Angels and devils, death and misery, shame and sorrow: it was all an act.

Sarah had stopped listening. She was a young girl again, in starched petticoats and ribboned bonnet, walking hand in hand with her sister past carved pillars toward the front of a church, gazing up at the fan-vaulted ceiling, at gilded paintings of stern figures. Their nurse held her baby brother, a squirming mass of white lace, while a minister recited the rite of baptism:

"Dost thou, in the name of this Child, renounce the devil and all his works?"

"I renounce them all," came the voices of the group assembled around the font.

It was the talk of the devil that had scared Rosina. She had run, out of the church and into the street, and Sarah had been too busy watching the minister to realize until it was too late. She remembered being rushed from the church in a flurry of skirts and angry whispers: *"You were supposed to look after her, Sarah!"* It took them several hours to find Rosina. She had been hiding in the graveyard and had fallen asleep beneath an oak tree.

"What's wrong with you, child?" their mother had demanded, shaking her. "Why do you have to spoil everything?"

But it was their mother who had spoiled

everything, Sarah thought. It was she who had made them what they were.

Sarah's eyes were on the Virgin Mary again when she realized the Ordinary was talking about her.

"Some may feel that such a woman is beyond understanding, beyond redemption, hardly human at all. We must place her as far away as possible from all other women, from all of us."

Nods from the gallery. A few of the prisoners on the bench in front had turned to look at her. She stared down at her hands.

"Hear the words of your Redeemer: the day is coming in which all who are in their graves shall hear the voice of their Judge and shall come forth; they that have done good, unto the resurrection of life; and they that have done evil, unto the resurrection of damnation."

The warder to Sarah's right scratched at her neck. A young prisoner at the front of the chapel had begun to weep.

"He cometh up, and is cut down like a flower. He fleeth also as a shadow . . ."

Sarah heard James repeating back the words. His voice was surprisingly clear and even. How foolish of her, to have thought he would be afraid.

24

At an early hour last night the Old Bailey, and the space around the angles of Newgate, were thronged with a clamorous multitude, including almost as many women as men, and among the latter persons apparently of every grade in society though, as in all such cases, the great mass was of the lowest order.

— *MORNING POST,* 2 MAY 1837

The banging began at four o'clock on Monday morning and grew louder over the next hour. They were building the scaffold.

As she waited for her cell door to be unlocked, Sarah heard two of the warders talking in the corridor.

"There must be ten thousand people out there."

"More, I reckon. It's the best attended execution this year."

"Groves says they're charging three guineas for a station at the windows opposite."

"Three guineas! Let's hope Greenacre puts on a good show for 'em!"

Even from within her cell, Sarah could hear the crowd, humming like a dangerous machine. James must be able to hear them too. What was going through his mind in his final hours? Was he sorry? For any of it? Did he picture her face, or did he think only of Hannah Brown's, the right side a mess of blood and bone?

At seven o'clock, as she scrubbed her stone floor, Sarah heard the buzz of the crowd mount to a roar. Then came another, and another. The people were cheering; they must have wheeled out the scaffold. By half-past seven, the noise from outside vibrated the glass in the windows of the breakfast room and the drumming resounded in her ears. Some of the prisoners climbed on top of chairs and pressed themselves up against the high windows, passing down information to those standing below. The sheriffs were there, they said, in their heavy gold chains and red robes, and the Ordinary too. And people in the crowd were shouting at the men in front to take off their hats so that they could see. Now Calcraft, the executioner, was here. Wasn't he a rum-looking blackguard! Was he half-sprung?

Would he botch the job again? Would he have to hang on to the man's legs to break his neck? Would he misjudge the drop and take his head off? So the women went on, inexorably, breathlessly.

The turnkeys were too busy watching the events themselves to bother chastising them. They did not notice, or affected not to see, as Rook slid over to where Sarah sat with her head bowed over her breakfast plate.

"Too scared to look and see, Gale? Thinking about when it'll be your turn? Don't worry. It won't come to that. I wouldn't let that happen to you, would I? No. I'll get you first."

Sarah glanced up at Rook and took in her smirk, her gray-tinged face. It was, it came to her, all a pretense: the claim to know Sarah's secrets, the claim she would finish her off. And all at once she did not care what this miserable woman might do to her. Nothing could be worse than this: this feeling of guilt and rage and distress that was rushing over her like a tide.

"Just leave me alone," Sarah said wearily. "Go on. Go and find someone else to play with."

Rook opened her mouth but was prevented from making any reply by Groves, who had pushed through the group of women and seized Sarah's arm. Without speaking, Groves guided Sarah past the others, down a flight of iron steps to the passageway that ran beneath Newgate. Through the grille of the gate, Sarah could see a light approaching along the dark corridor. It grew closer and closer and then, looming out of the blackness, a figure.

"James!"

His face as he turned toward her was stricken with horror. He seemed to stare right at her but not see her. In the candlelight, his skin was waxen and white as though it were already his death mask. His eyes were pinpricks of darkness.

"I kept my part of the deal, Sarah," he said. "I did what I said I would. May it keep me from hell."

And then he was gone.

She heard the stamp of the jailers' feet receding as they led him away. Then the deep and hollow toll of St. Sepulchre's bell marking the moment that James emerged onto the scaffold. As she slumped down onto her knees, a roar went up from the crowd. The show had begun.

By the time Edmund reached the Old Bailey, the road was almost impenetrable, packed with ballad singers, street performers, and groups of people laughing as though they were attending a bullbaiting or a country fair. He pushed his way through the throng, past a booth selling "Greenacre tarts" and currant wine, and knocked at the door to one of the houses that backed onto Newgate Street. The maid admitted him and he climbed the carpeted stairs to the top floor.

"Ah, the guest of honor!" a red-cheeked man shouted as Edmund entered the room.

Faces turned toward Edmund as he advanced into the parlor. Twenty people or more were standing in clusters about the room, chattering, drinking, laughing.

The red-faced man seized and shook Edmund's hand with vigor. "Well, well, Edmund. Quite the lawyer now."

"Mr. Belcher. It was kind of you to invite me." The man was a friend of his father. It was several years since Edmund had seen him and he had turned to fat, his chins spilling out from his linen shirt.

"What a case, eh? My friends and I have been taking bets this morning as to whether the Gale woman will hang before the month's end. Care to give us a tip?"

Edmund swallowed. He should not have come here. "I thought bets were normally placed on how long the hanged person will twitch for."

"Oh, that too! That too!" The man laughed, gobbets of spit flying from his lips. "Eleanor! Bring this man a drink!"

Edmund went to stand by the open window. Every other window in his field of vision was packed with people, as were the roofs of all the houses.

"Quite a spectacle, isn't it?"

A tall man with gray whiskers and a long pipe stood to his left, also looking out of the window.

"Your first time at the New Drop?" the man asked.

"No, no," Edmund said, although he had seen it only once before. His father had brought him and Jack here as boys and made them stand by this same window as the prisoners, five men convicted of conspiracy to assassinate the Prime Minister, were led onto the platform. The last man, weeping, had to be dragged. As they watched the executioner measure the men for the noose, his father had explained how the prisoners would have spent the night alone in the condemned cell, how they would have passed along Dead Man's Passage in the morning, lighted only by a single candle.

Here comes the candle to light you to bed,
Here comes the chopper to chop off your
  head.

Edmund wondered why his father had
told them all this. Did he think it was an
important lesson in the law, or had he
meant only to frighten them? The corpses
had been beheaded and their dripping
heads held up to the crowd. Edmund had
caught only a glimpse of the horror before
covering his eyes with his hands. The image, however, had never left him.

The gallows, which had already been
brought out, was the same boxlike structure
Edmund remembered. The black stage, the
crossbeam, the rope. This time, however,
there were two soldiers with spikes guard-
ing the gallows and black barriers had been
erected to keep back the crowds. Evidently
they were expecting trouble.

A great cheer went up. A small figure was
climbing up the steps to the scaffold: the
executioner.

"It's begun!" Mr. Belcher shouted.
"Everyone, it's begun!"

Two women pushed forward to the window. One raised double-barreled opera
glasses to her eyes.

"Calcraft is fastening the halter onto the

chain. It's truly ghastly!" She passed the glasses to her friend so that she could observe the ghastliness for herself.

"People from the crowd are being carried off," the second woman told them. "They must be crushed or overheated or overcome. It is too awful!"

It *is* too awful, Edmund thought. He moved farther away from the window and leaned his back against the wall.

At a quarter before eight, the bell of St. Sepulchre's church began to toll, low and hollow. Then the crowd gave a deep and sullen shout. Greenacre must have emerged.

Edmund remained standing against the wall. He wondered how much Sarah could hear of this. He closed his eyes for a moment. Then he opened them. He was not a boy anymore.

The Ordinary was reciting the Hangman's Psalm at the foot of the scaffold. His voice was audible even from where Edmund stood.

Fill me with joy and gladness;
Let the bones which thou hast broken
    rejoice.
Hide thy face from my sins.

Edmund made himself watch as the executioner stepped forward and covered Green-acre's face with a white hood. The noise of the crowd had dropped to a murmur that rose again as Calcraft slipped the noose over Greenacre's head and tightened it beneath his chin. For a moment, all was quiet.

"Amen!"

The trapdoor shot open and there was a collective gasp as Greenacre's hooded body dropped and jerked. For thirty seconds or so he writhed and twisted as though partaking in some strange dance. Gradually, however, the struggling slowed to only an occasional movement, then to a twitching. In the breeze, the body swung gently. The crowd was finally silent. The vengeance of the law had been accomplished.

25

"A fiend is here behind, who with his sword
Hacks us thus cruelly, slivering again
Each of this ream, when we have compast
 round
The dismal way; for first our gashes close
Ere we repass before him."
> — *The Divine Comedy,*
> Dante Alighieri, 1307

Two bright black eyes looked out from the corner of the cell. Sarah dropped pieces from her hunk of bread onto the floor and then watched a small gray mouse scurry across the stone slabs, take the crumbs in its tiny hands and nibble upon them, watching her all the while. Sarah tried to eat some of the bread herself but it stuck to the roof of her mouth, glutinous and tasteless. The surface of her cup of cocoa had congealed into a dark, greasy skin.

Since the hanging, the warders had mainly

left her alone to sew in her cell. Her face was puffy, her eyes still swollen, even though she had long ago ceased to cry. She felt dry and brittle like an old leaf, blown in the wind. The more she tried to shut out certain thoughts, the more they recurred: ugly visions at the edge of her consciousness, slivers of evil.

Miss Pike had brought in leather-bound poetry books for her: Wordsworth, Coleridge, and other good works. It was not those she thought of, however, but Dante and his circles of hell: the falsifiers hacked into pieces by a sword-wielding demon, dividing parts of their bodies as in life they divided others.

Now, when she closed her eyes, she saw not Hannah Brown, but James's bloodless face, his eyes black coals glinting in the dark as he stared at her through the grating. He would have been hanged anyway, she told herself, but there was always that doubt eating away at her, like a wasp through wood. Could she have done differently?

At ten o'clock Hinkley arrived to take her to the yard. "Come on, Sarah," she said. "It'll do you good to get outside in the fresh air."

Sarah remained sitting, not sure she had the strength to get up.

Hinkley walked over to her, her skirts swishing, and as she put out her arm Sarah thought she meant to pull her to her feet. Instead, she put her hand on Sarah's shoulder and squeezed it gently. In that moment it felt like the kindest thing anyone had ever done for her.

"Come now," Hinkley said. "You can't stay in here all day."

Outside, it was raining. Cold drops fell onto Sarah's upturned face and ran down her cheeks, mingling with tears that were themselves a mixture of grief, anger, and guilt. He could no longer hurt her. He could no longer hurt George. Why, then, did she feel such distress? Why should she mourn a man who had caused so much damage and pain?

She could have shut the door in James's face when he arrived on Christmas Day. Instead, she had invited him in; she had cooked the food he had brought and laid it out on the table, like a good wife. After dinner, as they sat by the fire eating nuts and segments of orange, George opened the present James had brought him. It was a tin spinning top painted with crimson and silver stripes.

James helped him to spin it until it was just a whirl of colors spiraling into a vortex of deep red.

In that instant, she had almost allowed herself to believe that it might all be for real. That they might be a happy and normal family together, despite everything that had happened, despite the blood she knew coated James's hands. Amid all the lies that had been told, it was the lies she had told herself that were the worst.

When Sarah returned to her cell, she was soaked through. Hinkley placed a towel around her shoulders and told her to dry herself. As she did so, she noticed that there was a small parcel on the stool bound in twine. She looked at Hinkley, who nodded, so she took up the package and unwrapped it. Inside were James's spectacles. She turned them over in her hand.

"He said he wanted you to have them," Hinkley said.

Sarah wondered what this meant. That she should look out for herself? Or that he wanted her to know he was still watching her? Although, for once, a fire had been lit in her room, she shivered.

Edmund visited in the morning. Sarah realized, with a twinge of surprise, that she had missed their meetings. They sat close together at the little table, their knees almost touching through the layers of wool and linen.

"I'm afraid," he said, "that I have not yet received a response from the Home Secretary. However, I think we should take this as a good sign. If Lord Russell intended to simply reject my recommendation then he would have done so quickly. I suspect that he's passed the matter to the King's Council so that His Majesty can approve the pardon."

"You really think so?" She felt a flutter of hope in her chest.

"I do. I understand that the King is in very poor health, so that may well be the cause of the delay. Or it may be that they are confirming that the law is as I stated it — namely that acting under duress, as you did, provides a defense to concealing a murder."

"And does it? Is that what the law says?"

"I believe so, yes. I'm sorry I can't give you a complete assurance, but this isn't an area that has been much tested in previous cases."

It all sounded so abstract: duress, defenses, and cases. And yet it was her life.

"But, Sarah, as I said, I think these are good signs and I'm fairly confident you will be pardoned. You must try not to worry."

Sarah smiled thinly. Try not to worry whether you will live or die. Try not to worry whether you will be saved or damned. Not for the first time, she wondered how a man who was in some ways so clever, could in other ways be so obtuse.

The following day was a Wednesday. That meant there would be mutton for dinner. Not that this was anything to look forward to. Meat was believed to excite the animal emotions of criminals and the small amount of meat that was served up was therefore made as unappealing as possible. It was usually more gristle and bone than flesh, and the prisoners had to gnaw at it with their teeth, like dogs. Sarah lined up with the other women to collect her food and then sat down at her usual space on the far table, staring at the stringy piece of mutton before her. She knew she had to eat to keep her strength up, but the sight and smell of meat — another dead thing — turned her stomach.

All at once, there was a shout and a loud clatter over by the kitchens. One of the prisoners had knocked a tray out of another woman's hands. Within seconds, the turnkeys were at their side, reprimanding them and ordering that the wasted food be cleaned up. Other women stood up to get a better view of what was happening and there was a hum of voices all around. In that instant, Sarah felt a shadow cast over her and she looked up just in time to see the flash of a knife as it approached her face.

It was not red Sarah saw then, but white — clear white. It was as though all the pent-up rage, despair, and frustration of the past few months were channeled into her and, rising like a tidal wave, she struck out and knocked the knife from Rook's hand, the force of her fury carrying her over the table and on top of the other woman, hitting her head against the wooden surface and digging her hand into the flesh of her face. She felt as though she were watching the episode from outside herself, from high up, above the people and tables. She heard screaming but was not sure whether it was hers or Rook's, or someone else's altogether and, in the moment before the turnkeys pulled her away, she felt utterly and blissfully free.

26

"The eye is the window of the soul, the mouth the door. The intellect, the will, are seen in the eye; the emotions, sensibilities, and affections, in the mouth. The animals look for man's intentions right into his eyes. Even a rat, when you hunt him and bring him to bay, looks you in the eye."
— Hiram Powers (1805–1873)

Edmund woke in a panic, clammy with sweat, certain that someone close by had shouted his name. The room, however, was empty, the bed curtains drawn.

Bessie was almost silent during breakfast and he could think of little to say. She looked at him reproachfully over the uneaten devilled kidneys.

"You're setting a bad example for Clem," she said in a low voice.

Was this a reference to his poor appetite, or to more serious failings? He could feel the dull throb of an approaching headache.

He needed to get out of the house.

"A consultation on a new case," Edmund told her, standing up, although, despite his best efforts, he had received no decent new instructions for weeks. He certainly could not admit he was going to the prison now that there was no real reason for him to do so.

"I hope you're being paid well for it," Bessie said, without looking at him.

When he did not reply, Bessie raised her eyes. "The butcher has asked us to settle our account. We haven't paid him for a month, Edmund."

"You mustn't worry yourself about it, Bessie. This is for me to resolve."

Edmund had been counting on receiving his payment from the Home Secretary as soon as his report was completed. Spinks, however, had refused to pay him so much as a shilling.

"You will get your money when His Majesty makes his decision," he had said, smiling like a cat. "Assuming, of course, that your report meets with his approval."

Bessie folded her napkin. "I don't see why you can't just ask your father."

Edmund tensed. "Perhaps you should ask him yourself," he said quietly. "Tell him that his son hasn't lived up to expectations."

"That's hardly fair, Edmund. I only meant —"

"I asked my father for help before. Remember that? And his idea of help was to allocate me this case."

Bessie looked down.

"Yes. So please, let me deal with this alone. I will find a way."

Edmund had been waiting in the lodge for a quarter hour when Miss Sowerton approached him. The expression on her face was unreadable.

"I'm afraid you won't be able to see your Miss Gale today. She's in the infirmary."

"The infirmary?"

"Yes, she's been fighting."

Edmund frowned. "I find that hard to believe."

"Yes, not such a lady after all, it seems," the warder said coolly. "And she certainly doesn't look like one now."

Edmund stood up, alarmed. "Is she badly injured?"

"Oh, don't concern yourself, sir," Miss Sowerton said. "A few scratches is all. The other woman is in a much worse state than she. Of course, Gale says it was all in self-defense. But then you know about her defenses."

"I must see her," Edmund said, trying to keep the panic out of his voice.

"No, not today," the woman said blandly. "Probably not tomorrow neither. There'll have to be an adjudication to determine what's to be done with her."

"I am quite sure," Edmund said, "that Miss Gale would not have attacked someone unprovoked, especially not now, while the Home Secretary is considering my report. I need to speak to her."

"As I say, Mr. Fleetwood, that won't be possible, not while she's in the infirmary. But don't you worry: they're taking good care of her for you."

The expression on her face shifted momentarily and he saw the glint of something beneath.

"It's molded on the face just after they die, you see," Mr. Cope said. "They use plaster."

Edmund had insisted that he be taken to the Governor's room, a carpeted palace in comparison to the rest of the prison, with green velvet curtains, old paintings of Botany Bay hung over the desk, and busts of murderers on a shelf beside the door. Although Edmund had tried to speak to him immediately about Sarah, the Governor had insisted on showing him Greenacre's death mask. His expression, eyes closed, was uncharacteristically benign, as though he had forgiven those who condemned him.

"You see that the nose is thicker than it was in life. The features are swollen: that's because the blood vessels burst when they hang."

For a second, Edmund had a vivid image of how Sarah's death mask would look, the delicate features thickened and contorted by the choke of the rope. He pushed it from his mind.

"Madame Tussauds is to use the mask to make a likeness for her waxwork collection," the Governor told him proudly, smoothing his hand over the cheek. "Several of our inmates have made it into her museum, but none yet into the Separate Room where the worst criminals are displayed. No doubt Greenacre will appear with his saw and cutting table." He laughed and mimed a sawing action.

"Yes, Mr. Cope, but I must speak to you regarding Sarah Gale."

The Governor raised his eyebrows. "What about her?"

"Miss Sowerton claims that she was in some kind of fight."

The Governor shrugged. "Yes, common enough in this place. They fight like cats, the women."

Edmund struggled to keep the impatience out of his voice. "Mr. Cope, you forget that I have spent much time with Miss Gale in the past few weeks, and I think it very unlikely that she would have initiated a fight. It is far more probable that she was attacked. Indeed, I suspect that she has been assaulted previously in your prison."

The Governor suppressed a yawn. "Forgive me, Mr. Fleetwood, but when you have seen as much as I have of these creatures, you cease to be surprised by any of the things they do. Some of them seem more like wild beasts than women. Did you know that we had a convict last week fashion herself a weapon out of a chiseled piece of bone? She tried to attack one of the ward ers with it, but fortunately was disarmed."

"Most fortunate, Mr. Cope, but what I'm trying —"

"What most people don't appreciate is the sheer scale of female criminality in this country. One-third of the convicts in this kingdom are women," the Governor continued. "And that doesn't take into account those who seduce men to commit crime. In fact, the real proportion is likely to be far higher, given that women are far more devious and thus likely to evade justice."

Edmund breathed out in frustration. "Will it be you who carries out the adjudication?"

"Myself and the matron, yes. Don't worry, Mr. Fleetwood, we will consider all of the evidence and if she was indeed the victim in this little scrape, then we will punish the other woman accordingly." He set the death mask down on his desk. "You know that Greenacre's head has been sent to an esteemed medical surgeon for examination."

"Oh, yes?" Edmund said, distractedly.

"Yes, we do this with all of the most serious cases. The surgeon is to examine the brain for any abnormality."

"I see. And the rest of the body is . . . ?"

"Buried in quicklime in the passage that connects Newgate with the Old Bailey," the Governor said.

"Of course. Dead Man's Walk."

"There's a rather neat symmetry to it, is there not, Mr. Fleetwood? For the dismemberer to be buried without his head?" He chuckled again.

"Yes, I suppose there is. I understand that Sarah, Miss Gale, is in the infirmary. I would like to speak with her."

"No, no, Mr. Fleetwood. We can't have visitors in the infirmary, as much for your sake as for the prisoners'. All sorts of nasty ailments you could catch. She'll be out of there soon enough, no doubt. And then of course she'll be leaving us completely, one way or the other."

"Yes," Edmund said, turning to leave.

"Although of course," the Governor said, "if she is hanged here, she will never truly leave. For she'll be buried within the walls, together with Greenacre." He smiled. "Together even in death. That's fitting, isn't it?"

Edmund made his way to the Old Bailey and pushed his way through the clusters of worried relatives and bewigged barristers. Eventually, he found Morris, deep in discussion with some other clerks outside the main courtroom.

"I'm tellin' you, Mr. Fleetwood, I've been doing my best to swank solicitors into sending briefs your way, but this Edgeware Road business has made people nervous as hens. Word's got out you've recommended our Miss Gale be spared, and there's some none too 'appy about it. Plus there's some pleece officer goin' 'round telling everyone you're a gulpy."

"Gulpy?"

"Dupe. Idiot. No offense, sir. You must 'a riled 'im."

347

Edmund gave a tight smile. "Feltham. He didn't appreciate my interfering with his investigation. But surely not everyone believes the word of a crooked police officer. Surely some people see that the conviction was unsound and that my recommendation was right."

"Oh, there's plenty want to employ the celebrated Edmund Fleetwood," Morris said, gesturing toward the throng of poorly clothed, pinch-faced men and women waiting outside the court. "But they mostly can't pay so much as half a crown."

Edmund wended his way home, his hands in his pockets, thinking. Who had divulged the news of his decision? Spinks? When he arrived at his chambers, he found Bessie in a blue floral visiting dress — it was Thursday, her "at home" morning.

"Well, I have been snubbed," she told him as soon as he had closed the door. "Hardly anyone visited today. Miss Pinkerton merely left a card. You know the cause of it." She folded her arms.

Edmund removed his hat and gloves. "Yes, I suspect I do."

"Mrs. Whipple, your colleague's wife, condescended to visit — all airs and graces. She told me that you have sided with a woman everyone believes to be a wicked criminal."

"Well, everyone is wrong. And it will be proved."

"Will it? Will it, Edmund? Why are you so sure she's innocent? Because she tells you so? A woman will say anything to save her neck. Surely you know that."

"Bessie, you really don't understand. I know you're upset, but please do not comment on my cases when you have no knowledge of them."

"But, Edmund, I have to comment when your work begins to affect us, me, our lives."

"Will our lives be so much the poorer without visits from the Miss Pinkertons of this world?"

"It's not just visits, Edmund. What will this do to your practice if people think you are sympathizing with the worst kind of criminal? You were hardly besieged with work before all of this started, and now . . ."

Edmund ran his hands through his hair. "I know, Bessie. I know that very well, but I'm confident that the truth will out. That people will come to accept that I have acted rightly."

"But I ask you again how you know this Gale woman to be speaking the truth? Remember she has not only herself to save, but her child. I'd do or say anything for

Clem. I'm sure she would do the same for her son."

Edmund did his best to keep the annoyance out of his voice. "Bessie, I understand why you're concerned, and I'm sorry you've been snubbed — it's wretched, it really is. But these people are wrong and will be shown to be so. Miss Gale has been the victim of gross prejudice and of our supposed justice system. The police manipulated the evidence, the newspaper men have slandered and lied about her — you've seen the things that have been written, Bessie. Even her own lawyers undermined her. I cannot fail her as well."

Bessie looked down. "Is she pretty?"

"What?"

"Is she very pretty? They say she is handsome."

"Bessie, what a thing to ask. What does it matter if she is handsome?"

"It's just . . . well, you have spent so little time with us recently. Clem misses his father. I miss you."

"I'm sorry, Bessie. I know I've been . . . absent." He was stung with guilt. He had, he reflected, been away much of late: at the prison, at the library, or locked in his study, working. He had begun to remind himself of his own father. He kissed her forehead.

"This is something that I have to do, but it will be over soon. And then things will get better. I'll get more work — good work. I promise."

As he stroked her hair, his eyes alighted on an envelope on the mantelpiece, resting against the mirror. In its reflection he could see his name, written backward. He pulled away from Bessie and picked up the envelope.

"Oh, yes," she said, "that came for you while you were out. Flora said that a woman delivered it. A woman in a gray dress."

27

"O dreadful is the check — intense the
    agony —
When the ear begins to hear, and the eye
    begins to see;
When the pulse begins to throb — the brain
    to think again —
The soul to feel the flesh, and the flesh to
    feel the chain."
               — "The Prisoner," Emily Brontë

She shifted to try to reduce the pain. The manacles cut into her wrists and whenever she made the slightest movement the iron cuffs bit deep into the already damaged flesh. Sarah could feel the blood on her back drying and sticking to her clothing. She thought she could taste blood in her mouth. She could see nothing at all.

Immediately after the attack in the dining hall the previous day, Miss Sowerton and the two rough-looking warders had dragged her down to the basement. She had fought against them at first, insisting it was Rook who had started it, shouting that Rook had been out to get her since the start. That, of course, had been a mistake. There was nothing worse, in this place, than a rat.

"You can protest your innocence all you like," Miss Sowerton had said, "but I saw through your act a long time ago, and I think it's time you admitted what you did."

That was when they had taken her to the dark cells.

First, they bound her wrists. Next they manacled her so that she was facing the wall. Then they tore the dress from her back so that she was naked from the waist up.

She had stopped protesting by this point. Fear had made her numb, for she realized what they meant to do.

From behind her, she heard Miss Sowerton's voice. "You think you're better than the others, Gale. You think you're better than us. But you're nothing. You're nothing at all." She spoke then to one of the warders. "Start with ten."

She had tried for as long as she could not to cry out. One stroke, two strokes, three. She clenched her teeth, clenched her whole self, and tried to stop herself from feeling as the leather whip tore into her flesh. Four strokes. A cry burst from her lips. *Imagine you're somewhere else. Imagine you're outside your body.* That was what she had tried to do with her father. It had never worked then, either. Five strokes. Were they going to kill her here? She could feel the skin of her back splitting, the blood running. Six. *Breathe slowly. Stay calm.* Seven, and she could no longer keep the pain in, but it burst forth as a scream and a howl and all dignity was gone as she begged and pleaded for them to stop.

"Oh, I'll tell her to stop," Miss Sowerton said, "when you confess what you did to that woman. You going to tell us?"

"I've already told."

"You mean the lies you told the lawyer? I don't believe them. Rook says she heard you were there."

"No."

"No?"

Sarah saw George's face before her. She saw Rosina.

"No. Rook's bluffing. She doesn't know anything."

A pause. Then: "Ten more lashes."

"Please, God, no. No!"

Did anyone hear her screams outside the cell? Could Lucy hear her? Could God? If He could, He must believe, as these women did, that she needed to be taught a lesson.

At some point she lost consciousness. When she awoke, the darkness was so complete that she did not know whether her eyes were open or shut. She would not even have been sure she was alive, were it not for the searing pain that scorched along her back. The warders had shackled her to a low wooden bed and left, sealing the doors so that not a single beam of light reached her, nor the slightest sound from outside.

Would they come back? she had wondered. Would they flog her again, or apply some new torture? Or would they simply leave her to die?

The cell stank, of mold, piss, and vomit, perhaps her own. She could hear the squeal and splash of rats in a puddle of something in the corner. In her exhaustion and fear, Sarah felt her mind turning in on itself. She began to believe that it had all been pointless. She should have simply accepted what fate threw at her rather than trying to fight it, for what difference had she made anyway? The planning and the weighing and the worrying had all been futile because she would die here, in the dark. Her torn back, untreated, would become septic and poison her blood, or the warders would return and

finish her. They would claim she had suc-
cumbed to a fever — that was common
enough — or they would say that she had
hit her head against the wall in a rage.
Perhaps Miss Sowerton would say that,
before her death, she had confessed to having killed Hannah Brown herself. And then
all of it would have been in vain.

Was this how Hannah had felt before she
died? The terror, the pain, the hopelessness.
Or perhaps she had no idea of what would
happen to her.

Sarah drifted off again, into sleep or
unconsciousness. She awoke to see one of
the warders, holding a lamp. The light, after
such darkness, blinded Sarah and she could
not look into the woman's face, but managed to rasp, "Please. Some water."

"Miss Sowerton wants to know if you've
anything to say." It was the gruff voice of
one of the two warders who had been on
duty in the laundry that day.

For a moment, Sarah considered saying
that yes, Miss Sowerton was right, she had
been there, she had helped James kill Hannah, had sawed her to pieces, mopped up
the blood. Indeed, she was so thirsty and
hungry, in so much pain, that she might at
that moment have admitted to anything.
But there must still have been some hope

within her like a glow of amber in the dying ashes of a fire, for she could not bring herself to do it.

"I beg you," she said. "Just give me some water."

She felt the woman hesitate, but after a moment she moved away.

"Don't leave me here!" she shouted at the woman's retreating form. "At least give me a candle!"

The warder did not turn, but continued toward the door, taking the lamp with her, its flame wavering as she walked.

"Please!"

The door clanged shut and Sarah was plunged again into utter darkness.

Sarah slipped in and out of consciousness, in and out of time. She had no idea whether she had been in the cell for hours, or days. At times she thought she was back in her childhood bedroom with Rosina, shut away in the dark for their misdemeanors. Once when she woke she sensed, as she had that time in her cell before, a presence. Above the squealing of the rats, she heard again the sound of labored breath.

"Hannah?"

No answer, but still the breathing: fast, then slow; fast, then slow. On it went like this, on and on. Sometimes Sarah was conscious and sometimes not, and often she was somewhere in between.

At some point it came to her that Hannah's silence was not hostile. She did not respond, Sarah realized, because she could not. She was dying.

"It's all right," Sarah said into the darkness. "It's all right, Hannah. It will be over soon."

And then a light. First just a beam and then a brightness flooding the cell with a whiteness so intense that it seemed to reach inside her head. She screwed her eyes tight shut against it, but she could hear a voice. A voice she knew well.

"In order to discipline the mind, you must discipline the body."

"I am not interested in why you decided to take her to the punishment cell, Miss Sowerton. Nor am I interested in why you lied to me."

"You might not be interested, Mr. Fleetwood, but if you report this —"

"If I report this to the Home Secretary, Miss Sowerton, that will be the end of your tenure as Matron of Newgate."

The matron glared at Edmund with such hatred he could almost feel her eyes boring into his skin. "The Home Secretary would understand my methods."

"On the contrary, he would be aware you were committing a criminal offense. The whipping of women was outlawed some years ago, as you know perfectly well. If I hadn't arrived when I did, she could have died."

A young, freckle-faced warder was with Sarah now in the next cell, sponging her back with brandy and dosing her with laudanum to reduce the pain.

"Gale exaggerates, as she always does," the matron said. "She suffered no great harm."

"She was in a collapsed state, her back is latticed with appalling cuts, and she has been left without food and water in complete darkness for nearly forty-eight hours. I would say that was assault with grievous bodily harm. I would say a jury would agree with me." His tone was measured, but there was steel beneath.

"Are you threatening me, Mr. Fleetwood?"

Edmund paused. "As you know, Miss Sowerton, we are awaiting a decision on Sarah's case. I anticipate that Lord Russell will pardon Sarah. I also anticipate that he will be most displeased if he finds that the prisoner he has set free has disappeared or been injured."

"What exactly do you mean, sir?"

He met the woman's cold-eyed stare. "You will keep this other prisoner, Rook, under lock and key and you will make very sure that no harm comes to Miss Gale. If anything happens to her, I will hold you personally responsible and I will do my utmost to ensure you are brought to account. Is that clear enough for you, Miss Sowerton?"

He was tempted to report her now, to prevent her from harming others, and merely to see the look on her pockmarked face when she found she had lost her power. That would be a risk, however. If the matron were not removed from post immediately, he dreaded to think what revenge she might exact. At least this way he retained some leverage over her and over this Rook woman. He would report them both once Sarah was safely out of Newgate.

"You will also ensure that Miss Gale is properly fed and given the medical treatment she needs in order to recover from her ordeal."

He saw the woman's jaw twitch. "Since you expect so much from me, you will at least have the goodness to say who told you the prisoner Gale was here?"

"As a matter of fact, I don't know, Miss Sowerton. The letter I received was anonymous." This was true.

"I would like to see that letter."

"You can't. I burned it." This was not true. He had preserved it, as evidence.

"Someone must have seen who delivered it."

Edmund shrugged. "No, apparently not. It seems no one was looking."

Flora had seen the woman, of course, but Edmund felt that, in this particular instance, he was entitled to lie.

Edmund walked back into the cell where Sarah lay on her side beneath a gray calico sheet. Her dark hair was unpinned and spread across the pillow. Her eyes were closed. The right side of her face was badly bruised, and a red cut ran across her cheek.

The young warder, who had been sitting on a stool next to the bed, stood up as he entered the room and put her finger to her lips.

"She's sleeping now," she whispered. "Best thing for 'er." Edmund nodded. "Thank you, Miss . . . ?"

"Hinkley. I'll look after her till she's moved to the infirmary."

"I'm sure you will, Miss Hinkley. I will

ask Miss Pike to look in on Sarah as soon as she can."

The girl nodded. It must surely have been her who brought the letter to his chambers, and yet she was younger and slighter than the woman Flora had described.

He paused, considering what to say. "Is there another warder, older than you — broader, perhaps, who has been kind to Sarah?"

Miss Hinkley frowned. "Not that I know of, sir. Kindness ain't exactly encouraged here. Especially not toward felons."

Edmund nodded. Perhaps, after all, Flora's description of the woman had been wrong. She had probably been drunk.

Edmund looked back at Sarah, her thin frame, her tangled hair, her damaged face, and he was seized with anxiety. Even if the Home Secretary lifted the death sentence, Newgate would kill Sarah. Whatever happened, she could not stay here.

28

"For now we see through a glass, darkly; but then face to face."
— 1 Corinthians, 13:12 (KJV)

Sarah held the piece of looking glass before her and stared at her reflection, the crack in the glass splitting her face in two. All that remained of Rook's attack was a purplish mark to the right of her eye and a thin red line running down her cheek, like a faded imprint of Hannah Brown's injuries.

For the past three days she had been in the infirmary — a long, dismal, whitewashed room with flaking paint and twelve beds, all occupied. During the day, the warders treated her back with vinegar and witch hazel and brought her thin broths and stale bread. At night, the walls resounded with the coughing of the consumptive and the crying of the lonely. Sarah's inability to sleep had hardened into something else, and she had begun to believe she might never sleep again. Each night, she lay awake, her eyes wide open in the darkness, thinking and waiting. How many more days before the Home Secretary communicated his decision? And would she survive long enough in this place to hear it?

Rook was in a bed at the other end of the corridor, her face still bandaged. Since Edmund's intervention, she had been kept under close watch, but how long would they be able to keep her at bay? She could almost hear the clicking of the other woman's mind calculating how she would revenge herself on Sarah, how she would evade the gaze of the night warder, or persuade her to look away when the moment came. And Sarah knew that next time Rook would not make a mistake: she would kill her.

Edmund was not permitted to visit her in the infirmary and Sarah had heard from him only once, by letter.

"I have spoken to Lord Russell's clerk," he told her.

Although he could not confirm to me the Home Secretary's decision in the matter, he gave me reason to be hopeful. Indeed, his words were that the Home Secretary had been "most impressed" with my report

364

and that a decision would be imminent. I have stressed to him the importance of removing you from Newgate as soon as possible.

Sarah had read the letter over and over. She had done everything she could think of, everything she could stomach, but perhaps it was not enough.

The hospital matron approached and held her hand out for the looking glass.

"Visitor here for you," she said. "The Gov'ner says you're to see 'im in the legal visitors' room, as it's important, 'pparently."

Edmund sat at a table by the far wall, holding a letter. "Please, sit down," he said to Sarah as she approached.

Sarah remained standing, however, her body tense.

"What does it say?" she asked.

Edmund unfolded the letter onto the wooden table and leaned forward, the better to view it. She could see that there was a sheen of sweat on his brow. In a clear voice he read the letter aloud.

Sir,
In response to your despatch of June 9th, I have the honor to transmit to you the

Secretary of State's decision in this matter.

Lord Russell was strongly impressed with the reasoning in your report and sympathetic to the plight of the prisoner Gale, who it seems acted under the control of the criminal Greenacre. He concurs in your submission that the prisoner Gale's actions do not warrant the death sentence in these particular circumstances. The evidence suggests that she only became aware of the murder after the event and was placed under considerable pressure to keep her silence.

However, Lord Russell cannot accede to your suggestion that a pardon would be appropriate. Whatever the emotional constraints acting upon the prisoner, she should — both in legal and moral terms — have spoken out about what all agree was the most atrocious crime. To fail to do so amounted to helping to conceal the murder. Had she reported her concerns to the relevant authorities, it would have avoided an expensive and lengthy police investigation. That she failed to speak out is testament to a weakness of character and of morals. The Secretary of State has therefore recommended to His Majesty that Miss Gale's sentence be commuted to transportation to New South Wales for the term of her natural life. He is pleased to report that His Majesty has accepted that recommendation.

As you know, it is the wish of Lord John Russell to diminish, as much as possible, the number of transports sent yearly to the Australian colonies; and his Lordship is desirous of concerting with the authorities there to ensure that they are not overloaded with convicts. However, Miss Gale is a particularly good example of a felon who cannot continue to be incarcerated in this country and for whom there is no viable alternative.

In order to ensure a speedy conclusion to this matter, I have personally arranged for Miss Gale to be taken aboard the next available ship. She will be removed within the course of the next week. Given the nature of the crime, it is not considered appropriate for Miss Gale's child to accompany her.

I am, Sir,
Your faithful and obedient servant,
Jelinger Spinks

As Edmund finished reading, Sarah sank down into the chair, her body limp, her legs no longer able to support her. Transportation for life, that substitute for death.

For a time, neither of them spoke. Sarah was dimly aware of the sounds around her — the scraping of pens and the hum of conversation — but it was as though they were far off, in another place altogether.

"I'm so sorry, Sarah," Edmund said. "I really thought . . . I really thought that they would do more than this for you."

She turned the words over in her mind, trying to comprehend them. *For the term of her natural life.* In a matter of days, she was to be shipped to the other side of the earth away from everything she knew. Away from Rosina. Away from George: her boy. She closed her eyes, unable to take in the enormity of it. The despair washed at her feet in waves. She had imagined and come to terms with the possibility of a short prison sentence, but not this. Not after everything she had said and done, everything she had risked.

"I will not cease to fight for you," Edmund said. "It is not the end."

Sarah stared at him, hardly hearing.

"All those meetings," she said after a time. "All those words. I told you my story. You said it would make a difference. I betrayed James. And for what? For this?" She jabbed her finger at the piece of paper, suddenly furious.

"Why did you make me feel there was hope?" she said, tasting the salt of tears running into her mouth. "Why did you come here and make me feel again, when they were only ever going to kill me, one way or another?"

Edmund flushed. "I thought Lord Russell meant to look properly at your case. I miscalculated the odds . . ." He trailed off. "But it is better than hanging. It is better than staying here, in Newgate."

"Is it? I'm to be sent away from everything I know. Everyone I love. *From my own son!*" She put her hands on her forehead. "Sent away on a convict ship for months on end, and, if I survive the passage, what will happen then? Do you suppose Australia is an inviting place? Do you suppose they send people there for their own enjoyment?" She laughed. It was as though she were on the edge of a precipice, staring down.

Edmund did not say anything. He looked, she thought, as if he himself might cry.

It had begun to rain again. She could hear the raindrops falling against the window like pins.

You fool, she thought. You utter fool.

■ ■ ■ ■

Edmund walked back to his chambers in a
heavy downpour of rain, not bothering to
hurry or to keep out of the rivers of water
that slaked down the gutters and poured
from waterspouts and rooftops, turning the
streets into streams of filth. He carried the
letter in his hand. Horse-drawn cabs over-
took him, splashing water onto his trousers.
He barely noticed.

When he reached his study, he rolled out
the letter from the Home Secretary. In the
rain, the ink had run so that some of the
words were now indecipherable. The post-
script from Lord Russell at the bottom of
the page remained clear, however.

As you may know, I discussed this matter
with your father, and he agrees that, in
these circumstances, a woman cannot be
pardoned.

29

"The best chess-player in Christendom may be little more than the best player of chess; but proficiency in whist implies capacity for success in all those more important undertakings where mind struggles with mind."
— "The Murders in the Rue Morgue,"
Edgar Allan Poe, 1841

Edmund awoke in a foul humor. He had slept little and thought much. Looking back to his initial meeting at the Home Office, he realized he had been played: he had been used as a pawn. The Minister had never intended to take his investigation report seriously — he had simply wanted to give the impression that he was doing something. Edmund decided to go and see Lord Russell immediately.

It was a bright morning but the ground was still wet underfoot as he made his way through the Temple Gardens, emerging into the sunshine of Essex Street, silently rehearsing the words he intended to use before the Minister.

He arrived at the high stone building shortly before ten o'clock and asked a liveried porter to inform the Minister he wished to speak with him.

"Is he expecting you, sir?"

"No, I confess I have no appointment, but it's important that I see him as soon as possible."

The man looked at him impenetrably. "He knows your business, I take it."

"He does."

The man disappeared behind the tall oak doors, leaving Edmund standing in the wide portico. Five minutes passed and no other visitor arrived. Edmund paced the deep red carpet of the entrance room, hands behind his back.

He looked up to see the porter returning with the clerk, Mr. Spinks, who smiled unconvincingly.

"What can we do for you, Mr. Fleetwood?"

"I received your letter regarding Miss Gale and the Minister's decision. I was . . . surprised. I wished to discuss it with Lord Russell. There are certain matters that he may not have appreciated."

Spinks folded his hands. "I assure you, his lordship is fully apprised of all the facts. But if you would come this way . . ."

He opened a door onto a long corridor of polished wood lined with pictures of former Ministers, bewigged and austere. He stopped at a door midway down the corridor and knocked lightly. When Edmund entered he saw that Lord Russell was sitting at his large desk, various papers spread in front of him.

"Edmund, come in. I apologize for the disarray. You find me in the midst of my work on the Offenses Against the Person Bill."

"It is I who must apologize, my lord, for arriving here uninvited, but time is of the essence and I wished to speak with you regarding the Sarah Gale matter."

"Indeed. And what a matter. I congratulate you on your report excellently drafted, if I may say so. That is the wondrous thing about you young gentlemen of the bar: you have such a fine turn of phrase."

"I am grateful, my lord. And of course —"

"Please sit down."

"Thank you. I was heartened that you commuted Miss Gale's sentence —"

"Tea?"

"No, thank you. She is of course relieved that the penalty —"

"Spinks, move these papers for me, will you?"

"My lord," Edmund said firmly, "surely justice in this situation demands that she be pardoned entirely."

Lord Russell looked up at Edmund over his glasses. "Justice in fact demanded that she be *hanged.* It is I, exercising the King's Prerogative of mercy, who have spared her that fate. You cannot realistically demand any more."

"And I say again that I am highly respectful of your lordship's decision. However, I wanted to make sure you were fully aware of the facts. Namely, that she was coerced into acting as she did. She had no choice but to assist Greenacre or she would have risked her life and that of her child. In those circumstances —"

"I read your report. I read the affidavit. And, as I say, they were admirably drafted. However, fine words butter no parsnips. I did not ask you to look again at the investigation but at the punishment the court awarded. I thought my instructions on this matter had been clear. The reality is that this woman, who was not tied to Greenacre by the lawful bond of marriage, helped to conceal a murder. A horrific murder of an innocent woman that has shocked the nation. Whatever her reason for not speaking out, it is plain that she has no defense. The judge reviewed the matter and confirmed that he believes the conviction was correct, albeit that he has some sympathy for her plight. Mr. Spinks has also looked into this for me and we are quite certain on the point. Is that not right, Spinks?"

The clerk stood with his hands folded. "That is correct, my lord. Coercion provides no defense to aiding and abetting a murder."

"There is no clear authority on it either way," Edmund said. "It would be open to you to find that in this case it did provide a defense."

"Mr. Fleetwood," Lord Russell laughed, "these are hardly the correct facts on which to establish new law. For a start, you have only her word that she was coerced."

"Miss Pike spoke for her. And one of the policemen who arrested her had some doubts."

"Yes, yes. But none of these people actually *saw* anything. That's correct, isn't it, Spinks? None of them saw anything firsthand. There were no eyewitnesses. It's all . . . conjecture," he said, waving his hands in the air to indicate the vagueness of it all.

"Her son witnessed the threats."

"Her son? He's a young child, isn't he? Not exactly a reliable or appropriate witness. He'll say whatever his mother tells him to."

"But, your lordship, with the greatest respect, if the jury had been presented with evidence that Miss Gale had been coerced, they might not have convicted her."

"They might have; they might not have. But there is no right to any appeal or retrial, so the matter is immaterial. The fact is, she had the opportunity to give a statement saying all this, or to direct her counsel to do so, but she did not."

"Because she was afraid for her life. She was afraid for her son. And because she was represented by the same lawyers who took their instructions — and payment — from Greenacre."

Edmund was doing his best to keep his tone level but he was furious.

The Minister had gone back to his papers. Without looking at Edmund he said flatly, "The decision I arrived at is the correct one. There has been no miscarriage of justice. The outraged public will not be further

376

outraged by the pardoning of a woman they see as a murderess; Mrs. Fry and her lot will see I have made some adjustment for the woman's circumstances. Everyone is happy."

Edmund refrained from saying that Sarah herself was very far from happy.

"You are aware, my lord, that she will be separated from her young son if indeed she is transported."

"If, my dear sir? *If?* The matter has been decided and has been approved by His Majesty the King!"

Edmund thought this unlikely. The King, it was said, was far too ill to be able to give any thought to such matters.

"Indeed, and of course Miss Gale is most grateful, but one wonders whether it could at least be agreed that her son should travel with her."

"On a convict ship? How long does the voyage to New South Wales take these days, Spinks?"

"Approximately five months, my lord."

"Five months indeed, packed together with criminals of all types. Hardly a fitting environment for a young child."

"But the alternative may be the work-house."

This possibility did not appear to have occurred to Lord Russell. He tutted. "A convict ship or a workhouse. Poor boy. Not that workhouses are quite as awful as Mr. Dickens would have us believe."

"So you will permit her son to travel with her, my lord?"

Edmund thought of George's thin little face, his wide blue eyes. He thought with a stab of pain of how Clem would feel were he to be wrenched away from his mother.

The Home Secretary sighed. "I will consider it when I have a spare moment."

"I have heard," Edmund said, "that other women have been permitted to take young children with them on the voyage."

"*Other women,* Mr. Fleetwood, have not been convicted of concealing a notorious murder! One can hardly imagine she has been a good mother to that child."

"On the contrary, she is entirely devoted to him and, I believe, has sacrificed much for him."

"Her reputation, certainly, for he was born out of wedlock, wasn't he? Now, was that all?"

Edmund hesitated. "Will you publish your decision?"

"The decision, of course, but not the reasons for it. We never do."

Edmund stood up, considering his words

carefully. "If I were to find clear evidence, beyond her own testimony or that of her child, that Miss Gale had concealed the crime of necessity, would that make any difference?"

Lord Russell laughed again, without mirth. "Well, you're certainly determined. One might almost have thought you were the woman's advocate rather than an investigator commissioned by the Crown. My advice to you, sir, would be to get on with your criminal practice. It's a harsh environment out there, is it not?"

Edmund trudged up the stairs and entered his study to find Morris sitting in his chair with his feet on his desk.

"So, she's to be boated, is she?"

"Yes, Morris, boated. Within the next week."

"A lifer an' all." He whistled.

"It is highly unjust."

"Yes, sir. I imagine you would think that. But bear in mind there's many who cross the herring pond for far less. One of Mr. Chippenham's clients was sent over for stealing a couple of silver spoons, and only twelve, 'e was."

"Well, perhaps Mr. Chippenham should have done a better job of defending him."

"Indeed, sir, indeed. Anyway, time to make some tin."

"Tin?" Edmund felt tired.

"The needful, the rhino, the ready."

"Money."

"Money. You told me to get you some work, and I 'ave just the thing to cheer you up — a tax matter."

"Fraud?"

"Of a sort, yes."

Edmund took the bundle of papers that Morris handed him and began to go through them. He could not, however, concentrate on the words. After a time, he looked up.

"The boy with the silver spoons, Morris."

"What about 'im, Mr. Fleetwood?"

"Did he ever come back?"

Morris tilted his head. "As far as I know, he's still there," he said, pointing at the floor.

"In the ground?"

"No, sir. On the other side of the earth."

30

"What are young women made of?
What are young women made of?
Sugar and spice and all things nice;
That's what young women are made of."
— Robert Southey, circa 1820

"The King is dead! Long live the Queen!"

So shouted the newspaper sellers as Edmund made his way up Fleet Street on the way to the prison.

"Alexandrine Victoria proclaimed Queen of England!"

Edmund bought a copy of the *Morning Chronicle* from a boy of about ten years old, and stopped in a doorway to read the black-bordered front page. For months, the Royal household had maintained that the King was perfectly healthy, although rumors had seeped out of his illness. The article confirmed what Edmund had suspected: that King William would have been far too ill to consider Sarah's petition. Lord Russell had made the decision on his own.

Edmund looked at the sketch of the new Queen, a small, determined-looking figure. Perhaps he could petition her to keep Sarah in the country.

First, however, he needed to seek support from someone who should have been helping Sarah from the start.

Newgate's library was an unpainted, stone-walled room with a high ceiling and a large window that looked onto the inside of the prison. Lining the walls were bookshelves filled with dusty, worn volumes, their titles disintegrating into their spines: prayer books, hymn books, lives of the saints.

The Ordinary sat at a desk, cutting pictures from a thick book with a pair of scissors. He looked up as Edmund approached and then returned to his cutting.

"Mr. Fleetwood. You find me removing dangerous images from our reading materials."

Standing by the desk, Edmund could see that the book was a medical text and that the pictures that the Ordinary was removing were anatomical drawings and sketches of the human body.

"You think it harmful for prisoners to see

representations of the human form?"

The Ordinary scowled. "It is not a matter of thinking; it is a matter of knowing. Remember that I am well acquainted with the nature of these criminals."

"Yes." Edmund found himself wondering what the man intended to do with the pictures he was dissecting from the book.

"Can many of the prisoners read?" Edmund asked.

"There are a handful who can read and write tolerably well, but the vast majority are barely literate."

"Do you attempt to teach them while they are here?"

The Ordinary looked at him incredulously. "And equip them with the means to carry out more pernicious crimes? Certainly not."

Edmund pressed his lips together. "Thank you for agreeing to see me. I wanted to ask for your assistance."

"Oh, yes?"

"You may be aware, Reverend, that the Home Secretary has commuted Miss Gale's sentence, but to transportation."

The Ordinary did not look up.

"You may also be aware," Edmund continued, "that Miss Gale has a young son. Four years old. I have requested that the Home Secretary grant permission for George to be able to travel with his mother, but so far that permission has not been granted. I believe it may make a difference if you, as a man of the cloth and of high moral standing, lend your support to my request. There is not much time — she is to be taken to the boat in the next few days — so it is important we act quickly."

The Ordinary stopped his cutting. "It is as I feared," he said.

Edmund frowned. "And what is it that you feared?"

Dr. Cotton put down his scissors and exhaled. "I have had the privilege of working at Newgate for many years. In that time, I have seen all manner of criminals: the misguided, the deranged, the erring, and the truly evil. There are many in the last category who are women. Clever women. Deceitful women. Women who would make you believe they were made of sugar and spice, but whose flesh is rotting from within, whose souls are as rancid as month-old butter."

Edmund felt his jaw clench. He knew what was coming.

"She is very clever, your Miss Gale. She knows what to say to convince a man and she has evidently worked her sorcery on you. I assume she has manufactured a story to make you sympathize with her. Stories, Mr. Fleetwood, are dangerous things." He pointed to the walls around them. "That is precisely why we ensure that there are no stories here: no novels, no fiction. Only clinical texts, religious tracts, and, of course, the Bible."

Edmund managed to refrain from pointing out that the Bible itself was full of stories, many of them horrible, several involving dismemberment.

The Ordinary continued. "You will permit me to say that I am rather more experienced than you in the ways of the world. I see through Miss Gale as I do all of them. It is not my assistance she needs. It is God's. And He will only have mercy upon her soul if she confesses to her crime and truly repents."

Edmund pressed his lips together. "She denies any active involvement in the crime, Dr. Cotton. She was not there." He separated the words for emphasis.

The Ordinary picked up his scissors again. "Sir, if that is what she still claims, then there is nothing either you or I can do for her. There are some souls that we cannot reach."

"You refuse to lend your support to my request?"

"Mr. Fleetwood, for the prisoner Gale's son, his mother being transported is probably the best thing that has happened so far in his sorry little life. One might even say it was an act of God."

Edmund stood and walked from the room, hearing only the sound of his own footsteps and the slicing of paper.

Edmund had communicated the Home Secretary's decision to Rosina by letter the previous day, but she had not replied. He needed to see her. The streets of Covent Garden were dense with people, vehicles, and animals, and by the time Edmund reached Rosina's house, she was already at the door, on her way out, a basket in one hand. George wore a white cap and patched clothing; she, a pale green print dress and white mantle.

"Miss Farr," Edmund said. "I must speak with you."

"We're just going to the market before it closes," she told him. "You'll have to come with us." She did not smile.

It was after seven o'clock when they reached the market, but it was still busy with people trying to complete their week's shopping. The steps of Covent Garden theater were covered with heaps of vegetables and fruit — sacks of apples and potatoes, bundles of wilted rhubarb, asparagus, and broccoli. The flagstones were stained green with leaves and petals trodden underfoot. As they walked, George bent down to the pavement and picked up discarded and crushed flower heads, which he stuffed into his pockets.

Rosina made her way from fruit seller to dairyman to baker, feeling fruit for bruises, smelling and tasting the butter before buying, and continually checking that George was still close to her. She did not speak to Edmund and refused to let him carry her basket.

As the light faded, they walked together to a coffee stall at the side of the market and sat on wooden stools among the charcoal smoke. George took the crushed flowers out of his pockets and began to lay them on the table.

Rosina kept her eyes on her coffee and refused to meet Edmund's gaze.

"I know you must feel that I've failed your sister," he said.

"It's not you that's failed her, Mr. Fleetwood." She held her cup in both hands and Edmund realized that she did so because her hands were shaking. He saw all at once that she was not, as he had thought, angry with him, but trying as best she could to hold herself together.

"You've done more for Sarah than anyone else and I'm sure she knows that. It's just that . . ." She swallowed. "It's just that this isn't how we expected things to play out."

Edmund shook his head. "That's my fault. I should have prepared her for the worst. I just thought that . . . Well, I thought they would listen to me and they didn't."

Rosina set down her cup and put her hands up to her eyes to stop the tears.

Edmund felt a wave of sadness wash over him.

"Rosina, I know that things seem desperate, but at least she'll be out of that hellish place. And there are still steps we can take. First, as I said in my letter, I asked the Home Secretary to give urgent consideration to allowing George —" The boy, hearing his name, looked up, and Edmund stopped himself. "Well, you know what I have asked."

"You said they did not listen to you."

"Exactly. That is why I'm here now, or at least that's part of the reason. I think you should write to the Home Secretary yourself. If you set out in your own words why it is important . . . why you may not be able to support him . . . he may have some sympathy. But you must do so at once."

She gave him a look, which he could not at first read. "Mr. Fleetwood, I've already done that."

"You have?"

"Yes, of course — as soon as I received your letter. I explained how I wouldn't be able to support him and how he might end up being a burden on the Parish. They might listen to money if they won't listen to sense."

He smiled. She was so like her sister: quick as powder.

"There's also the possibility," Edmund said, "of submitting a last-minute petition for Sarah's case to be reconsidered, but I would need some new piece of information. If I could only find some proof that Greenacre threatened her, then I might be able to convince the Home Secretary to look at the matter again. It's possible that our new Queen may have more fellow feeling with Sarah. If she would take an interest, then we could stop Sarah being taken on that boat." He looked at Rosina. "Is there nothing you can think of that might help me?"

She held his gaze for several seconds, unblinking. "I can't say any more than my sister has already told you. If there were anything you could use, she would have mentioned it. You collect those up now, George," she said, helping him scoop the flowers from the table.

Edmund looked at the child. How much did he understand of what was going on? He hoped, mercifully little.

"You often find presents for your mother, don't you?" he asked him.

The boy looked at Edmund warily with his large blue eyes.

"Did you dig something up for her once, in the garden?"

George looked first at his aunt and then back to Edmund. "Yes," he said, nodding. "Some rings and some coins from the fairies. We made them shiny." He grinned at Edmund, pleased with himself. Edmund smiled sadly back.

31

"Our deeds still travel with us from afar
And what we have been makes us what we
    are."
    — *Middlemarch,* George Eliot, 1872

"I tell you, I'd sooner die than go out there and be eaten up by wild animals."

"Or by the natives. They say they skin white people and boil 'em up in pots."

As Sarah sat holding her breakfast bowl, she could hear the whispered conversation of the prisoners on the table next to her.

"And that's assuming you get across. You might die at sea and be thrown into the cold ocean for the fish to nibble out yer eyes."

"Oh, hush, Mary! It's not so bad," an older woman said. "I've had friends go out there and come back in one piece, and with both eyes in their heads."

In four days, Sarah and twenty other prisoners — "the transports" as they were now known — would be transferred to the ship at Woolwich: the ship that would take them to Australia.

Sarah stared down at her bowl of stirabout: a stodgy mix of oatmeal and Indian meal, and she thought of all the breakfasts she had made for George, of all the times she had spooned food into his mouth, of the times she had given him her own food so that he might not go hungry.

It had been four days since she had learned she was to be transported, but still she could not fully digest the truth of it: she was to leave her sister — her best friend — and her own child. She would never see them again. How had she got it so wrong?

"Surely the food on the boat can't be any worse than this muck." Boltwood held up her spoon and turned it over so that the congealed matter dropped back into the bowl with a soft plop.

Since learning that the ship was to board in only a few days, the convict women had talked of little else. In nervous whispers, they speculated as to what might become of them. What would their living quarters be like? How cramped, how damp? Some said that things were much improved in recent years. Others warned that things were still bad enough. It all depended on the boat —

whether it was one of the new merchant-
men or a creaky old vessel fit for nothing
else; it all depended on the winds; it all
depended on the captain — whether he
stuck by the rules or sold off half of the ra-
tions and starved the convicts; it all depended on the crew — whether they were
decent types or the sort who would have
their way with the women whether they
liked it or not. And into this maelstrom,
several of the women were bringing young
children; one, a baby.

Although Sarah would at that moment
have given anything to take George with
her, she knew that a convict ship was in fact
no place for a child. There was little scurvy
these days but there were the other diseases
— cholera, dysentery, ship fever. If one
convict fell ill, then many of the rest would
follow. And then there was the story, told
nightly, of the *Neva,* the convict ship that
had gone down in the Bass Strait in '35,
taking almost all of its crew and human
cargo with it.

Lucy was also to go to New South Wales,
for a term of seven years. As Edmund had
predicted, she was acquitted of murder but
convicted of concealing the birth.

"At least it means we'll get to be together,"
she had whispered the previous evening.

"You're the only real friend I've got."

But you hardly know me, Sarah had thought. You know only the small pieces of me I have chosen to show. If you knew the whole story, you would hate me as the others do.

Sarah's attention returned to the women whispering on the next table.

"Yes," a red-haired girl was saying, "I heard the black ones carry sticks and knives and whenever they see a white woman they butcher her straight off."

Mary nodded. "And there's poisonous snakes and huge spiders bigger than London rats."

Miss Sowerton walked over to their table. "Kindly keep your mouths shut save as is required to get the food in."

The women grumbled but ceased their conversation.

"At all events," Miss Sowerton said in an undertone, "never mind your spiders and snakes: I'd be more worried about something a little closer to home." She jerked her head toward Sarah.

Sarah felt the other women's eyes settle on her, like flies. Since her fight with Rook and her escape from the dark cells, the other inmates looked at her in a new way: more fearful, perhaps more respectful.

"Not surprising they won't let her take her son with her," Miss Sowerton murmured.

Sarah met the woman's stare. What can you do to me now? she thought. I am being wrenched away from my own child, and you think your words can hurt me?

"You mustn't be cast down," Miss Pike said when she visited Sarah that afternoon. "The fight is not over yet."

Miss Pike's pale face was even whiter than usual and her eyes were red-rimmed behind her glasses. She began to remove items from a bag: a few books, a flannel petticoat, some woolen stockings, a calico dress.

"I have this morning delivered a petition to the Home Department," she said in an enforced sprightly tone. "A petition signed by two hundred people, Sarah — Mrs. Fry included — insisting that Lord Russell grant permission for George to travel with you. It's simply ludicrous to separate a child so young from his mother, and Lord Russell knows it. It is all political posturing. I cannot believe that he will really —"

"Miss Pike." Sarah put her hand on the woman's arm. "If the petition doesn't work. If I really do have to leave George behind, will you help him? Will you help my sister?

They won't have enough to live on."

Miss Pike's eyes filled with tears. "Sarah, what a ridiculous question. Of course we will help them. But it will not come to that."

"They mean to make an example of me, Miss Pike. I'm the monster, remember? You said it yourself."

Miss Pike shook her head and blinked away her tears. "If there are any monsters in this whole affair, it's the bureaucrats, playing politics with children, for heaven's sakes." She abandoned her air of levity and her face seemed to droop. "We claim to be able to make a difference with our petitions and our visits and our meetings, but those who make the decisions are not listening."

"You've made a great difference to me," said Sarah. "You've made me feel as though I'm not entirely alone. You helped me see what I had to do."

Miss Pike averted her eyes and nodded. Sarah wanted to say something more to her — to show her the full hand — but it was too late for that.

"You know, Sarah," Miss Pike said, a little more confidently, "you must think of this as an opportunity for reformation. A chance to redeem yourself before God and in the eyes of society."

Sarah smiled at her cheerlessly, thinking

of how the prisoners had regarded her in the dining hall. "You're very good, Miss Pike, but I doubt others will allow me the opportunity to redeem myself, as you put it. I might be on another continent, but they won't forget who I am or what I was convicted of."

Miss Pike busied herself with folding the items of clothing she had brought with her. "You don't know that; really, you don't. Lord Russell and his imbecile advisers might not understand the importance of second chances, but remember that you're going to a place where many are trying to escape their past. There would be no future for the colony if people were forever judged by their previous crimes. You must trust in God and you must do what you can to set things right."

"I will do my best," Sarah said, but she doubted one could ever really escape the past. She had tried to shed the abuse of her childhood, but had become entangled in a relationship defined by violence and humiliation. She had wanted to be a good mother to George to cancel out the sins of her own mother, but now she was deserting him altogether. It was as if the damage within her radiated outward, drawing in and scarring everything around.

She picked up the dress that Miss Pike had brought. It was of the same calico fabric as the garment that had been passed to the jury box during the trial. *"Clear proof, we say, that the prisoner Gale knew about the murder and helped to conceal it."*

No, while she would like to think that you could simply turn a page and begin writing on a blank white sheet, Sarah suspected that your deeds followed you wherever you went, like a shadow.

That night, as she slept, Sarah felt warm water washing about her bare feet. She was on a boat: not a convict ship but a steamer of the type that carried people down the Thames. The boat was sinking and people all around her were filling vessels with water to bail it out. Some used bowls and buckets, but others used strange objects: old shoes, silver teapots, feathered hats, and wooden boxes. Rosina was there too, using a coal scoop to sweep water over the side as fast as she could. She was weeping and begging Sarah to help: "We'll all go down!" she was crying. For George was beside her, she realized, clinging to her wet skirts, the water reaching to his knees. Sarah searched about desperately, but she could find nothing with which to catch the water. She tried using her own hands, but the water slipped through her fingers and the boat sank lower and lower until the water was up to her chest and she had to pick George up to keep his head above the water.

It was only at that point that she realized that the water was red. Indeed, it was not water at all, but blood. Warm blood.

32

"That Testimony which is delivered to induce a Jury to believe, or not to believe the matter of Fact in Issue, is called in Law EVIDENCE, because thereby the Jury may, out of many Matters of Fact, *Evidere veritatem;* that is, *see clearly the truth,* of which they are proper Judges."

— *The Englishman's Right: A Dialogue between a Barrister at Law and a Juryman,* Sir John Hawles, 1764

The letter arrived first thing. Edmund walked quickly through the Temple Gardens, the letter in his hand, rehearsing in his mind what he would say to Sarah in the same way that he might prepare his speech before a day in court. He found, however, that he could not form coherent sentences.

He announced himself at the prison lodge and waited in the legal visitors' room, watching solicitors hunched over their papers, speaking in low voices to their sullen or weeping clients. Through the narrow window, Edmund saw morning shadows stretch their tall fingers up the gray stone wall opposite. Pigeons cooed in the yard. A clock ticked loudly.

Ten minutes passed, twenty. He began to grow anxious. Was it possible Sarah had been taken onto the ship early? That he had missed his last chance to see her? Or perhaps something else had happened. Maybe Rook had attacked again.

But at last she appeared, even frailer and more delicate than before, walking behind a heavily built warder with a fleshy face. The warder met his eye as she led Sarah to him, seeming to wish to convey something to him. "Here she is," was all she said.

Edmund pulled out a chair for Sarah, opposite him.

Once Sarah had sat down, Edmund drew his own chair in close. "I bring news."

She looked up at him with such hope and trust that he felt that his heart might burst. "The Home Secretary has agreed that George should travel with you."

Sarah closed her eyes and put her hands over her face. "Thank God," she whispered. "Thank God." She began to cry, silently.

He drew out his silk pocket handkerchief

and pushed it into Sarah's hand. After a moment, she pressed it to her face and held it there as she tried to calm herself.

They sat for a minute or two without speaking. He could smell her — an animal smell mixed with lavender — and hear her breathing above the beating of his own heart, which was now so loud that he had the ridiculous idea that she could hear it.

When she spoke, her voice was cracked. "Edmund, I don't know how to thank you."

It was the first time she had used his Christian name. It struck him full force in the chest like a fist.

"It wasn't only me," Edmund said. "Miss Pike's petition, your sister's letter . . ."

She shook her head. "I'm not just talking about that," she said. "You've done more for me than I ever anticipated — more than I deserved. And I know that, when I last saw you, I must have seemed very ungrateful."

"I never expected gratitude. That's not why I did this. I wanted . . . I wanted . . ." He floundered. "Well, at first I just wanted to solve the riddle — to work out why you had kept silent. To prove myself clever, I suppose. But then I realized that it wasn't about me: it was about you. It was about getting justice for you. And in that I've failed utterly. If I'd made a better case —"

"Please," she said. "Please don't blame yourself. You saved me from the rope. You have ensured my son will travel with me. And I lied to you."

"You lied because you were terrified; I understand that. What's important is that you told me the truth eventually. I'm just sorry I raised your expectations. It was naive of me to think that a full pardon was possible. I realize now that it was all about public opinion, not about justice; about giving the appearance of fairness rather than the thing itself. I shouldn't speak like this, of course, but this is perhaps the last time we'll meet, and I wanted to be entirely honest with you."

She met his eye and then looked away. For some time there was just the sound of others talking, pens whispering on paper, chairs scraping, the clock ticking. Sarah sat with her head bowed.

"This isn't necessarily the end," Edmund said. "If I could find something that would support your story, it might be possible to get the Home Secretary or perhaps the authorities in Australia to look at your case again. And if you were to be granted a conditional pardon, you could return to England. I won't stop looking — I promise."

He put his hand over hers.

Sarah raised her eyes to his. "You must forget about me. You must return to your old life."

What life? Edmund wanted to ask. "I can't do that," was all he said.

"You think you can't now, but you'll forget all this soon enough. You'll have other cases."

"Not like this," Edmund said. "Besides, the Home Secretary is unlikely to give me a further commission after I dared to question his judgment in this one." He gave a wry smile.

"This has damaged your reputation, hasn't it?" Sarah said. "I've spoiled things for you."

"No, no. There are those who mutter that I shouldn't have recommended a pardon, but they can say what they like. They don't know the truth."

Sarah closed her eyes for a second. When she reopened them, a tear rolled down her right cheek. Edmund resisted the urge to reach out and stop its descent with his finger. There was so much he wanted to say to her and yet, even now, when it was almost too late, he could not bring himself to tell her how he felt. He was not even sure he would be able to verbalize it were he to try.

"Time!" Miss Sowerton shouted. "Prisoners, move to the doorway!"

"Sarah . . . listen," Edmund said, still desperately trying to find the right words to convey what he meant.

Sarah was looking away. "Edmund," she said, "if you should ever see things differently, if you should ever cease to think well of me, please remember that I wanted . . . that I've always greatly respected you."

"And I you," Edmund said. "But, Sarah," he folded his hand over hers, "I won't come to see things differently. I've never seen so clearly." They were not the right words, but maybe they were enough.

Sarah smiled: a thin, sad smile. She squeezed his hand and then rose to leave. One last glance, and she was gone.

■ ■ ■ ■ ■

Part Three:
Crures

■ ■ ■ ■ ■

33

"On the 26th June 1837 the first prisoners were received on board at Woolwich to the number of thirty one with seven of their children from Newgate and from that time to the 12th July we almost daily continued to receive from the various prisons in England and Wales to the amount in all, of one hundred and forty three prisoners and twenty nine children, the last eleven and one child arriving from Newgate."
— from the medical journal of Surgeon Superintendent William Leyson, 1837

They started out just after dawn, leaving Newgate in silence, their feet crunching on the gravel as they were led to the Black Maria coaches. On the silent streets, the horses' hooves rang out and the wheels whispered, carrying the prisoners on toward the Thames. On Ludgate Street, a driver brushed the gleaming coat of his horse. By

Puddle Dock, a maid emptied a bucket into the roadway and then looked up to watch the cabs pass.

The women were led down to lighters on the Thames, London's silent highway where the water sloshed darkly. None of them spoke. The lighters glided ghostlike along the murky water, past Queenhithe Stairs and Southwark Bridge; past mudlarks — small, dirt-spattered children — already starting out to find some treasure in the stinking riverside mud. The convicts stared at the black water below and listened to it lapping against the piers and the echoing arches of the bridges of the Thames.

As the lighters slid farther down the river, the women heard the occasional cry of the last revelers of the night before and the sounds of the first barrows and carriages making their way past shuttered windows.

Just after the Thames bent away from Greenwich, the hulk of a huge ship cast a long shadow on the water. As the lighter-men slowed the boats and moved toward the hulk, the women realized that the enormous dark shape that rose out of the water before them was their vessel, a three-hundred-ton barque, square-rigged.

Built in Calcutta from fine Burmese teak and sheathed in copper, she was sold on the stocks to Henry Wellesley, First Lord Cowley, and now bore his name. In her fifty-year career she had borne many cargos: wheat from Carolina, sugar from Grenada, spices from the East Indies, timber from Norway. Now, reduced to a convict carrier, the ship was moored at Woolwich Quay, straining like a frustrated beast against the ropes that tethered her to the bank. Each of her three masts — foremast, mainmast, and mizzen, moving from bow to stern — was rigged to carry three square sails, which flapped idly against her masts.

The well-scrubbed quarterdeck was enclosed by a brass rail that glinted in the early morning light. Two of the private guards stood talking. The others remained in their living quarters, which had been built into the area below. On the forecastle, between the mainmast and the bow, half a dozen seamen were playing at cards, smoking, or watching the fishing lines hanging over the catheads. Gulls screeched around the vessel, passing under the stern windows and appearing again at the bows.

The bottom deck of the ship, the orlop, was usually reserved for cargo. For this trip, however, it had been adapted. Partitions had been erected to create three self-contained areas. Forward and aft were the stores, stacked with provisions for the voyage: fresh water, ale, brandy and rum, cutlings, molasses, salt beef and hams, fowl in pickle, potted herrings, spices, oatmeal, sugar, and tea.

The middle partition, between the stores, was by far the largest. The hatches that led to it were fitted with a grating that could be bolted down from above. Deep shelves had been attached to each side of the hull and covered with sack cloth. Here, in the airless dark, the convict women and their children would sleep.

Sarah's eyes followed the length of the boat, crossing the portholes, closed and silent. Some of the other women were weeping quietly. They descended unsteadily from the lighters and waited in a huddle on the quay.

Then Sarah heard a sound that seemed entirely out of place: children's voices. She saw that a small group were advancing toward them, picking their way through the mud. Near the front was Rosina, wearing her best dress and a straw bonnet. In one hand she carried a bag; in the other, she held George's hand.

"Rosina," Sarah said when they were near enough to hear her. Close up, she could see that her sister's eyes were red with weeping, her complexion blotched pink and white.

Rosina put her arms around Sarah and then pulled back, her hands still on Sarah's shoulders, to look at her face.

"My sister. My big sister," she said. "I can't believe this is happening. It can't happen. It's not too late, you know."

Sarah shook her head sharply. "No, Rosina."

George stood next to them. Sarah squatted down to his level and held his hand in both of hers.

"Hello, darling boy. I'm so sorry I've been away for so long. But we're going to be together now."

George squinted at her, confused.

Rosina bent down too so that all three were crouching close together.

"Georgie, remember that present we got for your mama?" George looked at her absently for a few seconds and then reached into his breeches and removed a coin, which he held in his closed palm for a moment before offering it hesitatingly to Sarah. The old King's head had been rubbed away and, in its place, a message had been inscribed in tiny lettering: "From your sister, who will always be with you, in lightness, and in dark."

The words faded as Sarah's eyes clouded

with tears. How had it come to this?

Groves appeared at Sarah's side. "You have five minutes before you leave," she said gruffly. "You must put your things on the boat."

Sarah stood up. George attached himself to her leg.

"It's all right. I'm not leaving you," she said.

Five minutes. What do you say when you have five minutes to speak to your sister — the one person who has ever truly loved you and you know you will never see her again?

"I've packed a bag for you," Rosina said, passing it to Sarah. "George's clothes, his red spinning top, and his doll; some food too: apples, boiled beef, and a loaf. And here, this is for you." She passed her a plum-colored woolen cloak.

"But this is yours, Rosina."

"Well, then, it can remind you of me." She kept her eyes on the muddy ground. "I can't bear it, Sarah. God, I can't bear it."

Sarah put her arms around her sister's neck. Rosina's sobs were loud in her ear, her tears wet against her own cheeks, and she gripped tight to her sister's juddering body, unable to recall when anyone had last held her like this. George clung to both of them. And that was how they stayed for their five minutes.

When Sarah moved away from Rosina she saw that there were several other family groups saying their good-byes: men with tired, drooping faces; older children weeping. But there were some women whom no one had come to see off. Rook's friend, Mary Boltwood, stood on her own, her arms clutched around herself, staring out at the riverbank. Maybe it was better not to have anyone to leave behind.

Rosina bent down to George and kissed him on the cheek. "You must be a brave boy for your mother," she said, her breath catching. "You're going on a long journey."

"Are you coming too?" he asked.

"No, poppet." Sarah could see Rosina was trying not to cry again.

George looked intently at his mother and then at his aunt. "But we'll see you when we come back?"

Rosina looked despairingly at Sarah.

"Yes," Sarah said. "We'll see her again." Sometimes it was easier to lie.

Sarah felt a firm hand on her shoulder.

"It's time now, Gale."

When Sarah looked in Groves' face, she was surprised to see that the warder's eyes were full of tears. For a moment she thought perhaps it was the stinging wind, but then something occurred to her.

"It was you, wasn't it, Miss Groves?"

"What was me?"

"It was you who got me out of the dark cells. It was you who got the message to Mr. Fleetwood."

Groves met her eye. "You'll have to look out for yourself out there," she said. "Better than you have here. Now say good-bye to your sister."

Sarah turned back and hugged Rosina one last time. "This is the right thing," she murmured in her ear. "It couldn't have been any other way."

A grim-faced guard led them up a plank and onto the huge vessel, George gripping Sarah's hand tightly. The water, as she looked down, was mud-choked and still, the color of clay. Once they were on deck, she stared back to the small group waiting on the quay. Groves waited with them, watching, but not waving. Rosina stood to the right of the clutch of people, a lonely figure in green.

Sarah lifted George up onto her hip and pressed her face against the side of his, feeling the brush of his lashes on her cheek. Together they waved until a bell rang out the hour and they were herded with the other prisoners into the darkness below decks.

34

"Eyes will not see when the heart wishes them to be blind. Desire conceals truth as darkness does the earth."
— Lucius Annaeus Seneca

The whistle screamed, gray plumes of smoke blew past his window, a shower of smuts hit the roof of the carriage, and they were off. Thanks to Morris, Edmund was traveling to Birmingham to prosecute licensing offenses — dull as ditchwater, but a reliable line of work. Moreover, it got him away from home, where he felt increasingly like a prisoner, kept under constant observation. He knew that Bessie watched him and worried. He knew that she perceived his obsession but said nothing about it. Her gaze made him feel a heavy, sickening guilt. It was best to stay away.

The train sped past the jagged sides of houses torn down to make way for the railway, past smoking factories and brick chimneys and on toward the countryside. Occasionally, Edmund glimpsed fragments of other people's lives: a woman sitting in a doorway feeding a baby, a group of ragged children, waving.

Edmund turned his attention to the pamphlet on his lap: "Emigration to New South Wales." He told himself that the research was for Rosina. In part, it was. However, as he read more about the Government scheme, he increasingly thought it might be an opportunity for him. London was awash with criminal barristers, all vying for scraps of work. Australia, on the other hand, had crime aplenty and very few lawyers. Surely, out there it would be much easier to succeed.

Edmund stared from the window at the trees and ditches and lines of wooden houses. The journey itself would be the hardest part: he had heard that the vessels were overcrowded, the food terrible, and the voyage long. Better — far better — than a convict ship, however. He felt a crushing sensation in his chest at the thought of Sarah boarding the ship with George. Miss Pike had assured him that conditions were much improved: the boats were of a better quality, the prisoners were no longer kept shackled below decks, and — since surgeon-superintendents had been put in charge of the prisoners' health — most arrived alive. Many still spoke, however, of the lechery of the crew; the rapid spread of disease; and the survival, despite the new regime, of the old breed of captains who flogged or starved their convict cargo.

As the train hurtled through a tunnel, Edmund glimpsed the outline of his features in the train window. He should have thought of a way to save her.

When Edmund returned to London that evening, he made the mistake of broaching the subject of Australia with Bessie.

"Thirty-six pounds for a man and wife, and five pounds for each child aged one to seven."

Bessie did not respond, but continued to dissect her broiled chicken.

"It is said," Edmund continued, "that there are very good opportunities for criminal barristers out there."

"I'm sure there are," Bessie said. "It's full of criminals. All the more reason not to go there."

"That's very shortsighted of you, Bessie."

"Is that so, Edmund? And why this sudden enthusiasm for Australia? Why not

America, for example? Or France?"

"Their legal systems there are quite different. I would need to retrain."

"I see. And of course this has nothing to do with Miss Gale."

Edmund felt his cheeks grow hot. "No, Bessie, it has nothing to do with her, save to the extent that it was because of her sister that I was reading of the scheme in the first place. I'm simply raising it as a possibility."

"Very well. I'm simply rejecting it as a possibility."

"Because of Miss Gale?"

"Because it's on the other side of the earth and is full of people *like* Miss Gale."

"As we have discussed previously," Edmund said quietly, "it is in fact my view that Miss Gale is innocent."

Bessie attacked her chicken with additional vigor. "Well, evidently she was good at acting the victim."

"What do you mean by that?" Edmund snapped.

"She was an actress — you knew that, didn't you?"

An icy shiver ran up Edmund's back. "That doesn't make her a liar."

Bessie looked up from her plate. "She used to be part of a troupe in the East End. It was in the Kent papers while I was staying with my sister."

There was a longer silence. Then Bessie said softly: "You didn't know, did you?"

Edmund took a drink of his wine. "No, she didn't mention it. But then I didn't ask about all of her previous positions. There were more pressing matters to discuss."

Edmund stared at the candle flame, the flare of white within red. When he looked at his wife, Edmund saw that she was gazing at him with what might almost have been pity.

After dinner, Edmund took a cup of spiced wine to his room and changed into his evening attire. The Season was still in full swing and there was only so long he could avoid it, and his father.

Standing before the looking glass to tie his black satin cravat, Edmund wondered if what Bessie had said was correct. Could she be inventing stories merely to rile him, or had Sarah really been an actress? She had never mentioned it, but perhaps she had not thought it relevant. Strictly speaking, it was not.

Edmund took a hansom cab to Hanover Square and waited in line to be announced by the liveried footman, staring at the austere family portraits and fine porcelain figures that adorned the hallway. As soon as he entered the ballroom, he knew it had been a mistake to come. The glittering room was awash with women overdressed in white crepe and lace pelerines, and dull men, fitted out in doeskin breeches, velvet waistcoats, and bright-gold buttons. Footmen in powder-blue jackets circulated the room with trays of glistening glasses, and a string quartet played a quadrille. Within a few minutes of his entering the ballroom, his father had clasped his upper arm and steered him into the refreshment room and toward a man with very little hair and a wide face the color of a boiled ham.

"Edmund, this is Montague Squires. A great friend of mine — and," he added in Edmund's ear, "adviser to the Lord Chancellor on judicial appointments."

"Ah, the famous son. Arthur has told me you've been delving into the criminal underworld," the ham-faced man said, looking him over as if to check for dirt or blood. "Tell us: are the women of Newgate really so wicked and depraved as is claimed?"

Was this it now, Edmund wondered. Was he to be an exhibit? The criminal *pièce de résistance*?

"Many are more sinned against than sinning, I believe."

"Yes, I understand that you recommended that the Gale woman be pardoned entirely. Can that be true?"

Edmund sighed inwardly. "Yes, that's correct. But," he said quietly, looking at his father out of the corner of his eye, "it was not my recommendation that he followed."

Edmund managed to slip away to the punch bar, but there too he was accosted by people wishing to talk to him about Newgate and the penal system and the moral depravity of the lower classes. A man with luxuriant dark whiskers tried to engage him in conversation about phrenology, claiming that the criminal mind demonstrated itself in the shape of the skull.

"The low-intentioned have low brows and a broader forehead," the man assured him. "The men tend to have an ape-like cast to their face."

"And what about female criminals?" Edmund said, not bothering to keep the sarcasm from his voice. "Does this apply to them too?"

"Oh, yes, most certainly," the man replied. "Indeed, the female criminals are the most easily recognizable by dint of their animal features and dark complexion."

Edmund pictured Sarah — her fine nose

and milk-white skin. He had not been aware until that moment of quite how much he missed her.

He walked out of the ballroom and down a corridor leading to a large dark room lined with glass display cases. Stepping closer to them, he saw that the cases were filled with insects — butterflies, moths, and glossy beetles, each stuck to white cardboard with a pin through the heart. Little nameplates were fixed beneath each specimen — *Mantis religiosa, Actias luna, Latrodectus mactans*. He had the distinct feeling that someone was watching him. Turning, he saw only the round glass eyes of a stuffed white fox staring blankly at him out of its glass case. A shadow moved against the back wall.

"I should have known to find you among the dead things."

"Father. Are you following me?"

"What are you doing wandering about back here?"

"I . . . came the wrong way."

His father leaned against the wall, a crystal tumbler in his hand.

"Bad news about that woman — Gale. But at least you spared her the Newgate jig, eh?"

Edmund did not respond.

"They were never going to let her off entirely, Edmund. You should have seen that. This is perhaps the best outcome."

"And I suppose that's what you advised Lord Russell." Rage welled up within him but he managed to keep his voice steady. "Tell me, what made you think it was appropriate to interfere?"

"Interfere?"

"Lord Russell told me you approved of his decision."

"Edmund, I simply responded to a question John asked me at a dinner we attended. I could hardly have refused to answer."

"What was the question?"

"Something along the lines of: did I agree that the common man would be angered by the pardoning of a woman who had helped to conceal a murder?"

"And how did you answer?"

"I said I could see that, in circumstances where the individual had not been entirely exonerated, the public might balk at such a decision."

"So because one cannot show that someone is innocent, they are guilty? Do you know *nothing* about the criminal law?" The blood rushed to his cheeks.

"Edmund, Edmund. It is about appearances, is it not? Lord Russell's question was

426

not about the rights or wrongs of the matter, but about whether it would *seem* to the man in the street that justice had been done. His view, with which I agreed, was that most people would think it wrong to grant an absolute pardon to a woman whom they perceived to have aided, or at least turned a blind eye to, another woman's murder. I suggested, however, that they might accept transportation as an appropriate punishment. It was mere conversation."

"No, it was a woman's life."

"And she is alive, is she not? You spared her the gallows, Edmund. Don't forget that."

"Had it not been for your intervention, she might have been spared a terrible journey aboard a convict ship. She might have been *here,* in London!"

"For heaven's sakes, Edmund, don't be so naive. John wasn't going to simply free her, no matter how good your report. He was minded to hang her regardless. You should thank me for recommending a middle way."

"*Thank* you? Thank you for what, exactly? You leaned over my shoulder for the entirety of the investigation and then, when my report evidently didn't meet with your approval, you went direct to Lord Russell and put forward your own views. Why didn't you just get yourself appointed to the bloody role in the first place?"

"Edmund, you have completely misinterpreted the situation."

"You claim to have recommended me to the role for the benefit of my career, and then you intentionally humiliate me, just as you always have!"

"You've had too much to drink," his father said shortly. "You are saying things you do not mean."

"On the contrary, Father. For once in my life, I'm speaking plainly to you. For once in my life, I am telling you what I actually think."

His father looked about him, as if to check that none of the dead animals in their cases had come to life to bear witness to this conversation. For a moment, he seemed poised to say something important, but he simply said, "Edmund, go home and get some rest. You'll see this very differently tomorrow."

"No," Edmund said. "I will not see it differently. It's perfectly clear what you've done. And I was a fool to have ever accepted the commission."

35

"As the credit due to a witness is founded in the first instance on general experience of human veracity, it follows that a witness who gives false testimony as to one particular, cannot be credited as to any."
— *A Practical Treatise of the Law of Evidence,* Thomas Starkie, Esq., 1833

The captain, Master Williams, was a tall, broad-shouldered man. When young, he had been considered handsome, with his regular features and ash-blond hair. Age and the sea had not been kind to him, however. His face was now angular and harsh, his eyes narrow slits of blue. He was appropriately revered and feared by his men, never drinking with them, only alone in his cabin where he kept several bottles of good madeira and port. If he had a woman or family at home, no one knew of it. He was not one for small talk. His language was all of the masts and the sails and the wind and the seas.

Some of the men who had voyaged with him years before remembered a violent temper rising like a storm when provoked. Although it did not display itself now, he gave the impression of a man keeping a tight rein on his emotions, ready to rear up and bite at any moment, should the occasion require it.

He walked toward the women, into the wind, his blue coat flapping open.

"Ladies," he said, although he knew full well they were not. And Sarah guessed, as soon as she heard his voice, at what sort of a man he was.

"Welcome aboard the *Henry Wellesley,* your home for the next five months, all being well."

As he spoke, he walked around the groups of women, who moved closer to one another.

"Quite a few sea rats, I see," he said, bending down so that his face was level with that of a boy of about eight, who clutched his mother's arm in terror.

"Well, you should know that all aboard this boat must work, no matter what their age or inclination. I'll have no dawdlers."

He scanned the wide frightened eyes of his audience, who remained silent.

"You should understand that there's a law on ship as firm as that on land. There are clear rules and clear punishments for those that break them. You will obey orders from myself and my men immediately. If you do not, you will live to regret it. I'm a fair man, but I'm also a hard man. Do not cross me."

He stopped at the break in the quarter-deck.

"I have a crew of twenty-one men working under me. I'm responsible for their direction and discipline, so if any of them misbehave — I'm sure you know what I mean — you tell me.

"We wait here for a week or so while the other convicts arrive. Then we sail via Tenerife to pick up fresh water. None of us wants to be drinking Thames water for the whole journey." He spat over the side.

"From Tenerife we make round the Cape of Good Hope and from there we cross six thousand miles of ocean without sight of land. It's a tough life on board ship, but if you follow my orders and those of my men, you'll get on well enough. I cannot, however, tolerate insubordination. You've managed to escape England with your lives. Make something of them here."

With that, he turned and strode away.

A few of the children whimpered. Rain

began to hit the surface of the river, causing the water to rise up in silver rivulets like the ridges on a washboard.

"What's this?" said the first mate. "A fight?" He was a scrawny man, all sinew and elbows, with an anemic freckled face, a pointed chin, and lank red hair.

"I won't be in her mess," Mary Boltwood shouted, pointing to Sarah. "She's a murderer!"

"Is she, now?" said the man, raising his eyebrows. "That makes a change from the thieves and whores we usually carry on board. You'll all work together and live together. Whatever you were and whatever you did in England is of no consequence. You're all the same here: you're all dirt."

Once all of the women had been divided into groups of six, they were issued with bedding and cooking and eating utensils. Each mess was given a keg and horn tumbler and a kettle for tea-making. Each woman received a bed, pillow, and single blanket plus two wooden bowls and a wooden spoon. They were also handed a bundle of clothing. Sarah carried her things to her allotted bunk and laid them out: a couple of linen shifts, a cotton cap, a neckerchief, a pair of worsted stockings, a brown serge jacket, and a petticoat. An image flashed before her of Hannah Brown's wedding dress laid out across her bed: a burst of red on white.

"Beautiful, ain't it?" Hannah had said. "Cost a pretty penny, too."

"I'm sure," Sarah murmured.

"Yes," Hannah said, "it's an expensive business, as it turns out, this getting married, what with the flowers, the food, the silk stockings, and slippers. I've had to buy some of the things on credit. James's credit, if the truth be told."

Sarah made no comment.

"He'll understand, won't he?" Hannah asked. There was a catch in her voice. "I'll tell him when the time's right. I just didn't want to vex him with it before the wedding."

"Oh, yes," Sarah replied. "I'm sure all will be well."

Sarah should have felt sorry for her. She should have warned her what kind of a man James was. She should have told her to take her dress and run and run and run.

But instead she had thought, *It should be me.*

At eight o'clock they were sent to bed. In their bunk, Sarah and George lay close together, listening to the unfamiliar sounds of the timbers creaking and the wind singing in the ropes.

"Is it ghosts, Mama?" George said after a time.

She hugged him closer to her, marveling at the warmth and wonder of him, breathing in his little-boy smell. "No, darling. I know it sounds strange out there, but it's just the wind and the water. We're quite safe."

"Will you tell me a story?" he asked.

Sarah thought for a moment. "There was a little boy called George," she whispered, "and he was very brave."

Drawing upon the stories she remembered from her own childhood — the stories she had whispered to Rosina in the dark — she told him about a boy who traveled the seas and encountered giant whales and beautiful mermaids, who found crystal caves and pirates' treasure. She whispered until she could feel his body relax and hear his breathing slow. Then she lay back next to him, staring into the gloom. Was it deceitful to pretend this was an adventure when she knew that they would encounter not mythical beasts, but danger, deprivation, and storms? Maybe she was as bad as her own mother, telling her daughters that their flight to London was an exciting trip, not

the beginning of their descent into the gutter.

Sarah thought of Rosina as she had last
seen her. She tried to print her face on her
memory so that she might never lose it, but
it was Hannah Brown's split face that came
to her in the darkness, her wound as it was
described at trial: the crescent shape of the
moon.

36

"Let us have no lies, stories, fibs, or whatever you may call them. There are no white lies, they are all black. Any trying to deceive is a lie. Drop all lying and deceiving, or it will be a habit that will grow on you. 'Speak out the truth fearlessly, and shame the Devil,' people say. Why shame him? because he is the father of lies."

— *Loving and Fighting: Addresses Delivered in Sunday and Ragged Schools,* George E. A. Shirley, 1871

The main room in Peele's Coffee House was furnished like a drawing room, with mahogany booths, sanded floors and dark wood paneling. Newspapers, magazines, and books were piled on the shelves. Several men sat smoking cigars and reading. Edmund took his usual place and nodded to the servant, who returned a few minutes later with a cup of coffee and a copy of the

Morning Chronicle, freshly ironed.

"In fact," Edmund said, "it's not today's news I wish to read but that from some months ago. I understand that you keep such copies?"

The man led him to a shelf at the back of the room, which held carefully cataloged copies of regional newspapers. After some time, Edmund found the article from the *West Kent Guardian* that he was looking for.

The female prisoner Gale seems perfectly overcome with anxiety. Little is known of her previous history. It is said, however, that some years ago she was a supernumerary at one of the east-end theatres, and that she then went by the name of Winston or Wiston. She afterward was "under the protection" of a well-known barrister.

So Bessie had not invented the story. Sarah had been an actress. Of course, he had not specifically asked her whether she had worked as anything other than a nurse and seamstress. He had intentionally not directed the questions about her past too narrowly, but had instead allowed her to talk about herself. He had always been told that the fewer questions one asked, the more open the interviewee was likely to be. In this case, however, it seemed that the interviewee had selectively cut pieces of information. Why would she have done that? To avoid admitting she had fallen into prostitution? The line between actress and whore was often a thin one, and it was quite possible that she had wanted to avoid any discussion about that part of her life.

Edmund wondered too about the barrister referred to in the article. If even the *West Kent Guardian* could refer to him as "well known" it must be someone of whom he himself had heard. Perhaps that was why Sarah had not mentioned this either.

He told himself these omissions did not matter. As his father had said, everyone lied. That she had not told him these things did not mean that she had been dishonest about the murder itself. And, Edmund reflected, who was to say that the information the newspaper had printed was correct? The mere fact that something was written down did not make it true. Many of the stories that had been printed about Sarah and Greenacre were simply lies.

Still, it would not hurt to find out who this barrister was, if indeed he existed at all.

There was no journalist's name on the newspaper article — no indication as to who had written the piece. He had an idea who would know, however. Glancing about the room to check that no one was watching, Edmund ripped the page from the newspaper and folded it into his pocket.

"Am I wrong in thinking, Morris, that you occasionally drink with journalists?"

They were sitting by the fountain in the heart of the Middle Temple watching little sparrows wash and shake themselves, the water springing in silver droplets from their feathers.

"You are not, sir," Morris said, drawing on his pipe. "I like to damp my mug in a wide range of circles."

"Know anyone from the *West Kent Guardian*?"

"Don't think so. Why d'you ask?"

"One of their journalists wrote an article about Miss Gale. I would be interested to talk to that person. It might be in their interests too."

Morris raised his eyebrows. "And what might it say, this harticle?"

Edmund took the crumpled page from the pocket of his waistcoat and handed it to Morris, who read it slowly, following the words with his forefinger.

"You think 'er being an actress means

she's been playing a part for you — is that it?"

"I'm more interested in the fact she was supposedly under the protection of a barrister. She didn't tell me that. It may be nothing, of course."

Morris nodded slowly. "This is for yer own information, is it?"

"It is."

"I'll see what I can do, then," Morris said, folding the piece of newspaper into his own waistcoat pocket.

Edmund dipped his fingers into the water, and a sprinkle of goldfish swam to the surface. "I'd be obliged if you could be discreet."

"Mr. Fleetwood, I am always discreet. I see nothing. I hear nothing."

The gleaming maroon stagecoach shot out of the yard, several small, tattered boys running behind it and gradually tailing off as the coach picked up speed.

Edmund sat on the outside, next to the driver, listening to the brass work on the horses' harnesses jangling like little bells as they cantered over the stones, past dustmen and milk women with pails, past men walking early to work and drunkards stumbling late to their beds. Out of London to where the roads opened up, past market gardens and the outlines of new houses, all the while keeping up a pace that turned the passing sights into a blur of white and gray, the stagecoach a streak of red through it.

At Tunbridge Wells, the coach stopped at the Rose and Crown Inn to change horses. As the horses were unharnessed and taken to the trough, steam rising from their silken backs, Edmund went into the inn and bought a hot meat pudding and a pint of ale. A short time later, they set off again, with fresh horses, for Rochester. He took out of his pocket the slip of paper that Morris had handed him the previous evening and which stated only: "Ezekiel Breakspeer, Rochester, Kent."

When they arrived at the town, Edmund descended from the coach and looked about him at the High Street lined with redbrick buildings, and the ancient crumbling castle rising in the distance. Few people were about so he entered the Victoria and Bull Hotel, where he sought directions from the publican. Following the road, he came at last to a shabby cottage with a bowed front and dingy little windows. Outside the house a woman was feeding a clutch of hens.

"Ezekiel?" she said. "He'll be writing at this hour, I should think. Upstairs."

Edmund took the steps to the garret room, where he found a slight man with quick black eyes sitting at a small desk in a smoke-filled room, puffing on a cigar.

"Mr. Breakspeer?"

"That's me. And who might you be?"

Edmund stepped into the room. "I'm investigating, or was investigating, the Edge-ware Road murder. I came across this article that I understood you wrote." He removed the scrap of paper from his pocket and passed it into the journalist's ink-stained fingers.

"Yes, I remember."

"I wanted to find out if you knew who the barrister was — the one whom you refer to as having protected Miss Gale."

"Ah," the journalist said. "Well, there's a reason I didn't print his name. Libel. Trouble. And for the same reason I'll require some persuasion to provide you with his name now, particularly as I notice you haven't given me yours."

Edmund had brought some persuasion in the form of a one-pound note, which he laid on the man's desk.

Ezekiel nodded. "Very well. Fleetwood."

"I'm sorry?"

"Fleetwood," Breakspeer repeated, pocket-ing the money. "He's a senior barrister in the Middle Temple. Apparently he's looked after her for several years, one way or another."

Edmund was silent for a moment.

"And his first name?" he asked softly.

"Arthur. Arthur Fleetwood. Maybe you've heard of him."

37

"However this may be, there can be no doubt of the fact that by some means or other men contract at a very early age and retain through life a strong disposition to believe what they are told."
— *A General View of the Criminal Law of England,* Sir James Fitzjames Stephen, 1863

By the time Edmund returned to London, it was Saturday evening. His father was not at home, the butler informed him. A crown and a quiet word later, however, Edmund knew where to find him. He walked through Haymarket and the east end of Piccadilly and the Quadrant, down to Windmill Street, where the pavement swarmed with opera-hatted gentlemen, beggars, prostitutes, and black-cloaked barristers. Within a short time, he reached his destination on the corner of Little Argyll Street and King

Street: the Argyll Rooms. Edmund climbed the stairs to the second floor so that he could look down from the balcony onto the huge ballroom, fifty feet long, hung with crimson flock wallpaper, and lighted by three chandeliers. Below him, dancing men and women swayed and swirled in reds and purples and blues.

He attracted the attention of a serving-man: "Have you seen Arthur Fleetwood?"

"I couldn't say, sir."

"Oh, come now. He's here somewhere." Edmund handed the man a bright coin. The evening was proving to be an expensive one. The serving man led him into an exquisitely furnished anteroom. From the center of the ceiling, a chandelier dripped crystal, the bright droplets reflecting in the mirrors on each wall. Dark velvet ottomans and matching chairs were placed around the room with colored cushions scattered upon them. Edmund saw his father sitting in the far corner of the room, his arm around a woman in mauve taffeta. As he approached, his father removed his arm and stood up. He was evidently about to make some pleasantry but saw the expression on Edmund's face.

"Edmund. Let's not talk here."

"Why not? It seems a suitable location:

full of corruption and artifice."

His father looked about him, uncomfortably. "It would be better if —"

"If what? If I didn't raise the matter of you keeping Sarah Gale as your whore?"

His father's female companion touched his arm and left them together.

"Edmund," his father said in a hushed tone, "I understand why you're angry, but please be aware that I had your best interests at heart. And hers."

Edmund gave a short bark of a laugh. "Oh, of course. Just as you had my best interests at heart when you duped me and Jack into leaving our mother all those years ago."

"I hardly see what that has to do with it."

"Don't you? You've used me in this to further your own interests just as you used me back then to distress Mother. And the hypocrisy of it! You cast Mother out for her moral failings, and then embarked on a relationship with a woman who, in your own words, was little more than a prostitute."

"Edmund, please keep your voice down."

"Good God, is that still all you care about? What people *think*? Your precious reputation?"

"And what do I have, Edmund, aside from that? What do you think would happen to my reputation were it to be discovered that I once consorted with a prostitute-turned-prisoner? I had to keep it quiet. I also couldn't stand by and see her sent to the gallows. So I persuaded John that the matter needed to be investigated."

"And then you suggested that he appoint me to the role of investigator so that you could keep a close watch on my progress and influence my decision-making."

"That's not exactly how it —"

Edmund cut him off. "I couldn't fathom it at first. Why would you claim to me that she was a woman of lax morals, a woman capable of doing anything to suit her own ends? But then of course I understood: you knew that would steer me toward the opposite conclusion."

"You have always been contrary, Edmund," his father said quietly. "And you've always sided with the weaker party."

Edmund shook his head in disbelief. "You know, the amusing thing is that I thought I'd been selected for the job because of my legal skill and powers of analysis. I now realize I was chosen for my naivety. Well, it turns out you were right. She had me. I believed her."

His father took him gently by the shoulder. "Edmund, my dear boy, calm down, will you? Of course that's not the reason. I've always respected your legal acumen; that's why I suggested you. You and I both know she's innocent."

Edmund remained silent, his breathing fast and shallow.

"For God's sake, Edmund. Sarah is many things, but she's no murderess and no conspirator. You saw that just as well as I did. And did I think you might be sympathetic to her? Well, yes, I did. You've always been a softhearted boy; you've always liked to rail against injustice. And I knew when we spoke after the trial that you recognized the evidence against her was weak."

"You knew I would be taken in by her." Edmund moved nearer to him. "And I was. I truly was. But now my eyes have been opened."

"Edmund, you are wonderfully mistaken. You must consider your position carefully. You know that if you report this, my career will be finished. Yours, too, perhaps."

"How dare you threaten me?" Edmund stepped farther toward his father so that their faces were inches apart.

His father spoke softly, almost inaudibly. "I'm not threatening you, Edmund. I'm simply pointing out facts. If you go to the Home Secretary about this, he will have me disbarred, and he will think you a fool. And what will happen to Sarah? They may reopen the whole investigation. What effect do you think that will have on her?"

"It strikes me that she is a good deal more resilient than she might at first have appeared."

"She's a good woman, Edmund."

"So you say. What else have you been hiding from me?" Edmund said. "Have you taken the liberty of doctoring the evidence? Bribing the witnesses, perhaps?"

His father puffed his cheeks and blew them out. "No, Edmund. I have done no such thing. If you've missed anything it's because you've failed to see it. Just as you've failed to see that a trip to Australia is better than a hanging. Do you honestly think I have it in me to go about destroying evidence or coaching witnesses?"

Edmund stared at him, unblinking. "I think you're capable of doing anything in order to protect yourself and your own reputation." He picked up his hat from the table. "The irony is that none of this would have happened if you'd looked after Sarah properly."

"What in the devil's name do you mean?"

"If she hadn't been near destitute, do you think she would have stayed with Greenacre? She had nowhere else to go and no one else to turn to."

His father looked suddenly ill, the color sapped from his face. "I did support her at the beginning. But it became too difficult. I had other priorities."

Edmund snorted. "What? Other mistresses? You abnegated your responsibility to Sarah just as you did Mother. You left her at the mercy of a tyrant. And then, instead of supporting her publicly, instead of going to Lord Russell directly and speaking in her favor — as you could easily have done — you drag me into your grubby subterfuge. All in order to keep your name out of the gutter. You're little better than Greenacre." He turned to leave.

"Oh, Edmund," said his father weakly. "You're in love with her, aren't you?"

Edmund did not answer. He walked back out into the noisy street, his ears hearing not the noise of the crowds but the words of Jelinger Spinks.

"Take nothing on its looks; take everything on evidence. Even the things you think you know."

Once back at his chambers, Edmund closed the door to his study, cursed at his buttons, and threw off his jacket, leaving it lying on the floor. How could he not have seen it? He had always known that his father acted only in his own interests, so he should have guessed that he had a very particular reason for recommending him for this case. And Sarah: she must have known who he was when they first met, and yet she had said nothing. She had deceived him right from the start. How much of what followed had been lies? All he had was Sarah's word that she had been coerced into remaining silent, and, thinking back, was that even what she had said? He unlocked his bureau and searched frantically for the interview notes. Finally he located the correct notebook and the correct page. Reading back over his scribblings, he saw that what she had in fact said was that she had "no choice." No choice but to do what?

A chill ran through him as the knowledge seeped in. He had allowed himself to see what he wanted to believe, to be guided by what he wanted to be the truth, rather than what was. And it was he who wrote the words in the affidavit and report, not her; he who mangled the information to present the picture he believed was right.

Edmund opened the top drawer of the bureau and took out a decanter of French brandy. He removed the crystal plug, poured a large measure into a tumbler, and took a strong gulp, relieved momentarily by the burn hitting the back of his throat. He slumped down onto the sofa, the tumbler in his hands. He had been chosen not for his knowledge but for his gullibility, and he had proved his worth by believing the story he was told. Not only believing it, in fact, but formulating it. *"He coerced you, didn't he?"*

Swirling the golden liquid in his glass, he could not quite believe it was all an act on Sarah's part. The distress had been real, palpable. It was just the reason for it that eluded him. What had really happened?

Edmund was still sitting on the sofa, revolving the possibilities in his mind, when, half an hour later, the door opened and Bessie entered with a rustle of silk and the scent of carnations: the perfume he had given her some time ago. When had he last bought her a gift, he wondered absently.

"I thought I heard you come in," she said gently. "You move around us like a spy these days."

"I'm sorry. I needed some time to think."

"To think about what?"

He looked at her tired face and thought momentarily of telling her — about his father, Sarah, everything. But of course he

452

could not. If he abandoned the pretense of being a decent lawyer and a good husband, it would all fall apart.

Bessie's eyes alighted on the mess of papers and notebooks that lay on the open bureau. "Oh, Edmund, you're not still ruminating about the Edgeware Road case, are you? I thought that was all over?"

"It is," Edmund told her. "It is over."

But it was not over. It had only just begun.

38

"A lively and fresh run fish will appear twice as big as he really is, whilst a large but dull one will sometimes deceive his pursuer into the belief that he is weak and powerless, and then in a fit of desperation he will show his real size and capabilities by breaking away with a long line towing astern."

— *Manual of British Rural Sports,*
John Henry Walsh, 1856

Sarah half woke, clinging to sleep in the warmth of her bunk and, for a few moments, could not remember where she was. She wondered at the light rocking motion and the gentle sloshing sound, muted as though she were back in the womb. Then she emerged fully from her dreams and realized where she was: caged in a floating prison.

"Larboard watch, ahoy. Rouse out there,

you sleepers. Rise and shine!" It was the boatswain, waking the crew.

A short while later came the sound of the men washing down the decks and polishing the planks: a din of stones and swabs and shouts, the wheeze of pumps, and the clash of buckets.

Next, she heard the jolt of the hatches being opened and the bang of tubs of salt water being set down for the women to wash with. At six o'clock they climbed the steps to the deck to hang out their bedding on the bulwarks and rigging. As Sarah pegged out her own sheets and breathed in the morning air, she listened to the conversation of a group of women nearby.

"It's true. She said that in Australia we'll 'ave more opportunity."

"More opportunity for whoring, most likely. That ain't my idea of opportunity."

"No, not just that. Most of those out there are the waifs and strays who've survived the passage, so they can't demand good character in the same way as your London madam. This is a chance for us, girls."

Mary Boltwood, struggling to hang out her bedding, snorted. "Don't you believe it. Prejudices and pettiness is everywhere."

An older woman reached up to help her peg the sheets. "Yes, and so's dirty linen. If they're too partic'ler 'bout who they employ, they'll be washin' it themselves."

Sarah was carried back to her final conversation with Hannah Brown, the day she had gone to collect her belongings from the house. After looking at the wedding dress, they had descended the stairs and stood awkwardly by the door, Sarah holding her bundle of things.

"You know," Hannah had said, "if you're looking for a position, I could do with some help at the laundry. It's hard work, but it pays fair."

Sarah stared at Hannah, incredulous. It was Hannah, after all, who had ensured that she and George were thrown out.

"She doesn't want you here after the wedding, I'm afraid, Sarah. She considers herself the lady of the house now."

Hannah Brown: a lady! She was an uneducated washerwoman. Did Hannah now feel guilty that Sarah was being left in biting poverty, kicked out of the house in the depths of winter with a young child, or was she mocking her? Well, she wanted neither this woman's pity, nor her derision.

"That's most kind of you, Miss Brown," she said coldly, "but I'll get by just fine on my own. I always have."

Thinking about it now, however, it seemed

to Sarah that Hannah Brown had been making a genuine offer, one woman to another, and she had been too proud to see it. Sarah reflected that she had only James's word that it was Hannah, not he, who had decided that she and George should leave. It was quite possible that it was just another of his games, setting the women against each other. In fact, it was more than possible: it was exactly the sort of thing he would do.

The women formed into their messes for breakfast. Each group was issued with tea and sugar and each person was given a pot of burgoo — gruel mixed with sugar and butter. George and Lucy ate theirs eagerly, but Sarah managed only a few mouthfuls. She was anxious now to set sail, despite the dangers that lay ahead.

During the day, the women were formed into work parties, and allotted tasks according to their skills. Former kitchen girls and maids peeled vegetables and prepared the food. Former seamstresses and bonnet-makers — Sarah included — were set to sewing new sails and mending clothes. They sat out on deck in the morning sunshine, the open air a blessed relief after the dank darkness of prison cells.

In the afternoon, twenty or so more

convicts arrived, many in a pitiful state, having traveled from all over the country shackled to the outside of prison carts. The first mate leaned against the boat, watching the women as they approached, eyeing them as he might a delivery of goods.

"Could you tell me how many more we're waiting for?" Sarah asked him.

"There's to be a hundred and forty in total, I believe," he said, turning to look at her.

"When do you think they'll all be here?"

The man's face morphed into a leer. "Keen to leave, are we? Scared they're going to think twice about letting you go?" A thin silver scar ran down his cheek, puckering at his mouth. "Don't you worry, Sarah Gale. We'll look after you."

The children had quickly sought each other out. While the adults worked, the boys and girls ran up the steps of the hold and played puss in the corner and hide-and-seek among the bunks and barrels and coils of rope.

When the pipe sounded for lunch, George returned from his new friends, breathless and red-faced. "Mama, we saw a monster."

"A monster?"

"Yes, like a man but with lots of legs."

"Where?"

"Where they put the sick people."

"The sick berth?"

"Yes. It was making this noise." George emitted a moaning sound.

"George, are you telling me lies? It's not good to lie."

He looked at her reproachfully, his pink mouth forming into a pout. "You tell lies," he said.

It was as though a cold wave had washed over her. "What do you mean, George?"

"You make things up. Like about the boy who goes to sea and finds a whale."

Sarah breathed a sigh of relief. He was talking about the stories she told him at bedtime, no more than that. "Yes, I suppose I do. But a story isn't the same thing as a lie. A story is something you make up to entertain someone. A lie is something you make up deliberately to trick them."

George looked at her in confusion. "What you told me to say about digging up the shiny things. Was that a lie?"

Sarah flinched. "Sometimes, George, only sometimes, we have to lie."

39

"There are also other situations, where it is highly necessary to deceive the adversary . . . But this mode of play should be reserved for material occasions, and not by its frequency give cause for its being suspected."

— *Advice to the Young Whist Player*,
Thomas Matthews, Esq., 1808

Dawn came on like a ghost, colorless and silent. Edmund awoke early, with a gasp. He did not remember what he had dreamed but Sarah's face was before him as he opened his eyes. He blinked and turned over. His wife was still asleep on the far side of the bed, curled in on herself like a child, her golden hair spread out over the pillow. He rose quietly so as not to wake her, washed quickly at the marble-topped washstand, dressed, and left the house. It was gray and quiet as he made his way eastward past the great dome of St. Paul's and through Cheapside, and the lamplighters were still running up their ladders to extinguish the streetlamps. It being Sunday, the City's warehouses and offices were closed and silent, wreathed in the morning mist. Here and there, housekeepers and porters were about, sweeping away the night's filth. Street children stooped and searched for anything they might be able to sell.

When he reached Cornhill, Edmund heard the clop of hoofs and turned to see the omnibus to Paddington approaching. He thought again of Greenacre, carrying the victim's head on his lap all the way to Stepney. Sarah could not have known that, surely. She could not have known that, and stayed.

Edmund turned left up Bishopsgate and soon saw the bright lamp of the police station. Inside, two police officers in uniform were writing at a desk. The place was silent save for occasional shouts from the underground cells, which the officers ignored.

"Can I help you, sir?" one of the men asked.

Edmund explained he wished to speak to Inspector Feltham and was led through to a back room, where the inspector sat in his armchair, puffing on his pipe.

"You're up early, Fleetwood. Something wrong? Had your pocket handkerchief swiped?"

Edmund would not rise to this. "I need to look at your file relating to the Edgeware Road murder."

"I thought you'd completed your investigation, sir. Your Miss Gale's already on the boat, ain't she?" He barely attempted to disguise the smirk on his face.

"Yes, she leaves in the next week. There's something in your records that I must check."

"What, exactly?" Feltham was interested now. Edmund should not have come.

"I want to be sure that I was aware of everyone to whom you'd spoken — that there was no one who might have seen something, but who had slipped through the net."

The inspector gave an exaggerated sigh. "Mr. Fleetwood, as I've told you before, we spoke to every man and woman on the street. Everyone was questioned. None of them had anything useful to say. Now, if you'll excuse me," he said, standing up, "I've other matters to be getting on with. Nasty attack on a young girl in Lavender Hill."

Edmund returned to the street, his heart racing.

They might have questioned all of the men and women, but what about the children?

He heard in his mind the sound of running feet.

Edmund traveled once more to Camberwell, to Carpenter's Buildings. He knocked at the door to number eleven. The neighbor, wearing a ribboned cap, answered the door. The smell of baking wafted from within.

She frowned, confused. "You want to see Greenacre's house again?"

"I'm sorry to bother you, ma'am. I'm looking for a young boy I saw here the last time I came: torn blue jacket, about ten years old. He seemed at the time to be following me."

She wiped her hands on her apron. "That's probably Bailey. He was fond of Sarah and often wanders 'bout the house. An odd little soul. His parents don't pay much attention to 'im."

"Where do they live?"

"At number eighteen, across the way. Don't expect a warm reception, mind. They don't much like authority."

Number eighteen was a dilapidated house

with soot-blackened walls and papered windows. Paint flaked from the front door. From inside he could hear the bawling of a baby. He hesitated and then knocked.

"Yes?" came a shrill woman's voice.

"May I come in?"

"What d'you want?"

Edmund pushed at the unlocked door. Inside, a woman sat beside a small spluttering fire, nursing a baby. At her feet was a young girl in threadbare clothing, playing with a doll.

"My name is Fleetwood. I'm looking for your son, Bailey."

"Is 'e in trouble?"

"No, no trouble. I just need to talk to him about a friend of his."

She looked at him coldly. "He ain't here."

"I'll pay you," he said.

"Boy!" the woman shrieked.

A dirty-faced child in a faded blue jacket appeared at the top of the stairs clutching the banister. As soon as he saw Edmund he was down the stairs and out of the door in an instant. Edmund did not stop to explain. He ran after the child as fast as he could, along the street, down a side road, off into an alleyway, catching sight of the boy's blue form hurtling around bends as he rushed along the filthy passageway. They were approaching the rookeries off Bowyer Lane now — a labyrinth of dirty, narrow lanes and decaying timber houses slanting into each other like a deck of cards. A lean pig scampered out of his way and two small children flattened themselves against a wall as he went tearing past, through piles of rotting refuse. Glimpsing a flash of blue falling, Edmund threw himself on the boy and took him to the ground. He felt his hands on the boy's torn shirt.

"I didn't do nothing. I didn't tell no one." The boy was breathing hard and shaking. Edmund relaxed his grip.

"It's Bailey, isn't it?"

The boy did not answer. He gave off the sharp smell of neglect.

"Listen, Bailey, I'm not here to reprimand or punish you, and I'm nothing to do with the man I suspect you're afraid of, James Greenacre."

As soon as he said the name, the boy tried to get up to run again. "No, please listen," Edmund said. "Greenacre is dead. He was hanged. And I wasn't sent by him. I'm a friend of Sarah Gale's."

The boy's wide eyes searched his face.

"I'm not going to hurt you," Edmund said. He had come armed — he removed from his pocket a twist of acidulated drops.

465

He unfurled the brown paper, removed one of the sweets and put it in his own mouth, then held the bag out to the boy. Hesitating, Bailey reached out a thin hand and snatched one of the sweets.

"You liked Sarah, didn't you?" Edmund was not sure why he was talking about her in the past tense.

"She were kind," Bailey said eventually. "She'd give me things sometimes."

"She would want you to tell me the truth about what you know."

"I don't know nothing," he repeated, his eyes round with fear.

Edmund smiled, his breath still labored. "You run fast, fastest round here, I'll wager."

The boy did not reply.

"You've been watching me, haven't you?" Edmund said. "You're good at watching. I'll lay a crown you see things the other children are too slow to see."

The boy nodded almost imperceptibly.

"That man, that man you're afraid of, he's dead now. Do you understand? He can't hurt you. Did he say he would hurt you?"

The boy looked around warily, and took another sweet in his hand. His nails were blackened with dirt. For some time there was just the sound of him sucking the sugar drop.

"Bailey, it's important you tell me what you saw, because you're the only person who did see. You want to help Sarah, don't you?"

The boy nodded eagerly and Edmund felt a twinge of guilt. "Were you at the house on Christmas Eve, Bailey? Did you see something?"

The boy pulled at his grubby shirt collar. "Mam locked me outside one night just before Chrissmas."

"Christmas Eve?"

The boy nodded. "I was sitting on the steps."

"Yes?"

"I 'eard shouting come from in Mr. Greenacre's 'ouse."

"Who was shouting?"

"Mister and some woman. Maybe the lady which come a few weeks before. I got closer to the door to lissen, which was when *he* comes out. He didn't see me, mind. Just hooked it."

"Greenacre?"

"Yes. It was snowing by then and I tried to get back into our 'ouse but the door was locked."

"So?"

"So I crawled inter the little shed in the front of Mr. Greenacre's garden. There were nowhere else for me to go, see . . ."

"And what happened then?"

"I saw 'er comin' up the drive."

Edmund's stomach dropped. "Saw who, Bailey?"

"Miss Gale, sir."

He felt as though he were falling from a great height. "Sarah? You're sure it was her?"

"I'm sure, sir. It were dark, but I've seen 'er so often . . ."

"What time was this?"

"Late. Ten o'clock, p'raps?"

"Could you hear or see what happened inside the house?"

"There were more shouting. I could only 'ear part of what they said. They used bad words."

"Two women?"

The boy nodded.

"What did they say?"

His urgent tone must have frightened the boy, as he shrank back and murmured, "I don't know, sir. I don't know nothing."

Edmund tried to keep the panic out of his voice. "Bailey, please try to recall what was said. You won't get into any trouble."

The boy appeared to think for a moment. "The other woman, she called Sarah a bold-faced slut and a whore too. Things like that."

"And Sarah? Could you hear what she said?"

Bailey shook his head. "She were more quiet. She called the other woman a liar, I think. They was juss fightin'. And then they stopped."

Edmund closed his eyes. "Did you see Sarah leave?"

"No, I never. I went back home then and Mam let me in." Edmund took out his handkerchief and rubbed the sweat from his face. He felt slightly delirious and wondered if he were falling ill.

"Did you see Greenacre return home?"

The boy shook his head.

"And you promise me you're telling the truth?"

"Wish I may die if I ain't. I'm just sayin' what I saw."

After a time, Bailey said, "This won't get her into trouble, will it? She were always kind to me."

Edmund stared at the boy briefly and then handed him the rest of the bag of sweets. He bent closer toward him. "It was good that you told me this, but it's important you don't tell anyone else. Do you understand?"

The boy nodded.

They wandered together back to Carpenter's Buildings. The lane was deserted, dust, straw, and scraps of paper blowing up and down it in the breeze. After the boy had returned to his home, Edmund stood looking at Greenacre's house with its windows shuttered against the world. So Sarah had been here on the night of the murder. What had she seen and done? Was she in the house when Hannah died? Had Sarah herself killed her?

If he had looked closely he might have seen the clues, the mismatching pieces. Instead, he had chosen to create his own picture — a picture that was entirely wrong. He had criticized his father for his hypocrisy, but he was just as bad: skewing the facts to meet his own ends. The torn bill in the window flapped in the wind and a door creaked. A man came out of one of the adjoining houses and stood in the pathway staring at him, his arms folded. Edmund had been so certain and now the ground shifted beneath him, as though he were at sea. He pulled his jacket collar closer around his neck and walked back along the silent street.

40

"I closed my lids, and kept them close,
And the balls like pulses beat;
For the sky and the sea, and the sea and
    the sky
Lay dead like a load on my weary eye,
And the dead were at my feet."
— *The Rime of the Ancient Mariner,*
        Samuel Taylor Coleridge, 1798

Early the following morning, the first mate ordered all of the women to line up on the quarterdeck for the surgeon to examine them. Sarah's flesh goose-pimpled in the morning air. She pulled her shawl tighter around her.

"New regulations," the surgeon said as he walked along the row of shivering women. He was a slight man, perhaps forty years old, in a black uniform with large brass buttons. "Before we leave, we are required to check that you are fit to make the journey.

There have been complaints."

Complaints, Sarah assumed, from the authorities in Australia, tired of receiving convicts riddled with disease and incapable of work.

The surgeon tried to inject authority into his voice, but he sounded nervous. She wondered if this was his first voyage or whether he knew what he was in for. He made his way along the line of women who stood bracing themselves against the wind, wrapping capes or wretched pieces of material around them. Pausing at each one, he asked respectfully for the woman to open her mouth as he placed a stick on her tongue so that he could see inside. He looked carefully at their hands and arms, leaning in close and asking questions quietly. Then he nodded, scribbled something in a little notebook, and moved on.

Sarah noticed that, as the surgeon carried out his inspection, so the crew were carrying out theirs: looking over the women as though they were horses at a fair, muttering to one another and sniggering. Evidently they were picking out their choices. She reached her hand into her cloak and felt the reassuring cold touch of metal: the knife that her sister had concealed there, resourceful to the last.

When the surgeon reached Sarah, he said, "Name, please."

"Sarah Gale."

She saw him tense. She thought he might ask her if she was "that Sarah Gale" but he merely glanced at her. She could not read his judgment.

"If you wouldn't mind opening your mouth for me . . ."

Close up, she could see that his face was still smooth. Dark hairs stood out from the pale skin of his wrists.

"Very good. Have you had any illnesses in the past year: Cholera? Typhus? Anything more personal?"

Sarah shook her head. If there was something wrong with her, it was not of her body.

"And is there any medical issue with which you need my help?"

Yes, Sarah thought, I would like you to stop the nightmares, the waking visions, the images of a dead woman's face that haunt me day and night. I would like you to look inside my mind and tell me what is wrong.

But she said, as she had said to the judge at the trial, "Thank you, sir, but there is nothing."

The surgeon took her hand and turned it over. His touch was gentle. Then he let it drop and noted something in his little book.

He moved on.

At ten o'clock, the women and crew assembled on the quarterdeck for "church" — the captain's sermon. In other boats this might have been given by the chaplain, but there was no chaplain, and the surgeon was no public speaker.

"Blessed is he whose transgression is forgiven, whose sin is covered," the captain read, his hair blowing in his face. *"Blessed is the man unto whom the Lord imputeth not iniquity, and in whose spirit there is no guile. When I kept silence, my bones waxed old . . ."* Some of his words were stolen by the wind and carried over the water.

". . . Wash me thoroughly from mine iniquity and cleanse me from my sin."

The day had brightened and Sarah looked out across the prow at the millions of dots of light dancing on the Thames. Beside her, George squirmed.

"The eyes of the Lord are upon you," the captain was saying.

And what, Sarah wanted to ask, is the point of him watching us if he does nothing to protect us? If he just watches a father abuse his daughter without intervening? If he watches a man grind a woman into the ground without stopping him? If he watches a woman die without stemming the blood? She had been told all her life that God was watching her, but it never made her feel protected or loved, only guilty and afraid. She looked at George, still fidgeting beside her. She did not want him to grow up under the same burden. He deserved to be free. He deserved to be happy. Could she give him that, at least?

"Though your sins be as scarlet, they shall be as white as snow," the captain continued. *"Though they be red like crimson, they shall be as wool."*

It had always struck her as such a beautiful passage, but could scarlet sins really be whitened? Surely there would always be a dark stain on the snow. It had been snowing the evening that Hannah Brown had died. As the captain spoke, Sarah's mind slipped and returned to that night. All at once she was there, watching the flakes falling thicker and faster, her heart pounding, her mind screaming out:

What have I done? What have I done?

41

"Vidocq, for example, was a good guesser, and a persevering man. But, without educated thought, he erred continually by the very intensity of his investigations. He impaired his vision by holding the object too close. He might see, perhaps, one or two points with unusual clearness, but in so doing he, necessarily, lost sight of the matter as a whole."
— "The Murders in the Rue Morgue," Edgar Allan Poe, 1841

By the time he reached his chambers, the initial shock had worn off, leaving Edmund with a residual nausea. He knew he would have to tell Lord Russell that Sarah had been at Greenacre's house on the night Hannah Brown was murdered. He had presented a Government Minister with a report that was patently untrue and it was now his professional duty to correct it. The consequences of fulfilling that duty were, however, almost too painful to contemplate. Edmund presumed that the Home Secretary would order that Sarah be retried for her part in the murder, but he might simply direct that she be hanged forthwith. Lord Russell had evidently been reluctant to commute the sentence at all, and, once he discovered Sarah had not only lied during the trial but in her petition to him and during the subsequent investigation, he might decide to dispense with her as soon as possible.

Edmund felt a knot growing in the pit of his stomach. Sarah had deceived him — she had drawn him in and duped him, had looked into his eyes and lied. What was worse was that he himself was partly to blame: he had lost sight of what was real and allowed himself to become infatuated with the woman he was supposed to be investigating. Had she intentionally led him to believe that she cared for him, or had he just imagined all of that?

"Will you be dining with us this evening?" Bessie had opened his study door and stood before him in her light blue dress.

"I would be grateful if you would knock before just marching in here."

Bessie sighed. "Oh, for goodness' sake,

Edmund, what is it that you do in here that's so secret?"

"I am merely asking for some privacy."

"Privacy?" She gave a high laugh. "Edmund, I barely see you anymore. And I have very little idea of what goes on in your private life. You've done your best to ensure that."

"Can you blame me, when you are constantly spying on me?"

"Edmund, I'm not spying on you. I'm just trying to understand what's going on, to fathom what's happening to our marriage. You hardly speak to me these days."

Edmund did not respond.

"Is it her?" Bessie asked quietly.

"Is it who?"

"Oh, please don't play games with me. We both know who I'm talking about. Are you in love with her?"

"What a question!"

"Is it such a ridiculous question?"

Edmund exhaled and turned away.

"Is she in love with you?" Her voice was little more than a whisper.

Edmund laughed. "On the contrary, my dear, she has tricked and undermined me. She has played me for a fool. There! Are you pleased now?"

"Of course I'm not," Bessie said. "But I

did try to warn you. I told you she might well be lying but you wouldn't listen."

"Ah, yes. My wife: the legal expert. My wife: the investigator."

"Well," she said softly, "it seems I've been a mortal sight more observant than you."

Edmund felt a flush of anger and shame spread over his face. "Leave me."

"Edmund, please be reasonable."

"Please leave this room." He could no longer bear to see her — she seemed at that moment to represent everything that had gone wrong, all the ways in which he had failed, all the ways in which his father had controlled him.

Bessie stepped forward, her arms stretched toward him, and all at the same time Edmund, emotion rising within him, moved to push her away. The next moment she was on the floor, her face white with shock.

"My God, Edmund. What's happened to you?"

Edmund stared at her distraught face and then looked down at his own hands as though they were no part of him. "Bessie, I'm . . ."

Holding her skirts, she struggled to her feet.

"Bessie, I'm so sorry."

He shut his eyes. In a moment of clarity,

he saw that he had been ignoring and rebuffing her for months: his own wife. He was little better than his own father. "I'm so very sorry," he murmured.

But when he opened his eyes, Bessie had gone, leaving the door swinging open.

She did not appear for the rest of the evening. Edmund ate alone and then lingered outside the nursery door, listening to her speaking softly to Clem. He knew from the tone of her voice that she was reading him a bedtime story and he felt a rush of guilt as he realized he had not read a book to Clem for weeks.

He made himself up a poor sort of bed with his coat and some cushions on the floor of his study. As he lay awake, the dull pressure of an approaching headache between his eyes, Edmund wondered if perhaps he was going mad. He had tried to keep everything ordered in his mind: to consider the evidence rationally. But now his thoughts were confused fragments — snowflakes whirling in a blizzard.

As the night lightened into morning, he tried to recall the whole of Sarah Gale's history as she had told it to him: her lonely childhood, their flight to London, her life as a poor seamstress, her miserable marriage.

Perhaps, he thought, the entire thing had been a fabrication: a series of lies stitched neatly together to elicit his sympathies, to portray her as the innocent victim. Maybe, he thought with a shiver, Sarah knew all about his mother — all about his own feelings of guilt — and had chosen the role of abused woman for that very reason. Yes, she must have known, from what his father had told her, that it was the key to getting him to trust her.

Edmund watched the shadow from the candle dancing on the smoke-stained ceiling. He felt like a cat who had been outwitted by a mouse, but there was still time to claw her back.

42

"As Lightning to the Children eased
With explanation kind
The Truth must dazzle gradually
Or every man be blind —"
— "Tell All the Truth but Tell It Slant,"
Emily Dickinson, 1868

The first mate ducked belowdecks, and the women, sitting at the long deal table, grew silent.

"Prisoner Gale!"

Sarah's heart dipped. From around her came a rustling of whispers as she stood up from the table and came forward. The first mate stretched his thin, colorless lips into an unpleasant smile.

"You're wanted up there," he said, jerking his head in the direction of the deck. "You're to come with me."

He insisted on her climbing the ladder before him, and Sarah could feel his breath

on her neck, his eyes on her back. As they ascended, she heard voices above, and as the voices grew nearer, she realized that she recognized one of them.

When she emerged into the afternoon light, she saw him standing on the quarter-deck talking to the captain, solemn in his tall hat and black coat. His cheeks were flushed and his eyes shone a vivid blue in the sunlight. Edmund stared at her but did not smile.

"I need to speak with Miss Gale alone," he said to the captain. "It has been autho-rized by the Home Secretary."

The captain was holding and reading over a letter, which he then passed back to Ed-mund. "Very well. You may meet in my cabin." He gestured for Edmund and Sarah to follow him.

By the time they reached the cabin, Sarah could hear the blood pounding in her ears like the roar of the sea. Why was he here?

The captain showed them into the room, looked briefly and shrewdly from her to Ed-mund, and then left, shutting the door behind him. Sarah stood facing Edmund, trying to interpret his expression, but it was inscrutable: a closed book.

"Is something wrong?" she said eventu-ally.

Edmund inclined his head to one side. "Is anything right?"

She swallowed, trying to push down the panic that was rising within her.

"Is anything you've told me these past three months true?" he said. "Or has it all been lies — every word?" He spoke quietly, but his voice was cold and hard with anger.

"I told you as much as I could."

"You told me a pack of lies! And even now, standing here, you lie to my very face." He practically spat the words.

Sarah stumbled back against the wall.

"Do you know what this case has done to me?" Edmund said. His tone was even, but she could hear the violence coursing beneath. "Do you have any idea what it's cost me to stand up for you when the rest of London was baying for your blood?"

Sarah stared at him, unable to think of anything she could say at that moment that might help.

"Christ." He ran his hands over his face. "I've gambled everything in order to save you. And the whole time — *the whole time* — you were feeding me a lie."

"Edmund, I beg of you. Please understand that —"

"That what? Let me guess: that you had no choice? That you were so afraid of the demon Greenacre that you had to lie and cheat your way through our interviews? Tell me, at what point did you realize who I was? When we first met? Or did you know even before that? Had you discussed with my father how you planned to dupe me?"

"No, of course not. I hadn't heard from Arthur for months. I suspected from the beginning that you were his son, but I couldn't ask, not at that stage: you represented the one chance I had of escaping the death sentence. And then . . . well, and then it was too late. Believe me, I wanted to tell you. My conscience has been almost more than I could bear —"

Edmund laughed. "Spare me the theatrics, Miss Gale. Or is that Miss Wiston, the leading lady? I don't want to hear about your tortured conscience or your terrible past. I want to hear the truth about what happened that night. I want to know what your role in it was. And before you attempt to construct another story, let me tell you that I have an eyewitness who saw you arrive at Green-acre's house on the night Hannah Brown was murdered."

Sarah's stomach dropped. "What?"

"Yes. Someone who saw you enter the house shortly before ten o'clock, which would have been around the time Hannah

Brown died. Explain that." He folded his arms.

Sarah shook her head. "It wasn't me."

"Is that the best you can do? It wasn't you? How, then, do you explain why the witness says he saw you?"

For several seconds, Sarah was silent, the possibilities and repercussions revolving in her mind.

"He saw someone else," she said eventually.

"Is that right?"

"Yes, Edmund, it is."

"I don't think so, Sarah. I think he saw you. I think you went to the house and, at the very least, helped Greenacre dismember and dispose of the body. Or perhaps it was you who killed her. Heaven knows, you had a motive."

Sarah put her hand to her throat. "You don't believe that. You know I couldn't have done that."

"Do I? Oh, a week or so ago I might have thought so, but now I don't know. I have no idea who you really are. While you, it turns out, know me all too well: indeed, you've been wheedling bits of information out of me since the beginning, the better to manipulate me."

"That's not true. You *wanted* to tell me

about yourself. You wanted someone to talk to."

Edmund shook his head, his eyes curiously dark. "Enough. You must tell me the truth."

Sarah felt almost numb with fear. If she remained silent now, it would be the end. She would hang. But maybe she would anyway. "I can't explain it," she said quietly, "but I was not at the house."

"You will have to explain it to a jury."

"Please, Edmund." She pressed her hands together. "I cannot go through that again."

"You may not have to. The Home Secretary may not even give you that chance. He may simply reinstate the death penalty."

She felt her heart contract. "You don't need to tell him."

"You cannot really expect me to keep quiet about what I now know?"

"You don't know anything."

"I know what the evidence tells me."

"The evidence tells you nothing. Your witness is mistaken."

"This witness has no reason to lie. He saw you approach the house and enter it." His tone was that of the barrister in the courtroom.

"Edmund." She tried to steady her mind, to find the right words. "You yourself once told me that a person may think he has seen something he cannot possibly have seen."

"In some circumstances, yes, but how on earth do you explain how someone may see and identify a person he knows if it is not in fact that person?"

As he reached the end of his sentence, Edmund's expression changed. She saw with a terrible rush of emotion that he had answered the question for himself. For a few seconds they simply stared at one another.

"Your sister."

"No."

"Yes," he said wonderingly. "It was your *sister* he saw, wasn't it?"

Sarah felt her eyes fill with tears and fought them back. "No."

Edmund still stared at her, unblinking. "That's why you failed to defend yourself at the trial. It wasn't Greenacre you were protecting at all. It was Rosina."

"No." She shook her head.

"It was *her* the boy saw. In the darkness, he thought Rosina was you."

"Please, Edmund," Sarah said. "That's not who he saw."

"She killed Hannah?" His tone was incredulous now. "Why?"

"You've misinterpreted this." Sarah's voice was hoarse.

"Oh, I don't think I have. I think I'm finally seeing what really happened. I think that's why you're trembling."

He was right: she was shaking uncontrollably. She clutched her arms over her chest to try to still herself.

Edmund kept his eyes on Sarah. "Rosina killed Hannah Brown and then left the house. Greenacre returned and found Hannah dead. He knew that everyone would believe it was him who had murdered her . . . maybe he even believed that he himself had caused the injury that killed her, so he disposed of the body. He was telling the truth all along when he said that he'd come home to find her dead."

"James confessed," Sarah said. "You told me that he admitted to having killed her."

Edmund shook his head. "Greenacre 'confessed' at the very last minute because he thought it was the only means by which he might secure a reprieve. That doesn't mean what he said was true."

Sarah did not — could not — reply.

"Is that why you went back to him? To make sure he'd gotten rid of the evidence that might have incriminated Rosina?"

"You've got it all wrong," Sarah said, trying to slow her breathing. "It wasn't Rosina that your witness saw. This boy, whoever he

489

is, merely imagined that he saw someone who looked like me."

"Sarah, stop; think about this. I will have to tell the Home Secretary that there is a witness who believes he saw you that night. It's my professional duty to do so and also to tell him that I believe that the witness is mistaken and that it was your sister who was at the house the night Hannah Brown died."

"You don't have to tell him anything," she whispered. "How will it help to tell him anything? Hannah Brown is already dead. James is already dead."

"Why did she kill her?" Edmund asked, seeming not to hear her. "Greenacre suggested she was mad: was he right?"

"The boy is *mistaken.* He doesn't know what he saw. No one will believe the word of a child, in any event. You don't need to tell the Home Secretary. Please, Edmund." She could hear the tremor in her own voice.

"I can't go along with that, Sarah. Dear God, I can't pretend I don't know."

"Yes, you can."

"What, and leave a dangerous woman on the streets?"

"She's not dangerous," Sarah said quietly.

"No? Then why did she kill Hannah Brown?"

490

"She didn't."

Edmund breathed out in frustration. "I know what you're doing, Sarah, and I know why you're doing it, but you're making a mistake. The truth will out eventually, and the longer you fight against it the less likely the Home Secretary or a jury are to show mercy to you and Rosina."

Sarah gave a half smile. "Mercy? I don't expect mercy. I don't expect kindness. I was stupid enough to expect it before, but I don't expect it now."

"And yet you expect me to stay silent? Do you have any notion of what would happen to me were it to be discovered that I'd concealed all of this? I can't do it."

"You can: for George."

Edmund looked at her quizzically. My goodness, she thought, did he still not see it?

"If Rosina and I are both imprisoned or hanged, he will be all alone."

Edmund was silent.

"Your own mother was taken from you," Sarah said. "You know how that feels. Would you wish it upon another child?"

"Don't turn this on me." He was angry again now. "Don't make this about me. I have my own obligations."

"To whom?" Sarah asked. "Lord Russell?

Do you really think he cares about justice? He cares only for his own reputation. The case is already closed so far as he's concerned. You don't need to reopen it." She could hear the desperation in her own voice.

"Maybe he doesn't care about justice, Sarah, but I do. That's why I came into this in the first place."

"And what is justice, Edmund? Is justice killing one woman for the death of another? Is it punishing one woman for trying to protect another? Because that's what will happen."

"Justice is about fair dealing, not about concealing the truth simply because it's inconvenient. Whether or not your sister meant to harm Hannah Brown, the fact is that she's dead and the man who was convicted of her murder —"

"Is also dead."

"And might not be had you admitted what truly happened."

"But you yourself told me that his having mutilated the body was enough of itself to warrant the death sentence."

"Probably, yes, but that wasn't for you to decide. It was for a court, considering all of the relevant information."

"A court that would have sentenced Rosina, James, and me to death for the same crime. I ask again: is that justice? Is that fairness?"

"And I tell you again, it was not for you to decide. And it's not for me to decide now. My duty is merely to report what I now know to the Home Secretary."

"Edmund, I beg of you, please don't do this. If not for George, then for me. Surely you must feel some sympathy, some fellow feeling —"

"You know perfectly well how I feel about you. You've made very sure of that."

"That's not fair. I never —"

"Oh, please. At least have the goodness to be honest now and to admit it was just part of the act."

"Edmund, it was never an act. What you've understood about how I feel toward you . . . that's true." And she realized as she said it, that it was.

He shook his head. "You were acting out a charade, just as you played the role of victim."

"The role in which you cast me! You wanted me to be the innocent victim who you could rescue, just as Miss Pike wanted me to be the abused woman, just as the public wanted me to be a crazed murderess."

"And what are you really?"

She blinked. What was she? "I'm just . . . I'm just the same as anyone else. I look after those I love."

Edmund met her eye. "And you expect me to do the same by covering up for you." He put on his hat. "But I won't. I can't."

He turned from her and walked through the doorway, a gust of cold air rushing through it as he left.

43

"I have no way, and therefore want no
  eyes;
I stumbled when I saw. Full oft 'tis seen,
Our means secure us and our mere defects
Prove our commodities."
> — *King Lear,* Act 4, Scene 1,
> William Shakespeare

Edmund took a passenger steam packet from Woolwich back to London, past the docks, past bowed dwellings, collapsing in on each other, past church steeples, warehouses, arches and bridges, laborers carrying casks, and women carrying children. The closer the steamer came to the heart of London, the greater the river traffic, and by the time Edmund caught sight of the grand arches of Waterloo Bridge, the Thames was a riot of little rowboats, skiffs, and skerries.

At the bridge, Edmund alighted and climbed the steps to the terrace beneath

Somerset House. His mind still swirled like the river with its competing thoughts: was Sarah right? Had he himself cast her in the role of the downtrodden woman? Only it turned out that, ill-used though she might have been, she was no innocent. The only real victim was Hannah Brown — beaten and rejected by Greenacre, then killed by his lover's sister.

Although he was tired and already covered in dust from the dry road, he made straight for Rosina's house on Hart Street. When no one answered his knock, he entered the grocer's below, approached the counter, and spoke to the shopkeeper — a short, rotund man with a round, red, shining countenance like one of his own apples.

"You might try St. Paul's church by Covent Garden," the man said as he poured some sugar into a twist of paper. "She often takes her little charges to the garden there."

Edmund walked down Garrick Street, past the tall, grand houses of Bedford Street and entered the church garden via the west entrance. It was a pretty place with young birch trees, a horse chestnut tree, and neat flowerbeds. Within a few seconds, Edmund caught sight of Rosina in a pink dress and straw bonnet, seated on a bench some distance from him. He watched her talking to the two girls seated either side of her and thought for a moment that it was simply impossible that someone so apparently open, so full of life, could have killed another woman. For some time, he stood watching her as she got up and strolled about twirling her parasol. Eventually, when he was a few feet away from her, perhaps sensing that she was watched, Rosina looked up and saw Edmund.

"Oh!" she said in surprise. Within a second, however, her look of puzzlement had faded and her expression grown fixed and afraid. She understood why he was there.

Edmund held her gaze, but said nothing. He heard Rosina urge the little girls to go and play on the lawn "so that I may talk to the gentleman." When they had run off, she approached and stood before him, her face closed.

"The main thing I don't understand," Edmund said, "was how you could have allowed your sister to go through all of this — the arrest, the trial, the sentencing, the imprisonment — and not say a thing. Would you have stayed silent forever?"

Almost imperceptibly, she shook her head.

"So you admit it?"

"I admit nothing."

"Well, that's unfortunate."

"How so?" She spoke softly, but there was a tremor to her voice.

"Because I have a witness who believes that he saw your sister arrive at Greenacre's house shortly before Hannah Brown died. On the basis of that evidence, it is very likely that Sarah will be tried and convicted of murder. Or the Home Secretary might simply reinstate the original death sentence."

The blood rushed to Rosina's face. "You don't believe her capable of murder." She spoke almost in a whisper. Close up, Edmund could see that the irises of her eyes were paler than Sarah's, the color of dark honey flecked with gold.

"No, I don't, as it happens," he said. "But it won't be me who makes the decision. It will be Lord Russell, who is already hardened against her, or twelve men who will have been told that she lied at the original trial and is lying again when she denies murder. Will you keep your silence even then?"

Rosina closed her eyes. Her eyelids were a pale, mauvish color, like a fading bruise.

"And if I were to tell you now," she said, "that it was me who went to the house, that it was me who killed Hannah Brown, but not intending to do so, what would happen then?"

"Well," Edmund said, "it depends on exactly what happened."

Rosina said nothing. The blood had now drained from her face, leaving it white as ash.

"If," Edmund said, "*if* one could convince a jury that the killer had not intended to cause serious injury, then it would be manslaughter, not murder. That might mean a sentence of transportation or imprisonment rather than the death sentence."

"And for the person who had not spoken out?"

This time it was Edward's turn to remain quiet.

"It would be the same sentence, wouldn't it?" Rosina said, opening her eyes. "*Both people would be transported or imprisoned.* Perhaps" — here her voice broke — "both would be hanged."

Edmund ran his hand over his face. She was right. For this time the jury would know for sure that Sarah had concealed the crime. This time they would know that she had sat through the original trial and kept quiet about everything she knew. She would hang.

Something of his distress must have shown on his face, because Rosina said urgently,

"There's no need for you to change your report. Sarah's already on the boat. It's all already been decided."

"On the basis of a lie!"

She shrank away from him.

"How? How did it happen? How could it possibly have happened?"

He had spoken in a raised voice and Rosina glanced over at the two girls who were still playing near the flowerbeds.

For a few moments, she did not speak. "Supposing . . ." she said finally, "supposing I *had* gone to James's house on Christmas Eve."

"Yes?"

"Supposing Sarah had specifically told me not to interfere, but I'd been unable to simply do nothing. I'd done nothing before, you see, when Sarah needed my help. Supposing I'd been so angry with that wretched man who had put her and George out on the streets in the middle of winter. After everything he'd put her through, after every mean thing he'd done, making her believe they might one day marry, keeping her ashamed and afraid and isolated." Rosina looked at him. "You remember what it was like then, don't you? Freezing and wet, and they had nowhere to go. I was living in as a governess so they couldn't stay with me.

Instead, they ended up in that hovel in Walworth, surviving on the crumbs he gave her. And then, on Christmas Eve — on Christmas Eve of all days — he tells her he's cutting off all financial assistance. He won't even pay for the lodging house. And he tells her it's because of Hannah Brown."

"What do you mean?"

"James told Sarah that Hannah had insisted that he stop providing her with any help. He said she'd made it a condition of going through with the marriage: she didn't want him supporting another woman and her child, not even for a few weeks while Sarah got back on her feet, not even if it meant they starved. So supposing by the time I got to the house, I wasn't thinking rationally. Supposing I intended to give James a piece of my mind — tell him all the things I'd wanted to say to him for so long."

"And supposing he wasn't there," Edmund said.

"Yes. And supposing Hannah Brown *was*. She wouldn't have been very pleased to see me, would she? Especially if James and she had been fighting, and especially if James had told her that it was because of Sarah that he was leaving her."

"I imagine she would be very distressed," Edmund said carefully.

501

"You would imagine that, yes," said Rosina. Her cheeks were flushed pink now and she spoke more rapidly. "You'd imagine, wouldn't you, that she'd be tear-stained and distraught, with her clothes all disarranged, so that if I asked her where James was, she'd say he was probably with my sister and that she was welcome to him. She'd probably say that my sister was a bitch and a whore and a devilish sly one at that."

"Why would she say that, Rosina?"

"Because James had said that it was *Sarah* who told him about Hannah claiming credit in his name at that shop. I tried to tell her that it wasn't true — that Sarah wouldn't have done that — but she wouldn't listen; she just kept on about Sarah having ruined everything for her and about it being Sarah's fault that James had broken off the marriage. I couldn't help it; I lost my patience with her then. I told her that it was nothing to do with my sister — that if James had ended their relationship it was because he'd come to his senses and realized she was a dried-up old washerwoman, and that no amount of money would make it worth his while. Such cruel things I said, but I believed, you see, that it was *her* who'd ensured that George and Sarah were cast out."

"And was it?"

Rosina shook her head. "I don't know. I believed it then, but now I wonder whether it was just something James said to upset Sarah."

Edmund saw it now. Greenacre had set the women against each other, stoking the flames so that they would hate one another, all because of him.

"What happened then?" he said.

"I'm not sure what it was in particular that I said to set her off. I thought at the time she must have been drunk, but maybe it was just anger at having lost out on her one chance to be married. Maybe it was when I told her that, due to her, poor little George was going hungry, and how would she feel if that were her own child? It wasn't until the trial that I realized that of course she couldn't have children of her own.

"At all events, she threw herself at me. It seems ridiculous now, thinking of it. I can't quite understand how we went from just shouting to grappling, clinging to each other like strange dancers. Hannah somehow got her hands around my throat and I tried to pry her hands away but I couldn't, and I couldn't breathe — so I began instead to kick and kick at her legs until they gave way. She came down forward then, on top of me, and" — here Rosina put her hands to her head — "well, at the same time I managed to wriggle free from her grip and move sideways and then . . . and then we came crashing to the ground. I fell badly, onto my shoulder, but managed to get myself up and away from her." Rosina exhaled and let her arms fall to her sides. "I saw then that her body was wrong somehow, like a puppet dropped on the floor, the legs at odd angles. She was making a low groaning sound and, as I pulled her back, there came a noise that was somewhere between a grunt and a rush of air. That's when I saw her face. I saw what I'd done."

Edmund waited.

Rosina was looking away from him, toward the stained glass windows of the church. "She'd fallen onto the coal box, you see, and the handle had pierced her eye." She shuddered at the memory of it. "A mess of red and white, blood and bone. The other eyelid was still half-open, but the eye itself was unseeing — blind.

"I told myself she was just stunned. I shook her, I spoke to her sharply, I splashed a cup of water in her face to try to revive her, but it only dripped from her chin, the water droplets mixed with the blood."

Rosina was speaking almost in a whisper

now. "I thought of calling for a physician, but suspected it was too late. I thought briefly of running for a police constable, but I . . . well, I knew what that would mean. I stood there for a long while in a sort of daze, and then I thought I heard the sound of footsteps on the path."

"And you ran."

Rosina hung her head. "Yes. I took one last look at Hannah, sprawled across the stone floor, and left by the back door."

For a moment, neither of them spoke.

"Was Hannah Brown dead when you left her?"

"I'm not sure."

"What did you think would happen after you left?"

"I assumed James would raise the alarm: fetch a surgeon or a constable but of course he didn't."

Edmund nodded. "Because he knew how it would look."

"I don't think he was even sure what to make of it himself," Rosina said. "He told Sarah he didn't think he was responsible, but he wasn't certain. He'd given Hannah a beating, remember, and his memory of the whole thing was clouded by liquor."

"And of course Sarah did nothing to dispel his fear that it was his doing."

Rosina's gaze wandered uneasily. "I don't know what Sarah said to James when they were alone. And I don't know what he did when he was alone with Hannah. It's possible she was still alive when I left and he himself finished her."

Edmund shivered at the memory of Dr. Girdwood's words: "Greenacre slit the woman's throat shortly after death — possibly while she was still alive."

"And Sarah knew. You told her everything."

Rosina did not reply.

"Is that why she agreed to take Greenacre back?" Edmund asked. "So she could convince him of his guilt and ensure that he disposed of the body?"

"No." She shook her head. "Sarah went back to him because, for reasons I can't begin to understand, she still loved him, or felt something for him. By the time she returned to his house, he'd removed all signs of what had happened. We knew he must have disposed of the body, but we didn't know *how* he'd done it. When the papers started reporting the discovery of the body pieces, we suspected, we feared, but Sarah didn't know for certain until the police told her."

That fitted. That would explain why Sarah

was so distressed when she was arrested; that and the struggle she must have had in her own mind as to whether to allow the blame for the murder to be pinned on Greenacre.

"And then she kept quiet about what she knew in order to protect you," Edmund said.

Rosina lowered her eyes. "You mustn't think it was easy for her, or that she approved of what I'd done, but, well, we've always looked after one another. And it wasn't exactly as though James had treated her well."

"No," Edmund said. "He'd treated her very badly, in fact, and now this was to be his punishment."

Rosina looked up quickly. "It wasn't like that at all."

"No? It seems to me that it was the perfect solution to allow Greenacre to take the blame. After all, it was he, wasn't it, who set Hannah and Sarah against each other? He told Sarah that it was because of Hannah that he was throwing her and George out without any money, and he told Hannah that it was because of Sarah that he was calling off the marriage."

Greenacre had played a game, Edmund thought. A game that had gone disastrously wrong, leaving a woman dead and himself in the frame for her murder.

"I never meant for any of this," Rosina was saying. "I only ever meant to speak out on behalf of Sarah, and I've ended up destroying everything for her, for me, for George."

Edmund did not respond. She looked at him. "Could you just say that it was me? That Sarah had nothing to do with it? She's already been through so much. She doesn't deserve any of this."

"You think I can simply lie to the authorities to protect Sarah?"

"Well, what purpose would be served by telling them? It won't save anyone; it won't help anyone. It won't bring Hannah Brown back. It will just be another needless death."

"It's not for me to decide," he said shortly. "The most that I can do is ask that they take pity on Sarah."

"Oh, and you think they will listen to you? Did they do as you asked last time?"

Edmund felt his cheeks grow hot.

"I don't care anymore what happens to me," Rosina continued, "but I care very much what becomes of Sarah and George. She didn't ask for this — she was just trying to protect me. And George — Mr. Fleetwood, he's just a child."

Edmund turned away from Rosina. "This is not my fight," he said, not looking at her. "You have to live with the consequences of your actions."

"I know that, and I am — I have been for many months — but you'll also have to live with the consequences of yours, and one of them will be that George is left at the mercy of the Parish."

Edmund said nothing, but his mind was summoning up images of the workhouse, of a tiny coffin.

"Promise me that you'll look after him," Rosina said. "If you must do as you claim, then please tell me that you'll make sure he's provided for."

"You cannot *bargain* with me. You cannot make any demands of me! I am the investigator. My duty —"

"Was to investigate Sarah's petition," she interrupted him. "And you did that. You completed your report and you sent it to the Home Secretary and he made his decision and now Sarah and George are on a boat ready to travel to Australia. None of that needs to change. Please. Please." She put out her hand as if to touch him, but then, perhaps seeing the look in his eye, let it drop. "You're a good man, Mr. Fleetwood. Your father's done nothing for

George, but I know you will."

A cold feeling ran through him. "What do you mean by that?"

"George: he's your father's son. Your half brother."

Edmund stared at her. Of course. That was who George reminded him of: Clem. He looked like Clem. Darker and thinner, but the same sharp chin, the same lips, the same large knowing eyes.

Edmund walked back to his chambers like a blind man, almost unaware of where he was going.

What on earth was he to do now? If he failed to report Sarah and Rosina, he would be in grave professional jeopardy, but if he informed the Home Secretary of his findings, it was quite possible that both would be hanged, leaving all alone the boy who it now transpired was his brother.

When Edmund arrived at his chambers, he found them unnaturally silent. The shutters had not been closed, there were no voices in the nursery, and no candles had been lit in the hallway. By the time he opened the door to his study, he knew with a cold and heavy certainty what he would find there. On his desk, propped up against his copy of *The Law of Evidence,* was a card.

Edmund,

I do not know what is happening to you. I have tried to understand but, time and again, you have shut me out. I cannot and will not put up with your behavior. I have taken Clem away for a time. I will contact you when I feel able to do so.

Flora has left, having not been paid for over a month. She seems to have taken the cutlery in lieu of payment.

Do not try and look for us. You will not find us.

Your wife, Elizabeth

Edmund sank down into his chair, his head bowed forward. He could not blame Bessie; he had associated her with his father and, in so doing, had begun to act like him. He raised the card to his face. It smelled faintly of carnations.

When Morris entered the room the following morning, Edmund was lying across his desk with the side of his face resting on a partially written report.

"A late night, sir?"

Edmund sat up abruptly. There was a blotch of black ink on his cheek. His jaw ached and his mouth felt like the inside of an old glove. He tried to reply, but no words came.

Morris eyed the half-empty decanter on Edmund's table. "I 'ave just the thing."

He disappeared and returned a short while later holding two metal cups, one of which he stirred and passed to Edmund.

Edmund sipped at the concoction and gagged. "For the love of God, what is this?"

"The solution to all your problems."

"If only that were true, Morris." He looked at the dark liquid swirling in the cup. It smelled of peppermint and nutmeg with a whiff of something metallic.

"Private issues, Mr. Fleetwood?" Morris sat on the edge of the desk.

Edmund frowned. "I've been carrying out some further investigations."

"Regarding our Miss Gale?"

"Yes, regarding Miss Gale." Edmund pressed his palm against his forehead. "It transpires that she has not been entirely truthful with me."

Morris cocked his head to the side as a bird might do. "Not truthful about what, exactly?" He threw back the liquid in his own cup and grimaced.

"Let us just say that her original conviction was probably correct, albeit for the wrong reasons."

Morris gave a low whistle. "And you think she should be punished?"

"No, Morris. I don't think that, as it happens. But it's not for me to decide. Justice requires that I inform the Home Secretary of my findings."

"Does it?" Morris raised his eyebrows. "I always thought justice meant giving people what they deserve." He paused. "But then I'm not a lawyer. I leave the law business to you gentlefolk."

"Yes," Edmund said uncertainly, toying with the metal cup.

Morris got up, tipped his hat, and went toward the door. "You 'ave a little ink, sir. On your cheek. You may want to look in your shaving mirror."

Edmund rubbed his face and called him back. "You understand we haven't just had this conversation."

"Mr. Fleetwood, as you know, I see nothing, I hear nothing."

By the afternoon, Edmund had nearly finished his letter to the Home Secretary. In the kitchen, he found the heel of a stale loaf, which he toasted over the fire with one of the few remaining forks and ate with some Dutch cheese, swallowing it down with a glass of port. The many previous drafts of his letter burned in the grate. There was a knock at the front door, which, given Flora's departure, he knew he would have to answer himself.

When Edmund pulled open the door, he was surprised to see his father, looking uncharacteristically disheveled. He could smell the tobacco on his clothes, his hair.

For a moment Edmund simply stared at him, and then said, coldly: "What do you want?"

"I wanted to apologize."

"Right. Anything else?"

His father glanced nervously about him before saying in a low voice, "Sarah had nothing to do with your appointment. She had no idea that's what I intended to do. She certainly didn't ask for it."

"Then why interfere?" Edmund said at normal volume.

"I was trying to help."

"No, you were trying to protect your own reputation."

"That's not true, Edmund. I felt I owed it to her to try to assist her."

"By using me."

His father glanced again about the lane. "May I come in?"

"You may not."

"Edmund, this is ridiculous."

"No, what is ridiculous is how you've behaved. What is ridiculous is you having kept your wife in misery and near poverty as a punishment for her 'downfall,' while you lived with a woman you yourself have called a prostitute. What is ridiculous is how you then left that woman and your own son in penury rather than acknowledge them."

"Edmund, please keep your voice down."

Edmund laughed. "And even now, all you care about is appearances. Well, you needn't worry. I don't plan on telling Lord Russell about your involvement with Miss Gale. It wouldn't serve any purpose."

"No. No, it wouldn't, but I am grateful all the same."

"Don't be. It's not for your sake that I'm keeping quiet about it."

"For Sarah's?"

"No, for my own. I've made enough of a fool of myself over this case. I don't need the world to know that the only reason I was appointed was because my father was attempting to pervert the course of justice."

His father seemed unable to find a response to this. He tapped his cane awkwardly on the ground. "Have you made up your mind as to what you will say about her?"

"I have."

"And?"

"And you can read about it in the newspapers the same as everyone else. Good day, Father."

Edmund shut the door and walked back up the stairs, feeling lighter than he had done all day.

44

"Presently the fox is thrown among the hounds, and soon torn limb from limb, and eaten. Such is the finale of this exciting sport, in which the energies of so many have been long engaged."
— *Manual of British Rural Sports,*
John Henry Walsh, 1856

"It's all over, Lucy," Sarah whispered as the two women sat side by side on her bunk, shrouded in the darkness of the orlop.

Earlier in the day, the cattle pens and poultry boxes had been loaded onto the ship — cows that snorted with fear and a swarm of squealing pigs, which seemed to know that they were doomed to die. Now, as night fell, Sarah heard the shrill scream of one of the pigs, perhaps being butchered for tomorrow.

"What are you talking about?" Lucy asked.

"Edmund — the lawyer — he knows now

what happened on the night of Hannah Brown's death. That's why he came today."

For a long time they sat silently amid the coughing and mutterings of the other women.

"What *did* happen, Sarah?"

Sarah looked at Lucy. In the dim light, she could just about make out her sharp features, the whites of her eyes. Could she tell her? She had kept her secret for so long — hardly even discussing it with her sister — that it seemed impossible to say the words.

"It was Rosina who killed Hannah," Sarah said finally. "She didn't mean to, but she did." And once she had said it, the rest came out in a torrent: the growing hatred she had felt toward Hannah, the shame she had felt at living as an unmarried mother, James's goading, her outpouring to Rosina on Christmas Eve. She had been sitting at the garret window watching the snowflakes falling, thinking about Hannah and James, when, in the yellow glow of the streetlamp, she saw a cloaked figure approach the house. She knew from the way the figure moved, hurriedly, head down, that it was her sister, and she had run down to let her in, before Rosina could knock. Her cuffs were red with blood, her cloak wet with the snow.

"She wouldn't tell me at first what had happened, but I worked it out soon enough. I gave her one of my dresses to wear while I washed hers, but, though I scrubbed and scrubbed, the stains would not come out. In the end, I burned it in the grate. Rosina had to buy a new dress, which she could ill afford, but she would have lost her situation, of course, if she were not respectably dressed. That was why, later, I pawned Hannah Brown's silk dresses. For the money. James had given them to me, saying that Hannah had left them in lieu of payment. But of course I knew what had really happened. I knew that I was pawning the possessions of a dead woman." She closed her eyes. "I pawned her wedding dress, Lucy: the dress she never got to wear." Beneath her closed lids she saw it again — red as ruby, red as blood.

"And it was because of me that she died." Saying it aloud after all this time made it all seem suddenly real and clear, not the shadowy nightmare in which she had been living since that night.

"What d'you mean, because of you?"

"Rosina was angry on my behalf. She went to see James just after I told her that he'd cut me off, and that Hannah was the cause of it. If I hadn't told her about what James and Hannah had said . . . if I'd left James long before, as I should have done, none of this would have happened. That's why I say because of me. Because of me Hannah Brown died. Because of me Rosina will now hang. Because of me George will be left all alone."

Lucy turned her face toward her and then looked away. In the half-light, Sarah could not interpret her expression.

"You remember that first night you spoke to me at Newgate?"

"Yes."

"I was going out of my mind with despair in that awful place. I thought my baby had died 'cos of me."

Sarah waited.

"And you helped me," Lucy said. "You didn't have to, but you spoke to me: you told me it weren't my fault, that I shouldn't feel guilty. Well, this weren't your fault neither. It weren't you who struck the woman, just as it weren't me who stopped my baby's heart. You're a good person, Sarah."

"Good? Lucy! How can you say that? After everything that's happened? I concealed a woman's death. I let James go to the gallows for it rather than speak out. Good! I am very far from good. I am bad to my very bones. Mr. Price saw it. The Ordinary saw it. Rook saw it, too."

"Oh, and they know you, do they, those Prices and Cottons and Rookses? They can believe what they like, but they ain't spoken to you like I have, have they? I know you, and I know how much you love your little boy and your sister. *That's* why you did what you did, isn't it?"

Sarah shook her head. "I allowed James to go to his death believing he might have killed Hannah, even after he himself insisted I'd had nothing to do with it all."

"Why *did* he say that?"

"That was what we'd agreed. That was our contract. I would deny I knew anything about him beating Hannah or disposing of the body. He, in return, would state that I knew nothing about it. Of course, James didn't know what had really happened. And he never knew that I didn't keep my side of the deal."

"It wasn't much of a deal."

"No, but still, he maintained until the very end that I played no part in the murder. I'm not sure why he did that. Maybe, after everything he'd done, he felt he owed me something." Maybe, she thought, there had been a tiny sliver of goodness in him after all.

"And yet I let him hang in place of my sister."

"He would have swung anyway, wouldn't he?"

"Maybe. Probably. But there's always that tiny possibility that he wouldn't have. That he would have been reprieved, as I was. And the thing is, Lucy, I keep going back to that night, to the night she died, and trying to work out whether I could have done anything differently. Whether I should have told Rosina to go at once to the police; whether I should have told James what had happened; whether I should have reported it to the police myself. But of course I couldn't have done any of those things. I couldn't have done anything different from what I did."

She imagined it as a dicebox that had been shaken and shaken and, each time, the numbers came out the same. It would always have ended like this.

"Maybe Mr. Fleetwood will see that," Lucy said. "Maybe he'll understand you didn't have a choice."

"But I did have a choice, Lucy. I had a choice as to what I did, and I had a choice as to what to say to Mr. Fleetwood, and I chose to deceive him. He was one of the very few people who tried to help me — who was willing to listen to me — and instead of trying to explain, I lied to him. I felt I had to. No, he won't protect me now. He's a proud man and I've tricked and humiliated him. Whether or not he believes it was my fault, he'll make sure that I pay."

After Lucy had gone to bed, Sarah lay on her bunk next to George's sleeping form, listening to the creaking of the ship and the lonely whine of the wind in the ropes. Maybe tomorrow they would come for her, to take her back to Newgate. Newgate, where Rook still waited, like a snake, coiled; where Miss Sowerton still presided. And she would no longer have Edmund to keep them at bay; she would no longer have his threats to stop Miss Sowerton from dragging her back to the dark cells or from simply unleashing Rook on her, like a dog at a rat. She was foolish to have feared the rope — to have imagined that the worst would be a slow strangulation before a crowd of thousands. She wouldn't make it as far as the scaffold. She would die in the dark, alone.

And, when Miss Pike found that she had lied to her, would she keep her promise to help George? Would she pity the son when the mother had betrayed her, or would she simply leave him to his fate in a Parish workhouse? Sarah stroked George's hair as he slept, knowing it might well be the last time she ever did so.

It was always the waiting that was the worst. She remembered lying in bed in the pink-papered room of her childhood, knowing that soon enough she would hear her father's footsteps, the rustle of cotton as the sheet was pushed back. She remembered sitting alone in the kitchen at Carpenter's Buildings waiting for James to return, wondering whether he would be inebriated but elated, or just drunk and vengeful. She remembered staying awake at night, crouched by George's cot, convinced that tomorrow would be the day that she and James were arrested. She remembered staring from the window at the falling snowflakes, wishing that something would happen to prevent James from marrying Hannah. But she had not wished for that. She had not imagined a floor awash with blood, a body cut into pieces.

Maybe tomorrow they would come and end it all.

Edmund sat by a window in Peele's Coffee

House, watching drops of water trickle down the glass.

A waiter appeared with a cup of steaming coffee, which he set down before Edmund. Staring into the swirling black liquid, he rehearsed in his head what he would say to Lord Russell when he reached the Home Office with his new report.

"My lord, I am duty-bound to inform you that new information has come to light . . ."

"I regret that my original report was premised on facts that have since turned out to be incorrect . . ."

"Unfortunately, it seems that I was misled and, in turn, misled you . . ."

He took out his inkpot and pen and, on a sheaf of paper, jotted down a few alternatives, but none seemed to work. How to find the right words?

He took a sip of the hot coffee and sat for a minute staring at the raindrops; at the people rushing past outside, scowling into the wind and rain; at two small boys who had broken free of their nursemaid and who were jumping in puddles, laughing with pure joy.

Eventually, the words crystallized in his mind. Drawing out a new white sheaf of paper, he began to write.

45

"Wash me thoroughly from mine iniquity,
　　and cleanse me from my sin.
For I acknowledge my transgressions: and
　　my sin is ever before me.
Against thee, thee only, have I sinned, and
　　done this evil in thy sight."
　　　　　　　　　　— Psalm 51 (KJV)

There were now one hundred and twenty-nine convicts aboard the *Henry Wellesley:* lock-pickers and card sharpers, housebreakers and horse stealers, all crammed into the orlop for the last night before they left England.

Sarah had spent the day in a state of suspended terror, growing more nervous with each hour that passed. Why had they not yet come for her? Was the captain waiting until the last prisoners arrived from Newgate, so that she could be sent back at the same time? Or perhaps Edmund was punishing her by playing her as he believed she had played him: waiting until the very last minute to reel her back in.

As Sarah readied herself for bed among the low chatter of women and howling of infants, the message came. She was to attend the captain's room.

This is it then, she thought. This is the beginning of the end. She was overcome by a great weariness, a feeling of leaden sadness that began as a heaviness in her chest and spread down her body. In the near darkness, she sank down on her bunk next to George's sleeping form, all energy and spirit draining from her like the final grains of sand running through an hourglass. The captain must have received a letter from Edmund or a command from the Home Secretary himself. Either way, she was finished. They all were.

For several minutes she stayed by George, watching his chest rise and fall and breathing in his smell: warm milk and marine soap. She pressed her lips against his cheek. What would happen to him without her there to look after him? She had ruined everything — she had played it all wrong. In trying to save her sister, she had forfeited her son.

"I'm sorry, George," she whispered. "I'm

so sorry."

Sarah climbed the ladder to the main deck, her chest tight with fear.

On deck, everything was quiet and still. There was only the occasional cat's paw of wind and the slosh of gentle waves slapping the boat. Even the stars had hidden, and the night was as black and wet as ink. Sarah stood outside the captain's cabin, her heart pounding. She rested her closed fist against the door for a second and then knocked twice.

"Come in."

When she pushed the door open a crack she saw only darkness. She pushed it farther and saw that the captain was sitting at a small wooden desk lit by a stump of candle in a pewter pot. He was making notes on a graph. As Sarah stepped through the entrance, the door swung shut behind her with a thud. The captain put down his pen and blinked.

"Well, don't just stand there, woman. Come forward." The candlelight illuminated his face from beneath, casting dark shadows under his cheekbones.

Sarah stood with her hands clasped behind her back, looking at the floor. She could tell he was appraising her.

"I have received a letter to pass to you," he said. "As you are a convict, I was obliged to read it first." He held the letter out and Sarah stepped forward to take it from him.

At first, Sarah was unable to focus on the words. Her hands shook violently despite her attempts to still them and the sentences were mere tangles of black ink lines on white. Gradually, she began to understand.

11 July 1837

Dear Miss Gale,
Having carefully reviewed the issues about which we spoke at our last meeting, I have come to the view that little purpose would be served by taking matters further. Arguably, they have gone far enough. As you yourself said, the case is closed. Ultimately, James Greenacre paid the price for his misdeeds.

Yours will not, I suspect, be the only eyes to read this letter. I will therefore say simply that you and your son have been forsaken and betrayed by many people and that I do not intend to add to their number. Heaven knows, I have already made enough mistakes.

I wish you and George the best for the voyage and for your new life in Australia.

No doubt your skills as a nurse will be greatly valued there. I am sure that you realize how close you came to not having this opportunity. Make the most of it.

Yours very truly,
Edmund Fleetwood

Sarah felt heat rush to her face and a choking sensation in her throat. Was this another trap, or was he really letting her go? Her eyes glistened wet in the darkness like black opal. She realized that the captain was studying her. She turned her face away, afraid that the flush across her cheek would betray her.

"You're a nurse?" he said.

It took a moment for her to understand that this was a question. Edmund's words still swam before her eyes and blood roared through her head. "Yes," she said eventually.

"You should be helping the surgeon then."

Sarah pictured the knives glinting. The needles. She thought again of her mother's sick chamber with its potions and powders.

"I'm not sure that the other women would be happy to be treated by me."

"They'll be grateful to be treated by anyone at all if they're ill. You will report to the surgeon tomorrow for duty."

Sarah nodded. "Yes, captain."

"The letter," he said. "Its meaning is not immediately clear to me. Presumably it is to you."

Sarah said nothing.

He looked at her hard. "What did he mean by 'taking matters further'?"

"I'm not quite sure," she said. "Lawyers have a strange way of speaking."

He raised his eyebrows. "Yes, indeed. Almost a code, you might say." He narrowed his eyes as though trying to make out something far away, and then waved his arm to indicate she was dismissed.

Sarah curtsied and walked back into the damp night air, fighting against a wave of relief and disbelief. She went to the gunwale, drew her cloak about her shoulders, and stared over the edge of the boat into the dark water. It was as though a weight was finally being lifted, leaving her light as a cinder: almost too light. She could not quite believe that Edmund had forgiven her despite everything she had done. Was he genuinely willing to let both her and her sister go free? Perhaps she had underestimated him. Perhaps he understood that no purpose would be served by punishing them further for a crime that had already taken two lives. Or maybe it was simply that he cared for her. And now she was leaving him behind.

As she stared at the dark water below, she thought of Hannah: Hannah Brown with her drab face and fancy clothes, who had wanted only to be loved, but who had been duped and used just as she had, and who had ended up bruised and bloodied on a cold stone floor. If only Sarah had understood. If only she had directed her hatred at the man who had sought to crush her rather than at the woman she saw as her rival. If she had spoken to Hannah — spoken to her truly — then they might have fought him together. They might have won.

The words returned to her from the captain's sermon: *"Wash me thoroughly from mine iniquity and cleanse me from my sin."* Could her own sins be washed away? Swallowed up by the great, deep ocean as they journeyed to Australia? As if in answer, the Thames glinted up at her, slate-gray and black.

The following morning, they received the last of the prisoners: a further eleven women and one child from Newgate. Barrels of water and of salt beef were loaded onto the boat, together with the remaining livestock

— cagefuls of squawking chickens and a tussle of goats. The crew ran about the decks calling to one another and preparing the boat for its voyage. The women, however, were unusually subdued and the air was heavy with fear.

After the eight bells rang out there was a shrill cry: "Make sail!"

Then came the running of feet, a race up the ratlines, and the unfurling of the topgallants high in the sky above them.

The noise as the ship began to move was deafening: ropes creaked, sails flapped, men shouted and ran from one side of the boat to the other, their feet clattering on the boards. Behind that rose a low wail from the women who were leaving behind them everything they knew — homes, families, histories. They clustered together in groups, some supporting one another, some with their arms around their children.

Sarah stood with George on the leeward side of the quarterdeck watching the retreating riverbank, feelings of relief and loss battling within her, droplets of rainwater hitting her face. She drew George closer to her and wrapped her woolen cloak about them both. Then, from the inside pocket, she removed the items that would remind them of home: the letter from Edmund, the coin

from her sister, and a pair of earrings, red
and gold.

46

"This above all: to thine own self be true,
And it must follow, as the night the day,
Thou canst not then be false to any man."
— *Hamlet,* act 1, scene 3,
William Shakespeare

9 December 1837

Dear Father,
I apologize for the delay in responding to your letters. Bessie and I have been traveling in Europe with Clem for the past month, having finally received full payment for my work on the Edgeware Road case. For that, if for nothing else, I must thank you.

What you have heard is correct: I have accepted a position as legal reporter for the *Times.* I am fully aware of your views on journalism; indeed you have voiced them many times. All I can say is that our thoughts on this, as on many other subjects, differ, and that I must now live my life as my own.

Contrary to your assumption, however, I am not leaving the Bar. Indeed, I have been instructed by a private individual on a significant new case.

It follows that I am no longer in need of financial assistance and am therefore returning to you the check that you enclosed with your most recent letter. I would request that you instead use your money to increase Mother's allowance. You have already punished her severely for mistakes far less serious than your own. I have asked you to do this several times before, and you have always refused. As I am now in possession of information that would cost you heavily, you can do me the courtesy of granting this one wish.

Lastly, you asked about Miss Gale. I have heard nothing. By now, however, she must be nearly there: on the other side of the earth.

Your son,
Edmund

HISTORICAL NOTE

The Unseeing is a work of fiction, based on fact. All of the newspaper extracts used in *The Unseeing* are real, as are many of the details of the crime itself and the subsequent investigation and trial. However, at some points, I have — like Sarah — twisted the truth in order to make a better story.

Although now largely forgotten, the murder of Hannah Brown caused a sensation at the time. It became known as "the Edgeware Road Murder" due to the first body part — the torso — having been found under a paving stone in a half-built house on the Edgeware Road on 28 December 1836. A week later, a lockkeeper at Regent's Canal in Stepney recovered a woman's head, the right eye "knocked out." The head was taken to Paddington Green workhouse, where the parish surgeon, Dr. Girdwood, matched it up with the trunk, before preserving it in a jar. On 2 February 1837, two laborers found a pair of legs sticking out of a sack in an osier bed off the Coldharbour Lane, Camberwell. It was the writing on the sack that allowed the police to trace the murder back to James Greenacre and, from him, to Sarah Gale. When she was arrested, Sarah had in her possession several items said to belong to Hannah Brown, including two gold rings and some carnelian eardrops.

During her final questioning by the magistrates, Sarah was reported to be shaking so much that she struggled to hold the pen to sign the deposition. At the trial, she gave only the short statement quoted in *The Unseeing,* and was said to have watched Greenacre intently throughout the proceedings. On 3 April 1837, Greenacre was convicted of Hannah's Brown's murder; Sarah, of aiding and abetting him.

Opinion was divided as to whether Sarah was a knowing accomplice or unwitting dupe. She continued to claim that she had known nothing of the murder, but the Home Office rejected her petition for mercy. She was transported to New South Wales, together with her son George, on 17 July 1837.

Sarah Gale's petition has disappeared and I do not know who was appointed to consider the case. This gave me the freedom to create Edmund Fleetwood. Similarly, although there were some reports of Sarah having a sister, I know nothing about her. Therefore Rosina, too, is a piece of fiction.

Sarah Gale survived the voyage to New South Wales. In 1849, she married a man called Job Noon and in 1850 she received a conditional pardon. She never returned to England. Sarah died in 1888, by which time she was said to have, "assisted hundreds of girls to lead a good life."

For those interested to know more about the Edgeware Road Murder, the transcript of the trial is available online (www .oldbaileyonline.org/browse.jsp?id=t18370 403–917&div=t18370403–917), as is James Greenacre's entry in the Newgate Calendar (www.exclassics.com/newgate/ng622.htm). In addition to the contemporary accounts, various works have been helpful to me, in particular *The Invention of Murder* by Judith Flanders (HarperPress, 2011), *London in the Nineteenth Century: "A Human Awful Wonder of God"* by Jerry White (Vintage, 2008), and *Women, Crime and Custody in Victorian England* by Lucia Zedner (Clarendon Press, 1991).

I am grateful to the staff at the British Library, Southwark History Library and the National Archives who helped me with my search for the truth about Sarah Gale. For all my research, I remain uncertain as to what role Sarah really played in the murder of Hannah Brown. I am quite sure, however, that she knew far more than she claimed.

READING GROUP GUIDE

1. From the beginning, we know that the Edgeware Road murder is a huge case, drawing crowds of people with its sensational and gruesome story. Why do you think people are both repulsed and fascinated by true crime stories?

2. Sarah uses her routine to cope with the fear and isolation of Newgate. Imagine you were in a situation where you were cut off from society and those you loved. What would you do to pass the time? How would you cope?

3. Edmund Fleetwood, when talking to his wife, says, "Maybe in order to gain her trust, I need her to think I believe her." Do you find this duplicitous? If you were in Edmund's position, how would you get Sarah to tell her story?

4. When do you think Edmund crosses the line between pretending to believe Sarah Gale and actually believing? Do you think he ever truly does trust her? Do you?

5. At one point, while interrogating Sarah, Edmund tells himself that she does not look like a criminal, but then asks if it is really possible to tell. Do you think it is possible to tell who is a criminal? Do you think any person can become a criminal?

6. Imagine you are Edmund investigating all of the witnesses. Who do you believe? Who do you think is lying? What are their motives?

7. Sarah reflects on some horrible things that happened to her in childhood. Do you think what happens in childhood, good or bad, affects who we become later in life? Are we able to change? Has something from your own childhood, either positive or negative, affected you as an adult?

8. Do you think James Greenacre is a villain? Do you think Sarah is? Explain.

9. When reading *The Unseeing,* we learn a

lot about the court system during this time period. Can you draw any parallels between the system in place in London and ours today? Do you think there is justice for the innocent and guilty? Is the system corrupt or in place to serve the people?

10. What did you make of Sarah's involvement with Arthur Fleetwood? How does it color Edmund's involvement with the case? What do you think of the father-son relationship here?

11. We discover that Sarah refused to defend herself to save her sister from the gallows and her son from destitution. Can you understand this? Is there someone who you would protect no matter what? Where do you draw the line?

A CONVERSATION WITH THE AUTHOR

The Unseeing is based on a true case. How much of the story is fact and how much your own imagining?

The Unseeing is very much a work of fiction inspired by a true crime. The newspaper excerpts that appear in the novel are real, as is much of the detail, but Edmund Fleetwood was not a real person, and while I know that Sarah Gale had a sister, I know almost nothing about her. The motivations I have given the key characters came partly from the historical documents, but partly from my own imaginings. At some points, I diverged from the known facts of the case in order to make the story more compelling and surprising. I agonized over this for many months, and it is one of the reasons that a key theme of the novel is truth/ deception. Some people will criticize me for playing with the truth, but, ultimately, I'm a storyteller, not a historian.

What type of research went into this novel? Did you find it difficult to immerse yourself into this time period?

I started off by researching the case itself (through newspapers, the National Archives, Old Bailey online, convict records, and pamphlets), then the criminal justice system and Newgate prison. I read prison diaries and parliamentary commissions, I searched for sketches and pictures, and I studied plans of Newgate to get a sense of what that prison might have been like. In terms of the streets outside, I read journalistic works such as Henry Mayhew's *London Labour and the London Poor,* the fiction of the period, guidebooks, newspaper reports, court reports, letters, and the journals and memoirs of those who lived in or visited London. Immersing myself in the time period wasn't really the difficult bit — it was leaving it. I realized I had to stop myself from researching and finish the darned book.

A lot of *The Unseeing* deals with the question of justice and what justice looks like. How would you define justice?

It's treating people fairly and transparently, not making decisions on the basis of preconceptions or prejudices. It's ensuring that all are equal before the law. That's far from the case in *The Unseeing,* of course, which is perhaps why I was attracted to the story in the first place.

Do you see any parallels between the justice system from your novel and our own current justice system?

In some ways, yes. The criminal justice system still has a long way to go in how it treats vulnerable people, the mentally ill, and victims of crime. There continues to be political and police corruption. The quality of legal representation you receive still depends on how much you can pay. But whatever we think of the justice system, we've come a long way from the early Victorian era!

Which character was your favorite to write?

It was Sarah. It took me a long time to get to know her, but, probably because of that, she's stayed with me. I also had a lot of fun with Morris, Edmund's clerk. I read lots of nineteenth-century slang to come up with his phrases.

What does your writing process look like?

It involves reading, writing, procrastinating, and panicking in about equal measure. The way I write has changed a lot as I've progressed as a writer, however. For *The Unseeing,* I created a relatively short synopsis and worked from that, but the novel changed drastically over the three and a half years in which I wrote the book, and I now know that I should have plotted it out in a far more detailed way and thought far more carefully about the characters' arcs. Every writer is different, but I think I work best when I know where I'm headed, even if the plot later changes. For my second novel, I'm working from a far more detailed plot structure.

Do you think, after the book ends, Sarah and George find a happy ending? What about Edmund?

I learned from newspaper reports that Sarah remarried in Australia and died an old woman, by which time she was respected within the community. Of course, I don't know whether that meant she was content, but it sounds like an improvement on her life in London. I would very much like to believe George led a long and happy life but have been unable to trace what happened to him. As for Edmund, I imagine him trying to make the best of things with Bessie and Clem, but I don't think he'll ever forget Sarah.

Who are some of your favorite authors?
Margaret Atwood, Toni Morrison, Sarah Waters, Shirley Jackson, Graham Greene. My favorite books generally have a crime at their center but aren't always classed as "crime" novels: they're explorations of why people end up committing terrible acts.

Are you working on anything new?
I'm currently writing my second historical crime novel, set on the Isle of Skye in 1857, a few years after the Highland Clearances. It's about a young woman named Audrey who goes to work for a collector of folklore and discovers that a young girl has gone missing, supposedly taken by spirits. Of course, that's not what she believes is going on. Again, the idea was sparked by a real case, but I haven't tried to base it on the case in the same way that I did with *The Unseeing.*

ACKNOWLEDGMENTS

This book never would have been written without the support, encouragement, and patience of my family, in particular my mother, Elizabeth, and my husband, Jake (technical adviser, title creator, tea maker, saint).

Thank you to Juliet Mushens for being the best agent in the business, and to Imogen Taylor for her editorial wisdom. Thanks also to my eagle-eyed copy editor, Yvonne Holland, to my wonderful publicist, Ella Bowman, and to the whole talented Tinder Press team.

In the U.S., thanks to Shana Drehs at Sourcebooks and Sasha Raskin at United Talent Agency for their excitement about and contribution to this story.

Thank you to Andrea Mason of Literary Kitchen for getting me writing in the first place and to Kirstan Hawkins and all at the Novel Studio, City University, for helping me through the first draft. Many people have been forced to read and comment on this book. Those who have given me particular assistance are Regina Alston, Athena Stevens, Eve Seymour, Steve Lambert and the Novel Studio crew, Hellie Ogden, and Sophie Lambert.

I am grateful to the various professionals who have given up their time to answer my bizarre queries, including Dr. Tom Wedgwood, Professor Allyson May, Professor Philip Steadman, Simon Elliott, and Alan Moss of History by the Yard. Thank you in particular to Chris Rycroft who alerted me to several historical inaccuracies.

Thanks, lastly, to Faith Tilleray for creating the most beautiful website for me and my book (AnnaMazzola.com).

ABOUT THE AUTHOR

Anna Mazzola is from Camberwell, London, not far from where the murder at the heart of *The Unseeing* took place. While *The Unseeing* is her debut, it has already won awards, including the Brixton Bookjam Debut Novel competition and she was runner-up in the Grazia First Chapter competition judged by Sarah Waters. Anna studied English at Pembroke College, Oxford, before becoming a criminal justice lawyer. She is currently working on a second historical crime novel set on the Isle of Skye. Visit Anna at www.AnnaMazzola.com or on Twitter @Anna_Mazz.